# ALIVE IN
# NECROPOLIS

RIVERHEAD BOOKS

*a member of Penguin Group (USA) Inc.*

*New York*

DOUG DORST

ALIVE IN
NECROPOLIS

RIVERHEAD BOOKS
Published by the Penguin Group
Penguin Group (USA) Inc., 375 Hudson Street, New York, New York 10014, USA · Penguin Group (Canada),
90 Eglinton Avenue East, Suite 700, Toronto, Ontario M4P 2Y3, Canada (a division of Pearson Canada
Inc.) · Penguin Books Ltd, 80 Strand, London WC2R 0RL, England · Penguin Ireland, 25 St Stephen's Green,
Dublin 2, Ireland (a division of Penguin Books Ltd) · Penguin Group (Australia), 250 Camberwell Road,
Camberwell, Victoria 3124, Australia (a division of Pearson Australia Group Pty Ltd) · Penguin Books
India Pvt Ltd, 11 Community Centre, Panchsheel Park, New Delhi–110 017, India · Penguin Group (NZ),
67 Apollo Drive, Rosedale, North Shore 0632, New Zealand (a division of Pearson New Zealand Ltd) ·
Penguin Books (South Africa) (Pty) Ltd, 24 Sturdee Avenue, Rosebank, Johannesburg 2196, South Africa

Penguin Books Ltd, Registered Offices: 80 Strand, London WC2R 0RL, England

The newspaper article quoted on p. 272, with some omissions and minor additions, is found in
*Lincoln Beachey: The Man Who Owned the Sky,* by Frank Marrero (Scottwall, 1997).

Library of Congress Cataloging-in-Publication Data

Dorst, Doug.
Alive in Necropolis / Doug Dorst.
p.      cm.
ISBN 978-1-59448-987-7
1. Police—California, Northern—Fiction.   2. California, Northern—Fiction.   I. Title.
PS3604.O78A79    2008              2008005817
813'.6—dc22

Printed in the United States of America
1   3   5   7   9   10   8   6   4   2

*Book design by Stephanie Huntwork*

In addition to the above disclaimer, I would like to stress that I do not intend any elements of this narrative to
reflect poorly on the real-life Colma Police, who were friendly, informative, accommodating, and unfailingly
professional.

Please note that I have taken liberties with history and geography whenever it suited my purposes. This is because I am neither a historian nor a cartographer but a fiction writer, and I like making stuff up.

FOR DEBRA

*How does one kill fear, I wonder? How do you shoot*
*a spectre through the heart, slash off its spectral head,*
*take it by its spectral throat?*

—Joseph Conrad, *Lord Jim*

A rare sunny morning comes to Colma.

The sky brightens over San Bruno Mountain, bruised blues giving way to baby-cheek pinks and teases of gold. Navigation lights blink, red and resolute, atop the radio towers that scar the broad, rambling summit. Sunlight creeps across the green valley in which Colma is nestled, wicking away the dew from the lawns of the city's residents.

Twelve hundred of these residents are alive. They do what living people do: work jobs, sweat on treadmills, make love, incur debt, celebrate birthdays, worry about aging, watch prime-time TV, pray, complain about the weather. Another two million of these residents are already dead. No one knows for sure what they do—if they do anything but lie mute, immobile, decaying—but some of the living have their suspicions.

As the sun makes its way across the valley, it shines first on the Cypress Golf Course. Underneath these seventeen acres of Bermuda grass and fescue is the potter's field where the beggars of cobblestoned San Francisco were buried in numbered graves and forgotten. Four golfers in primary-colored windbreakers take practice swings on the first tee, whipping metal-gleam arcs through the crisp morning air. A greenskeeper backs a long-bed golf cart out of the maintenance shed, and a lone golden-crowned sparrow answers the cart's reverse-warning beeps with a plaintive, unrequited song.

The first golfer tees up his ball and takes his stance with the light morning wind luffing his nylon sleeves. As he swings, his plastic spikes slip in the wet tee box, and he slices the ball dead right, a line drive into the pine trees and scrub. He mutters a curse, blaming himself for his first-tee jitters, but then the ball thwocks against something in the woods and caroms out, skidding ahead on the slick grass and rolling to a stop in the center of the fairway, just a choked-down 8-iron away from the green. He turns and grins as his friends moan their disbelief. *Lucky sonofabitch. Somebody's looking out for you today.* And they continue their round: nine holes, played twice. It never occurs to him that the brownish scuff on his ball did not come from a tree or a rock or a log, but from a misshapen human skull coughed up by the shifting earth of the fault-lined valley.

The glow of morning spreads over the easternmost cemeteries of Colma: Olivet Memorial Park; the Serbian Cemetery; Pet's Rest; and the two Chinese cemeteries, Hoy Sun Memorial and Golden Hills.

Across Hillside Boulevard.

Nocturnal gamblers emerge from the front doors of the Lucky Chances 24-Hour card house, slack and pale as fish in a bucket; they rub their eyes in the morning light, then collapse into their cars and drive away. All of them— the winners, the losers, the breakers-even—will be gnawed at by the *if onlys* until the next time they rest their elbows on the soft green baize and ante up.

The day advances into Holy Cross Cemetery, Colma's oldest, a former potato field blessed in 1892 as a Catholic cemetery to serve San Francisco. Skyrocketing land values had convinced city dwellers that death was best dealt with elsewhere, and it was roundly agreed that a ten-mile trip southward was not an onerous journey for the dead to make—a mere step or two, in fact, compared to the great voyages on which their souls had already embarked.

The sun rises higher. Cypress Lawn East. Hills of Eternity. Eternal Home. Home of Peace. Salem Cemetery. The Italian Cemetery. The Japanese Benevolent Society Cemetery.

Lawn mowers sputter and cough out puffs of blue exhaust, then rumble to life and prowl the gentle slopes of the graveyards. In the lots of the car dealerships that clot Serramonte Boulevard, beads of dew glimmer on the polished hoods and roofs and trunks, while strings of red, white, and blue plastic pennants flick in the breeze, hopeful as America.

Across El Camino Real.

The overnight clerk at the Zes-T-Mart prepares to go home. He is a heavily tattooed young man whose pierced ear and nose are connected by a length of steel chain, and he wears the afternoon-shift girl's name tag because he likes to head-fuck naive customers into wondering if his name really might be Mindy. He notices that, once again, several cartons of Chesterfields have vanished on his watch. He blames their disappearance on ghosts. He will never inform his manager of his suspicions, and he will never ask to see the surveillance tape to test his theory. This coming afternoon, though, he will crawl out of bed and join his four roommates around the house bong (a complicated maze of Habitrail tubes that once housed a gerbil named Happy), and, while watching smoke plumes rise from the mouthpiece, he will dreamily remark, "Dudes. When we die, we'll all smoke Chesterfields." And although his friends will burst out laughing, thinking it's just stony talk, he'll find himself happy to believe in ghosts who jones for nicotine and remain brand-loyal. It's the one belief he has that is unique and private, and thus absolutely unassailable.

The sun.

Across Cypress Lawn West, the Greek Orthodox Cemetery, Greenlawn Memorial Park, and, finally, Woodlawn Memorial Park.

The day rolls by, and one hundred twenty-two people are interred in Colma, this self-described "city-cemetery complex." Mourners lift their eyes skyward as jets taking off from SFO thunder overhead, drowning out somber-voiced pieties and whispered farewells. Solitary and rickety white-haired people struggle up the muddy incline at Pet's Rest to lay wreaths for departed cats, dogs, bunnies, goats, horses, ocelots. Four mortuaries, ten florists, and eight monument carvers within the city limits are open for business, ensuring that the dead are admirably furnished. One proprietor reminds a new employee to speak slowly and with pleasant, reassuring words when asking for customers' credit cards, and instructs her to up-sell only the lost, the desperate, the bewildered, the afraid, the stoic, the defeated, and the accepting. "Never the angry," he says. "It's best to avoid a scene."

At the end of the day, the fog sweeps into Colma, a cold Pacific breath that flumes over the coastal hills. It hunkers down for the night, thick and mist-filled, alive with visible eddies and chutes that are swept by the chilled wind. Night-shift police officers reporting to the station zip their Tuffy jackets against the cold and pin their badges to the outside. Through the night, they patrol the quiet streets, wait for intoxicated drivers leaving Molloy's to cross the center line on Old Mission Road. They intervene in a domestic dispute on Spindrift Lane, thwart lumber thieves loading a pickup behind the home-improvement warehouse, break up a fight at the movie theater. They run passing checks through the cemeteries and sweep their spotlights over the fields of granite and marble, chasing away copulating kids, who dart like sprites into the shadows behind mausoleums and obelisks and weeping angels, struggling to hitch up their pants or just running bare-assed with their bundled clothes in their arms and their exposed skin shining ghost-white.

The next morning, one of these officers—Wesley Featherstone, a twenty-seven-year veteran—will not report back to the station. His Crown Victoria will be parked underneath the grand stone archway that leads into Cypress Lawn East, the driver's door ajar and the alert tone pinging softly. Sergeant Featherstone will be slumped behind the wheel of the cruiser, one hand reaching toward the radio, the other clamped over his mouth. His eyes will be wide and panicked. A lock of his thin hair—once red, long since turned peachy gray—will dangle from his temple, hanging all the way to his chin.

Featherstone will be dead of cardiac arrest.

Four dead men will sit atop the archway and pass a jug of daisy-petal pruno to toast their success. One of them will take a deep swig, dribbling onto his powder-blue tuxedo jacket, then hand the bottle to a hard-looking man with bloody fingertips, who will push him off their perch. The man in the tux will slam facedown on the pavement, inches away from the cruiser's front bumper. He will yelp and howl and curse the persistence of gravity even as his shattered bones begin knitting themselves together again, as ghost bones do.

The rest of the gang will shinny down to the ground, and all four of them, laughing and swaying drunkenly, will gather around the car for a final round of taunting the sergeant's corpse. Then they will stagger off to catch some rest. Even the dead need a little shut-eye sometimes.

A twenty-year-old Salvadoran landscaper reporting early for his first day on the job will hop out of a pickup truck, slap a good-bye on the quarterpanel, and wave as his cousin drives away. As he passes under the archway, he will glance into the cruiser's windshield and discover the corpse. This will be his first up-close glimpse of death, of an empty, defeated body, and as soon as he is able to unlock his legs, he will sprint down El Camino, get on the first bus he sees, and head out of town, anywhere, he won't care. He will stare vacantly out a knife-scratched window as the bus rumbles through the foggy morning. The young man's name is Ángel María de Todos los Santos, and he will forever be haunted by the pop-eyed look of terror on Featherstone's face. He will come to dread the hour of his own death even more acutely, forever robbed of the ability to believe that God helps souls pass gently. He will not appear in this story again.

PART ONE

BOY THIRTEEN

# FERN GROTTO

It is a rainy night, eight months after Wesley Featherstone's life of devoted public service was honored with moist eyes, a dolorous wheeze of bagpipes, platters of cocktail franks and baked ziti, and, finally, a blast of crematory flame. Officer Michael Mercer, Colma Badge Thirteen, steers his cruiser through that same archway at Cypress Lawn, only dimly aware of how desperately he wants to be a hero, and not at all aware that he is about to become one.

Mercer is driving one of the department's new Crown Victorias. The vehicle in which Featherstone died is gone, auctioned off, parked in a citizen's garage somewhere down the peninsula. No one wants to patrol in a dead man's cruiser. Fortunately, the Colma P.D. is well-enough funded that no one has to.

Mercer snaps on the cruiser's alley lights. The rain-glazed grass glows an unearthly green in the halogen beams. Daisies shine blue-white and astral, scattered points of lonely, unconstellated light. Officer Nick Toronto, riding shotgun, radios their position, and they drive slowly through the cemetery, lighting up the night around them as they follow the looping pathways. Mercer, as always, is on the lookout for trouble, but all he sees is ordinary graveyard detritus: empty beer cans, tipped-over pots of withering poinsettias, an old boot with its sole yawning away from the upper, wet fast-food wrappers clinging to the stone of a family called Oyster. Mercer usually patrols solo, but Toronto is in charge tonight because Sergeant Mazzarella went home early with a case of the almighty shits, and Toronto assigned himself to ride with Mercer so he can relax, shoot the breeze, keep his mind off his hangover and his nicotine-starved nerves. Mercer doesn't mind the company, even though Toronto, who'd been his Field Training Officer, still makes him nervous and self-conscious.

"Close your window," Toronto says. "It's fucking raw out."

Mercer shakes his head no, even though he's cold, too. An Alaskan front is sweeping down the coast of California, and the temperature has plummeted in the hours since midnight. The weather report says steady rain and piercing winds throughout the Bay Area for the next three days. Right now, there are flurries over Twin Peaks, and an inch of snow has accumulated on top of Mount Diablo. The power company has imposed rolling blackouts because they say the grid is sputtering, overtaxed by all the switched-on heaters.

"As the ranking officer in this car," Toronto says, "I order you to close your window."

"Sorry," Mercer says.

"Don't be sorry. Just close it."

"Book says open."

"The Book doesn't take into account that I'm freezing my nuggets off."

"Book says open," Mercer says again. Toronto might be testing him, and Mercer is determined not to screw anything up. The Book, Mercer knows, is the safe way to go. The Book is The Book for a reason.

As they roll through the cemetery, they pass ornate Victorian mausoleums that are more spacious than Mercer's apartment, the opulent resting places of James Flood, one of the Comstock silver kings, and Claus Spreckels, the sugar baron. They pass the Hearst family and Lillie Hitchcock Coit. The quiet is disturbed only by the patter of rain, the sticky hiss of tires on wet pavement, the Crown Vic's eight-cylinder grumble, and also Toronto, who keeps on bitching about the cold and tapping an unlit cigarette nervously against the dashboard. He quit smoking three days ago to placate his girlfriend, but Mercer doubts he'll last long—and until Toronto breaks down and lights up, Mercer is braced for a bumpy ride. Toronto can be a surly sonofabitch when things aren't going his way.

Mercer steers back onto the cemetery's main loop and lets the car drift back toward the archway that looms over the entrance. He's about to joke that *things look pretty dead here tonight* when he spots a small, torn-up patch in the wet grass to his left, just off the road. Tire tracks—a pickup, maybe an SUV.

Left sometime after the rain started, so they're three hours old, at most. Mercer scans the area beyond the tracks. A darkened path weaves between the small, flat stones that pock the ground—foot traffic, he guesses, four or five people—and it runs about a hundred yards out to a decrepit part of the cemetery called Fern Grotto.

Hidden from view by an imposing stone tower and ramparts of ivy, broadleaf ferns, and sprawling hydrangea, Fern Grotto is a circular, subterranean vault that held hundreds of bodies in its walls before a flood turned it into a pond full of yellowed, floating bones. These days it's an empty, bramble-choked pit where Peninsula kids come to drink coconut rum from the bottle and screw. The grotto tower is an arresting sight: fifty feet high, with ivy snaking up its sides and converging at the top in a burst of green, an improbable tuft of vegetation that led Mercer, when he first saw it, to mistake the structure for an ancient, craggy-barked tree. A few weeks back, Mercer picked up two community-college kids (white male, 20; Asian female, 19) after he found them kneeling in the grass at the base of the tower. They were out of their heads on mushrooms and contemplating the enormous thing before them. "Lost souls," the girl had intoned, stroking the naked, woody vines tenderly, with beatific concern. "The clawing fingers of lost souls."

Mercer brakes to a stop. The vehicle is gone, and, he assumes, so are all of its occupants. Still, it's his job to make sure.

"I have a theory about life," Toronto announces, "and it's this—"

Mercer holds up his hand. "Wait," he says. He kills the engine. He listens.

"You need to hear this," Toronto says.

"Later."

"It's the answer to your problems."

Mercer points. "Torn-up grass. Foot traffic. Let's take a look." He gets out of the car, taking his flashlight with him. When Toronto doesn't follow, Mercer crosses to the passenger side and knocks on his window.

Toronto rolls it down. He leans his head back in mock weariness, and Mercer notices for the first time just how protuberant Toronto's Adam's apple is. Seriously, it's like the guy swallowed a golf ball.

"Boy Thirteen," Toronto says dismissively, "they're gone. No one's here."

"I want to check it out."

"Go ahead. I'll wait."

Mercer hesitates. He's acting like a typical rookie, he knows, chasing shadows while more seasoned cops roll their eyes. Toronto's probably right. No one with any sense would stick around on foot in weather like this. All Mercer has to do is nod, get back behind the wheel, and drive them to the station, and they'll be out of the cold and rain, and they can wait out the last two hours of the shift—*the stay-awake hours,* Toronto calls them—in the break room, where the TV will be tuned to hoops highlights or poker or some cable show about strippers.

"Changed your mind?" Toronto says. "Good, let's go."

Mercer rounds the front of the cruiser and is reaching for his door handle when the wind shifts and brings a sound to his ear. A sound. Barely audible, but it was there. He heard it. Something small, fearful, human.

"I heard something," Mercer says through the open window. He flinches as the sky shoots a frigid dart of rain down his collar.

Toronto taps his cigarette.

"Listen," Mercer says, and the sound comes again. "Hear that?"

"I hear not one damn thing," Toronto says.

"Hold still. Close your eyes."

Toronto stops tapping. "Of course, there's Option Two, in which you stop wasting my time and tell me what it is." He tucks the cigarette between his lips, where it hangs sadly, the paper splitting at the bends.

"Someone's out there," Mercer says. "At the pit."

The sound comes again, louder this time, edged with fear and punctuated by a raw, scraping retch. "Well, fuck," Toronto says. "I heard *that.*" He flicks the ruined cigarette out the window and joins Mercer in the rainy dark. "Fucking kids," he says.

Mercer radios in, using the pick mike on his jacket collar. "Colma, Thirty-three Boy Thirteen."

The dispatcher's voice crackles in his earpiece. "Go ahead, Boy Thirteen."

"On foot patrol, east side of Cypress Lawn. Suspicious circumstance." He tucks his keys into his back pocket to keep them from jingling, and he and Toronto quietly cover the stretch of green between the cruiser and the grotto. Mercer holds his flashlight away from his body; when situations go sideways, gunmen will shoot at the light. (You have to learn good habits and practice them. Take nothing for granted. As Sergeant Mazzarella likes to say, *Nothing will make you dead faster than an assumption.* Everyone wishes the sergeant would lighten up a little, but they also know he's right.)

A quick check around the perimeter of the grotto, the base of the tower. Nothing. The steel gate at the entrance to the vault is ajar. They hear the sound again—no, the *voice*, it's a voice—a whimper, then a feeble moan. From inside. Mercer feels his pulse quicken, feels his hackles rise. Any cop will tell you: trust the hairs on the back of your neck; when they stand up, you pay attention. Mercer uses hand signals: he points at Toronto, then at his own eyes, then at his back. *Watch my back. I'm taking lead.* Toronto, whose neck hairs must be sending him a less-urgent message, shrugs and waves Mercer forward. *Knock yourself out, Wonder Boy.*

Mercer passes through the gate. A blackberry branch catches his sleeve, and the thorns scrape down the heavy nylon as he pulls away. He steps into the clearing and shines his flashlight down into the pit. Shards of glass catch the light, sparkling amid the brambles and cast-off leaves. A pair of jeans is splayed over a tangle of thorns—flung from above, probably—and a white high-top Chuck Taylor hangs in some cascading ivy, looking as if its owner stepped out of it in midair. Crumbling brick steps, hardly more than a red trail of scree, lead down into the pit. The only sound now is the pattering drizzle. The fog, sheltered from the wind, hangs dense and still.

Mercer follows the path that circles the pit. To his right, built into the earth, are the small, rectangular compartments in which the dead once lay. Dark tendrils of ivy cobweb the openings. To his left, along the pit's rim, is a balustrade built from knotty, fist-thick birch limbs; in the bleaching glare of the flashlight, it looks to him like a fence of bones. Mercer steps quietly along the path, alert, coiled, ready to act.

He comes across a spot where leaves have been kicked away. Two empty tequila bottles lie in the dirt. Top-shelf stuff, Mercer notes. Stuff he can't afford to drink. Also on the ground are a wood-carved pipe and a scattering of cigarette butts.

In the dark ahead of him, someone coughs. Mercer shines his light on the path and sees nothing. He summons his command presence, straightening into a powerful posture and urging his voice to boom. "Colma Police," he says, feeling the authority resonating in his chest, his throat, his skull. "Identify yourself."

Another cough, and a sudden rush of liquid. Chunky, strangled, urgent sounds.

Slowly (too slowly—as Mazzarella would say, *the kind of slowly that'll get you killed*), he realizes the subject is lying inside one of the burial chambers. He shines his light along the wall into the far corner and sees bare legs protruding from one of the openings. The ankles are bound with duct tape that shines silver in the light. Toronto sweeps his beam across the area, scanning for other people, and Mercer hurries ahead, tugs away the curtain of vines that drape around the legs, and looks into the chamber. It's a kid—white male, probably mid-teens—and he's been shoved in headfirst, on his stomach. Naked from the waist down, and just a damp white T-shirt on top. Wrists duct-taped behind his back.

"I'm making contact," Mercer calls to Toronto. "Are we secure?"

"All clear," Toronto says.

Mercer touches the boy's calf. His skin, wet from the rain, is pale and blue-tinged. Mercer finds a pulse from the femoral artery, and it's slow, draggy, erratic. An earwig skitters across the kid's thigh, and Mercer sweeps it away.

Toronto comes up behind him. "Hypothermic?"

"Think so."

"So what should you do?" Toronto's voice is level, cool.

"Try to rouse," Mercer says, impatient. It's an emergency, not a goddamn training session.

"How are you going to do it? Sternum rub?"

"Of course not. Can't get to it. Can't move him."

"So how, then?"

"Rub somewhere else," Mercer says.

"Where? You going to rub his ass, for instance?"

"I'm not rubbing his ass."

"Whether you do or not, I'm telling everyone you did. You'll be known forever as Mike Mercer, Ass-Rubber. We'll get you vanity plates that say I RUB ASS."

"We've got a *situation* here. Let me think."

"Don't think. Just deal with it. Unless you need me to do it for you."

Mercer makes a fist and rubs his knuckles up and down the sole of one of the kid's cold bare feet. "Hey, buddy," he says, raising his voice. "Can you hear me?" No response. Mercer tries the back of his knee and elicits a dwindling, wordless groan. The air stinks of the kid's vomit, and Mercer has to pull away for a moment to gird himself.

"Let's get him warm," Toronto says. "I'll grab the blanket."

Mercer radios in. "I have a ten-forty-two, code three." *Medical emergency, request for ambulance, with siren, all due haste.* "Subject is a white male, about fifteen, unconscious, breathing. Subject is hypothermic, intoxicated, narcotics possible. Subject is on his stomach, inside a—what's the word?—a chamber, I guess, in Fern Grotto. Yes. The place with the tower. Subject's wrists and ankles are bound with duct tape."

"Subject's ass is boldly on display," Toronto offers as he heads out through the gate. "Subject lacks any kind of trouser."

While Toronto's getting the medi-kit from the cruiser, Mercer keeps one hand on the kid's clammy leg. He's got to talk, keep him alert, but words keep deserting him before he can push them through his mouth. A better cop, he thinks, would know just what to say. "Hang in there," he says. "Um, just stay with me. I'm a police officer, and I'm going to take care of you." He pauses, and the air around him turns empty, lifeless. Keep talking, got to keep talking. The foggy sky lights up in swirling red and blue. "Stay with me." Shit, he said that already, he's terrible at this, he can feel himself being terrible at this, and he can feel his brain slamming shut the way it sometimes does, and suddenly he doesn't have any words at all and in their place is that acute, straining, sweaty *empty,* proof that words always fail him in the most critical situations, always have, always will, and he imagines this kid lying there listening and lamenting the shitty luck that has put his life in the hands of someone so tongue-tied and lame. *Tough it out,* he tells himself in an internal command-voice, *just talk,* and he keeps his mouth working, and finally, after a few tentative syllables get choked off in his throat, the words dribble out again. "We're going to get you to the hospital. An ambulance is on the way. Stay with me. Just breathe, and stay with me." He hears Toronto's feet scuffing toward him through the leaves, and he shuts up so Toronto can't criticize his patter. He feels his panic ebbing, and then he is himself again, sweaty and not-unpleasantly-spent-feeling, still buzz-headed but back in the world, here, in this cemetery, in this cold, on this wet ground. Doing his job like he's supposed to.

Approaching sirens tear the air. Toronto removes the emergency blanket from the medical bag and shakes it open. They cover the kid with it, with Mercer reaching deep into the compartment to cover as much of him as possible. The air in the close space reeks of tequila and bile and moss and decay.

"Kid's fucked up," Toronto says. "He's seriously fucked up."

"Tequila."

"No shit."

"Narcotics, you think?"

"Maybe ketamine. This kid's *out*."

"I'm cutting the tape," Mercer says.

"Hold off," Toronto tells him. "Fire's almost here. If the kid dies, it won't be the tape that did it."

"Don't say he's going to die," Mercer says.

"I didn't. I said *if*."

"Because maybe he can hear you."

"Can *you* hear me? I said *if*."

Mercer reminds himself to breathe. "All right," he says. "So what are we looking at here?"

"I'm going to make an educated guess," Toronto says, "and say that it's ghosts. Ghosts drugged him and pantsed him, and had their ghost ways with him. Spooky, evil, sex-crazed ghosts."

"Be serious," Mercer says. "For one goddamn second."

"I seriously don't know," Toronto says. "You'd think sexual assault, but there's no sign. Not that I can see. It *looks* like this is just a fucked-up, taped-up kid that someone left outside. I'm going down to check the clothing for an ID. Stay with him." Toronto makes his way around the pit to the collapsed brick stairway; loose grit schusses ahead of him as he sidesteps down the slope. When he reaches the bottom, he high-steps over clumps of thorns to get to the discarded jeans. Mercer keeps his hand on the kid's blanketed legs and softly tells him again and again that he'll be all right, aware that this might be a lie.

As the fire engine's lights join the cruiser's in the sky, coloring the cloud bank, the kid mumbles a few syllables. Mercer leans closer to hear. Under his hand, the leg muscles twitch, then go slack, then clench in spasm. Then the back arches, and the head slams against the top of the chamber. Mercer pulls away as the kid's body convulses, legs kicking, arms jerking and straining against the tape. The blanket falls to the ground. A fecal smell fouls the air.

Mercer flicks open his knife. "He's seizing," he shouts to Toronto. "I'm cutting him loose." Toronto says something back, but Mercer doesn't hear. He steps closer to the twisting body, ignoring the stink. He aims the knife and saws once, the blade snapping through the tight-stretched tape, and the kid's arms swing free. Then Mercer does the legs. When the last filament of tape pops away, one leg kicks out before he can step clear, and the kid's foot crashes into his cheek. There's a green flash in his eyes and a sound like hammered metal in his head, and he staggers a few steps, then goes down. From the wet ground, he hears Toronto call his name, and he shouts back *I'm fine. It's all good.* He stays on the ground to rest. Let his head settle. The sirens cut out with final, staccato squawks, and Mercer imagines he can hear their echoes drifting away in slow, dreamy ripples.

The firefighters approach, a jumble of voices and heavy footsteps and clanks and jingles. As they pound past him, one of them tells Mercer to go back to sleep, they'll take it from here. Mercer wants to tell him to fuck off, but he can't get his mouth to work yet.

He opens his eyes and sees the firemen—six, at his first count, but once he blinks and straightens out his vision, he sees there are only five—clustered in a semicircle, blocking his view of the kid.

"Huh. Don't see this every day."

"Bitch getting him out."

"Careful. It's shit city over here."

"Need the spine board."

"Yup. Spine board."

"Can't do it without a spine board. No way."

"Let's go. Let's stop dicking around and do this thing."

"Is he alive?" Mercer calls.

"Ish," the paramedic says.

"What?"

"Alive-ish."

Mercer hears someone come lumbering into the clearing alone, breathing heavily. He slowly turns his head and sees Jerry Fahey, a retired fire volunteer who's been tagging along on calls again ever since his wife passed away. He's wearing a pale blue pajama top and threadbare gray sweatpants under an open wool overcoat, and his furry belly peeks out from between his pajama buttons. Mercer knows him well; he and Toronto often hoist beers with him at the Death's Door Tavern, just over the line that separates Colma from Daly City. Fahey's a dedicated drinker, his spuddy nose shot with blown capillaries.

Mercer pushes himself up onto his knees, rests, breathes, stands. He slaps leaves and dirt away from his jacket and pants.

"Boy Thirteen," Fahey says, "you look like shit."

Mercer puts his hand to his face. His cheek and eye have already begun to puff up. He presses gently around the edges of the swelling, testing the depth of the ache. "Kid seized," he explains. "Foot caught me."

Fahey looks over at the kid. He shakes his head. "Son, if a naked little boy is going to knock you down, you're in deep shit if you ever actually have to stop a crime."

"I'm aware," Mercer says.

Fahey bellies-up to the bone fence and calls to Toronto, who's still looking around in the pit. Gesturing toward the kid in the wall, he says, "This is one fucked-up way of coercing confessions, Toronto."

"It wasn't me," Toronto calls back. He's holding a black wallet. "It was Mercer. His girlfriend hasn't been putting out."

"You guys are a menace," Fahey says. "For all I know, you'll come after me one of these days. I'm going to padlock my belt buckle."

"You're not even wearing a belt, you fat, lazy bastard. Nice outfit, by the way. You on your way to prowl the playgrounds?"

And so on. Mercer doesn't feel like joining in. He's not very good at the insult game, and plus, he's just noticed sparkles of coppery light in his vision. He closes his eyes so he can watch them dance more brightly. He opens them again when Fahey's meaty arm thumps down over his shoulders, a sudden burden that nearly buckles his knees.

Fahey says, "I was just shitting you before. You know that, right?"

"When?"

"Just now. Naked little boy, deep shit, stop a crime, excetera."

"Right," Mercer says, and his memory pops back into place. "No problem. I can take it."

"You're fine," Fahey says. "You're going to be a good cop. I can tell." His breath is a rank cocktail of mouthwash and beer fumes. Mercer wishes the compliment didn't have that closing-time feel to it.

They watch as two firemen work the spine board under the kid's body. The paramedic stands behind them, directing, waving his hands. The other men lean against the wall of empty burial chambers, talking, laughing. It's one of the first things Mercer learned on the job: guys are always looking for a reason to stand around.

Toronto scrambles up the loose brick. He falls once and curses, then makes it up on the second try with a three-step running start. He knuckles a rhythm on the fence as he walks toward them. "Jesus," he says when he sees Mercer's face. "I told you to watch out for that."

"Yeah," Mercer says. "Well."

"Our boy has a name. His license is in there." Toronto hands him the wallet, and Mercer flips through the bills. Four twenties. A lot to leave behind, if money's a motive. "They dumped his jacket down there, too," Toronto says. "A nice one. Suede. Italian designer kind of shit."

"Bottom line, then," Mercer says. "It's not a robbery."

"Was that a pun? 'Bottom line'?"

Jerry swats Mercer on the back. "Good one, Boy Thirteen."

"Nick." Mercer sighs. "Jesus."

"Fine," Toronto says, sounding disappointed. "No, it's probably not a robbery. Maybe personal."

"I could use a jacket like that," Fahey says. "Update my image."

"Jerry, you could update your image with a fucking loincloth," Toronto says.

"What's that supposed to mean? I'm old? You're calling me old?"

"Of course I'm calling you old. You're old."

"It wouldn't fit you, anyway," Mercer says.

"The loincloth?"

"No, Jerry, the jacket."

"So now I'm fat, too," Fahey says.

"You've always been fat," Toronto says.

"I'm just saying the kid's tiny," Mercer says. "Plus, the jacket's, you know, evidence."

"No sense of humor, this one," Toronto says, pointing at Mercer.

"Kids today," Fahey says.

Toronto turns to Mercer. "Run the ten-twenty-nine. And tell them to get Funkhouser out of bed. We need a detective down here."

"Why don't you call in?" Mercer wants to rest a little longer. He wants to wait for his brain to stop rattling against his skull.

"You need to practice your radio skills," Toronto says, and he walks off with Fahey. Mercer can't tell if he's joking.

While he's on the radio, the kid is carried out past him on the spine board, and Mercer gets his first good look. He's short and slightly built. Dark hair with tight curls, cut short and thickly gelled. A thin, high-bridged nose centering a beardless olive face. Thin lips flecked with the same yellow-orange mess that's splattered over his T-shirt. Long, feminine lashes fringing his closed eyelids. All things considered, the kid looks pretty peaceful. It's sad, Mercer thinks, that this boy might die surrounded by a bunch of strangers who'll only ever know him by his medical condition, his bare ass, and his vital statistics.

*Last of David Ida Mary Adam Ida Ocean.*

*First of John Union David Edward.*

*Middle of P, Paul.*

*Date of birth zero-seven, one-three, eighty-eight.*

*Out of San Francisco. Street address: two-zero-one Buena Vista West.*

Dispatch calls; the kid comes back ten-thirty-one-A. Clear record, not reported missing. "Get a reverse and call the residence," Mercer orders. "Subject is en route to Good Shepherd Hospital."

Jude P. DiMaio is carried out of the grotto and into the cemetery just as the ambulance arrives and adds a third set of flashing lights to the scene. The kid is rushed off, the siren Dopplering away, and after the rest of the firemen file out, the grotto is quiet again: just the popping of cold drizzle on fallen leaves and waterproof nylon.

Mercer hears Toronto flick open his lighter and turns to see him with a cigarette in his mouth, cupping his hand to keep raindrops off the flame. "Thought you quit," Mercer says.

Toronto inhales deeply. "I did," he says. He snaps the lighter closed and exhales a long, satisfied stream of blue.

They stand in the rain at the crime scene, not talking. Mercer feels too tired to move, and his head is throbbing. Plus, the flashing lights in the sky keep attracting his attention, and every time he moves his eyes too quickly, a wave of dizziness hits him broadside. Yes, he's worried for Jude, and yes, he urgently wants to find whatever bastard taped him up and left him out in the wet winter night, but right now he wants more than anything else to be home in bed, warm and dry under three blankets, a bag of ice on his damaged face, the blinds closed and a beach towel draped over them to catch whatever light leaks through.

"Well, Boy Thirteen," Toronto says, finally, flicking away his first ashes as a reborn smoker, "I guess we ought to do some police work here."

Lillie Hitchcock Coit, San Francisco heiress and devoted patroness of firefighters, sits on the birch-wood fence and watches the officers walk about, collecting things and taking measurements in their methodical ways. Holding her honorary helmet from the Knickerbocker No. 5 in her flanneled lap, she basks in her contentment. The firemen have come, have extracted the boy from his predicament, and are rushing him to get medical care. How serene she feels. How satisfying to witness a good rescue. How good to have a short reprieve from all the worry about Doc Barker's gang and their seething cruelty.

She'd have preferred to see a fire, of course—the crushing wall of heat, the smell of one's own eyebrows singeing when one stands too close, the hot crash of collapsing timbers, the fearful shrieks of the trapped, and above all, the grace and valor of the firefighters who tame the chaos of flames—but there are precious few fires here, and one must take one's pleasure where one can, mustn't one? Without the small pleasures, there's little purpose in remaining here, is there? And she has no inclination to follow all those unhappy ones who chew their Roots and rush themselves into oblivion. No, she shall seek out the small pleasures, and she shall seize them, and to blazes with anyone who might be lurking about and intending her harm.

Small pleasures, such as racing into the grotto alongside the firemen. Such as watching the boy's chest rise and fall, however slowly, as he was carried out. And now, oddly enough, watching the policemen. The younger one is more appealing to her, more interesting. He's not a small man—he's square-shouldered and sturdy—but he moves with an inelegant, lumbering gait befitting someone much bigger and heavier. His face is scrunched in concentration as he rolls some sort of measuring wheel over the ground, and she admires the focus that comes with dedication to one's task. She sighs happily, perhaps even theatrically, and when she does, something strange happens: her officer spins around, as if he can hear her.

Oh, my.

Another one?

The policeman spins so quickly that he loses his balance on the wet grass, and Lillie quite unintentionally smiles at the sight: this young man, his arms wheeling, his heavy-browed face showing a determination not to fall over and a fear that he might have tipped too far already. Yes, she decides. Another one of her pleasures shall be to watch him. He is someone worth keeping her eye on, even if it turns out he's not a crosser. He did find the boy, after all, and she's glad someone did.

# GO WEST

Five in the morning. The sky is still dark, but Interstate 280 is alive with early commuters zooming north toward San Francisco and south toward Silicon Valley. The fog has thinned, and drivers hum along through the drizzle at sixty-five, seventy, seventy-five. Trees on both sides of the freeway flail in the gusting wind, and small cars skate back and forth within their lanes as they fight the gusts. When the northbound fast-lane drivers notice the cruiser in their rearview mirrors, they slow with a flash of brake lights, hurriedly flick their right-turn signals, and change lanes—some of them swerving—to get out of the law's way. "Nervous drivers," Toronto says. "Watch out for them, Boy Thirteen. A citizen with the yips is just as dangerous as one who's shit-faced."

"I'm aware," Mercer says.

Toronto is driving while Mercer rides shotgun, resting his eyes. He's taken three naproxens already, and the pain is still lingering in his head, a blunt ache. The swelling on his face intrudes on his vision, like a fingertip shading the corner of a photograph. Drowsiness fell heavily upon him the moment he got into the passenger seat, and it's a chore to keep his head up.

They're heading back to the station from the county crime lab in San Mateo. All the evidence they gathered, numbered, and stored in paper envelopes at the scene is now in the lab's night-drop box. There were thirteen cigarette butts in the grotto, two different brands. The pipe: recently used, charred residue still in the bowl. They won't get any prints off it—too porous—but they have the tequila bottles, and once those dry, the lab might get a partial they can work with. Their best hope, though, is for the kid to ID the perps himself.

Mercer opens his eyes as they pass a green Lexus. The driver is about his age, just shy of thirty, but already jowly and puffy-looking. He's riding with the dome light on and rummaging for something in the passenger seat, his attention alternating between the seat and the road. He wears a white dress shirt with suspenders and a bow tie, and a suit jacket hangs in the window behind him. Mercer watches him drift rightward across the lane divider. *Watch where you're driving, buddy,* he thinks.

The driver returns his attention to the road, pulls back into his lane, and notices the cruiser running even with him on his left. He meets Mercer's eyes and gives him a crisp salute. Mercer raises his hand in acknowledgment, a reflex, and immediately regrets it, unsure if that salute was a genuine gesture of respect or of condescension. The more he thinks about it, the more he suspects it was the latter.

"Asshole," Mercer says as the Lexus falls a few lengths behind them.

"What'd I do this time?" Toronto says.

"Not you. Guy in the Lexus."

"What'd he do?"

"Saluted. In an I'm-better-than-you way."

"You're jealous he's got money?"

"Fuck that," Mercer says. "That's not a life I want."

"Good," Toronto says. "It's not a life you have."

Mercer hadn't planned on a career in law enforcement. He'd simply been lost. He was years removed from college, sick of bartending and office temp work. His friends were finding jobs they cared about and women they loved and places to travel to, and Mercer could feel their attachments to each other slackening, which depressed him. Spooked by a creeping sense of his own irrelevance, he was drinking too much, sleeping too much, and getting dark-minded and hopeless in a way he feared might be permanent. One day, he forced himself out of bed shortly after noon and, while sipping the bitter dregs of his hyper-employed, dawn-rising roommate's coffee, he opened the newspaper and came across an article headlined A MIME EVERYONE CAN LOVE.

It was a feature piece about a cop in San Francisco, a former professional mime who practiced his art as he walked his beat. He'd act out routines that urged at-risk kids to stay in school, warned gang-bangers to watch their step on his turf, shamed traffic offenders, reminded church-bound pensioners and smack-drowsy whores alike to take vitamins and see a health professional regularly. The accompanying photograph showed him—in full uniform and whiteface—walking against the wind to the apparent delight of a kindergarten class. If you believed the residents who'd been interviewed, this mime cop had almost single-handedly restored order, goodwill, and civic pride to a troubled part of the city.

Mercer put down the paper. He eyed the half of a jelly donut that his roommate had left on the table. All the jelly had been scooped out, leaving a moist purple cavity in the dough, but Mercer ate it anyway. He leaned back on two legs of his loose-jointed chair and thought about finding a way to discover his role in this life, about making damn sure he didn't sleepwalk through it and die without doing anything. That cop had a good thing going. A job he believed in. A regular check and benefits. And, every day, chances to help people, fix problems, maintain order, be appreciated. He was a fucking *mime*, and everyone loved him.

Mercer wouldn't have a hook like that; he couldn't tap-dance, bust freestyle rhymes, or do ventriloquism or magic tricks. But maybe it would be enough to be a good cop, well-intentioned and effective. It dawned on him that he really could be a cop if he wanted to, and then it dawned on him that he'd had this revelation while eating a donut, and if that wasn't a sign, he didn't know what was. It felt like an inspired idea, one worth pursuing before it slipped his mind and he slumped back into his usual morose inertia.

And he did pursue it. Within two months, he'd quit slinging Cosmopolitans and mojitos at The Hard Ten Tavern on Divisadero, told the manager at the temp agency to chuck his file in the shredder, and enrolled in the Police Academy in Santa Rosa. His mother said she was torn; she worried about the dangers of police work, but she was happy to see him finding some focus. His friends—still the high-school crew, who'd gone on to expensive degrees and then to high-paying jobs, trust-funded leisure, or both—razzed him for weeks, until his best friend, Owen, declared that enough was enough, that they should respect Mercer's choice, and that no one should spark up joints or do lines anymore while he was in the room to spare him any ethical dilemmas. After some initial griping, they agreed, and they turned curious about his training, instead of dismissive.

It had been only a few months since Mercer had finished field training and gone full-time with the Colma agency, but already he knew he'd made the right decision. He loved the work, loved the rush he got from facing fear head-on, loved the camaraderie of a small group of people committed to watching each other's backs. Toronto had once told him the best cops were those who found their calling late, and the worst were the ones who thought they'd been born with a badge. "They're the motherfuckers with issues," he'd said. "Watch out for them." Toronto had come to the force after teaching English at a junior high school in East Palo Alto where knife fights were more common than mac-and-cheese lunch days. After that, he said, he'd wanted a job that let him carry a gun.

Speaking of life," Toronto says.

"I know. You have a theory about it."

"One from which you'll benefit greatly."

Mercer looks out the window as they speed past the Crystal Springs rest area. A sandstone statue of Father Junípero Serra overlooks the freeway, an eight-lane charcoal-colored swath of pavement. The missionary kneels with one arm extended, pointing westward, out over the coastal hills and toward the ocean. His facial expression is blank, his eyes flat, irisless, unreadable. *Go west,* he counsels, without offering any hint as to who should go, or why, or how far, or what one might find when one gets there. Could be paradise, could be sharks.

"All right," Mercer says. "Let's hear this theory."

"Are you ready?"

"What, do I need to take notes?"

"I want to make sure you're listening. This is *wisdom,* Boy Thirteen."

"Bring it on," Mercer says. "Let's get it over with."

"My theory about life is this: that you're only as old as the woman you're sticking it to."

Mercer blinks. "That's it? That's a theory about life?"

"It is. And it's a good one."

"Horseshit, is what it is." It's also typical Toronto: now that he has a twenty-two-year-old girlfriend, he'll proclaim that cradle-robbing is the world's greatest virtue. Still, he's so sure of himself, so matter-of-factly convinced of his own insight, that Mercer finds it hard to dismiss what he says out of hand. He also feels a stab of envy: Toronto will be going home to a hot, young girlfriend—an *acrobat,* no less—and Mercer won't. And he probably won't ever again. He has a sense that those days are over for him, and that he wasted them being shy and self-conscious and risk-averse. "How old are you, anyway?" Mercer asks.

"Thirty-seven. Thirty-eight next month."

"Didn't know you were that old." He'd figured thirty-four, tops.

"Which proves my point, doesn't it?"

Mercer supposes it might, which disturbs him, but then he reminds himself to be wary of the conclusions to which his mind steers him at this time of the night. Or morning. Whatever the hell this is. "I know where you're going with this," Mercer says. "Don't."

"All I'm saying is I feel great. I feel great, and you're a mess. I'm going home to have unspeakably acrobatic sex with Mia, and you're going home to screw somebody's grandmother."

Mercer's face grows hot. "Fuck you," he says, buying time while he figures out what he really wants to say. Then he decides that "Fuck you" *is* what he really wants to say, so he says it again. "She's nobody's grandmother," he adds. "She's nobody's mother. She's a few years older than you are."

"My point exactly. What the hell are you doing with her?"

He should never have told Toronto about Fiona. He's hardly told anyone. It's not that he's hiding her, it's just that he doesn't like to talk about his romantic life unless he has a good reason to, and he usually doesn't. He'd let it slip one morning at the end of his field training when he and Toronto were having drinks at The Death's Door, decompressing from the shift along with a couple of Daly City cops named Whitehurst and Gillis. Mercer had kept quiet; as the new guy, he was unsure of his place in the conversation. Talk had turned to sex, as it usually does, especially with cops. Gillis got laughs with his story about picking up a goth girl at a Laundromat in Belmont ("Turns out she thinks she's a vampire. Seriously. Bitch bit me."). Whitehurst griped about feeling cheated because the woman he was sleeping with, a notorious badge-chaser, wouldn't do oral anymore. Eventually they turned to Mercer, waiting for him to contribute. By then, he had three well whiskeys in him, and he let down his guard. "I'm kind of seeing someone," he said.

"Who is she?" Gillis asked. "Details. We need details."

"An ER nurse. At Good Shepherd."

"A nurse," Whitehurst said. "That's great. That's hot."

"Tits?" Gillis asked, gesturing with his hands to indicate sizes ranging from ample to pneumatic.

Whitehurst elbowed Gillis. "Of course she has tits, douchebag. She's a woman." He turned to Mercer. "She *is* a woman, isn't she?"

Mercer rolled his eyes. Earlier, when he'd mentioned that he used to work at The Hard Ten, he'd had to explain that no, it wasn't a gay bar; the owner had opened it with money he'd made at a craps table in Reno by betting every-thing he had on a hard ten on the hop. A stupid bet, laughable, but it had paid off. Every night Mercer had spent in that bar was a reminder that other people tended to be luckier than he was. "Yes," Mercer told the other cops, trying to sound as exasperated as possible, "she's a woman."

Toronto asked how old she was, and Mercer, determined not to hesitate because hesitating would suggest that he thought there was something wrong with the age difference, and he didn't think there was, not really. He'd looked Toronto squarely in the eyes and said, in the confident, matter-of-fact tone he'd learned at the Academy, "Forty-three."

Toronto had choked on his drink, or pretended to. "Holy Jesus on a wreck-ing ball," he said. "What's *wrong* with you?"

It was a terrible moment, one that Mercer knew well: when horror and shame hot-knife through you because you've tried to fit in and instead proved yourself to be the freak they suspect you are. He had stared into his half-empty glass and felt a drop of sweat strum his ribs, and he cursed himself for forgetting that it's usually best just to keep your fucking mouth shut.

The cruiser whizzes along through the dark clouds and green-black hills. Rainwater roars inside the wheel wells in staccato bursts. Toronto changes lanes to avoid a shred of a blown tire. Toronto asks again: "Seriously. What's the deal? You love her?"

"No," Mercer says, but it's more a reflex than a considered answer. You have to be careful, throwing around a word like *love*.

"So, what, it's the sex? She knows things young women don't?"

Mercer shakes his head. In truth, they don't have sex all that often, and most of the time it's routine, perfunctory. Friendly, though. It's always friendly. But passionate? Sweat and biting and wolf sounds and rolled-back eyes and fisted toes? Rarely. It does happen every now and then, but that just confuses him more.

"Is this a Freud thing? You have issues with your mom?"

"Hey," Mercer says. "I passed the psych eval, same as you."

"Make me understand, and I'll back off," Toronto says. "Really, fuck whoever you want. I'm just trying to help."

"I like her, that's all. We get along. Why does it have to be more than that? Why does it have to *mean* something about me?"

"Everything you do means something about you. You going to marry her?"

"How should I know?"

"If anyone knows, you should."

"It's just early, is what I'm saying."

"It's not early for her. She's got about eight minutes before her ovaries petrify."

"Who said anything about kids?"

"Has she?"

"She knows it's probably too late. She said she's made her peace."

"She's lying."

"Can we stop talking about this?"

"Last question: do you find yourself still looking? Shopping around? Sizing up every woman you meet as fuckable or non?"

Mercer sucks his lower lip, thinking. He says, "I don't have any other viable prospects right now."

"That's your problem. You worry about what's viable."

"How can you not worry about what's viable?"

"Fuck viable," Toronto says. "The only thing that ever feels viable is staying where you are. Mia and I aren't *viable*. I'm a thirty-seven-year-old cop. She's twenty-two and a circus tumbler and nuclear-fucking-hot. We weren't viable until I made us viable."

"Yeah, but will it last?"

"I'm getting a ring this weekend."

"You're getting engaged?"

"That's generally what rings mean, dipshit."

"You've only known her a few months," Mercer points out. He remembers Toronto telling him about his first night with Mia: it was during Mercer's field training, and they were in the cruiser together, parked down by the landfill. They were watching Hillside Avenue, Mercer manning the radar gun, and Toronto went on and on about this circus girl he'd picked up over tequila shots in a bar on Valencia. Mercer had learned something important that night: that there's a kind of man who can talk freely and in great detail about the sex he's had—positions, orifices, sounds, fluids, kinks—and there's a kind of man who can listen to it enthusiastically, without embarrassment, and that he himself was neither. He'd wished an intoxicated driver would come along so Toronto would have to shut up for a while, but no one obliged. When Mercer couldn't stand it anymore, he took down a silver BMW for doing forty-nine in a forty-five zone.

"She's going on tour in a few weeks," Toronto says. "I'm going to ask her before she leaves."

"A little insurance," Mercer says. "So she doesn't screw the Dog-Faced Boy. Or Humpy the Clown."

"Fuck off. That's not funny."

Toronto heads down the Hickey Boulevard exit ramp, and the sounds of the freeway traffic fade behind them as they cross the town line. He takes the right turn onto Hickey too fast for the conditions, and the cruiser fishtails in the empty intersection before he brings it back under control. "I meant that," he says. "Scared you."

The sky has brightened to a pewtery gray. Mercer closes his eyes and relaxes, lets the flash of adrenaline he felt during the skid drain away. He's pleased with himself. *Humpy the Clown.* Little by little, he's getting the hang of this job.

. . .

**K**icking through a patch of tall weeds nearby, Phineas Gage hears the screeching tires as a faint mosquito-whine, and all he sees of the cruiser when he looks up is a dim, whitish blur receding into the gray. It is a minor distraction; it lasts no longer than the time it took his tamping iron to pass through his head when the charge detonated. A quarter of a second? A tenth? It is a brief distraction that brings a flash of calm, and then the misery returns, dark and crushing and old. He feels the emptiness in his hands as something tangible, sharp and cold, and he is overwhelmed with this sense of *lack*. The words return: *My iron, my iron, my goddamn iron.* He concentrates harder, keeps his head down, slaps aside weeds, scans the ground closely. *My iron, my iron, my goddamn iron.*

He can envision it perfectly. Three feet long; an inch and a quarter in diameter. A perfectly balanced thirteen and a half pounds, custom-forged, darkly mottled with age and skin oil. They'd found it fifty yards down the rail line, cleaned the brain from it, and brought it to him at the doctor's house. After that, it never left his side. Throughout New England, where he exhibited himself on street corners for pennies. At Barnum's in New York. Across the equator on the steamer to Chile. Back and forth on the stagecoach between Valparaiso and Santiago, knocking the heads of any bandits fool enough to make a try. In the artichoke fields of Santa Clara, supporting him in the heat. In his sweat-slick hands on his deathbed in San Francisco. Into the ground with him. But now? Gone. His iron is gone, and he feels its absence like a ragged, yawning wound. Someone stole his goddamned iron. His hands sting with nicks from brambles and sharp-edged grasses. It has to be here, somewhere.

He storms through the field, through scrubby bushes and skeletal trees. He trips over something and falls; hot rage sweeps over him and his head pounds and his vision goes blood-red and star-spiked and then there is shouting, there is some woman kneeling in his path, digging for Root, crying for devil-knows-why, and there is more shouting and the foulest words he knows and he stomps onward, his mind clouded with fury. *My iron. My iron. Someone stole my goddamn iron.*

To hell with them all. They don't understand the need that scrapes him raw, over and over, and the rage that burns and burns. A quarter of a second? A tenth? However long it was, in that moment, amid the deafening boom and the drizzle of granite and the dry fall leaves and the burnt powder and the shouting Irishmen, in that moment, as it shot through his upper jaw and out the top of his head, in that moment, his iron was *part* of him.

Pooling in the air are pockets of the smell that remains when the Root takes effect. A hot smell of vinegar and creosote, a smell that leaves him queasy. To hell with them. The ones who go away and the ones who stay. All of them. He keeps his focus on the ground in front of him. *My iron. My iron. My iron my iron my iron my*

**T**oronto parks in the station lot. He and Mercer are the last ones in for the night; unless a call comes in, the cruisers will remain idle until the daytimers show up at six. Inside, Officer Carolyn Benzinger is sitting at her desk, typing up her incident reports. She's in her forties, tall and whip-thin and severely muscled. She's a fanatical runner who spends her vacation time competing in hundred-mile races that often kill an entrant or two. She's also the best the agency has on domestic-violence calls, expert at defusing anger but nail-gun tough when the situation demands. As they approach her, Mercer turns his head away. He doesn't want her to see his black eye. Doesn't want her to see how careless he was.

Benzinger, punching at the computer keyboard with her bony index fingers, doesn't take her eyes off the monitor. "If you're looking for Hatchetface, he's in the break room," she says. "Knock before you go in. He probably has his dick in his hand."

"Nothing new there," Toronto says.

In the break room, Officer Arthur Cambi is slumped on the couch, legs crossed at the ankles, one beefy arm outstretched as if it were cradling an invisible woman's shoulders. Part Filipino and part Italian, Cambi is a body-builder with a thick neck and a buzz cut that emphasizes his dolabriform head. His lower lip bulges with dipping tobacco, and he's holding an empty cup to spit into. He's watching TV with the sound muted—an exercise show featuring three ethnically diverse, tank-suited models on a beach, bouncing on their toes and jabbing punches into the air, one-two, one-two, one-one-one-two. Palm fronds sway behind them. Foreheads glisten; bleached teeth and new cross-trainers shine the same hot shade of white; ample-but-proportionate breasts hippity-hop beneath clinging spandex. Toronto and Cambi greet each other with flipped middle fingers.

"Any news on the kid?" Mercer asks. Cambi had met them at the grotto and photographed the scene while Toronto bagged evidence, Mercer paced off distances with the Roll-O-Meter, and Detective Funkhouser supervised.

Cambi spits. "You look like shit, Mercer," he says. "That's going to be one black motherfucking eye."

"I'm aware," Mercer says. "How's the kid?"

"Seriously. Your head looks like a fucking eight ball."

"Don't be a dick," Toronto says. "What do you hear about the kid?"

"Not much," Cambi says. "Parents haven't been reached yet. San Francisco's attempting to contact."

"That should only take a week or two," Toronto says. "Give those fuckers an address, a map, a compass, and a cab ride to the front door, and maybe, just maybe, they'll be able to pull it off."

Cambi laughs, then spits, a delicate *purt* that drops a string of brown saliva into the cup. The TV models begin throwing perky uppercuts. "Nice," he says.

"What are you going to do today?" Toronto asks him. "Besides jerk off."

"Jerk off again," Cambi says. "Then work on the car."

"Which is, more or less, also jerking off."

"Listening to that engine is better than sex. You should come over and check it out."

"Sorry," Toronto says. "I'll be busy having a life."

"Boy Thirteen?"

"I'm not much into cars," Mercer says. He always nods and tries to look interested when Cambi rhapsodizes about the Mustang, but he understands little of Cambi's lingo and cares even less. Only two cars matter to Mercer: the Oldsmobile that gets him around town and whichever Crown Vic he's driving on patrol.

"Maybe you should *get* more into cars," Cambi says. "What's up with that piece of shit you drive?"

"Is that even a car?" Toronto asks. "I thought it was some kind of modern-art piece. You know, commenting on what shitty things cars are."

Mercer's car is a beige 1983 Oldsmobile Omega that had belonged to his grandfather. It was hideous when it was new, and two hundred thousand miles haven't made it look any better. There are dents in all the doors and quarter panels and in the front bumper, all souvenirs of his grandfather's last few years of menacing other drivers on the roads around Fresno. Mercer's mother had doubted that these were accidents at all; she believed her father—always stubborn and ill-tempered—had simply decided that he was entitled at his age to drive wherever he wanted, regardless of whether another vehicle was already occupying that space. When he died, she offered Mercer the car. "I can't imagine why you'd want it, but it's yours if you do." He accepted, not caring that the Olds was a piece of shit, or that he hadn't known or liked his grandfather much, or that hot, humid days would conjure the smell of the old man's cigar smoke up from the upholstery, or that he'd be opening himself up to years of taunts from friends and strangers. Recently, he'd suggested to his friend Owen that the car might be approaching retro-cool; Owen shook his head sadly and said, "I still have so much work to do on you."

"It gets me where I want to go," Mercer says. "Engine's still good."

Toronto says, "Spend some money. You're a grown-up. You have a job now."

"He's still probationary," Cambi says. "He could still wash out and have to go back to work at the Big Throbbing Dick."

"It's called The Hard Ten," Mercer says. "It refers to dice."

"My big throbbing dick it does."

"Funny."

"And even if you *do* like girls," Cambi says, "how the hell are you ever going to get one into that car?"

"Boy Thirteen already has a girlfriend," Toronto says.

Mercer shrugs, trying to stifle Cambi's interest so Toronto doesn't go into detail.

"She's actually seen the vehicle?" Cambi says, incredulous.

Toronto says, "She likes it. Because it's an *Olds*mobile." He looks at Mercer with a crooked smile on his face, hoping for a response. Mercer gives him nothing. Cambi's eyebrows knot briefly, but Mercer can see he doesn't get the joke. Cambi's a straightforward guy. He's best when situations are simple, clear-cut, and in the center of his vision: a vehicle weaving across lanes; a shirtless drunk punching his wife. He's not big on interpretation or inference.

Toronto installs himself next to Cambi on the coffee-stained couch. The exercise girls begin a series of perfectly synchronized karate kicks. Cambi spits into the cup and says, "Shit, look at that. I could do karate."

"No, you couldn't," Toronto says. "You're too bulked-up. Nothing on you moves."

Mercer, having lost a coin flip with Toronto at the crime lab, retreats to a desk to cut the paper on the DiMaio incident. As soon as he calls a blank form up onto his screen, he begins to type. He likes the simplicity of the incident report, the orderliness of it. Information is placed in its allotted box. Victim's name, Last First Middle. Done. Victim's address. Done. And so on. The officer's statement: simple sentences that tackle one action at a time, direct, unambiguous. *Victim DiMaio was naked from the waist down. I made contact. V-DiMaio was unresponsive.* He's still learning to write these—he takes twice as long as Toronto does, and he still sometimes gets tangled up in details or can't get sentences to say what he wants them to—but he enjoys the process of reducing life to ironclad objectivity. Off duty, he practices by narrating events as if he were typing them out. *Friend Owen prepared beverages by mixing rum and mango juice and serving over ice. Juvenile male (approx. 6 y.o.) rode electric rocking-horse outside supermarket; cried when ride ended. Subject Fiona (W-F, 43) asked if I would like to establish permanent residence in her home; Subject expressed dissatisfaction with response.*

Eager to finish, he works quickly, hearing the sounds around him without registering them. Stabs of radio static, the coffeemaker bubbling and hissing, day-shifters arriving and bullshitting with each other—Mercer blocks it all out, withdraws, focuses on the task in front of him, this incident, these facts, this keyboard, this soft and steady flow of clicks with each press and release.

He jumps when Benzinger taps him on the shoulder. She shakes up a chemical cold-pack and hands it to him. "Come on, Mercer," she says. "Take care of yourself first. You should know better."

"Thanks," he says. He holds the pack to his swollen face. Tiny fingers of cold work their way under his skin.

"Sure you're all right?" she asks.

"I'll be fine," he says, enjoying the numbness that spreads over the left side of his face. "I've been hit harder."

She whistles, feigning awe. "Boy Thirteen, you are one tough hombre." She pokes him in the back. "Make sure you ice it for a while."

Mercer types with his free hand until he gets frustrated with his slow progress. Then he spends five minutes trying to figure out a way to use the rubber bands in the top drawer to keep the cold-pack on his face, but succeeds only in pinching the skin at his temples and losing some hair, so he pushes it to the corner of the desk and resumes typing two-handed. He finishes the report at three minutes to six, logs out, and joins Toronto and Benzinger, who are at the front desk, putting on their jackets.

On the desk is a basket of blueberry muffins that Lorna Featherstone, the sergeant's widow, delivered the afternoon before. She still visits, even though there's no Wesley to say hello to, just a framed black-and-white photo of him—tight-eyed and grim-lipped, his comb-over sprayed stiffly into place—hanging on the wall. She recently took up baking, and she has been bringing them the things that have emerged from her oven. None of it has been good. Her oatmeal-raisin cookies were scorch-bottomed, black and bitter; her scones tasted like she'd mixed up the salt and sugar; her lemon-poppy bread made a better doorstop than a dessert. Last night, Mazzarella swore that Lorna's muffins were what sent his GI tract haywire. They welcome her gifts, though, and they welcome her, even though most of the officers secretly would prefer that she not come around; Lorna Featherstone, with her lost eyes, her small talk that teeters on the edge of breakdown tears, her lipstick-streaked front teeth, and her desperate, failed muffins, is too much of a reminder that they're all at risk of going out on patrol and never coming back. On any shift, on any call, in any pursuit, you can get yourself killed and end up as just a photo on the wall. Or, if you're lucky, the honoree of a three-mile stretch of freeway.

Officer Landau, a day-shifter, comes through the door, and cold wind rushes in with him. Rainwater speckles his face and clings in droplets to his mustache. The midnighters don't think much of Richard Landau: he's fifty and paunchy and bald, too dumb ever to make sergeant, a gas burner who drives in circles around the quietest parts of town and whose greatest law-enforcement skill is his ability to milk a lost-property call for three hours. To his face, they call him Dick. Behind his back, they call him Dead Wood. The double entendres are intended. Still, though, Landau's one of them. If another officer were in danger, he'd get his shit together and help.

Landau wipes his feet, says hello, and reaches for a muffin.

"Take two," Toronto says.

Landau pulls his hand back. "Wait," he said. "Are these Lorna's?"

"Yes, Lorna made them," Benzinger says. "She was kind enough to make them and bring them to us. But these assholes think they made Mazzarella sick last night."

"Every one of those muffins is a loaded gun," Toronto says.

"And twice as heavy," Landau says, hefting a muffin with an exaggerated clean-and-jerk. He holds it in the air, wincing, his hand shaking under its mostly-but-not-entirely-imagined weight.

"Hey," Benzinger says. "Ease up. Lorna's having a hard time."

"No one's doubting that," Toronto says. "But these muffins."

"We should be cooking for *her*," Benzinger says.

"I heard she sold the house," Landau says.

Mercer says, "I read somewhere that you're not supposed to let someone who's grieving make decisions like that. For like a year or two."

"It's not my place to tell her that," Benzinger says. "It's not any of our places. She told me she didn't want to live there without him. What's even sadder is that she's moving into that shitty complex up by the freeway crossing. The Willows."

"That's where I live," Mercer says.

"No offense, Mercer," Benzinger says. "It's just that it's a shitty place."

"Why do you live there?" Landau asks him.

"Save money."

"For what?"

"For later." Mercer isn't sure, really. He might buy a house someday. Or go somewhere. Hard to know at this point, but as he sees it, that's not the worst thing in the world, to have a little bit of money and not know what to do with it yet.

"You be nice to Lorna," Benzinger tells him. "Help her out."

"But don't let her cook for you," Toronto says. "Unless I'm in your will. Am I in your will?"

"Not after that grandmother crack, you're not," Mercer says.

Benzinger punches Toronto in the shoulder, a solid whack. "What did you say about his grandmother?"

"Nothing," Toronto says. "I swear."

Landau tells them good-bye and heads for the locker room. In the doorway, he's met by Cambi, who blocks the older man's path, countering each of Landau's attempts to get past him, smiling wider with each move. "Move it, shit-heel," Landau says, finally, and Cambi mock-graciously steps aside and holds the door open for him. As he approaches the group at the front door, he packs his mouth with another dip. "*Shit-heel.* That's great. That's old school. God, I love fucking with him." He wipes his fingers clean on his cargo pants. "All right. Who's up for drinks at The Door?"

Toronto says yes and knocks fists with him. Benzinger begs off. "I'm out," Mercer says.

"Come on," Cambi says. "You found the kid. Calls for a celebration."

"You're not going to sleep," Toronto says. "You'll be way too jacked up."

"I'm wiped," Mercer says. "And my head's killing me."

"Tough it out," Cambi says.

"Yeah," Toronto says. "Shut up and die like an aviator." It's his favorite, all-purpose piece of advice, and he dispenses it often. He says it's from some astronaut movie, but Mercer's never checked up on that.

"Not today," Mercer says.

Benzinger zips her jacket. "See you tomorrow," she says. "Good job tonight, you guys." She opens the door, and a gust of wind blows in. Mercer feels the cold on his face and his exposed throat.

"Wasn't me," Toronto says. "It was all Mercer. If it'd just been me out there, the kid would be a corpse."

"I don't know why you're proud of that," Benzinger says.

"Not proud. It's just that a man doesn't take credit for someone else's work."

"What, and a woman does?"

"He didn't mean it that way," Mercer says.

"Not as far as you know, anyway," Toronto says.

"Well, congratulations, Mercer," Benzinger says. "You're a hero. Take that home with you and enjoy it."

"He's not a hero yet," Cambi points out. "If the kid bites it, Mercer's still just Boy Fucking Thirteen."

"Ignore him," Benzinger says to Mercer.

"I always do," Mercer says, playing cool, but he feels his face warming. He's uncomfortable with all the attention. "There's other news," he says. "Toronto's getting engaged."

"Oh God," Benzinger says. "Not again."

Mercer turns to Toronto. "You've been engaged before?"

Toronto takes a pack of smokes out of his pocket, smacks it against his palm, and loads one into his mouth. "What can I say?" he says, shrugging. "I've lived."

THREE

◉

# GOOD SHEPHERD

**M**ercer and Fiona had met eight months earlier on a Sunday night at Good Shepherd Hospital, a high-rise medical center that crowns a steep hill just west of the freeway. Fresh out of the Police Academy, Mercer was working swing-shift security for the hospital while he looked for a job with a local agency. That night, he was posted outside the emergency room, and as a cat's-claw moon rose over San Bruno Mountain, cars appeared one by one in the driveway and birthed the injured before him: a woman about Mercer's mother's age, whose fever-green skin shone with sweat and smelled like low tide; a paunchy man in basketball shorts with a blown-out knee; a drunk twenty-something bleeding through napkin-plugged nostrils. As the doors slid apart and the patients and their companions crossed into the dim purple fluorescence of the hospital, Mercer stood to the side and nodded greetings that went unseen.

He watched an airplane lazily curl in for a landing into the bright lights of SFO and listened to the soft static of the interstate until his drifting thoughts were interrupted by a black pickup truck with head-high tires squealing into the hospital driveway. The truck jolted to a stop just in front of him. A round-faced woman in the passenger seat opened the door and dropped herself to the ground. She was wearing denim overall-shorts, and her body jiggled when her sandals hit the pavement. The smell from the truck—alcohol, cigarettes, and sickness—settled around them.

The driver got out, slammed his door shut, and approached Mercer around the front of the truck. White male, late thirties, six-foot-six or -seven—at least a half-foot taller than Mercer—with a thick, sandy-brown mullet that dangled past his shoulder blades and a patchy beard that failed to hide puckery acne scars. He was wearing a faded black T-shirt with a tuxedo silk-screened on it: bow tie, ruffles, piped lapels. His walk had an angry man's purpose and a drunk man's wobble.

"It's his fault!" the woman shouted at Mercer.

"What is?" Mercer asked.

"My daughter."

"Hey, Rent-A-Cop," the driver said before Mercer could respond. "How about you get off your ass and help us."

Mercer quickly sized him up: big talk, nowhere near as tough as he thought he was, but intoxicated enough to try something stupid. He readied himself. *Go low. Use his height against him.* He'd never been a fighter, but he'd discovered a combative streak in himself at the Academy; he didn't *want* to kick anyone's ass, but if he had to, he would, and he'd enjoy it. "That's what I'm here for," he said, keeping his voice hard but level. "Ma'am, what's wrong with your daughter?"

"She's drunker'n shit," the man said.

"It's his fault!" the woman shouted again. "He let her drink."

"Didn't see you stopping her, Barb," the man said. "Some mother you are."

"Asshole. You are such an asshole, Glenn."

Mercer heard a groan from inside the truck. "Ma'am, let's get your daughter some medical attention right now. That's more important than assigning blame." He peered into the truck and saw the girl, a dark bulk wedged into the rear jump seats. "Young lady, are you all right?" he asked her.

The girl moaned, and he watched her pale hands move to clutch her stomach.

"No, she isn't all right," Barb said, turning on Mercer. "We need *help.* That's why we're *here.*"

"Can she get out of there?" Mercer asked.

"I got her in," Glenn said. "So, yeah. Probably."

"Should I find an orderly to help you?"

Barb and Glenn stared at him.

"I'm not allowed to touch patients," Mercer explained, "for reasons of liability."

"Then you better find someone who is," Barb said. "My Layla's in trouble."

"Don't look at me," Glenn said. "I fucked up my back getting her in."

"So you're saying," Mercer said, hearing his voice wobble, "that you won't help get this girl out of the truck."

"Not my *yob*," Glenn said, in a cartoon Mexican accent.

The girl in the back seat moaned again. Mercer couldn't tell if she was saying *Mommmm* or if it was just an animal syllable of discomfort.

"Do something, one of you!" Barb shouted. "It could be her appendix! She could die!"

"It's not her appendix," Glenn said. "She's just shitfaced."

"You're no doctor," Barb said to him. Then she leaned in and told her daughter that everything would be all right once someone got her the hell out of the truck. Mercer looked at the two adults and shook his head. He doubted that this was true.

Inside the hospital, he found an orderly, a short and wiry, light-skinned Latino whose name tag identified him as MOISÉS. Together they walked out to the truck, Moisés pulling a gurney along behind him, his tight-braided ponytail jouncing between his shoulder blades. When they arrived at the curb, Moisés surveyed the situation, tugging on the long, black hairs that made up a stringy soul patch beneath his lower lip. "What's wrong with her?" he asked.

"Fucked up and about to bust," Glenn told him.

"We have to get her out of there ourselves," Mercer said.

"You're not allowed," Moisés said.

"These two have declined to help."

The girl moaned again. Moisés narrowed his eyes, then exhaled deeply and nodded. "Just don't make any mistakes," he said to Mercer. "All right. How we gonna do this?"

"Lift from the knees," Glenn said, his voice suddenly generous with wisdom.

"Any injuries?" Moisés asked.

"My back," Glenn said. "I didn't lift from the knees."

They decided to shimmy Layla out the passenger-side door, with the smaller Moisés lifting from inside the truck and Mercer receiving her at the curb to guide her onto the gurney. Moisés climbed in the driver's side and wrapped his arms around the girl's chest, while Mercer took hold of her calves. They got her feet pointed out the door and slid her a few inches across the vinyl half-seat. She didn't resist, but her body was tight with pain. She was wearing new, indigo-blue jeans that were under serious stress, along with a snug white top splashed with purple-orange stains where she'd gotten sick on herself. Mercer felt embarrassed for her.

While they were maneuvering the girl, Glenn lit a smoke and Barb rattled off the story of how they'd come to be there: they'd been at a wedding up along Skyline, and Layla decided to wear her new jeans even though they'd bought them a couple sizes too small so she'd want to lose weight, not that she has, of course, and she'd have been able to keep an eye on her daughter if Glenn hadn't—

"Please," Mercer said. "We're busy here."

"Aren't you going to write this down?" she said.

"I'm security," he grunted. "We don't write things down."

Inside the truck, the girl groaned, and Moisés inched her forward, saying softly, "Okay, *mija*, you gonna be okay."

They counted together, and on three, they hefted Layla into a quarter-turn so they could bring her out on her side. Moisés shuffled forward in the cramped space, and Mercer eased her down onto the pad. He felt a quick, sharp spasm in his lower back as he twisted to reposition himself. "Stop," he said. He thought he'd heard a pop, too.

"Can't stop," Moisés said, his voice strained. "Got to give her to you. Ready?"

Mercer grunted and held the girl aloft while Moisés jumped out and ran around to join him. Together, they lowered her the rest of the way, carefully, Moisés supporting her head and neck as they made contact with the pad, no jolts, no jostles. They kept her lying on her side so she wouldn't aspirate if she vomited again.

Barb followed them into the building while Glenn went to move the truck to the parking lot. As soon as they got inside, the pager on Moisés' belt beeped. "Shit," he said. "Just take her to check-in. Don't let them make her wait."

"Got it," Mercer said. He pushed the gurney along the turquoise-tiled path that led to the waiting room and the check-in windows. The wheels clacked lightly over the tile seams. The fluorescent lights hummed, and the ceiling felt dollhouse-low. The skin at Layla's clamped waist looked purple. Barb breathed heavily and sniffled as she hurried to keep up.

A white-haired woman with a beaded lanyard attached to her glasses was at the reception desk. "This girl needs to be seen," Mercer told her. "Immediately." The receptionist called the nurses' station, and within half a minute, a purple door swung open and a nurse made straight for the girl, all business, the pockets of her cardigan heavy with medical gear. Her eyes were wide and intense, and Mercer trusted her instantly. This, he would find out, was Fiona, although at that moment he was more aware of her as someone who could help the girl. She was professionalism personified. Competence in a mint-green sweater.

"How much has she had to drink?" Fiona asked Barb, all business. Layla had curled into a tight fetal ball on the gurney, clutching her stomach. Mercer saw that she was wearing a pink butterfly-shaped barrette, and for some reason this made him even sadder.

"It might be her appendix," Barb said.

"I asked you how much she had to drink." Her expression toughened, and a furrow between her eyebrows deepened. (Later, Mercer would discover that the furrow never completely left her face; lingering in bed one lazy morning, he would trace it with his thumbnail and understand how much easier it was for him to trust people who understood worry.)

"It was Glenn," Barb said.

Fiona cut her off. "I don't care *who*. I care *how much*. Understand?"

"I don't know how much."

"Drugs?"

"I didn't—"

"Any. Drugs," Fiona said again, both words fist-blunt.

Barb squeezed her eyes shut and shook her head. "I don't know."

"All right," Fiona said, with obvious disdain. "We'll talk later. You, Security, bring her in. Room Six." Fiona led them through another purple door into an examination room, where Mercer parked the gurney and locked the wheels. She went right to work, snapping on a pair of latex gloves and palpating the girl's stomach. "All right, sweetie, just try to relax," she said, her tone softening. "What's your name?"

Layla moaned.

"It's Layla," Mercer said. "Like the song."

"Relax, Layla. I'm taking care of you now." Each time she prodded Layla's belly, the girl yelped in pain. "Those jeans have to come off, *stat*." Fiona tried to slide a finger under the waistband, but there was no give in the fabric, and when she tried to wriggle in more aggressively, Layla shrieked a high note. Mercer realized he was staring, and he turned away, assuming his work was done. Fiona stopped him. "Hang on. Hand me those, will you?" she said, pointing to a set of shears on a metal tray. The chill of the metal lingered on his fingers after he handed them to her. Fiona, using one hand to hold up the roll of blued skin around the girl's middle, worked one jaw of the shears into the waistband. Layla shrieked again, and then there was a sound like a toy-gun pop. Something whined past Mercer's face at eye level, and he jerked his head back. The flying object ricocheted off the wall behind him, pinged across the metal tray, and rattled to rest on the floor tiles at his feet. It was the button from her jeans, logo-minted in shiny silver. Mercer picked it up and put it on the tray.

Fiona was still working the shears, which had cut through the fabric as far as Layla's inner thigh. The girl was breathing more easily.

"Close call," Fiona said, without looking up at him. "I wasn't expecting that."

"No problem," Mercer said. It *had* been a close call. One inch to his right, and he might've lost an eye. One inch to his right, and his career as a patrol officer would've been over before it started.

"What's your name?" Fiona asked.

"Mercer. Mike."

"Sorry about the projectile, Mercer Mike. Thanks for bringing her in."

"It's my job," he said.

"No, it isn't."

"Oh," he said. "You're right. But Moisés asked me to."

She nodded. "Don't get in the habit," she said. "I'll have a talk with Moisés."

"Is that all? Is she okay?"

"She's extremely drunk. There's that." A flap of denim peeled away as she spoke, and Mercer saw more pasty, puffy flesh. A few fringes of dark pubic hair curled out from a pair of pink panties. He looked away, feeling like an intruder. "You can go now," Fiona said. "Layla and I need some private time. Girls only."

The next night, Mercer and Fiona would sleep together. On the day in between, Mercer attended Sergeant Featherstone's funeral.

He walked into the chapel at Woodlawn just a few minutes before the service began. He'd only met the sergeant once, on an overnight shift; Featherstone had seemed remote and distracted, but not unfriendly, and Mercer wanted to pay respects. He took a seat in the back row, not wanting to impose on the cops who'd known him for years, but Toronto, his face stone-serious, noticed him and waved him forward to join the group. Mercer's lower back was tight and aching—from lifting Layla, he guessed—and he hoped no one would notice him walking stiffly. He didn't want to look weak.

Outside, afterward, as the bagpipes shrilled and droned and Mercer stood with the officers offering condolences to Lorna, the morning fog was burning off, and the sun cast stubby shadows behind everyone—or, rather, behind the living.

All around them, the dead were watching, too: perched on top of mausoleums, gathered in loose groups on the grass, peeking up from Root-mining tunnels, many shaking their heads sadly. There were whispers about how strange it would be now to encounter Featherstone as a dead man. He had pledged that he would rein in Doc Barker and his gang, and they had allowed themselves to believe in him. He had tried, and he had failed.

Still, he had tried, and in tribute, Lefty O'Doul laid his mitt on the grass, removed his cap, and held it over his heart.

Emperor Norton stood on the top step of a nearby mausoleum flanked by two sitting mutts, his saber held high in salute.

Lincoln Beachey, the daredevil aviator, flew past and dipped his wings before crashing just over the next hill.

Ishi, the last Yahi Indian, knelt alone under a willow tree, chanting an ancient song of mourning.

Lillie Coit leaned against the chapel doorway, wearing her helmet and sneaking glances at the firefighters in their dress uniforms. She also kept an eye on a small group of men taking in the funeral from a distance, high on a hill above the chapel. She was ready to sound the alarm if they came down to wreak their customary havoc.

One of those four men was Doc Barker, whose freshly shaved fingertips were dripping blood over the jug of pruno in his hand and veining red trails over the granite slab on which he sat. Behind him, three members of his gang—Ruczek, LoPresti, and Eastwick—were playing a drunken game of mumblety-peg, laughing as they hurled an ivory-handled knife at each other's feet. Ruczek wore a top hat and a monocle and spats that he'd taken off some dead Fancy Dan that morning, and LoPresti's pocket bulged with a gold watch he'd snatched. Eastwick wore a belt that he'd stitched together from the leather covers of stolen Bibles. In between throws of the knife, the three were wondering aloud what they ought to do to Featherstone when he showed up dead.

"Can't believe Doc was ever worried about Sergeant Candypants," Ruczek said, just loud enough for Doc to hear. "We didn't even have to touch the guy."

"Shut up and play the game," Eastwick said. "Don't bother him."

Doc watched the half-staff flag as it flap-fluttered in a cool breeze that stroked what was left of his hair and hummed a flutelike note through the hole in his face. Irritated by the hum, he held one hand over it to block the wind. Goddamn his bad luck to get stuck with the body he had at the instant he'd died. Some folks got to be their young selves; some were older but not so goddamn damaged. No one as shot to hell as he was, that was for sure. No rhyme or reason to it—just rotten luck, as far as he could tell. He'd had a long time to get used to it, but it still burned his ass, that rotten luck.

He pressed his skinned fingers together, giving himself a deep, sweet jolt of pain. Goddamn fingerprints—maybe this time he'd dug deep enough that the skin would heal flat and pink and anonymous. Those whorls and arches had led the feds to Ma and Freddy at the lake house—Ma and Freddy, dead, shot to ribbons, and it was all his goddamned fault, always would be. He pictured Ma's face, her pale, doughy, lopsided face, and her blocky body jerking as each bullet found its home in her. *Forgive me, Ma. I'm so goddamn sorry.* But the voice he heard back wasn't her tray-of-lemonade voice, it was her swinging-the-two-by-four voice, and it said, *You done what you done, and you are what you done, and ain't no changing that,* and his vision went bright red and he heard himself roaring as he dug his crusted fingernails even deeper into the pulped pads of his fingers, and he knew the boys would quit their laughing and put their knives back in their belts, because they would know that Doc was ready, ready to get back to work. Ready to make other dead folks lose what they least wanted to lose. And feel some pain of their own, too—if all went well.

That night, Mercer was again stationed outside the Good Shepherd ER, bored, ignored, and oblivious to the dead—their suffering, their machinations, their dread. A few hours into the shift, Moisés came outside for a smoke. "How's the girl?" Mercer asked him. "The girl from the truck," he added, when Moisés looked confused.

"Fuck, man," Moisés said, shaking his head. "Was like moving a fucking piano."

"You know how she's doing?"

"She gone home. Must be okay." Moisés' fingers crept up to his soul patch and stroked. "I heard her pants exploded."

"Her pants didn't explode. How can pants explode?"

"Nurse says the pants exploded. Says you almost lost an eye."

Mercer nods. "The button shot off," he said. "That happened."

"Hey, what you think of that nurse? Fiona?" Moisés stretched out each of the syllables of her name.

"What do you mean?"

"I mean, what you think about that nurse?"

"Well," Mercer said. "She seems to do her job well."

"I think she likes you, man," Moisés said. "She says to me, hey, who's that new security, the one who helps with the fat girl? And I tell her I don't know you from nobody, and she tells me you're cute. She says you got good reflexes or else you lose an eye when the pants explode."

"They didn't explode," Mercer said.

"Explode, don't explode. Whatever, man. Nurse likes you."

Mercer thought back. He hadn't noticed anything flirty in Fiona's voice or demeanor, but he knew he tended to miss signals. He tried to remember the expression on her face as she'd asked him his name, tried to remember whether she'd held eye contact with him for a beat or two longer than necessary. His whole memory of the exchange was vague and blurred, but he felt excitement stir in him.

"So, you like her?" Moisés asked. "You think she's cute, too?"

"I hadn't thought about it."

"Bullshit. Bull*shit*. You can tell me. Cute, right? She takes care of herself, you know?"

"I don't know," Mercer said. "I guess so." It felt like a safe thing to say.

"You got a girlfriend?"

Mercer shook his head. He hadn't gotten laid in months. The last time was on his final night at The Hard Ten, just before he started at the Academy. He'd hooked up with a regular named Bonnie, a garrulous blonde with off-center eyes who was a decent shot at pool and who'd always tipped him well. She'd called him once afterward, but he'd put off calling her back for a couple of weeks, and after that it felt too late. Since Bonnie, nothing. Mercer wasn't a stranger to dry spells; in fact, the longer they went on, the more he'd forget there was any other way to live. He figured he ought to be troubled by this— this ability to drift unbothered into celibacy—but he also thought it came in handy. It kept things simple, kept need and ache and rejection and loss out of his life. Still, he was curious. This nurse.

"She likes you, man," Moisés said. "You should take her out."

"Maybe I will," Mercer said, feeling strangely confident.

The guard in the hallway agreed to trade his post for the price of a peanut-butter-crunch energy bar. From this new position, Mercer could see when Fiona took a break. An hour later, she appeared in the hallway, retying her ponytail. She glanced at him, then turned away and headed for the cafeteria. He felt himself blush, and a terrible thought struck him: Moisés had told her he was interested, and she was snubbing him. He was nothing to her. But then she stopped and turned back, looking as if she'd left something important behind. This gave him time to speak, and he found his voice just as she was turning away again.

"Hi," he said. All that time waiting, and he'd forgotten to plan an opening line.

She faced him, came a few steps closer. "Mercer Mike," she said.

"Fiona? That's your name, right?"

"Nurse Wells, to you," she said. Mercer must have looked taken aback, because she added, "That's a joke."

He hoped his smile didn't look as forced and self-conscious as it felt. "I heard our girl's okay," he said.

"She went home. Make what you will of that."

"The mom's a piece of work."

"I tell myself not to judge," Fiona said. "But I don't always listen."

"You getting coffee?"

He braced for her response, but she nodded. "I'm about to drop."

"I could use some, too," he said, feeling bolder. "Want company?"

A speaker in the ceiling crackled out summonses to two doctors, then fell silent. She looked up and down the hallway, which was, for the moment, empty except for them. "You don't have things to guard?" she asked.

"I'm due for a break. They'll page me if they need me."

"Good enough," she said, and they walked together to the east-wing cafeteria, which was quiet, the last of the dinner crowd having left hours before. The smells from the day's enchiladas and cheeseburgers and Cajun catfish clotted in the still air. A few coffee drinkers had spread themselves around the room, isolating themselves with space. One of them, a middle-aged man with bristly gray whiskers, hunched defensively over his Styrofoam cup and watched the wall clock blankly.

Mercer paid for two coffees, and they sat at a clean table. Fiona sipped her coffee, then pointed at him with the hand that still held the cup aloft. "You," she said, "and I don't yet know why I think this, but you seem a little smarter than your colleagues."

"Thanks. I think."

"I mean, they installed the path of blue tiles so security guys wouldn't walk into the walls." She paused and looked at him closely. "Joke," she said. "We do that here."

Mercer laughed. *Quit being so stiff,* he told himself.

"My point is, I don't think you're here to make a career out of hospital security. I'm guessing you're between jobs. And I'm guessing that you're—"

"That I'm what?" He was eager to hear how she saw him.

"Hang on, I'm thinking. Let's see. You're a music teacher?"

Mercer shook his head. "Can't play a note. Air guitar. Steering-wheel drums."

"Show me your hands."

He held them out to her, palms up.

"Okay, not construction," she said. "Nothing manual." She looked up at him. "Priest?" she asked, then answered herself. "No, you wouldn't be hitting on me if you were."

"Am I hitting on you?"

"Not very well," she said. "But yes, you are. You haven't drunk any of your coffee. You're just sitting there, listening to me."

"Maybe you're interesting."

"Please," she said. "So I give up. What are you?"

"I'm a cop," he said.

"A cop. Huh." She tilted her head, studied his face. "Yeah, I can see that. You've got the right haircut, at least."

Mercer ran his hand through his hair, a reflex. When he felt the thinning spot on the top of his head, he pulled his hand away. He didn't like touching it. "I graduated from the Academy a few months ago," he said, recovering. "Just waiting to go full-time somewhere. I'm a reserve with Colma. When somebody's sick, or they need extra help, they call me."

"Colma has police?"

"Sure."

"Keeping the peace in a city full of dead people," she said. "That's funny."

"Everyone thinks that."

"Everyone? So I'm not special? I'm mundane? I'm trite?"

"I didn't mean that," Mercer said, feeling his face flush. "I mean, you're right, it *is* funny. But people live there, too, so there's a need for law enforcement. The card room brings some trouble, for one thing."

"I've met a few Daly City cops when they've brought people here. Bunch of good ol' boys. One of them called me *Sugar.* Can I give you some advice? Don't ever call me Sugar. Unless you're dancing with me. Or I get old and broken down and I'm serving coffee in a truck stop. With a tank top and jiggly triceps. Then I guess it'll be all right."

"I don't see that happening."

"The dancing, or the truck stop?"

"Probably both," Mercer said. "I'm not much of a dancer."

"Every guy says that. It's mundane. It's trite."

Mercer raised his coffee cup and blew away steam that wasn't there. "So," he said. "Layla. When was she released?"

"We kept her overnight. That's all. They probably sent the nutritionist to talk to her, but I'll bet she and Mom are deep into a box of Ho Hos as we speak."

"And the alcohol?"

Fiona shrugged. "She's a kid. They'll do what they're going to do. If she ends up with us again, we might get the county involved. But you can't save everyone. That's the first lesson everyone here has to learn." Her voice was tough, but her face showed fatigue; the austere overhead lighting darkened the bags under her eyes. He liked the way it made her look, though: serious, concerned, committed. He studied her face. How had he not noticed that she was attractive? Gray-green eyes that held his, a steep-drop nose like that red-haired actress from *Boogie Nights* had. He registered the hints of crow's-feet and the shallow wrinkles uncoiling from the corners of her mouth, and for the first time he understood what people meant when they said someone's face had character.

He realized it was his turn to speak. "Got to feel bad for that kid," he said.

"There are a lot of problems out there in the world. I try to fix the ones I can." She lifted her purse from the back of her chair and rummaged around in it. He stole a look at her breasts: subtle swells underneath her cardigan, small and oval. "Here," she said, when she'd found what she was looking for. "A present." She dropped it into his hand. It was Layla's button. "The bullet you dodged last night."

"Thanks," Mercer said, taking it from her. "It was surprising, huh?"

"Surprising things happen in hospitals. Got to be on your toes."

"Same goes for cops," he said. "It's a good reminder."

Fiona nodded. "I should get back," she said, swirling around the last of the liquid in her cup.

"Me, too," he said, and they stood.

"Thanks for the coffee."

"I wanted to meet you."

Her smile seemed mysterious to him, as if she knew things he didn't. He had no idea how she would respond. The moment unspooled, quiet. His scalp tingled.

"You're all right," she said at last. "I like you."

"But I haven't said anything impressive." He immediately regretted saying it, could hear the naked insecurity in his words, but she didn't appear to notice, or mind.

They left the cafeteria and walked down the hallway. They passed a janitor who was whistling as he swabbed the floor in rhythmic arcs and a white-bearded man in an ancient overcoat who stood at the elevator doors, watching the lit floor-numbers count down.

"You're walking stiffly," Fiona said. "Your back hurt?"

"A little. From helping the girl out of the truck."

"You're not supposed to touch patients, you know."

"It was a tough situation."

She nodded, and they walked in silence until they reached her door. "Are you off at midnight?" she asked.

*This is it,* Mercer thought. The moment of connection, of pieces fitting into place. His head swam, and he got hard. He shifted his legs. He reminded himself to breathe and then nodded. "You?" he asked.

"Buy me a drink afterward, and I'll give you a back rub."

"I'd like that," he said.


They both had cars, so they followed each other down the hill into Broadmoor and stopped at a bar called Sadie's. Photographs on the wall suggested that it had been a bustling working-class watering hole back in the days when all men wore hats. Mercer and Fiona were the only people in the place, apart from the girl behind the bar and the two underage-looking boys with whom she was speaking animatedly in what Mercer guessed was Vietnamese. She disengaged from her friends long enough to drop a couple of longnecks in front of Mercer and Fiona, her long, fuchsia-painted nails clacking against the bottles as she set them down. She swept up their money and giggled her way back down the bar, where the bigger of the two boys, who had wispy, pointed sideburns running down his cheeks, had just said something terribly funny.

Fiona shifted her stool so that she was sitting directly behind him. She hooked her feet around the stool's footrest, anchoring herself, her legs spread around him. She began to knead the muscles around his shoulder blades, then paused and hopped her stool a few inches closer. Her fingers were strong, and she directed them intuitively to knots of tension that Mercer hadn't known he had.

"It's my lower back that hurts," Mercer said. "Just so you know."

"I'm getting there. Keep your freaking pants on."

As she moved lower on his back, her thighs tightened against him. She paused occasionally to take sips of her beer. When their bottles were empty, Mercer signaled for two more, and Fiona called out for two shots of tequila, all of which the bartender delivered without breaking her stream of conversation with the boys.

When Fiona declared the massage finished, Mercer turned in his stool and allowed himself to slump into her. "I'm melting," he said. "I've melted."

The smaller of the boys walked behind them on his way to the bathroom. As soon as he went through the door, the bartender leaned across the bar, her disproportionately large breasts resting on the scarred oak, and kissed the sideburn boy. Immediately, they began stabbing their tongues into each other's mouth. Mercer and Fiona watched.

Fiona ran her finger along the edge of Mercer's ear. "When in Rome," she said, turning his face to hers.

He kissed her, tasting the tequila and lime on her tongue, astringent and smoky and tart. He turned around in his stool so he wouldn't have to stretch his neck, and he put his arms around her. Their kiss went on long after the small boy returned from the bathroom, and the three kids snickered at them, the small boy most loudly. "Get a room," he said, not entirely under his breath.

Mercer inhaled deeply after he broke off the kiss. He waited for her to say something, but she didn't. He took her hand in his. It wasn't the right gesture—too safe, too polite—but he thought it might be something she'd like anyway.

"Two more shots," Fiona called down the bar.

*What for?* Mercer wondered. They were connecting, they were aroused, they were buzzed enough to dull their inhibitions. He'd started to imagine going home with her, peeling off her clothes and going to bed with her. The night felt poised on a moment of perfect balance, and he didn't want to drink any more. But the tequila appeared, glasses were clinked, liquor was thrown down, and pallid lime wedges were sucked and tossed onto napkins.

"I'm too old for you," Fiona said.

"No," Mercer said. "What does that even mean?"

"Don't evade," she said.

"Who's evading?"

"You are. And what it means is that I'm too old for you."

"You're not."

"Do you know how old I am?"

"It doesn't matter," he said.

"I'll be forty-three in November," she said, and Mercer could tell she was watching his eyes for the flinch, for the involuntary squint of surprise and discomfort. He held his expression steady, aware that he was tightly controlling the muscles in his face, determined to keep it clear of anything she could read as doubt or concern. He didn't know what he truly thought about her age, only that it didn't matter to him right now.

"That doesn't mean anything," he said. It was time for a bold move, he decided. "Let's go somewhere private."

"You're sure?"

"I'm sure."

She turned half-circles on her stool—left, right, left right. "I live in Pacifica. On the beach."

"It's settled," he said. "Your place."


**H**e drove behind her over the hills toward the dark ocean. They parked on a quiet street west of Highway One, and he followed her up a stone pathway that curved around a tangle of rosebushes. A motion sensor lit up the yard around them and cast twiggy rose shadows back to the street. As she was undoing the deadbolt, Mercer heard meowing and scratching from the other side.

Fiona pushed the door open, and a thin gray tabby backed away from its sweep. The cat spoke again, a high-pitched chirp. "Don't let her out," Fiona said. "That's Cricket. She was my dad's." She flicked on a row of light switches.

Mercer was surprised at what he saw. A bulky grandfather clock filled the entryway, and the living room was a crush of chunky, dark-wood furniture. An armoire took up an entire wall. High-backed and wide-armed chairs jutted into walking space. The rest of the room was taken up by a coffee table, a rolltop desk, and a wide, squat bookshelf with a small TV on top. The ceiling was high, and the west-facing windows offered a view of the ocean night, but the room still felt overcrowded to him, oppressive.

In the kitchen, she poured bourbon into highball glasses, and as they sat at the table—also dark and too big for the space—she talked. She'd grown up in Iowa, but she'd moved west after college and stayed. She inherited the family house when her father died four years ago; she'd sold it and put all the money into a down payment. Now Mercer understood: she'd kept all the Iowa furniture in remembrance of her parents.

"There was insurance, too," she said. "And I had some savings because I'd been engaged. To a bass player. A bass player! What was I thinking? After we broke up, I didn't go out, didn't buy anything, didn't do anything. You can save a lot of money when you're depressed." Her words were coming louder and faster; somehow her expression had intensified even as her eyelids drooped.

"Do you still have both your parents?" she asked.

"They're alive," Mercer said.

"There are two kinds of people in the world: the ones who've lost parents and the ones who haven't." She bumped her glass with her elbow, and whiskey sloshed out. Neither of them moved to clean it up.

"My father left," Mercer said. "I haven't seen him in years."

"That's not the same."

Mercer splashed another shot or so into both their glasses. At this point, why not?

"Do you like Buddy Holly?" she asked.

"I guess. Why?"

The house in Iowa was just five miles from the field where Holly's plane went down, she said. Her parents had been at his last show, and afterward, juiced with rock 'n roll and liquor, they'd taken a detour, parked the Plymouth behind a barn, and made love as snow blanketed the car and the heater pumped against the freeze outside. Her dad insisted that Fiona was conceived that night; when he got a few drinks in him, he'd tell people it must've happened around the same time the musicians' plane hit the cold-crusted ground.

Their legs were touching under the table, and she had one hand on his thigh. She took a drink, swallowed hard, and shook her head. "He'd say, 'The music died, but we got a gift of life.' How embarrassing is that? But that was Dad. A Buddy Holly fanatic. Had the same glasses. Requested 'That'll Be the Day' for his funeral." She kicked off her shoes, and Mercer followed her lead. Cricket came in and sniffed at his toes.

"I went to a funeral this morning," Mercer said. "A cop I did a shift with once."

"I'm sorry," she said. "You want to talk about it?"

"Not really," he said. This wasn't a time to be thinking about death.

"Good," she said. "I'm tired of talking." She picked up both of their glasses and put them into the sink.

*She needs this,* he thought. *I need this.*

The sleigh bed hulked in the darkened room. Mercer wondered if she understood how wrong all the Iowa furniture looked in this house. She closed the door behind them, shutting out the cat, who chirped in protest, and they took each other out of their clothes.

"This is all—" Mercer said, searching for the right word, "surprising."

"Surprising things happen at hospitals," Fiona said. "I told you."

"We're not in a hospital."

"Don't be literal. It's unattractive."

Cricket meowed at them from behind the door as they wriggled and rolled in the bed. Mercer was drunk enough not to be too self-conscious, and he focused on the call-and-response of the kissing, on the motion, on the rhythm, on the pulsating thrill of the new. He noted differences between her body and the younger ones he was used to—shallow wrinkles at the base of her neck, less firmness in her breasts than he'd expected, more flesh in her thighs, a rougher feel to her skin—but none of it bothered him, he just observed things and let them go, and that felt magical all by itself. When she'd rolled on top of him and he was about to come, all he was thinking was *I'm alive. I'm alive. I'm alive.*

◉

# FOUR

# THE WILLOWS

**S**leep. Sweet, refreshing sleep.

If only Mercer could get some.

He should be tired, with a twelve-hour shift behind him and the added bonus of head trauma, but he feels wide awake and jangle-nerved, replaying the events of the night in a loop, gauging and regauging the odds that the kid will survive. If Jude dies, it'll be Mercer's fault. He should've noticed the tire tracks on his way into the cemetery, not on the way out. Should've gone out to the grotto the moment he saw the footprints in the wet grass. Should've been more willing to charge out there alone.

He needs to shut down, get some sleep, get rid of this kick-drum headache, hit his next shift fresh. Carrying a mug full of five-dollar red wine, he goes through his sunrise ritual. He closes the blinds in his cluttered living room, shutting out the murky gray morning. He turns the thermostat up to sixty-seven, and the familiar scorched-dust smell of hot air from the floor vents wafts through the room. He tunes his stereo to KCSM's *Morning Cup o' Jazz,* and into the warm, sweeping air currents rise the sounds of a soft, placid piano over a tiptoeing bass line and a brushed snare. Relaxing. A good start.

Mercer moved to Colma when he got the full-time job so he could commit completely to his work and to the community he'd committed to serve. The Willows is the only place in town he can afford, though, and looking around now, he has to admit that Benzinger is right: it is a shitty place to live. It's a small apartment with thin walls, unrelenting noise, and a color scheme of dismal, soiled earth tones. Still, he has adapted. He rarely notices that the cocoa-colored shag rug is balding and stained. Or that his kitchen linoleum has darkened to the color of nicotine-stained teeth and is gouged with dozens of sinister-looking knife wounds. Or that there's a peculiar stink that drapes itself over the entire complex: a mix of exhaust, sick-sweet pine disinfectant, and, inexplicably, sauerkraut. Or that freeway traffic zooms by at all hours. He now sleeps with earplugs so he won't be awakened by racing engines and honking horns, or by the low-flying jets, or by the kids and moms in the complex who shout and laugh with the carefree indifference of people who live in daylight.

His answering machine is flashing a red *1* at him. He figures it's Fiona; on the nights he works, she calls to wish him sweet dreams before she goes to bed. He ignores the message; for now, he's going to sit with his wine and his music, relax, and try to get his head straight. Looking around the room from his place on the couch, he realizes it's a mess: stacks of newspapers and magazines, CDs and cases, even his softball gear, which hasn't been touched since he moved in and dropped it all in the corner. He should probably clean up at some point, he decides.

On the coffee table is his invitation to Owen's thirtieth-birthday party, which arrived in yesterday's mail. With the calligraphy on the heavy-stock envelope and the silken cobalt-blue lining inside, he'd at first mistaken it for a wedding invitation and was hurt that Owen and Mollie hadn't told him first. Inside, though, he found a card with a pair of crossed croquet mallets embossed in gold, and underneath them, in rich blue ink:

*An Evening Garden Party in Honour*
*of Owen O'Dowd's Exiting His Reckless Youth*
*and Passing into Respectable Adulthood,*
*Albeit Reluctantly.*

*White attire required.*
*(Seriously. Don't mess with my theme.)*

Owen, turning thirty. And Mercer, just a few months behind him. Thirty. Three-zero. Goddamn. *Thirty.*

Owen has a lot to show for his thirty years. A house in San Francisco's Seacliff neighborhood, near Baker Beach. A commercial real-estate portfolio. Travels on all seven continents. Crowd-pleasing tales of large-scale marijuana cultivation and DEA-evasion. A perfectly timed ride on the dot-com wave. Unshakable self-confidence. A ten-year relationship with Mollie, who is the sort of beautiful, self-assured, intelligent, and trustworthy woman all of Owen's friends wish they could find. Another thing Mercer envies: Owen's certainty, from the moment they'd met in a drama class at Pomona, that she was the woman to whom he'd commit himself.

Mercer gets up to play the message from Fiona, thankful that he at least has someone who cares enough to call and say good night. He smiles as he listens to the whispery lilt of her voice, the voice of someone who will be overtaken by sleep in minutes. He imagines her lying in bed in the dark, the phone tucked between her neck and shoulder, the down comforter pulled up to her chin, waves breaking and ship lights twinkling in the distance. She loves the ocean unconditionally, she once told him. It's why she spent all her money on that house: she'd found the place where she fit.

Near the end of the message, she coughs and clears her throat. It's an ugly sound, and it takes him by surprise. He shuttles the message backward and listens again, and when her voice turns croaky and she coughs and she clears her throat, something dark rises in him, and he thinks, *She's too old,* and he knows he's not being fair, he's being petty, he's being a complete shit, he knows it shouldn't matter that Fiona isn't Mollie or even Toronto's nuclear girlfriend, but now his brain is looping the thought *she's too old she's too old she's too old* and the goddamn wine isn't settling him down and when the machine clicks off—*End of messages,* the polished female voice tells him—he forces himself to sit and relax and breathe. He touches his cheekbone. The bump has risen even more, and hardened, too. The skin over it feels stretched so tight that any more swelling might snap it open.

After a while, he takes the phone off the hook, closes the bedroom door behind him, undresses, puts in his earplugs, and dumps himself into the bed. Lying on his back, he stares at the water stains on the popcorned ceiling, a sprawling mural in shades of mud and rust commemorating The Willows' rich tradition of half-assed maintenance. He's more spin-headed than he planned to be, and he reprimands himself for drinking too much. He'll wake up feeling shitty and dried-out. Assuming he sleeps at all.

Toronto sits up in Mia's bed, a queen-sized mattress laid on the bare, fake-parquet floor of her apartment. He puts his hands behind his head and leans back against the wall, which is refreshingly cool against his skin. The apartment is small and dark, a low-ceilinged, subterranean junior one bed-room just north of the Panhandle. The lone window—banded with rust-flecked iron bars—offers a view of passing feet, empty half-pint bottles, trash from the barbecue and fried-chicken joints, the rattly wheels of the Grove Street Cowboy's shopping cart. Mia has repainted the apartment a bright sun-rise orange with sponged-on spirals of yellow, which ought to help brighten the mood more than it does. There's a dead asparagus fern on the window ledge, a withered claw of crispy brown fingers, the latest of Mia's botanical failures.

Still, as gloomy and cramped and cluttered and dead-ferned as the place is, Toronto is completely content to be there, because Mia is there, and they've just made love, and now he's watching her as she moves through the bedroom, freshly showered and naked. He's enjoying the taste in his mouth—the taste of her, mixed with his own whiskey breath, which she claims to hate even though he can tell it turns her on. He feels a pleasant sense of emptiness. Of being but not-being. This warm, melty after-sex feeling must be something pretty close to what Buddhists are always talking about. Goddamn if he doesn't feel like Sid-fucking-dhartha watching the river flow by.

He's a little hurt that she felt the need to shower, that she's going out into the world cleansed of him. But he knows he'll be in her mind all day, regard-less; she's just had, what, six orgasms by his count. Toronto firmly believes that if you're going to do anything, you should do it well, and nowhere is this credo more important than in matters of sex and love. He knows how to go down on a woman, that's for sure; he is one primo top-dog righteous major-league cunnilingus genius. It's all about giving and patience and stamina and focus and creativity, and he has all that *down;* he knows how to please a woman, not like ninety-nine percent of the male population, who think sex is just squeeze a tit, penetrate, blow a load, and roll over. Sex is all about giving. And getting, too, sure, but the best sex happens when you lose track of which is which.

He briefly drifts into a mellow drowse, then wakes again to hear Mia humming as she combs her hair in upstrokes, scalp to ends. She's standing in front of the mirror she found on the street; it's losing its silver, and her image looks like it's coming through a fog. He thinks he recognizes the song, but can't quite place it—a minor-key melody that twirls across two octaves, more energetic than melancholy, accepting the sadness of the flatted third without wallowing in it. The melody fits her; she's young, and she hasn't dealt with any real pain or loss yet, but when she does, she'll handle it with more grace than most.

"What's that song?" he asks her. He needs to know, needs to have the CD, needs to be able to listen to it at home, in the car, at the gym, everywhere.

"What song?"

"The one you were just humming."

"I was humming?"

"Yes, you were humming."

"How did it go?"

Toronto tries to hum it back to her, but he can't get past the first few notes, and even those sound wrong to him. "Something like that," he says. "It went on from there."

"I don't know. Must've just been in my head." She sets the comb on her dresser and faces him. "How was your shift? Anything happen?"

"We found a severely fucked-up kid in one of the cemeteries," he says. "Got him to the hospital."

"Is he all right?"

"I don't know," he says. "It's out of my hands." He raises his hands in the air and waves them. *See? Empty.*

She doesn't pursue it. He explained to her early on that he doesn't talk about work when he's not on duty. It's *his* time. He'll give a two-sentence police-blotter rundown of a call, fine, or a longer narrative if he saw something funny, like the guy with the frozen trout wedged up his ass gimping along El Camino, but the moment you get emotionally invested in any of these citizens' lives, you're ordering up an economy-sized bucket full of trouble, extra crispy.

"Long day today," she says.

"Every day's the same length, sweetie."

"Don't be a dick. You know what I mean."

"Got time for lunch? We could meet."

"I don't think so," she says. "We're running tech. We'll probably work straight through."

"I'll bring you something."

"Don't worry about it. They'll have hummus and stuff."

Mia performs with the Ashbury Street Traveling Psychedelic Circus. No lions and tigers, but lots of acrobatics, tightrope-walking, clowning, juggling, dance, and liquid-light projections. It had started out as a Summer of Love freak show, but over the years they turned mainstream hippie-lite, and now they perform at universities, civic centers, and corporate campuses. Mia had, in fact, run away from home to join them; she'd had a blowout with her parents when she was fifteen, vowed never to talk to them again—a pledge that was still intact—and hitchhiked from New Jersey to San Francisco. The circus was on tour when she arrived, so she lied about her age and spent a few months cocktailing at bars all over town, quitting whenever the boss or the other servers or the customers treated her badly. She's tough, she's unsentimental, she's self-sufficient. Mia does not take shit. Shit will not be taken by her. Ever. Toronto likes that about her, even if it is partly a pose. Either way, it's a hell of a turn-on.

Mia turns and walks toward the closet. The adhesive under the cheap flooring crackles under her steps. Suddenly, she yawps in pain; she hops, clutching her left foot in both hands—and Toronto immediately forgets that she's hurt, marveling instead at her balance, her flexibility, the gorgeous angle at which her knee is bent.

"Fuck," she says. "Fuck, fuck, fuck."

"Again?" he says. "We just did."

"Funny. God*damn*it."

"What happened?"

"I stubbed my toe on one of my fucking Rollerblades. God, I'm tripping over everything."

"That's because you have too much stuff in here. Too much clutter." He keeps his own apartment as empty as possible; he likes the feel of austere spaces, and he likes not being burdened by possessions. Plus, he never maims himself tripping on shit.

Mia whips her head around. "Don't tell me what to do," she snaps. There's a fierceness about her, and God, it's *hot*. She's hot. And tough. And smart. And, for fuck's sake, she's an *acrobat*. This is the woman he has to marry.

"I'm just saying you have too many things," he says.

"This works for me. I have a system." Mia lowers her foot to the floor, tests her weight on it. She winces.

"Clutter isn't a system. You should clear this place out."

"Why? Because you don't like it?"

"Because then there'll be room for me."

She looks at him, her dark eyebrows knitting together, little ridges of concentration appearing in her forehead. She stands there, motionless except for the gentle rise and fall of her small, taut breasts as she breathes. Then one corner of her mouth inches upward, as if she's testing out a new smile for the first time. "What are you getting at?"

"I don't need much room," Toronto says, "because I don't have as much shit as you." Just the essentials: TV, coffee table, ashtray, mirror, couch, bed, a minimum of kitchenware. And five books—never more. If he buys a new one, an old one has to go. *The Sun Also Rises* is untouchable; so is Jim Thompson's *The Killer Inside Me*. Everything else cycles through. Most of the cops he knows think he's a freak because he reads, but Toronto decided long ago that he doesn't give even the smallest fraction of one acrobatic flying fuck what they think.

"It sounds like you just invited yourself to live here," Mia says.

He finds his pack of cigarettes on the floor next to the mattress, flips it open, and shakes out a smoke. He lights it, playing the pause in conversation to maximum effect, then exhales. "Maybe that's exactly what I did."

She crosses over to him, not putting much weight on her injured foot, and she plucks the cigarette out of his hand and drops it into an empty wine bottle, where it hisses out. "You told me you quit," she says.

"I did tell you, and I did quit."

"It's poison."

"Got to go somehow."

"If you're going to live here, you have to quit and *stay* quit. I don't want to breathe that shit."

"You're saying you want me to live here?"

"Maybe."

"I should be here with you. I don't like you living here alone. I don't like the brothers shooting dice every night on the sidewalk."

"Will you shut up about the dice?" she says. "I walk by, and those guys don't even notice me."

*Bullshit*, he thinks. *Everybody notices you.* "Dice games are fine until there's an argument and somebody pulls out a goddamned weapon and before you know it, someone else takes a bullet in the goddamned skull. And of course every single one of the homeboys will lie to the cops about it. Tell a hundred different stories so no one's ever convicted."

"So, what, you're going to protect me from a bullet?"

"Given the opportunity," he says, "yes, I will."

She lowers herself to the mattress and lies on top of him. "I love you," she says, the tips of her hair painting wet strokes on his cheeks. Just out of the shower, her hair is espresso-brown; it dries a few shades lighter. If she's getting a lot of sun, she's told him, it'll lighten nearly to auburn. He hasn't seen that yet, but he wants to. The circus will be touring the Southwest states, and he can't wait to see her come home with all that sun in her hair. At the same time, though, he catches himself wishing she had hurt her foot more seriously so she'd have to stay home. With him.

"Your foot's all right?" he asks.

"Fine. A bruise."

"I wish you weren't going."

"I'll be back."

"And we'll live together."

"Yes," she says, "I think we will."

He wishes he had the ring already; he'd ask her to marry him right now, butt-naked and suffused with giddy, peaceful, postcoital warmth. Better that he doesn't, though; that's more or less how he proposed to both Jill and Cinda, and obviously he hadn't been thinking straight. They'd both turned out to be disappointments, fickle and weak women who were afraid of the hard work it took to be in love and didn't appreciate how committed he was. He wants to do *everything* differently with Mia, to avoid making any of the mistakes he might've made with the other two, and that means he's going to propose properly, traditionally, on bended knee, and fully clothed. He's a traditional guy, after all, a man who honors and respects romance, and he'll wait until he gets the ring and finds the right place to pop the question, and for now he'll just go down on her again.

He rolls her onto her back—she laughs as she rolls, a squeaky, chittery laugh—and he kisses her neck and works his way down her body. Her skin is still warm and soft and lime-scented from the shower.

"I have to go," she says, slapping him lightly.

"No, you don't," he says.

He'll miss living in Upper Noe, which is a hell of a lot nicer than this pocket of the Western Addition—sunnier, warmer, no homeless guys shitting in doorways, no shattered forties all over the sidewalk—but this way, he can keep Mia safe, walk her home from the bus stop after sundown on nights he's not working, keep the craps-shooting brothers from hassling her. And the sooner he starts saving money, the better, because he's going to take her on one hell of a honeymoon. New Zealand, maybe. Or Tahiti. Or Nepal. He'll take her to fucking Antarctica, if that's what she wants. Then he clears his mind of all these thoughts and focuses on her, on the taste of her, on the warmth of her, on the shape of her, because if you're going to do something, you'd better focus and do it well.

Mercer wakes up, disoriented, his heart beating furiously, as something wet slides up his cheek. Fiona's face looms above him; she's too close for his eyes to pull her into sharp focus, but he can see she's sticking out her tongue. She licks him again, then says something he can't hear.

He pulls out his earplugs. "What?"

"I said, you taste salty. You're sweating." She pulls back, and Mercer's image of her sharpens: her oval face; her striking nose; fine hair the color of driftwood, hanging to her shoulders; and those wide, gray-green eyes trained on him. He feels like a spoon she's trying to bend with the force of her will.

He wipes his cheek dry, then looks at the clock and groans. "I was asleep," he complains.

"Well, now you're awake."

"You know the rule. I need to sleep."

"I tried to call. Line was busy."

"That would've woken me up, too."

"Don't be such a tight-ass. I wanted to see you. I had a rough night." She traces a finger over the swelling on his face. "Looks like you did, too."

"There was an incident," Mercer says.

"I gathered," she says. She takes his chin in her hand, gently turns his head left and right as she looks into his eyes with a probing, clinical gaze.

"It's just a bruise," Mercer tells her. "Don't worry."

"Did you lose consciousness?"

"No."

"Were you dazed? Any short-term-memory loss?"

"I just got my bell rung, is all."

She nods toward the mug on the night table. "You shouldn't be drinking."

"I needed to sleep."

"And someone should've made sure you stayed awake. Don't they teach you guys anything? You don't screw around with head trauma."

"Enough. Stop."

"All right," she says. "I'll stop. But tell me what happened." As he tells her about the kid, in roughly the same language he used on the incident report, she continues to look him squarely in the eye, still evaluating him.

"You left out a part," she says, once he's finished.

"What part?"

"The part about how your face got involved in this incident."

"He had a seizure while I was rendering aid. I got kicked. I fucked up."

"Don't be so hard on yourself."

"I'm not being hard on myself. It's a fact. I was careless."

"It happens. Don't make yourself feel worse."

"Long run, it'll make me a better cop."

"Whatever," she says.

He takes some satisfaction in her knowing that he won't budge on this. *She understands me,* he thinks.

"Where'd they take him?" she asks.

Mercer sits up, suddenly clearheaded. "Good Shepherd," he says.

"Want me to call?"

Mercer nods. He should have woken her up, gotten her to call earlier. As she heads for the living room, he calls after her. "DiMaio," he says. "His name is Jude DiMaio. David Ida Mary—"

She reappears in the doorway with the phone in her hand. "Please," she says. "I know how to spell."

He tries to listen in, but she's speaking quietly and he can't make out the words and his ears are ringing a little, besides. She comes back into the bedroom, stone-faced, walking slowly. She sits on the edge of the bed in a slump-backed posture, facing away from him, one hand to her forehead. She sighs deeply, and Mercer's stomach sinks. Neither of them speaks. The heating ducts clank and rattle.

"Just tell me," he says, finally. When she doesn't respond, he adds, "I can handle it," though he can feel pressure building behind his eyes, pressure that he knows will push out tears if he's not careful. Thing is, he's not a crier. Never has been. Maybe the kick to his head did scramble him up a little.

She turns to him and blinks. She opens her mouth to speak, then closes it, as if she can't decide what her first word should be. She blinks again, and this time it looks deliberate, forced, oversold.

"He's all right, isn't he?" Mercer says.

Her pinched lips broaden into a smile. "He'll be fine," she says. "Serious but stable."

"Fuck you," he says. He's surprised to hear the words in the air between them.

"Whoa. Over the line."

"I'm sorry," he says. "I can't joke about it yet."

"It'd be better if you could."

"I know," he says. Their jobs are similar in this way. When you're exposed to tenth-floor jumpers, vehicle ejections, and kids left outside to die, you have the right to laugh at whatever the hell you want to. You laugh at the appalling and the horrific and the tragic so you can keep going back to work, just like normal people do.

"He's going to be all right," she reminds him.

He nods. Then he pulls the pillow out from behind his head and whacks her in the shoulder with it. A tiny feather floats away from them and drifts to the floor. "There," Mercer says. "I feel better now."

"Good. Because it's all going to be okay. He'll recover, and we'll all continue living the rest of our lives, and you'll always know you helped a kid when he needed it most." She leans in and kisses him on the cheek, which returns the tears to his eyes. He fights them back, closes his eyes, and swallows.

"There's more," she says. "Guess who his father is."

"Tell me."

"No, guess."

"I hate guessing. You know I hate guessing."

"I think that kid kicked all the fun out of you."

"Just tell me."

"Fine," she huffs. "His father is Marco DiMaio."

Mercer runs the name through his head. "I don't know who that is."

"He makes movies. He's a director."

"Never heard of him."

"Yes, you have," she says. "He won an Oscar. Remember *The Hallelujah Dogs*? About the Gulf War? And *Stockholm Underground*. That was his most recent."

Mercer shrugs.

"We saw *Stockholm Underground* together."

"Huh," he says. Sometimes his memory isn't what other people expect it to be.

"It was one of our first dates."

Then he remembers. They saw the movie at Embarcadero Center, had a drink afterward, then walked out to the water behind the Ferry Building and watched black waves roll as the wind made them both squint and leak tears. Of the film, he mostly remembers feeling bored. There was snow; there were blond actors he had trouble telling apart; and there was a plot about a thing that had been stolen, though you never got to see the theft or even the thing itself, which made the whole movie seem pointless. Admittedly, he'd been distracted, caught up in the rush of a new relationship, of sex both recent and imminent, of her experience and her clean, mild-soap smell.

"There's a lot you don't pay attention to," she says.

"I remember," Mercer protests. "The movie where nothing got stolen."

"Plutonium. Plutonium got stolen."

"I didn't see any plutonium."

"It doesn't matter. The plutonium was only important in that it brought the diplomat and the taxi driver together. It was their relationship that mattered."

"I think," Mercer says, "that I like movies where the plutonium is important because it's plutonium."

"Don't get upset."

"I'm not upset," he says, but he can feel the edge in his voice, too, and he's not sure where it came from. "I don't care about the father. Look what he let happen to his kid."

"That makes no sense," Fiona says. "You can't blame the father for this."

"Maybe not," Mercer said. "But you never know."

"Lighten up. You saved Marco DiMaio's son. It's a great story."

"It's not a story," he says. He doesn't want to think about the kid as just another anecdote, and he doesn't want her to, either. Jude P. DiMaio is a flesh-and-blood sixteen-year-old boy who's just been through hell. He can feel his anger rising; he knows it's unjustified, but he can't let go of it. "That's what Toronto does," he says, "and it's bullshit."

Then she's checking out his eyes again. "Hey, Officer Mood-Swing," she says. "You're talking like somebody with a concussion."

"I don't have a concussion."

"Actually, I don't think you do, either," she says. "Maybe you're just a grumpy old man." She hugs him, drops a soft kiss on his forehead. "You need some sleep," she says, into his hair.

The tears come back in a rush, and a few of them make it out onto his cheeks. What's *wrong* with him? "That movie sucked," he hears himself say. He wipes his face dry.

"Don't tell DiMaio that when you meet him," she says, smiling.

"I'm not going to meet him."

"Of course you're going to meet him. And I'll meet him, too." She runs her fingers through her hair, tilts her face toward an imaginary camera, crimps her lips into a pout. "Maybe he'll find a role for me. A *femme fatale*."

She's trying to make him laugh, and it works. He feels himself unclench. "A *femme fatale*, huh?"

"A glamorous, dangerous, immoral, and ruthless woman," she says, reaching under the sheets, running her hand up his leg and through the leg of his boxers, "who seduces a naive and trusting and idealistic younger man."

"Mmmm," he says.

"And destroys him," she says, and she squeezes his balls, just hard enough to widen his eyes and make him utter a sound that has no vowels. She stands up, smiling. "Look at the time," she says. "I have to get to work. And, remember, you have to sleep. I don't want to keep you from your precious sleep."

"Stay. I'll sleep after."

"Good-bye."

"Wait," he says. "You said you had a rough night."

"Don't worry about me," she says. "I'm feeling better." She kisses him deeply, then breaks free. She pauses in the doorway and strikes a silent-film damsel-in-distress pose, palms together beside her cheek, head tilted, eyelashes batting theatrically. "My hero," she says. He throws the pillow at her and misses. She laughs and disappears.

He hears the front door close. The apartment is quiet and dark, but he's wide awake again. And now with an insistent hard-on, too.

Once, when he and Toronto were lamenting how hard it could be to get to sleep after a night of action, Mercer had joked about using masturbation as a shortcut to dreamland. *When in doubt, rub one out,* he'd said, and Toronto had stared at him. "Not me," Toronto said, his tone judgmental, withering. "Not since I was fifteen. That's sexual energy, man. You can't waste that on *yourself.*"

Well, Mercer decides, he's not Toronto. He can do things his own way.

So he does. And though the faces of the women in his mind's eye keep changing, he's comforted that Fiona's is one of them.


**H**e wakes up again when he hears someone trying to open his front door, scrabbling at the lock with a key, twisting the knob back and forth, rattling the thin door in its frame. "Fuck off!" he shouts. He swings himself out of bed—he's light-headed and nearly falls—and he stomps toward the door, disappointed that the carpet is muting his furious footsteps. A man needs his goddamned sleep.

He undoes the bolt and yanks the door open, and a plump woman with a clear plastic rain bonnet over a head of gray hair stumbles into his apartment with her hand still on the knob. She holds her position for a moment, bent over as if she's scanning the carpet for loose change. Then she straightens, clutching her shoulder. It isn't until she steps back out onto the cement landing that Mercer sees who she is: Lorna Featherstone.

Shame hits him, blunt and crushing as a bullet into Kevlar. His face turns hot. Is she hurt? Did she hear him tell her to fuck off? Does he stink of wine? And what's she doing at his door, anyway?

"Officer Mercer?" she says. She's wearing a gray raincoat, and the rain bonnet is tied snugly under her chin. Thin trails of water wind down its surface and, after hesitating at the pink-trimmed edge, fall in drops onto her coat. She's not carrying an umbrella.

"Mrs. Featherstone?"

"What are you doing in my apartment?" she asks.

"Excuse me?"

"I don't understand why you're in my apartment," she says. "Did the chief send you? But why wouldn't he send you with clothes?"

Mercer realizes with alarm that he's standing there in the open doorway in a T-shirt and boxers, and that he has a mild case of morning wood, which his shirt doesn't hang low enough to hide. With both hands, he stretches the shirt downward as discreetly as he can. "I don't understand," he says. "This is my apartment. I live here." Still, doubt flickers in his sleep-slow mind: is he in the wrong place? He glances behind him at the living room. No, it's his place, and it's a mess. He turns back to her and sees that she's surveying the scene inside too, and that it makes no sense to her.

She points at the brass number screwed into the front door. "Apartment Eight," she says. "This is the apartment I'm moving into." She shows him the key, which has a scab of masking tape marked 8S in red ink.

"This is Eight North," Mercer says. "You want Eight South." He points across the parking lot and a row of waist-high hydrangeas to The Willows' south building. It's identical to the one in which he lives. Same two-level structure, same concrete landings running the length of the building, same weather-blackened roof tile, same drab, mourning-dove-gray paint. He hands the key back to her, and she stares at it as if it's a meaningless piece of metal. She seems shorter and squatter in his doorway than she does at the station.

Neither of them speaks. Raindrops plunk through the gutter pipes. She opens her purse and drops the key inside.

"I'm sorry," she says. "I'm new here."

"It's all right, really."

"I'm confused. I get confused all the time."

"Is your shoulder all right? Are you hurt?"

"I've woken you up," she says. "You need to rest. You were in a fight."

Mercer touches his hand to his eye. "It was an accident," he says. "I'm fine. Do you want to come inside?"

"Wesley hated it when I woke him up. When he was working nights, everything had to be quiet in the morning. I had to take the phone off the hook, catch the teakettle before it whistled, not open the garage door. If the doorbell rang, he'd be furious—"

He finishes her sentence in his mind: *just like you were.* Again he wonders if she can smell the wine on his breath. "Is your shoulder all right?" he asks.

She looks down at her galoshes. "You're trying to unwind, and I'm bothering you. I know. I was a cop's wife. It was the only thing I ever was." The unspoken question hangs there between them: What is she supposed to be now?

"Please don't be sorry," he says, afraid she'll start crying. "I'll get back to sleep, no problem. Do you want coffee? I could make you some coffee."

She clutches her right shoulder. "I think I hurt my arm," she says. "When the door opened."

"Oh God," Mercer says. "I'm sorry. I thought you were someone trying to break in. I was upset. I'm still on edge. From work. I'm so sorry."

"It's not bad," she says, flexing her elbow. "Nothing's broken. See?"

"But your shoulder."

She moves her shoulder up and down, forward and back, her range obviously limited. She tries to flash him a carefree smile, but he can tell she's in pain.

"Let me give you some aspirin, at least," he says.

"Don't you worry about me. I can take care of myself. I'll be fine."

"Maybe you should see a doctor."

"Not today. I have too many things to do. Busy, busy, busy."

"My girlfriend's a nurse. I could ask her to come look at you tonight."

"I won't be here tonight," she says. "I'll be at the house. One last night in the old house. Wes and I lived there for thirty-six years. It's empty. The movers came yesterday afternoon." Her words tumble out in a rush, and Mercer realizes he's speaking to a person who is using every resource she has to keep herself together.

"Did the movers take your bed? Do you need a place to sleep? I can stay at my girlfriend's. The place is a mess, but I could clean up."

"I have a cot," she says. "I can rough it. I want to be there tonight. I want to listen to the house."

"I'm very sorry about your loss," Mercer says. "I didn't know Sergeant Featherstone well, but everyone says he was a good officer and a good man."

"Thank you, dear," she says. "That's nice of you to say. Now go back inside. You must be freezing, standing there half-dressed."

"You're sure you're all right?"

She snaps her fingers. "I have an idea," she says. "You must need a bathrobe." Before he can tell her no, he's never owned one, has never felt the need, she says, "I'm going to get you a bathrobe once I get settled. It'll be a welcome present." She smiles.

It makes him uncomfortable, her worrying about him instead of herself. "You're the one moving in. I'm supposed to welcome you."

She waves him off, and he catches a grimace on her face as she moves her arm. "Never mind that, Officer Mercer. I'm glad we'll be neighbors."

"Me too, Mrs. Featherstone."

"Lorna. Please."

"Lorna. And you can call me Mike."

"I'm sorry about barging in on you."

"It's an easy mistake to make," he reassures her. "I'm sorry about your arm. If there's anything I can do."

"Put some ice on that face of yours," she says.

He watches as she trudges along the narrow, winding path to the south building. Mercer is about to turn away when he hears a rumble and clatter; from nowhere, a man and a woman appear on the path, roller-skating downhill and dangerously fast. They're holding hands—they'll clothesline her if they're not careful—but Lorna shows no sign of noticing. Does she even have her eyes open? He opens his mouth to shout, but by then the skaters have swooped past her—*how? he didn't see them raise their arms*—and they've cut a sharp turn into the parking lot, all rattling wheels and laughter and carefree togetherness. He should flag them down and deliver a stern warning, but instead he finds himself gawking at their clothing—she in a long, swirling blue dress, he in a dark gray suit and checkered cap—and then they've spun into the street without looking for traffic and disappeared down the hill. Idiots. No appreciation of risk, no consideration for safety. And why they were in costume he has not one goddamn clue. *Ghosts?* he thinks, and he shakes his head. God, he's tired. Nearly brain-dead. He watches Lorna walking, slowly and stiffly, in obvious discomfort, trying to keep her shoulders square. Quite a morning so far, he thinks. He's been out of bed all of five minutes, and he's already maimed an old woman. Imagine what he'll be able to do with the rest of the day.

An hour later, Mercer jolts awake immediately, miserable, when the doorbell rings. He ignores it, but it rings again, and then the knocking starts: big, loud, not-fucking-around knocking. *Kill me now,* he thinks. *At least then I'll be able to sleep.* He steps into a pair of sweatpants and trudges toward the door.

Outside is a black man, fortyish, with a woolly black beard that has a few curls of gray in it. The man stares at Mercer's bruised face for too long, then thrusts a clipboard at him. "Morning," he says, more a declaration than a greeting. "Movers." He's wearing a clear poncho over navy-blue coveralls with a patch that reads BEAUFORT BROS. MOVING on one breast. The name *Terry* is stitched in script on the other.

"You're in the wrong place," Mercer says.

Terry checks his clipboard. "Featherstone?"

"Wrong apartment."

"You're not Featherstone?"

"No."

"Says Apartment Eight."

"This is Eight North."

"Like I said. Eight. That's where I'm at, and you're telling me you ain't Featherstone."

"You want Eight South."

Terry looks at the clipboard. "Says Eight North." He holds it up for Mercer to see, pointing to the address with an index finger that has a split down the center of the nail.

*Shit,* Mercer thinks. Lorna has given everyone his address. He'll probably start getting her mail. "There's been a mistake. Mrs. Featherstone lives in Eight South."

"You sure?"

"I know my name. It's not Featherstone."

"Lucky for you. That's a funny name."

"The south building is over there." Mercer points.

Terry turns and takes in the sprawl of the complex. "No wonder she don't know the difference. It's all one big ugly-ass place." He whistles down the stairs to his crew, who have slung open the door to the moving truck and are fixing the loading ramp into place. "Wrong building," he calls. "We got to go over there." The men, all in matching, rain-darkened coveralls, murmur and slide the ramp back into the truck. "Sorry for the trouble," Terry says. "What kind of people don't know where they're staying at?"

"She just lost her husband," Mercer says.

"Shoot," Terry says. "I'd give anything if my old lady would get lost."

*That's not funny,* Mercer wants to say.

"Looks like someone beat you good." Terry points to his own, un-bruised eye.

"No one beat me good," Mercer says. "I had an accident."

"I woke you up, huh?"

"Yes."

Terry taps his watch. "Well, you can't sleep away the whole damn day." He walks down the cement steps, the metal railing vibrating with each heavy footfall. "Even if you did get your ass beat."

# JUDE, AWAKE

**H**is vision drifts toward focus but does not reach.

It is warm. It is dark. White noise breathing in the space around him. Soft, streaming percussion: water thumping glass. *Rain.* The word a revelation. *Rain.*

The memory: rain, sweet cold needles from the sky, pure and frigid, spiking him over and over; he can savor each burst of feeling, icy and electrifying. Also a faint echo of citrus on his tongue. Voices twirling in and out of phase, then pulling tight into themselves, compressed into tiny-box squawks. A flame, contorting, bending and springing back into place. Pressure against his lips. Time vanished and forgotten; a sequenceless tumble of feeling.

And this: a dead-drop, rag-limp, into the black of lonely.

But also: a blaze of green. An electric-green slash through a field of white-gold, and a face, pale. A narrow female voice with his name in it. Flickering orange ghosted onto her white skin, and pressure, lips, and then another word: *Reyna.* Reyna, Reyna in the rain, and Reyna receding. The dead rag-drop, and Reyna receding, a pinprick of green light down a tunnel of black, and gone.

Now: salted metal in his mouth and aches, aching, brutal blunt aches in his legs, back, arms, shoulders, neck, tongue. Like every muscle was removed, wrung slack and dry, put back red and ruined. A thought, now, of turning over to his side, and a sudden crush of pain. A liquid angel voice filling his head: *Sleep, chile, you need to rest yourself up. Ain't no need to rush. Just sleep, child, sleep.* Yes: still, still, keep still, still for the sweet liquid angel. Still.

. . .

**F**iona sleepwalks through the first few hours of her shift. It was a tough night for her: she'd woken up again and again with racing thoughts she couldn't still, thoughts about Mike, about babies, about growing old alone, about opportunities forgone. Even when she slept, she had bad dreams that kept her doze shallow and fitful. Mike, turning into other men—her high-school boyfriend; her mailman; the anesthesiologist with the shaved head whose name she can't remember—and she would try in vain to tell them things. Sometimes they spoke to her in a language she couldn't identify. Sometimes she could not get her mouth to move. Sometimes she spoke, but they ignored her, and there was menace in their silence. A terrible night, and she is dragging.

On her first break, Fiona takes the elevator to the fifth-floor Pediatrics wing. The hallway is lined with framed watercolors of kittens, puppies, and horses, along with children's art projects. Hanging in the sunroom is a mobile made from dozens of strung-together God's-eyes; it nearly reaches the floor, and it sways gently back and forth, a pendulum of yarn and Popsicle sticks set in motion by a drafty ceiling vent.

At the nurses' station, she tells them that her boyfriend is the one who found Jude, and that she promised him she'd check in on the kid. She tries to keep the boast out of her voice.

"You dating a cop?" one nurse says. "Brave girl."

"Or stupid," another says.

She knocks quietly on his door and gets no answer, so she eases it open. The blinds are drawn, blocking out the meager gray light from outside. Raindrops pop against the window glass. The fluorescent lights emit a faint hum. She watches him from the doorway; he's on his back with the blankets pulled up to his neck, comfortably asleep. His breathing is quiet and smooth, feathery brushes of air passing through his nostrils. Clear fluids drip from three IV bags. White-green blips on a monitor trace the beating of his heart. The faintest shadows of facial hair grace his upper lip and chin; his cheeks are baby-bare and pallid. She says his name quietly, but he doesn't stir.

The speaker in the room comes to life: a beep, a crackle, a female voice summoning a doctor to Recovery. Jude's eyelashes flutter, and he makes a few sleepy-kitten noises in his mouth, then stills. *He might have died if it weren't for Mike.* The force of the thought surprises her. She knows better than to get melodramatic. She's helped keep hundreds of people from dying; it's not her-oism, it's a *job,* it's what she's *supposed* to do. But this morning she'd felt inten-sity in his concern for Jude, a passion that she rarely saw in him, and maybe that's why she's surging with pride now, too. For a moment, she feels on the verge of tears. This is what happens when you love someone. She actually thinks the sentence in full, hears it in her own voice. *This is what happens when you love someone.* She's lucky to have found Mike. He's a work in prog-ress, for sure—guarded, stubborn, inattentive—but he's also compassionate, well-meaning, and self-sacrificing, and it's been years since she's been involved with anyone like that. Years. Or maybe ever.

She thinks again of her dreams, the ones with babies in them; she could have been dreaming one at the same moment Mike was discovering this boy. *Be careful,* she tells herself, *that's the magical thinking again,* but the thought is there, announcing itself urgently, and she can't ignore it: *we could have a fam-ily.* They could. She feels sure of it now. He might not know it yet, but he could be a great father—even though his own father, from what she can tell, was remote, mostly absent, relentlessly glum. Maybe even *because* his father did so little for him. He'd be nervous and uncertain—she can picture his bunched eyebrows, his clenched jaw, that blankness she sees in his blue-silver eyes when he goes somewhere else in his head—but all he needs is someone to help him get past the fear. And if there's a time for them to try, it's now, isn't it?

Fiona is startled when a voice behind her says, "Hello." She turns to find a stout woman in her late fifties with bowl-cut, white-blond hair. The woman is wearing a tan pantsuit and a cream-colored turtleneck and carrying a banana and a container of yogurt. Enormous round glasses with lime-green frames sit atop her tiny nose, and the effect is disorienting.

"Did the other nurse go off duty?" the woman asks.

"No," Fiona says. "I just wanted to see how he's doing. My boyfriend's the one who found him."

"Oh," the woman says, lifting her glasses and peering at Fiona's ID tag. "Nurse Wells, his parents will be very grateful."

"So you're not—"

"His mother? No. The DiMaios are out of the country. His mother is flying back right now. I'm a neighbor. Gracie Hankin-Cherry." She offers her hand for a shake. "You might have heard of me? I'm a realtor? Very Cherry Homes?"

"I think so," Fiona lies. The woman has an air of ridiculousness about her. The hair, the clothes, the name, the inappropriately salesy tone of her voice.

"I sold the DiMaios their house. Right next door to me! They're wonderful people."

Fiona gestures toward Jude in the bed. "He's through the worst of it."

"The doctor said he's much better, yes."

"What's he like?" Fiona asks.

"The doctor's very young," Gracie says. "Too young, if you ask me."

"I meant Jude."

Gracie adjusts her glasses. "Oh," she says. "He's smart, like his father. But maybe a little—" She glances at the sleeping boy, then mouths the word in an exaggerated way: *SPOY-YULD.* "His mother does everything for him."

"Any trouble?" Fiona asks. "Anything that would make you expect something like this would happen?"

Gracie again steals a look at Jude, then motions for Fiona to lean in close. "He smokes pot. In the backyard. I smelled it once when I was gardening."

Fiona wants to tell her that doesn't mean a thing. He's a kid. That's what kids do. That's not what landed him here.

"When my kids tried that stuff," Gracie goes on, "I took them down to the police station myself. This is what happens with drugs. Bad things. People turn into animals. I've never understood it." She sighs theatrically. "I suppose it's my fault. I should have said something to his parents. I'm just not the kind of person who likes to intrude into other people's business."

Fiona suspects that this is something Gracie has chosen to believe about herself and not at all the truth. This is an odd woman who believes it's the rest of the world that's off-kilter. "I should be getting back," Fiona says. Her break is nearly over, and truth be told, she's eager to get away from Gracie Hankin-Cherry.

If a woman like her can raise kids, Fiona certainly can.

Gracie, who is blocking her path to the doorway, pulls a business card from the pocket of her jacket. "If you're ever in the market."

"Thanks," Fiona says, walking around her. "But I like it where I am."

Mercer and Toronto arrive at the hospital during the evening visiting hours. The air in the lobby is the same as Mercer remembers: cool and empty, with a faint metallic bite. In the gift shop, bright Mylar balloons promise hope and good cheer and shining retail empathy.

Detective Funkhouser now owns the DiMaio investigation, but he told the officers to get as involved as they wanted, and for Mercer, that would mean *deeply involved*. Funkhouser's months away from retirement, anyway, so he's not exactly a ball of fire. In their meeting with the detective, Toronto offered to come along to the hospital for Mercer's protection. "You see what this kid's already done to him," he said to Funkhouser, and the two of them had a good laugh over it. Mercer wasn't able to come up with a good retort, so he stood there quietly and waited for the hilarity to exhaust itself.

Near the bank of elevators is a small waiting room painted jade green, with a matching carpet that has been worn threadbare and gray by pacing feet in well-defined pathways. Mercer looks into the room and sees a man in his mid-thirties sitting with two young boys. The man is bleary-eyed and slump-shouldered. The younger boy—five or six, by Mercer's guess—is filling in a page in a coloring book with a blue crayon, lost in his own world. His brother, a couple of years older, swings his sneakered feet through the air as if he's pumping himself higher and higher on a playground swing. The father silently places a hand on the older boy's corduroy knee, and the swinging legs go still. A grandparent dying upstairs, probably. Mercer remembers when his grandfather—not the Olds driver, but Grandpa Mercer, his father's father— was dying of lung cancer in a San Jose hospital. In a similar-looking waiting room, he'd watched as his father rocked back and forth and mumbled to himself, then got up and punched the vending machine until its plastic shield cracked. It was shortly after that that he left Mercer and his mother for the first time.

In the elevator, Mercer leans against the rear wall.

"So, your girlfriend works here?" Toronto says.

"Not over here," Mercer says. "In the ER."

"Caught you," Toronto says. "That's the first time you didn't deny she's your girlfriend."

"I don't know if she is," Mercer says. "We've never formalized it."

"Too late," Toronto says. "That's a confession, in my book."

"Like hell it was."

"It's my book, not yours."

"Your book's as full of shit as you are."

"I have an idea. Let's go visit your girlfriend when we're done. You can introduce me."

"I'm not letting you anywhere near her."

"Come on. If she's not your girlfriend, you won't mind if I pop her."

"Fuck off," Mercer says. "Anyway, what about your theory?"

"Mia's so hot that I've got some leeway."

"So, what, it's *average* age that counts?"

"Good question. Could be the mean, or the median. I forget which is which. Anyway, five hundred times with Mia and once with your old lady, that's an imperceptible uptick. I'm safe."

"You're safely an asshole," Mercer says.

"It's part of my raffish charm," Toronto says. "Chicks dig it."

Mercer's not in the mood for this; he has a headache, and the strobing fluorescent light in the elevator is making it worse. He wants to be focused when they meet the kid.

The doors open, and the hospital smell—urine, disinfectant, fear—immediately assaults them. Mercer is glad he hasn't eaten in a few hours. Along the hallway, hushed voices filter out from behind cracked doors, electronic games beep and chirp and make cartoon fighting noises, and medical hardware pings and clicks. Somewhere ahead of them, a child is crying. The air is cool, and the corridor feels crowded even though no one's in sight; a chill darts across Mercer's shoulders, and he shakes it away. The nurses' station is empty, which he finds strange, but a few steps past it he hears a file-cabinet drawer roll closed, and he turns to see a dark-haired nurse pop back up to her feet. Her sudden appearance is unnerving to him: first no nurse, then suddenly, poof, nurse. He's feeling antsy. Jesus, he's got to get some sleep.

"You're here for?" the nurse asks. Her teeth are impossibly white, her nails blood-red.

"DiMaio," Mercer says.

"Five fifty-four," she says.

The door to Jude's room is closed.

Mercer knocks, two quick raps. The woman who opens the door is not much older than Fiona, tan and trim with wavy ash-blond hair. Her denim shirt and tan slacks both look freshly pressed. Her eyes are red and puffy from a recent cry. A silver cross around her neck points attention to her lightly freckled cleavage. He struggles not to steal a glance. *It is highly unprofessional to scope out a citizen's rack,* Toronto said the other night, drawing laughs as he mimicked Sergeant Mazzarella, *unless you receive the citizen's consent to do so.*

"Mrs. DiMaio?" he says.

"Yes. Susan. I'm Jude's mother." She looks at his black eye but doesn't comment.

"I'm Officer Mercer, Colma Police. This is Officer Toronto." They flash their badges. "We're investigating the assault on your son last night."

"Are you the ones who found him?"

"We are, yes."

Her hug startles him; she moves so suddenly that his hand goes down to his side to protect his weapon—a reflex. Then, feeling foolish, he pats her on the back, once, twice.

"Thank you," she says, when she releases him. She hugs Toronto, too, who accepts it gracefully and flashes Mercer a raised eyebrow over her shoulder.

"We'd like to ask Jude a few questions, if he's feeling up to it," Toronto says.

"Who would do this to him?" she says. "He's a good kid."

"We'll do our best to find out," Toronto says.

She raises a hand to her chest, says she feels terrible, feels like it's her fault. She shouldn't have left him alone to go to Belize with Marco. But he's such a responsible kid—an A student, plays the cello, volunteers—and they've never had any problems before. She and his father are very worried; as soon as he wraps shooting, he'll get on the next plane home.

"Can we come in?" Toronto asks.

"Yes, yes," she says, backing into the room and holding the door open for them. "Of course. What was I thinking, keeping you out there?"

"It's all right, Mrs. DiMaio," Mercer says. "Just relax. We're here to help."

"Please don't upset him," she says.

Jude is in bed, on his back, his arms outside the blankets. Mercer thinks he sees a look of familiarity pass across the boy's face, as if he recognizes Mercer but can't quite place him. Mrs. DiMaio settles into a chair that's pulled close to the bed, while Mercer and Toronto remain standing. Jude's hair sticks together in tufted oil-and-gel clumps, and when his mother tries to run her hand through it, he jerks away.

Toronto introduces himself and Mercer, and as he speaks, the boy's eyelids flicker, then come to rest on the far corner of the room, aimed at nothing.

"They're the ones who found you last night," Mrs. DiMaio says.

"You're a lucky man," Toronto says.

A puff of air escapes the boy's nose, as if lucky is the last thing he considers himself, but he nods.

Toronto asks, "Do you feel up to answering a few questions about what happened last night?"

Jude raises a hand—the one with the IV tube plugged into it—and scratches at a pimple on his chin. "Okay," he says. "I can do it." His voice is deeper and fuller than Mercer expected. It seems too big for him.

Toronto's questions are direct, methodical, calm but firm. Does he know who assaulted him? Does he remember being in the cemetery? In a vehicle? Does he remember anyone he was with? He works backward in time, trying to determine the last thing Jude remembers. To all of his questions, Jude answers that he can't remember, doesn't know.

Finally the boy closes his eyes and lies motionless, like a child who believes that if he can't see you, you can't see him. Mrs. DiMaio smiles nervously at them; Mercer can see the little muscles in her cheeks quivering.

"Jude," Toronto barks, and the boy's eyelids spring open. The force of his voice visibly unsettles Mrs. DiMaio. She's about to speak when Toronto holds up his hand, hushing her. "Jude, you need to tell us who did this to you. Or if you can't remember, then think about whether there's anyone you *think* might have done this. Come on, buddy. Clock's running. Case like this, every minute that goes by lets the bad guys get farther away."

"I'm really sorry," Jude says, voice pitched higher. "I can't *remember* anything."

"One more time," Toronto says. "Do you have any idea where you were before the cemetery?"

"Officer—" Mrs. DiMaio breaks off.

"We're almost finished," Toronto says. "Jude? Any idea?"

"No." He squinches up his face, as if he might soon cry. "I'm sorry."

"You don't have to be sorry," Toronto says.

"I'm not trying to make your jobs harder. I know you're trying to help."

"Don't worry about us. If you don't remember anything about last night, then we have to figure out the last thing you do remember. Do you know where you were in the afternoon?"

"Home," Jude says. "I guess."

"Doing what?"

"I don't know."

"Were you practicing?" Mrs. DiMaio asks. She turns to Mercer. "He plays the cello. He's very good. He's played in—"

"Ma'am," Toronto says, "we need him to answer for himself."

Mercer wonders if she's going to call a halt to the interview. He can tell she wants to.

Toronto continues. "So, what were you doing at home?"

"I don't know." Jude's voice rises, turns younger. "I'm sorry. Everything's gone. Everything's just *gone*. I want to tell you, and I *can't*."

"Mrs. DiMaio, did you notice any evidence of a home invasion? Did anything look out of order?"

"No. Not at all."

"Can you remember seeing any of your friends yesterday, Jude? Anyone who could help us fill in what you don't remember?"

Jude shakes his head no.

"How about Wilson?" his mother asks. "Would Wilson know?" She turns to Mercer. "Wilson's been his best friend since they were little," she explains. "They're in the school orchestra together."

Jude rolls his eyes, then squeezes them shut; both Mercer and Toronto catch it. *Get a clue, Mom*, that eye roll said. *Wilson's not my friend. You don't know me.* Mrs. DiMaio doesn't appear to notice. She's still looking at Mercer as if she expects congratulations for thinking of Wilson, as if she's the one who's going to bust this case wide open.

Mercer takes down Wilson's name and address. The Book says you write down Wilson's name and address, so you write down Wilson's name and address. As he writes, he imagines Mazzarella saying with his usual deadpan melodrama, *Nothing will make you dead quicker than not writing down Wilson's address.* He feels a smile threatening to break loose, but he forces his lips back into a line. *Wilson Whitaker, 855 Commonwealth St., San Francisco.* Laurel Heights. Another kid with money, probably.

"I don't feel well," Jude says. "Can we stop?"

"Let me clarify something," Toronto says. "You don't remember being in any kind of vehicle?"

Jude shakes his head.

"Do you have a car?"

"He has an SUV," Mrs. DiMaio says. "A Prospector. It was his sixteenth-birthday present."

Mercer bristles. You could buy a whole fleet of '83 Olds Omegas for what a Prospector costs.

"Did you drive it last night, Jude?" Toronto asks.

The briefest of hesitations. Then: "I don't remember."

"Mrs. DiMaio, do you know where the vehicle is?"

"No," she says. "I didn't look in the garage when I got in from the airport."

"Is there someone who could look now?"

She nods, picks up the phone on the stand next to Jude, and dials out. A minute later, she says a terse "Thanks," hangs up, and shakes her head. "It's not at the house," she says. She turns to her son. "Jude, honey, what happened? Were you carjacked?"

"Jesus," Jude says. "I told you, I don't know."

"Anything you can tell us will help," Mercer offers. "Even if it seems insignificant."

"I can't tell you what I don't remember," Jude says. His voice has taken on an adolescent whine. "Don't you think I feel bad enough right now?"

"Does anyone else have permission to drive the vehicle?" Toronto asks.

Both DiMaios shake their heads.

"All right. We'll take a stolen-vehicle report when we're done here. A few more questions, though, Jude, and I think it'll be in your interest to answer them as best you can."

"That's what I'm doing," Jude says.

"Sure you are," Toronto says. "Were you drinking last night?"

"I don't know."

"Really?"

"Really."

"Here's the thing," Toronto says. "We've seen your blood work. And there were bottles at the scene. So it's hard for us to believe that you weren't drinking."

"I said, I don't know."

"Any drugs?" Toronto asks.

Jude's eyes flash in his mother's direction—quick, subtle, no head movement, but involuntary and revealing. "No," he says, "no drugs."

"I can understand that you think you're going to get in trouble," Toronto says, "but you're not in trouble. You're not going to get in trouble. Not with me, not with Officer Mercer, and not with your mom—right, Mrs. DiMaio?—because she understands, just like Officer Mercer and I understand, and all three of us hope *you* understand, that you're the *victim* here. Right now, the important things are for you to get your strength back and for us to find whoever it was that almost caused your death. Because that's exactly what someone did. Do you understand that you almost died? That someone wrapped you up in duct tape and left you outside to die?" Toronto's voice is blunt as a fist, and Mercer hears the fed-up teacher in him coming through.

All three adults in the room watch Jude, waiting for a response. "I'm tired," he says. "I need to sleep." He clamps his eyes shut, closes his mouth, lies motionless. Toronto keeps his eyes level with Jude's, waiting for the boy to open them again. Several uncomfortable seconds pass before Toronto says, "Let's go outside and talk. Officer Mercer, Mrs. DiMaio, could you follow me, please?" He leaves the room.

"I'm not comfortable with him," Mrs. DiMaio says quietly. "I don't like his manner."

"It upsets him to see bad things happen to kids, ma'am," Mercer says. "It upsets all of us."

They join Toronto in the hallway, and Mercer closes the door behind them. "I know I'm stating the obvious," Toronto says, "but he knows more than he's telling us."

"How do you know?" Mrs. DiMaio says. "He's a good kid, and—"

"You need to face reality, ma'am. Good kids make mistakes. We see it all the time. The important thing is for him to *stop* making this one. Let's be clear about this: if Officer Mercer hadn't found him, you wouldn't have a son right now. Either he took the ketamine—or whatever it was—on his own, willingly, or someone slipped it to him, maybe even forced it on him. Either way, he's not letting us get any closer to figuring out who furnished it."

Susan nods, and the stiffness leaves her shoulders. She's given in.

"You see?" Toronto says. His face has reddened.

*Don't rub it in,* Mercer wants to say.

"Yes," Mrs. DiMaio says.

"Do *you* want to find out what happened? Because I know we do."

She nods, looking like she's about to cry.

"I'd like to talk to him without you in the room," Toronto says. "He might be holding back because he doesn't want to upset you. Something about the drugs, maybe. Or it could be sexual in nature."

"Oh, God," she says. "Don't even suggest." She raises a hand to the cross around her neck, strokes it between two fingers.

"It's my job to suggest. I didn't do this to your son, ma'am. I'm just trying to find out who did."

"All right," she says. "But I want Officer Mercer to do it."

Toronto looks irritated, but he agrees, and Mercer feels a wave of anxiety roll through him and crash in his stomach. "Go to it," Toronto says to him. "He's all yours."

"Are you sure?" Mercer asks.

"You heard the lady."

Mercer goes into the room and closes the door behind him. Jude is snoring lightly, his head tilted to face the window. It's pitch-dark outside now, and the lights from the parking lot cast a salmon-pink glow on the wall over his head. Mercer takes the chair Mrs. DiMaio was sitting in. "Jude," he says softly. "Jude? It's Officer Mercer."

No response. From the chair, Mercer watches him, watches his chest rise and fall, thinks about what the kid has been through and what he'll have to go through: going back to school with all the whispers and glances, viewing line-ups, testifying, learning to trust in people again, and all while being sixteen, which is hard enough on its own. Mercer hardly recalls anything that happened while he was sixteen; most of his childhood memories seem like they've been obscured by a gray depressive haze.

As Jude's breathing deepens and slows, Mercer decides not to wake him up. He knows what it feels like when all you want is for the whole goddamned world to just leave you the fuck alone. *Trust your gut,* Mazzarella likes to say, and Mercer's gut tells him to shut it down for the night, to let the kid rest. If Jude's protecting someone, that means it's someone he either cares about or is scared of. In both cases, it's someone who's likely to stay nearby. They've got time. They can be patient.

He takes one of his cards out of his breast pocket, and, just below the gold-embossed badge (he had to pay extra for the embossing, but it makes the cards look more impressive), he writes *Call any time —Mike.* He hesitates briefly before adding his cell number. He sets the card on the table by the bed, leaning against a pitcher of water. When he stands to go, the chair scrapes on the floor, and he looks up, expecting to see Jude awake, but the boy's eyes remain shut.


Phineas Gage is looking for his tamping iron underneath a row of chairs upholstered in red velveteen when all of the light drains out of the cavernous room. Startled, he gets up from his knees, and he is struck by the sudden change in the air: it smells damp and earthy, and it is thicker, heavier, difficult to move through. He recognizes it, without knowing why, as *expectation,* and he realizes that he must be among a large group of the living. As he makes his way out to the aisle, he notices that the seats are occupied by those gray-washed blurs. They make him uneasy, but the urgent words fill his head again, *my iron, my iron, my iron,* and he drops himself to all fours and crawls along another aisle, ignoring the blurry gray feet, looking, looking, always looking.

A sudden noise booms from all around—strings, a bruising chord played by an orchestra of gods, everywhere and nowhere in the dark, and Gage leaps to his feet as the low strings rumble and thrum and the high strings sweep shrill arcs. He is still bewildered when the far wall bursts into light— shockingly bright blues and greens that twist and pulse as the music pumps— the entire wall a swirling canvas of light and color, and he is entranced, and the words in his head turn softer as he watches the wall of light showing people—people, thirty feet high!—running down a street, one chasing the other—and he watches, helpless and slack, until the wall erupts in a flash of orange and a crushing boom shakes the floor under him. An explosion. Sounds like *the* explosion. *His* explosion—

—and he is there again—

—his head punched backward—

—shredded skin and pulped bone—

—he can smell the gunpowder—

—dry autumn leaves—

—Irishmen shouting, shouting—

—dust and rock raining down—

—clatter of metal—

—and the rumble rolls through his head, loud and unstinting—

—and then he is crawling on hands and knees, crawling amid the dark and the intolerable rumble, crawling madly and falling to one side and another, the world shaking and every bone in his head turning to dust from the roar—

—then, falling through a doorway into quiet—

—breeze and soothing mist—

—smooth indigo sky—

He rolls over on his side, on the grass, yes, there is grass under him, soft grass. Rest. He needs to rest. Can't think, can't search, just rest. He closes his eyes.

When he awakens, he sees the hard faces of four men standing over him. On one of the faces, the right side has been blasted away. Even in the dark, he can see pinks and grays in the grotesque cavity. As he stares into this man's eyes—one of which rolls loosely—he feels a rush of empathy, of comradeship; they are brothers of the grievous head wound. "Brother," Gage says.

"What did he say?" asks a ratlike man in a top hat.

"Brother?" the wounded man says, and his laugh is sharp and serrated. "You ain't my brother."

Gage is suddenly afraid. If only he had his iron. If only his *iron iron iron*—

A bulky, olive-skinned man pushes his way close and goes nose-to-nose with Gage's face. "This is where you give us everything you have, so we only hurt you a little."

"I don't have anything," Gage says. "That's the problem."

He hears the sound of the blade sliding between his ribs several seconds before the wave of pain hits him, pain that turns the world red and leaves him gasping. The big man grabs the front of Gage's shirt and twists. Gage feels knuckles pressing against his lower jaw as his gut burns.

"Let's try again," the big man says.

"Wait," Gage says. "Feel. Here." He points to his cheekbone and to the soft spot at the top of his head. To his surprise, the big man releases him and runs his fingers over the places where Gage's skin stretches over gaps in bone.

"Hey, Doc," the big man says. "This guy's got a hole in his head, too."

"Blasting," Gage whispers. "My iron—"

"Difference is, yours healed up, didn't it?" the man called Doc says. "Hell, that just makes me madder."

"You should give us something," the rat-man informs Gage. "Now."

Gage tries to hold his hands out to show the men how empty they are, how empty he is. He feels another blade sink into a soft part of him. His eye follows the knife handle that protrudes from his stomach to the hand that holds it to an arm to Doc's horrible face.

"You know what happened to my brother?" Doc asks, and Gage feels drops of fluid spraying onto his cheek. "My little brother? He ended up with seventeen goddamned bullets in him."

Gage feels the rage coming on, and he wouldn't try to stop it even if he could; it is feverish and violent and as comforting as an old friend. He thrashes against the hands that hold him down. Blades flash in moonlight, and he feels himself being punctured over and over in a flurry of limbs, and he does not care because pain is simply pain, it can be withstood, and afterward he can go on with his search. The search is all that matters. He opens his mouth and what comes out is a string of curses; he curses Doc, he curses Doc's brother, he curses Doc's mother, and he laughs when he hears himself accuse Doc's whole family of all manner of unnatural sexual practices. He laughs; pain is just pain, and a knife is just a knife, but an iron is an iron. "Make him stop laughing," Doc's voice says, which makes him laugh even harder. Doc's voice tightens, rises in register, takes on a note of desperation. "Make sure this sonofabitch *hurts*. Make sure he remembers us."

Some of the wounds are already starting to heal—he can feel the warm tingling deep inside him—but they are quickly reopened as the knives fall again and again; new holes are made in him, holes from slashes and thrusts and plunges and twists, but Gage cannot stop laughing and doesn't want to. He laughs and curses and laughs until the pain turns the world from red to black, and, for a short and glorious and peaceful instant, he feels himself cease to exist.

The cold and wet weather system has stalled right over the Bay, so the night cops expect a long, boring shift—the kind that makes twelve hours feel like twenty-four—but the calls come in a steady stream, leaving them without much downtime. Mercer, Toronto, Benzinger, Cambi, and Sergeant Mazzarella spend the night driving from call to call, traffic stop to traffic stop, backing each other up in different combinations, a smooth choreography of order and procedure.

They receive a report of an unidentified naked male running across the golf course; Mercer responds to the call with Benzinger, and they shine their lights across the neat green fairways but find nothing. "Good," Benzinger says. "The last thing we need is another hypothermic naked guy." The two of them split up, with Benzinger driving off to back up Toronto on a traffic stop (busted taillight; driver on probation, subject to search), and Mercer joining Cambi at Molloy's, where Mrs. Vovek from the trailer park is at it again, skunk-drunk and harassing patrons at the bar. Mercer arrives as Cambi is guiding the tall, bone-thin woman out the front door.

"They are all racists," Mrs. Vovek shrieks, pointing back to the bar with spindly arm, spindly hand, spindly finger.

"No," Cambi says. "They just want to enjoy their drinks without you yelling at them."

"Don't call me a foreigner," she says.

Cambi pauses, but keeps his grip. "I didn't," he says.

"I speak English as good as you do."

"As *well* as I do," Cambi corrects her. Toronto gave him grammar pointers a few nights before, and Mercer can tell he's eager to show off what he learned.

"Racist," she says. "Bastard racist. You hate me because I am Magyar."

"Ma'am, nobody hates you. And I don't want to arrest you for being drunk and disorderly, but you're giving me very good reasons to do it. All I want you to do is go home and stay home. You're intoxicated, and you need to stop bothering people."

"Cam," Mercer says, "you need a hand?"

"Oh, look," Mrs. Vovek says, her eyes narrowed at Mercer. "Another racist. Tough bastard Nazi racist with a uniform."

"Mrs. Vovek," Cambi says, "I'm going to let you go home, just like last time. You know how to get home, right? Go home. Go to sleep. Stop bothering people."

She jump-steps away from him, then turns back, testing whether he'll chase after her. Satisfied that she's free, she turns and lurches down Mission.

"And don't call people Nazis," Cambi calls after her. "It makes them not like you."

She flashes a middle finger behind her just before she turns the corner. Cambi rolls his eyes at Mercer.

"You think it's safe to let her walk?" Mercer asks.

"It's only another block," Cambi says, "and she's a pro at this."

"I never knew you were a racist."

Cambi laughs. "What the fuck *is* Magyar, anyway?"

"That is one sad woman," Mercer says.

"No shit," Cambi says. "Speaking of sad, Fahey's in there. He's trying to read a book, and Pat says he's been on the same page since happy hour."

"Jerry reads books?" Mercer asks.

"He's trying, anyway. He might be doing better at drinking."

"Pat knows to get him a cab, right?"

"It's on the way. I told him to make sure Fahey gets into it, even if Pat has to stuff his fat ass in there himself."

They're interrupted by a radio call: someone has reported sounds of a disturbance in progress up by the movie theater. They respond to the call together, maintaining radio contact between the cruisers as they rev along J. Serra to the shopping center at the top of the hill. A pimply kid in a bow tie points them toward the scrubby field in back, where they shine their lights over dead grasses and muddy ruts and wet mounds of trash. They reconvene at the edge of the parking lot, where the flashing lights have attracted a cluster of gawkers.

"Nothing," Mercer says. "Don't see anything. Don't hear anything."

"Yup," Cambi says. "Ghost call."

Later that night, well after the bars have closed, when the roads are dark and the radio's quiet, Mercer finds Toronto parked in the driveway to Woodlawn with his dome light on. Toronto has his posse box up on the steering wheel, leaning on it as he writes intently. Mercer pulls up to him, rolls down his window.

"Hey, ass-bag," Toronto says, without looking up. *Ass-bag* is the current insult of choice at the station. The previous week's favorite was *dick-weasel*. Toronto holds up a hand. "Hang on a second. Have to finish a thought." He scribbles a few more words, adds an emphatic period, then looks up. "Did Fahey get home all right?"

"I just checked at Molloy's," Mercer says. "Cab took him home. I'll go by his house later, make sure things look all right."

Toronto shakes a tin of snuff and loads his lip.

"What's up with that?" Mercer asks.

Toronto spits into a soda can. "Mia got pissed about the smoking again," he says. "I'm going to try it this way."

"Great," Mercer says. "Think she'll stay with you once you have to get your jaw removed?"

"Thanks for caring," Toronto says. He spits again. "I can't believe you didn't get anything from the kid."

"He wasn't ready to talk."

"You don't help anyone by being soft. I taught kids like him. He's smart, and he's charming enough to make sure you never get what you need from him. All that *I'm sorry I don't remember* bullshit? It's just stonewalling that sounds like an apology. He knows grown-ups are suckers for contrition."

"He might mean it."

"He might. But I doubt it."

"I'll talk to him again."

"You and Funkhouser will have to work it yourselves. I have too much other shit going on. If he wants to protect people who nearly kill him, fine with me. Fuck it, I say."

Mercer nods. He doesn't try to explain that he saw honesty in Jude's sadness, that he felt a connection with the kid. Best thing to do is change the subject. "What are you working on in there?" he asks.

"Field-interview cards."

"Yeah? From tonight?"

"I did tonight's. These are extra."

"What do you mean? What's extra? Who'd you contact?"

"No one."

"But what's the card about?"

"What it's about," Toronto says, "is the chief and his fucking quotas."

Chief McCandless recently instituted a monthly quota of field-interview cards for all patrol officers. The idea is to make sure everyone is patrolling actively and engaging with citizens. All the officers agree the quota is a pain in the ass and an insult to their professionalism. In Cambi's words, it's *a dick-weaselly idea.* Mercer hasn't tallied up his monthly total yet, but he's sure he's made his number already. When you go by The Book, quotas like that aren't a problem.

"I can't believe he has us doing this," Toronto says. "This shit's for guys like Landau. Sits on his fat ass all day, and the only contact he makes is with his fucking shift wife."

"Maybe he fills out a card for her," Mercer says.

Toronto laughs. "I can just see it. *Action taken: stuck it to an alcoholic hag. Took pill to get it up.*"

"So, what are you doing? Making up your contacts?"

"Fuck yes. No one's ever going to look at these. All that matters to Mc-Candless is the count."

"Let me see."

Toronto hands him a card, and Mercer reads aloud. "*Name: Clarence M. Oyster. Address: 1370 El Camino Real.* Thirteen-seventy? That's not residential."

"No shit. Keep it up, you'll take Funkhouser's job."

Mercer thinks. "Thirteen-seventy is Cypress Lawn."

"Correct."

"Who is this? A transient?"

"No," Toronto says. "Fixed residence."

*Oyster,* Mercer says to himself, and he remembers where he's seen the name before. "This is a dead person."

"In a manner of speaking," Toronto says.

"What manner is that?"

"Most of them. Well, all of them, really."

"You're saying you field-interviewed a dead guy."

"If it helps you to think of it that way, yes. I'm going to say that I made contact, and this citizen and I had a pleasant conversation about the weather and about how he had no information whatsoever about any crime that may have ever been committed. Ever."

Mercer laughs. "What else do you have?"

Toronto hands him a dozen more cards. The subjects' addresses: 1000 El Camino: Woodlawn. 2101 Hillside: Hoy Sun. 1601 Hillside: Olivet. The name on the last one is *Chesapeake Sid.* Address: 1905 Hillside.

"No," Mercer says. "Don't tell me. Pet's Rest?"

Toronto spits into the can, then smiles at Mercer. A wet flake of tobacco is stuck to his front tooth.

"You're kidding," Mercer says. "Chesapeake Sid? What, a dog?"

"Sid was a horse. A fast and loyal horse. I believe he was a racehorse who then had a long and admirable career in stud."

"You're writing out a field-interview card that says you contacted a horse."

"There's no box on the form for 'species.'"

"A dead horse."

"Do you like the name? I made it up myself."

"A *fictional* dead horse."

"I was feeling inspired." He takes the card out of Mercer's hand and reads from it. "'*Subject spoke in a language foreign to me. I thanked him and gave him an apple, which he ate eagerly.*'"

"*Eagerly*'s an adverb," Mercer says. "You told me not to use adverbs."

"Sometimes you have to break the rules."

"You won't catch shit over this?"

"Over the adverb?"

"Funny. The false report."

"These will get filed away and ignored. Unless my dead people start committing crimes."

Mercer laughs. He wouldn't have the guts to try a stunt like this, and Toronto's doing it without any worry or guilt. Mercer feels looser just being around him.

"Made your number yet?" Toronto asks him.

"I haven't counted, but I'm in good shape," Mercer says.

"Fucking rookie," Toronto says.

Another cruiser pulls off the road and crunches over the gravel toward them. Cambi rolls down his window.

"Hey, Hatchetface," Toronto calls.

"Hey, you dick-weasels," Cambi says. "Let's get some coffee. I'm about to drop."

"Dick-weasels?" Toronto says. "That's so last week, Cambi."

"Yeah," Mercer joins in. "You're such an ass-bag for not knowing that."

# THE NEPTUNE SOCIETY

Your problem is, you're not playing the odds," Owen says, looking at Mercer over the rim of his martini glass. In the dimly lit room, his blond eyebrows and eyelashes are nearly invisible, and his skin looks strikingly white. "You're not meeting anybody, so how could you possibly find someone you want to be with?"

Mollie laughs at him. "Mike's problem is that he has too many friends telling him what his problem is."

It's early on a Friday evening, and the three of them are sitting at Neptune, a South of Market bar and grill. Mollie, a public defender, works at the nearby Hall of Justice; Owen meets her there for happy hour every Friday, and Mercer and their other friends join them when their work schedules allow. The room is washed in swimmy aqua light, and at the center of each black Formica table is a votive candle in a blue-green glass holder. The air is full of warm, buttery smells: potpies, grilled rosemary chicken, burgers, and onion rings. Mollie has changed her hair since Mercer last saw her; it's now a deep, dark purple-brown, shot through with streaks the same color as the candle flame. It's a more dramatic look for her, and Mercer thinks it's a good one.

"It's possible," he says, "that I just don't like meeting people."

Owen runs his hand through his fine blond hair, which he's worn longish and swept-back since high school. "You see what I mean?" he says to Mollie. "You see how he gets?"

"Don't be a jerk," Mollie tells him.

"You're dropping the ball, Mollie," Owen says. "You're supposed to find someone to set him up with."

"I'm looking. He's not for everyone."

"Hello," Mercer says. "I'm right here." He's hardly offended; they've been practicing this act for years, and he actually finds it comforting. Plus, he likes the idea that he's not for everyone.

"Sorry," Mollie says. "We're terrible."

"Mostly her," Owen says.

What Mercer wants to tell them is that they don't need to worry about him being alone. Maybe saving Jude has boosted his confidence, or maybe he's so sleep-deprived that he's feeling loose and reckless, but in these last couple of days, he's been less worried about what it means to be with Fiona, aware that he doesn't *need* to be with her, that he's *choosing* to be. On the drive up to the city tonight, he thought about telling his friends, finally, that she's more than just the one-nighter he casually mentioned last summer—as long as the moment felt right. And the warm, fragrant air and their smiling faces and the beer in his stomach have him thinking that it does. He's looking forward to meeting Fiona at her house later, cooking dinner together, settling in for a movie and sex and sleep. And even if he ends up lying awake, as he usually does, he'll be happy listening to her breathe, feeling her warmth folded into him, listening to the waves, watching the cobwebs wiffle in the moonlight on her ceiling. "I don't need to be set up," he says.

He expects a dramatic pause, but Owen responds right on the beat. "Of course you do," he says, straightening the fold on his turtleneck. "You just don't like to believe you do." Owen is Mercer's oldest friend, and these are their roles: Mercer, prone to long stretches of exile from women, and Owen, relationship-savvy and duty-bound to fix this defect in him.

"I don't," Mercer says.

Mollie grins. "Spill," she says. "There's someone new?"

Mercer sips his stout and shakes his head. "Not exactly new."

"Hang on," Owen says. "Who is it?"

"It's not a big deal," Mercer says.

"'Someone not exactly new,'" Mollie repeats. Her forehead crinkles in thought.

"Did you backslide?" Owen asks. "I thought we agreed that all the girls in your blond phase were deadweight."

"Oh, that's kind," Mollie says.

"We *agreed*," Owen tells her.

"We did," Mercer confesses.

"And it's not the one from the bar," Owen says. "And I can't imagine you're going through another Harold-and-Maude thing. So who's left?"

Mercer's head starts to buzz, and he breaks into a sweat. He tries to take another sip of his beer, but all that's left is foam that won't come loose from the bottom. He shakes the glass, pointlessly. He realizes they're waiting for him to talk and puts the glass down. "She's not *that* old," he says, trying to keep the wound out of his voice.

"Oh, great. Nice one, Owen," Mollie says.

"I didn't know," Owen protests. "I'm sorry, Mike. I'm an asshole."

"So you're with her?" Mollie asks. "*With her* with her?"

"I think so."

Owen sips his martini, eats an olive. "You had concerns," he says, still chewing, "about the age issue."

Mercer shrugs. It's not as if the worry is gone; it's just living farther back in his head than before.

"When do we get to meet her?" Mollie asks. "Are you bringing her to the party?"

Mercer imagines walking into their house with Fiona and having everyone see them as a couple. The thought freezes him. All at once, he has lost his sense of what he wants to do.

"No one's going to judge you," Mollie says.

"That's right," Owen says. "You're not going to be the center of attention. I am. I'll make sure of it." He pauses, as if trying to divine a more complex reason for Mercer's silence. "You're coming, aren't you? Tell me you don't have to work. This party is much more important than work."

"I'll be there," Mercer says. "We will."

"What's her name?" Mollie asks.

"Fiona," he says. He rarely says her name aloud, and it feels odd in his mouth; still, he feels good. Less burdened. "You know," he says, feeling the ease come back into his voice, "when I got the envelope, I thought it was a wedding invitation—"

Mollie interrupts him. "Don't say the W-word. Someone here has a problem with it."

"Honey," Owen says, "we don't have to go and *literalize* our relationship just so we can get a nice set of steak knives. We already *have* a nice set of steak knives."

"The fascinating thing," Mollie stage-whispers to Mercer, "is that he really does think he's amusing."

While they grouse at each other, Mercer's thoughts drift again to the party. There'll be dozens of good-looking, unattached girls—there always are at Owen's parties—and if he goes with Fiona, he'll miss feeling that sexual buzz of possibility, that chaotic zoom of hormones and *maybe, just maybe.* This is the trade-off, of course: opportunity for certainty. Risk for safety. It's a deal that Owen happily made a decade ago. There's no reason Mercer can't make it, is there?

"I need a refill," Mercer says. "You two ready for another?" They are: Owen, another martini with three olives; Mollie, another glass of zinfandel. Owen hands him a fifty, and Mercer hesitates before taking it. Then, a quick calculation: Owen has a house and multiple income streams and time for adventure tourism; Mercer has student loans that have just come out of forbearance, a crappy apartment that stinks of sauerkraut, and a job that on any given night could end with him getting himself dead.

He takes the crisp new bill and turns away.

**W**hen they started elementary school together, Owen was a misfit— short, frail, uncoordinated, too smart for his own good. Mercer wasn't big, but he was reasonably athletic, and he was willing to scrap to defend himself and others. During middle school, though, when hallways and classrooms and cafeteria tables became arenas for the Darwinist games of the nascently sexual, Owen passed Mercer in the hierarchy. Somehow, he was more comfortable with the new rules than he'd been with the old. He revealed a knack for smooth conversation, for making anyone laugh and feel important, for enjoying people when they were in his presence and not taking it personally when they left.

Mercer spent those same years feeling as if his skeleton might jump out of his skin and run away. He'd turned self-questioning and awkward in sixth grade. In seventh, his father had a very public breakdown at work on the HP loading dock, was hauled away as a 5150, and split town a month later, leaving Mercer's mother to work three jobs to keep the house. Los Altos was money- and status-obsessed, and he felt everyone's eyes examining him even more closely. He found a comfortable orbit around Owen, and he stayed in it.

With their group of friends, he could relax; with other people, he learned how not to be noticed and how to answer a question in a way that invited no further ones. This, he realized, was good training for law enforcement: chopped sentences, a slate-faced gaze, an imperviousness to people searching for your weak spot. Giving away no more than you want to give.


**D**rum-and-bass music thumps gently through the bar, and couples chatter through it. Pool balls thwack as three spiky-haired guys in T-shirts and ratty jeans play a game of Cutthroat. A group of men in drag sit at a table near the bar, gabbing about home improvement projects. Mercer smiles to himself. It feels good to be in the city. The air feels lighter here, somehow. For the first time, he realizes how restrictive it is to live in Colma, where he has to worry about maintaining a façade of professionalism. Besides, this is where his friends are. Ten miles can be a lot farther away than you think.

He finally flags down the bartender, a girl he notices every time he comes to Neptune—she's tall, nearly his height, strawberry-blond, attractively wide-set eyes, always wearing black. She reminds him of those creamy-skinned women who dance in a line behind a preening Irish guy on PBS, their feet snappity-popping at a million miles an hour. He's never tried to chat her up, though. All those years of bartending, and he never got comfortable with small talk. Sure, the old-timers on the barstools liked him, the gray-haired guys with their thick noses and gin blossoms and bassett ears and hairy hands clutching buck-fifty PBRs, but they would've liked anyone who'd listen to them and nod every now and then.

Mercer orders for Owen and Mollie and gets another pint of stout for himself. The girl takes the money with a mechanical smile that flashes and fades before he can even thank her. He heads back to the table, expertly balancing the three drinks, grateful that he's old enough not to be bothered by the little snubs anymore.

Owen and Mollie are talking animatedly, leaning in close to each other, and they pull away when he arrives. "About this party," he says. "What's with the croquet?"

"What's with the croquet is that we'll be playing croquet," Owen says. "And we're going to light the yard up. Bright as Pac Bell. Lights everywhere. Lots and lots of lights. Croquet and food and cocktails and bands and dance floors and bad behavior—"

"He's trying to out-Gatsby Gatsby," Mollie says.

"I'm not trying to out-anyone anyone. I'm throwing myself a big goddamn party."

Mollie glares at him.

"And by that, I mean that Mollie and I—Mollie, the great love of my life, and I—are throwing me a big goddamn party."

"Thank you," she says.

"Are you going to wear those?" Mercer asks. For some reason, Owen is wearing leather pants, and Mercer has been been waiting for an opportunity to razz him for it.

"No, everyone's wearing *white*." Owen sips his drink contemplatively. "Oh, wait. Were you making fun of my pants?"

"Was," Mercer says. "And am."

"What's wrong with my pants?" He stands up from his chair and does a wide-armed spin, showing them off. One of the pool players has to step back and wait for him to sit down before he can get to his shot.

"Leather?" Mercer says. "You're kidding."

"I think he looks good in them," Mollie says. "He's got a great ass."

"They're incredibly comfortable," Owen says. "You should get yourself a pair."

"Not likely," Mercer says. "You can wear things like that. I can't."

"You could if you wanted to," Mollie says.

Mercer shrugs. He wears things that are comfortable and simple. Nothing that attracts scrutiny. Dark, solid-colored T-shirts, jeans, navy work jacket, plain black shoes. All he needs.

"Feel how soft they are," Owen says.

"I'm not feeling your pants."

"He doesn't want to feel my pants," Owen complains to Mollie.

"You know he has buffer-zone issues," Mollie says.

"Again," Mercer says, "I'm right here."

"You really don't like touching people, do you?" Mollie asks. "But don't you have to when you're working?"

"That's different. It's my job," Mercer says. A pat-down is a pat-down. A rear-arm finger-flex is a rear-arm finger-flex. They're procedures, that's all. Procedures that help keep you safe. As Mazzarella says, *If you can't physically control a suspect, you're going to get yourself dead.* And he likes how it feels to control an interaction, to take the power from someone, especially from someone who doesn't want to cede it to you.

Loud greetings are called to them from across the bar, and three other members of the Friday-night crew pull up chairs around the table. Johnny Gruenberg, Johnny Kang, and Heath Kinnicutt all graduated from Los Altos High with Mercer and Owen, and each of them has spent his twenties profitably. Johnny G started a business making high-performance toe clips for bikes and recently hit big with some pro-rider endorsements. Johnny K is getting his MBA at Berkeley; his family has business contacts all along the Pacific Rim, and he'll be making money hand over fist as soon as he graduates. Kinnicutt is a writer; he's been working on his second novel for a few years with the cushion of a trust fund. Mercer bought his first book, even shelled out for the hardcover to support his friend. Never finished reading it, though. It's an eight-hundred-page tome called *The Shenanigan Tapes,* about an enigmatic rock star named Richard Shenanigan who disappears after recording a disk that makes shadowy government forces think he's a threat. Or something like that. It *sounded* interesting, but—like that Stockholm movie—nothing ever seemed to *happen.* The book was a tangle of fragments that never converged into a story, as far as he could tell. He'd put it down, then lost it in one of his apartment moves.

Kinnicutt has aged more noticeably than the rest of them. His hair, which he wore long throughout high school, is now just a close-cut ring around his head and a scrubby little island of brown fuzz over his forehead. He's been putting on weight, and he's looking particularly bloated and slack and exhausted lately. When Kinnicutt takes off his jacket, Mercer checks his wrists and notes that he's still not wearing his Medic Alert bracelet. Not a good idea for a diabetic who insists on drinking, but really, you can only raise the issue so many times.

Owen, as usual, finds a way to say what Mercer wants to but can't. He asks the two Johnnys if they found Kinnicutt sleeping under a truck.

"I don't look any worse than Mercer," Kinnicutt says. "Mike, who popped you?"

Mercer checked his eye in the bathroom mirror earlier; there's just a hint of puff around it, but the bruise has turned a greenish yellow around the outside and remained purple at the center. It's resolving well, but that's an alarming combination of colors to see on a face. Especially your own.

"He got it in the line of duty," Owen says.

"Our Officer Mike," Mollie swoons. "A hero. Go on. Tell them."

Mercer demurs, but everyone at the table clamors for the story, and he gives in. Owen and Mollie, who've heard it already, interrupt to fill in details and to emphasize the parts they like best. Mercer includes the new developments: the tox report confirmed ketamine, and a lot of it; the kid's lucky he didn't suffer respiratory failure. No matches for the prints on the bottles. No sign of the stolen vehicle.

Is the kid out of the hospital? they want to know. Does he remember anything? Did someone slip him the drug? Was he, in so many words, butt-raped? Will Mercer get to be in a movie? Will his friends? He reminds them that this is serious; it's not about cameo roles, it's about tracking down a person or persons responsible for battery and kidnapping, maybe even attempted murder.

"To our buddy, Officer Mike, who saves lives," Owen says, leading a toast.

"We're proud of you," Mollie says.

"To Officer Mike," the rest of them say, clinking glasses, and Mercer drinks with them, feeling guilty for enjoying the attention so much.

Kinnicutt pushes his bulk up from his chair. "Gentlemen," he says, "shall we go have a conversation with Hank?"

"Sure," Owen says. He and the two Johnnys all stand.

"Go," Mollie says, waving them away and sounding put-upon. "Go talk to Hank. Mike and I will stay here and converse like adults."

*Hank* is what they call the red-crystalled sticky bud that grows on land Owen owns north of Mendocino. It's named after the border collie owned by the one-eyed ex-Coastie who oversees the growing. This is information that Mercer would rather not know, but sometimes people forget he's in earshot. In general, though, they do a good job of walling him off, and he doesn't have to feel as if he's betraying his oath.

Mercer leans back in his chair and asks Mollie what kinds of cases she's working on.

"Still misdemeanors, mostly. I had a hearing today for a client who's charged with possession of a completely trivial amount of pot—and, of course, resisting arrest—and the D.A. won't budge. The cops are being assholes. They want to make an example of this guy for some reason."

"He must've pissed somebody off."

"I hope you know that when I complain about cops, I don't mean you."

"I know that. Everyone's got a job to do."

"But that's not what we should be talking about," she says. She swirls her wineglass, then slides it to the center of the table and leans in closer. "We should be talking about you."

"What's to say?"

"You saved a life. Think about everything that kid might go on to do. Even if it's not much, at least he'll have a chance to do it. And it's because of you."

Mercer shrugs. "Don't get dramatic," he says, although even as he speaks he can feel that his nonchalance is a lie.

"It's real," she says. "It's more real than anything the rest of us have done."

"Your work's important."

"I didn't say it wasn't. I know I help people. I just meant that you've done something real and tangible and good."

He stares into his beer glass, avoiding her gaze. "Thanks," he says. He looks around the bar, suddenly distracted by the music and voices and clatter and, standing in a crowd of at the bar, a woman who looks a little like Shelby Laswell, an ex of his from college. Round face, nut-brown hair, sweetly crooked mouth. But a long, upturned nose, where Shelby's was a button. He wonders where Shelby is now. It hits him that as he gets older, he'll be asking that question about more and more people.

Mollie looks over her shoulder to see what has his attention, then turns back.

"Your hair looks great," he says.

"Thank you," she says. "I love what you've done with your eye."

He wants to say something quick and clever, but he can't think of anything. Even with people he trusts, his best friends, he feels like he's a step behind.

"I can't wait to meet Fiona," Mollie says. "She's a nurse, right? So she's also someone who helps. You have that in common."

Mercer nods. "She's good at what she does. Takes it seriously. You'll like her. She's down-to-earth."

"Does she want to have kids? Oh, don't look so surprised. It's a reasonable question."

"She might," he says. "But we don't know what we're doing yet."

"You didn't learn that in health class?"

"Funny."

"It's good to see things falling into place for you. I've been worried sometimes. But now? You like your job—you light up when you talk about it—and tonight you're talking about Fiona. I know that's hard for you. No, it's nothing to be ashamed of; some people are more open than others. Frankly, Owen could learn a thing or two about self-restraint from you. But I digress. My point is, I'm glad to see you like this. We want you to be happy. You deserve to be."

"I don't know that anyone really *deserves* anything," Mercer says.

"Well, I do," she says. "Quit thinking so damn much."

Mercer thanks her and knocks back the rest of his beer as Owen and the guys return from the alley, red-eyed and laughing. They're followed by some new arrivals—two guys, two girls, all friends from their high-school years. They converge on the table, and once the hellos are said and the hugs and hand slaps dispensed and the new arrivals have gone off to cadge more chairs from around the bar, Owen sits back down next to Mollie, and Kinnicutt drops himself next to Mercer.

"I just had a great idea," Owen announces. "We'll all go in on a big piece of land up north, and we'll put in a village of yurts. We'll be able to take vacations together, or just get away whenever any of us needs to. It'll be great. It'll be all ours."

"What if you can't afford land?" Mercer asks. "Or a yurt?"

"We'll build extra. Guest yurts. All shall be welcome."

Kinnicutt raises his glass. "To all of us!"

"To yurts!" Johnny K says.

"And guest yurts!" Owen says.

After the toast, Kinnicutt turns to Mercer. "So," he says. "Have you met Marco DiMaio?"

"Not yet."

"Are you going to?"

"Possibly," Mercer says. "I don't want to make a big deal of it."

"Dude's a fucking genius," Kinnicutt says. "You ever seen his movies?"

"One or two," Mercer says. "Not really my style."

Kinnicutt opens the leather messenger bag slung over the back of his chair and pulls out a copy of *The Shenanigan Tapes* in paperback. He pushes the thick book across the table to Mercer, bumping the candle in the process. "Can you give this to him?"

Mercer doesn't pick it up. "I'm not comfortable with that."

"Come on. It'd be sweet if he optioned it. Dude's the right guy to make this thing. Fucking genius. Plus, fuck, the money, you know?"

In high school, Kinnicutt had been noted for his speaking ability, his meticulous but lightning choice of words, his perfect diction. This slack, sloppy speech is affectation hardened into habit, and it bothers Mercer to see his friend wasting a skill that he himself would give anything to have. "It's unprofessional," Mercer says.

"Unprofessional, fuck. This is how the business works. He knows that. He won't give a shit."

"My priorities are the boy and the investigation. Helping a friend comes after."

"That's too bad," Kinnicutt says, sounding irritated.

"Just take the book, Mike," Owen says from across the table. "It's the only way he'll shut up."

Mercer thinks for a moment, then accepts the book. "I'll give it to DiMaio if it feels appropriate. No promises."

"Thank you," Kinnicutt says. *About time,* his tone implies.

Mercer checks his watch. He still has half an hour before he meets Fiona, but she worries if he's even a little late. "I have to roll," he says.

"Stay awhile," Johnny K says. "You have to tell these other guys about the kid."

"We're just getting started," Owen says. "Where's your spirit?"

"He has a date," Mollie says.

The hoots and whistles fly around the table, just as they have since high school—since middle school, even. Mercer feels himself redden.

"Go," Mollie tells him, shooing him away. "Don't leave a lady waiting." She winks at him, and Mercer feels a flush of gratitude that he's lucky enough to have good friends in his life. He picks up his jacket from the back of his chair, zips up, and says his good-byes.

The Oldsmobile is parked a few blocks away, and Mercer takes in the neighborhood around him as he walks. South of Market is still sleepy, trying to rouse itself from its tech-binge hangover. Some long-dark doorways are lit up again, but FOR LEASE signs still abound, hung on gated entries and pasted into dusty windows. The Pan-Asian restaurants specializing in colorful cocktail infusions have vanished; the Cajun place is long gone. The upscale burrito joint: closed, its street-level picture window exposing a high-ceilinged space that's empty except for plaster-dust drifts on the floor. It looks like a museum exhibit of Failed Promise. A skinny, middle-aged black man in a watch cap attempts to direct cars into parking spots that once were scarce; the cars glide past him and ease into open spaces farther down the block.

Mercer looks up to the freeway that rumbles above him and sees a billboard image on a space that was blank the previous week except for the shreds of former ads that scabbed its surface. Now it shows a photograph of two people looking toward Downtown, many times larger than life. A husband and wife, retirement age, the ruddy-faced man with one arm draped around the woman. His free hand is intertwined with hers, and their skin—his pink, hers sun-honeyed—and their wedding bands and the man's white-white hair all shine in the glow of oncoming headlights. The woman's hair is an insistent, too-brown brown. The man looks caught in the middle of a laugh; his wife's smile is prim, reserved, perfectly symmetrical. His barrel chest strains the fabric of a navy-blue golf shirt, while the woman is stylishly thin in a white, sleeveless blouse. A photo taken on a cruise, Mercer guesses, snapped in the sunny flush of afternoon shuffleboard and umbrella drinks. Over the blue-blue cloudlessness of the sky behind them, the words *Remembering Leslie* shine in white italic type. He's not sure if Leslie is the man or the woman, but one of them must be dead, and the other is alive and grieving and demanding that the city of San Francisco share the pain.

The billboard will stay in place through the winter and spring. Month after month, people will Remember Leslie, even those who can only remember the billboard because they never knew the person. And then, one day, Leslie-and-Spouse will vanish again, leaving behind them that scabby, dirty-white panel. Nearly all the drivers and pedestrians—including Mercer—will feel relieved, subconsciously glad to be rid of a responsibility they never wanted. For a week, the space will remain empty, a blank screen waiting to be blessed with an image. Then, overnight, an ad for a clothing chain will appear, an artsy black-and-white shot of a distracted, dark-eyed young woman. Her hair will be in after-the-beach saltwater clumps, her low-cut white top held closed over her breasts by one loop of a thin lace, her stomach and midriff an expanse of gray-toned young flesh. Drivers will slow as they pass beneath her. Some will goggle; some will peek just long enough to avoid a rear-end collision; some will indulge a brief fantasy in which her drowsy attention settles on them; some will strain to see if that patch of dark is pubic hair or just a clever shadow and will remind themselves to check again the next time they pass; some will harrumph at the company's wanton flesh-peddling; and the task of Remembering Leslie will be left to the few whose duty it has been all along.

On this night, though, Mercer is seeing Leslie for the first time, and he idly wonders if this memorial is the beginning of a new trend, a cityscape devoted to images of the dead. Maybe in the future there will be projections of the departed floating over the city, holographic ghosts haunting the skies. Then he pulls himself back into the now and looks at the thirty-foot-high smiling Leslie-and-Spouse and their twined fingers and thinks, *This is what it means to be with someone. You grow old together, and one of you dies, and the other one of you is left so desperate and lost that you'll drop thousands of dollars on a bill-board no one else wants to see.* But maybe that's not a bad thing. Maybe that's the very point of all this living: making a bond that's strong enough that you don't care what other people want or don't want to see, hardy enough to out-last death. This is the thought that is tumbling in his head like a satellite adrift when he comes across his car.

Someone has torn off the radio antenna—probably a crackhead, impro-vising a pipe. He's not happy about it, but when you drive a beater like the Olds, you don't sweat the little things. He gets into the driver's seat, starts the en-gine, and as the blue smoke cloud gathers around the car, he checks the radio reception. KCSM is coming in with some static, but it's listenable. He makes his way onto the freeway and points the car in the direction of the ocean.

# SEVEN

# THE GREAT THING ABOUT ALMOST DYING

The great thing about almost dying is that it frees you. You don't care so much what people think anymore. So all the questions from parents and doctors and cops, all the tears and the shouting, all those half-assed text messages from your ex-best-friend Wilson pretending he cares if you're all right, all the time you had to spend listening to the young priest your mom called in to convince you that you were in need of *spiritual guidance,* none of it matters. None of it. Anyone who doesn't get you can just fuck off. The last twenty-four hours, Jude's parents have hardly even *tried* to talk to him. He likes it that way.

Jude is sitting in the back seat of his father's Saab, his parents in front. As soon as they pulled out of their driveway, he pulled his cap low over his eyes and clapped his headphones over his ears. The bass thumps like hell, the high end is rich and clear, and the noise-suppression circuitry makes the world outside his head cease to exist. It's just him and the music.

They're off to spend the day with the Robersons, family friends who own a vineyard in St. Helena. The trip is a surprise. He hadn't found out until his father woke him up this morning and told him. Jude doesn't mind, though. He likes going for walks by himself through the rows of grapes. Walking and thinking, sometimes smoking a joint and letting his mind really wander, surrounded by rolling hills and a warm wind and quiet.

And he has a *lot* to sort out. Did Reyna really kiss him? Did she try to stop Bobby and the other guys from taping him up? He remembers laughter, he can hear it in his head, the way it came to his ears in waves, but he can't tell if her voice was part of it. If he could just talk to her, he'd ask her straight out: does she like him, or is she just leading him on, making him the butt of a bigger joke? Would she pick him over Bobby?

She could. She might.

A memory returns: Jude, pulling her aside in the cemetery, trying to tell her that she's smart, and she should listen to the part of her that wants to make something of herself, the part that wants to study architecture and make insane buildings that will fuck with everyone's heads, just like she told him. Trying to tell her that she doesn't have to waste her life, that Bobby may be cool and Bobby may be a bad boy and Bobby may be fun, but Jude is *going* places, Jude is going to *achieve,* and she can, too. Trying to tell her that he thinks he loves her, and loves her so much that it's okay if they don't end up together as long as she's living a fulfilling life, as cheesy as that sounds. Only, his mouth won't form the words that he wants it to. All he can produce is slurred mumbles and clouds of breath steam.

Next time—if there is one—he won't get so fucked up.

If he could talk to her, he'd ask her straight out: *what's between us? what happened that night?* But she hasn't been answering her phone. She might be avoiding him. Or she might just be lying low because the cops are involved—he wouldn't blame her, if that's what she's thinking, but it doesn't make the situation any easier for him to figure out. And he can't talk to anyone else about all of this, because, let's face it, what happened to him is absolutely fucking *humiliating.* Who's he going to talk to, anyway? Wilson? His mom? His dad? Not a chance.

The bass in his headphones rumbles and slaps and thumps, and it carries the melody under the crashing power-chord guitars, and it is free, it is so goddamned free and amazing. He's listening to The Bloody Clerks, a punk band from San Diego that Reyna loves. If he stays very still and his dad doesn't keep hitting so many goddamn bumps—*Jesus, Dad, are you fucking blind?*—he can feel the heavy bass making his lips vibrate, and in those vibrations he can feel Reyna's lips pushing against his, kissing him as he fell down into the black. He can feel them, even though he's not entirely sure it really happened.

They could get together. Secretly, if they have to, and they could do it behind everyone's backs, do it in his car and in his bedroom and in his dad's screening room and in closets at parties and on the beach and even back in that cemetery, anywhere they can steal a few minutes alone. The next time his dad is shooting somewhere cool, he'll take her there and they'll do it on the set and in trailers and maybe he'll even put a handheld camera on her. She'll joke to the lens: *Bobby who?*

*Drink up, handsome,* she had said in the cemetery, when she handed him the orange juice.

*Handsome.*

Her lips pressed against his. That's the memory he has (or thinks he has, anyway), so that's where the fantasy starts: the pressure of her lips, and then her spiked tongue tasting like tequila and steel. Her skin smelling like smoke. Her cold hands holding his head in place. And in this version, the one he's directing, they're alone at the pit, high and dreamy, but he lifts her shirt and her nipples are hard in the cold and rain and she unbuckles his belt and un-buttons his jeans and she's rubbing him and asking if that feels good and then he's in her mouth and he can feel the metal against him and his hands are running through her spiky hair and then she shucks off her jeans and asks *are you ready?*

His dad jams on the brakes, jolting him out of the scene. He looks out the window. They're on the Carquinez Bridge, coming up on the toll crossing. His mom looks back, checking up on him, and Jude gives her the most innocent *Hi-Mom* smile and crosses his arm over his lap, then bounces his head in time to the music to tell her *everything's okay but I'm not going to talk right now.* She gives her gullible little Mom-nod, because she can't know what's going on his head, which is now this: Reyna on top of him, grinding, writhing. Her bare wet tits are gorgeous, and straggles of her hair, white-blond and green, hang over her tiny beaming white face. God, he's about to burst, about to come right in his jeans, he's never been so in love before—he doesn't even need to touch himself, he can do it all with his mind—and at the last possible moment he opens his eyes, stops the film so he doesn't slop a big mess all over himself. Try explaining *that* to Mom.

When his eyes refocus, he sees two visions of his father in the driver's seat. From the back, he's brown-sueded shoulders and a balding head with brushy, severe salt-and-pepper hair. Framed in the rearview mirror, he's just a pair of dark and intense eyes under thick, gray-shot brows. Those eyes are aimed straight ahead at the road, as if he's contemplating how to orchestrate the traffic before him. Then the eyes dart rightward, toward Jude's mother, and when his eyebrows rise, Jude can tell it's for emphasis, that he's just said something to her, explained something he assumes she doesn't understand.

His father's a serious man. All business, at home and on the set. Some actors love him—they hail him as a genius on talk shows and in magazines—but many others have stormed off his sets. Some websites say he once slugged Mickey Rourke. Put him down with one punch.

Jude's father's eyes turn back to the road as the car swings a left turn, and as they straighten out of it, Jude's mom throws him another glance over her shoulder. Jude shuts his eyes again immediately. She's been careening between anger and tears since he got out of the hospital, and he never knows which one he's going to get. He doesn't want either.

The bass is pumping in his head. Each song's faster and more furious than the one before. He's got to get himself a bass and a huge amp and make music like this. It'll be an easy transition, cello to bass. It won't be long before he's making the ceiling shake. He'll join a band. Write songs. Play sweaty, pissed-off, chaotic gigs as Reyna watches him from side stage, amazed at his talent.

Yes: he could win her. Maybe he already has. If only he could remember.

They've been going uphill for a while, which is strange because the Robersons' vineyard is in the valley, but he opens his eyes, sees fields of grapevines on their little crucifixes, and figures his dad is stopping for another one of his VIP tastings at some winery that he'll refer to as "a hidden gem." Fine. Jude can stay in the car. He's got music in his ears and Reyna in his head.

So he's not concerned when the car slows and gravel crunches under the tires. The driver's-side door opens and shuts—he feels this more than he hears it, feels the vibrations of the frame and the pressure change inside the car. He can feel his mom's eyes on him, waiting for him to acknowledge her so she can say *Hold on, they'll just be a few minutes,* but he keeps his eyes shut—*If I can't see you, you can't see me,* he'd believed when he was little—and then her door opens and shuts and she's gone, too. Then, because his arm is resting on the door, he can feel the locks *snick* shut, and what the fuck is that all about? Do they think something's going to come out to the car and *get* him? Do they think he's *helpless?* Or did they just forget he's there? Idiots.

He looks out the window. They're in front of a building like a French château surrounded by smaller outbuildings. There's a sign on the front lawn that says *Seven Oaks* in script. Another stupid, pretentious winery. He's about to close his eyes and visit Reyna in the graveyard again when he sees the heavy wooden door of the main building open, sees his parents walking back to the car with two men in baby-blue polos, and these guys—one black, one white, both bearded—are enormous, linebacker-sized and tough-looking. His dad aims his key ring at the car and there's another *snick,* and then his dad is pulling the car door open and yanking the headphones off Jude's head. Without them the world is loud and trebly and overwhelming. His dad's voice is ice when he says, "Let's go."

The blueshirts flank his father at the door. His mom stands at the edge of the driveway, removed, looking out across the greening hills.

"Let's go," his dad says again. "Now."

Jude slides out. "What's up?"

"You're staying here," his dad says.

"What do you mean?"

"I mean you're going to walk inside with these two gentlemen, and you're going to stay here and get treatment."

"Treatment?" Jude says, stunned. "What are you talking about?"

"We're not going to sit around while you throw away your life," his dad says. "You're going to clean up your act and get back on track."

"No," Jude says, and that surprises him, because he's not used to saying no to his father.

"What did you say?"

"I'm the victim," Jude says. "I'm the one who almost died."

"Exactly. And you were the one who put yourself in that position. By getting drunk. By doing drugs. By hanging out with these people, whoever they are."

"You don't understand," he says.

"You're right. I don't. Because you're not telling us what happened."

"I don't need *treatment.* This is a mistake."

"Don't make this hard, Jude," his mother says. "It's for your own good."

Adrenaline floods him. "This is *fucked,*" he says, and he looks left and right, animal instincts taking over, but the linebackers have him cornered. An escape plan: dive back into the car and out the other door. But what then? Hide, and live off the land in the Napa hills? No, he'll go along, trust these guys; they'll realize he's smart, he'll talk to them and enunciate well and use his best vocabulary, and he'll smile and show them he's a good kid. He's only ever been drunk a handful of times, and he's smoked maybe a thousandth as much pot as most kids he knows, and it's *insane* that he's the one being blueshirted into a place called Seven Oaks.

"We'll bring your things later," his dad says.

"Be good," his mom says.

Suddenly there's a muscled brown hand firmly around one of his wrists, a white hand around the other. They lead him up the stone path to the big oak door. He feels small, compliant, gutless.

"Jude, my name's Clinton," the black one says. "Like the president."

"I'm Duane," the white one says.

"This is all wrong," Jude tells them.

"I know you don't want to be here," Clinton says, "but this will be your home for a little while."

"You're going to get the help you need," Duane says.

"I don't *need* help," Jude says. What he needs is to see Reyna again, to make sure she knows he didn't rat out Bobby and the other guys. To hear her call him *handsome* again. A panicked thought: she won't know he's here. She'll think he's avoiding her, avoiding them. Maybe she'll think he did talk to the cops, or that he's too much of a pussy to face Bobby again. Maybe it's over. Maybe that one beautiful, distant, lost, dark, trippy moment—which might not even have existed—is all he'll ever have.

"Everyone needs help," Clinton says. "It's just a question of what kind and how much."

Behind him, Jude hears the revving engine and his dad's commanding voice. "Get in, Susan. Don't make it worse."

"Marco," she says.

"Clean break," his dad says. "Like we discussed." And then a door slams shut.

They *discussed* this.

As he nears the building, sounds flood over him: his dad's car calmly crunching the gravel as they drive away; three crows in a yellow-leafed tree jawing at him; his ears ringing; Clinton saying something in a maddeningly even voice; the iron creak as Duane pulls open the door.

He thinks: his father has no idea who he is.

He thinks: his mother sold him out.

He thinks: no one loves him.

He thinks: he's alone.

He thinks: his headphones. His parents have driven away with his sweet, sweet headphones, and that is just too fucking much. The thought buckles his knees, and he starts to cry. His vision goes blurry and swirling as Clinton-Like-the-President and Duane lift him up and carry him inside.

Sitting on a slab of black marble in the shade of a palm, Doc twirls his knife—his thumb guiding, his sore pink fingers flipping—and gets it spinning faster and faster, finally so fast that he can hear the *whick-whick-whick* of blade slicing air. He twirls and twirls, letting his vision relax into a blur, letting his thoughts drain away until his mind is comfortably empty. Time passes, although he can't tell how much; he twirls until he hears Ruczek's high, nasal voice, and he looks up to see the boys trudging up the slope to meet him. "Well?" he says as they gather around.

They shrug, mutter. Still no sign of the guy. They've looked around, they've asked, they've knocked the heads of people who looked like they might know something. But nobody knows nothing.

Has to be six months, a year—a long goddamn time, whichever. "Where the hell is he?" Doc says.

"Maybe he's not coming," Ruczek says. He pulls off his boots, flexes his swollen gray toes in the grass.

"How can he not be coming?" Doc says.

"How should I know?" Ruczek says. "I didn't write the fucking rule book."

"There's a rule book?" LoPresti asks.

"Don't be a moron," Doc tells him. "And don't you be one, either," he adds when he hears Ruczek snicker.

"No need to get sore," Ruczek says.

Doc catches him by the ascot and reels him in, knocking off the smaller man's hat and forcing his face right up against Doc's gaping wound. Ruczek strains to pull away, a reflex of disgust, and Doc feels a stab of pleasure. "My head hurts, is all," he says. "I got a shotgun hole in it for all goddamn eternity, case you haven't noticed. Haven't you noticed?"

"Oh, yeah," Ruczek smart-asses back. "But you can only tell up close."

"Why are you so worried about this guy?" LoPresti asks. "He's just a cop. A *dead* cop."

"Ain't worried."

"You look worried."

"Well, I ain't."

"He's being *cautious*," Eastwick says.

"That's right," Doc says. The big man doesn't talk much, but he always knows what to say. Smart guy. Freddy would've liked him. Ma, too.

"Still," Eastwick says, "he can't be any more of a threat now than he was before, can he?"

"And he wasn't much of a threat before," Ruczek says.

Doc hurls his knife end-over-end and buries it to the hilt in the palm bark. "Look," he says. "I don't like to leave a job half done. That's how Ma taught us."

His fingertips twitch when he pictures Ma—they're crying out to him—and he rubs the pad of his thumb against the knife blade. He can feel the long, clean, satisfying cut as it opens. "She taught us a lot. I ever tell you how she taught us not to be scared of nothing? No?" So he tells them: a blast-furnace afternoon the summer Doc turned ten. Pa, drunk like usual, face-down on the table with flies licking sweat off his skin. Ma called all four boys outside—Herman and Lloyd and Doc and little Freddy—where she stood in her ratty brown apron, holding Pa's rifle. Said she had a lesson for them. Led them down the road to a sun-scorched ruin of a wheat field, and when Lloyd asked her what this lesson was all about, she said, *It's about the four of you running. One side of this field to t'other. Now.* They'd stood there, not believing her, until she shouted *Go!,* and they all took off, their eight feet beating clouds in the dry dirt and flying across the burnt-up stalks. Ma fired shot after shot at them, reloading quicker than you could believe. The air popped and whined and Doc's lungs were burning, but they all made it to the other side, with Herman carrying Freddy the last fifty yards. Ma put the rifle down and called them back. *Now you seen the worst. Nothing ever going to be scarier 'n that. Y'all are my boys, and no boy of mine's going to be a piss-pant coward.* Lloyd was bleeding from getting winged in the leg, but Ma said sorry and bandaged him up, so it wasn't a big deal.

The lesson took. You get a lesson like that, you don't panic when, for instance, you're on a job outside Kansas City and your pal gets gut-shot by a bullet that burned a stripe across your chest on the way. No, you stay calm and grab both bags from the teller's hands and *then* shoot your way out to the idling car. A lesson like that, you *definitely* don't get scared when some clown of a cop gets an idea to come after you with a pocket full of Root.

Eastwick scratches the back of his knotty bald head. "Maybe," he says, "maybe he was so scared that he got here and took the Root first thing."

"If he ain't here by now," LoPresti says, "you got to figure."

"Yeah," Doc says. "Probably. Just keep your eyes open."

"Meantime, let's go find a goddamn bottle," Ruczek says.

"You read my mind," Doc says.

When Ruczek bends over to pick his hat up off the grass, Doc boots him in the keister and sends him sprawling. It's the little pleasures that keep a dead man going.

It feels like morning, but the sky is still black when Mercer finds himself suddenly wide awake, his mind arcing with shooting-star thoughts. He slides out of bed, hoping he won't wake Fiona, who is on her side, huddled under blankets and snoring softly. The old bed creaks, and she mutters in her sleep *No, I won't, it's mine* before trailing off into quiet again. He creeps into the bathroom and clicks the door shut behind him.

He snaps on the light, which comes as a shock. The bathroom tile glares pink at him. He keeps his eyes squinted as he takes a leak, enjoying the relief but aware that something in his head doesn't feel right. A swishing sensation, back and forth, then a downward diagonal crash as he feels his vision trying to split and diverge, an ocean swell rushing from one ear to the next. There is a trebly clank and clatter as his head brings down the towel rod, although it's more surprising than painful, and then he's on the floor, cheek pressed to cold tile, wondering what the hell just happened.

He pushes himself into a sitting position, back to the cool wall, and he holds his hands over his face, listening for sounds of Fiona stirring. Just as suddenly as the wave hit him, it fades away, although he can still feel himself trembling. *It's nothing serious,* he tells himself. *You're not dying. Sit. Wrap your arms around yourself and hold tight. It'll be morning before too long.*

◉

# EIGHT

# VAPOR TRAILS

Toronto and Mia hike up Mason Street, striding into a swift chill wind. It's a clear night, and when they crest Nob Hill, they have a sky full of stars to admire. Orion here, Big Dipper there, Cassiopeia there. A blue-pearl moon. Venus shining high over the bay. He hugs her roughly. "All for you," he says.

"Shut up," she says. "Don't get cheesy on me."

"Seven weeks. Long time to go without you."

"You'll survive."

"You never know," he says. "That's why you have to seize the moment."

"I'll seize your moment," she says, and he feels her hand on the front of his pants.

"Not on the street, you won't. I'm not letting SFPD pop me for a lewd-and-dissolute."

"Can I do that to you later?"

"You'd better," he says, "after what I just spent on dinner."

Even after climbing the steep hill, even after the rich meal and the huge bar tab, neither of them is breathing hard. Energy and stamina, they've got it; they're *formidable* together. The thought gets him hard, and he has to adjust himself. Then he surreptitiously pats his jacket pocket to make sure the ring is still there. Ninety-one hundred bucks. He's not letting this rock get away from him.

He'd wanted to give it to her the moment they sat down at Farallon, but he kept his cool, from the first round of mojitos through the last glass of port. He'd let her believe it was her going-away dinner. Even though she wasn't leaving for a week, he sensed that the idea of being apart was stressing her out; she'd been grumpy and distant before the alcohol relaxed her.

*What are you having?* she'd asked.

*Get whatever you want,* he'd told her.

*I just asked what you're having.*

*Monkfish. It's like lobster.*

*I know what monkfish is,* she'd said. *I'll get the salmon.*

*Babe, salmon's the same everywhere. You should get something special in a place like this.*

*Why is salmon on the menu, then?*

*For people who don't know any better.*

*I like salmon,* she'd said, folding her arms like a stubborn little girl. *I like it, and I'm getting it.*

*It's your night, babe. Whatever you want.*

That was the point: to get whatever they wanted, to splurge, to make the night memorable. He ordered the white Bordeaux Graves that the sommelier touted—a hundred bones for the bottle. They got a ridiculous appetizer—a jumble of seafood entombed in a pyramid of aspic—just because she was amazed anyone would make something like that and wanted to see it. Three desserts, because each one sounded too delicious to pass up.

And now: the big finish. He leads her along California Street to the Fairmont Hotel, dramatically lit and impressive in its stateliness, its solidity. A line of well-dressed people wait behind a doorman who's piping for cabs. Another doorman greets them as they walk into the lobby, which is high-ceilinged and bustling with executive types, European tourists, society-page people in formal wear.

"What are you up to?" she asks, taking his hand.

"You'll see," he says. They pass by the registration desk—they're not checking in, not yet—and he leads her along a red-carpeted hall to a staircase down.

"Are we going to the Tonga Room?" she asks.

He smiles. Months ago she mentioned that she'd never been there, and he'd decided it would be a good place to propose. It would show her that he pays *attention.* Holds on to every word she says.

He pays the cover, and just as they enter the bar, a monsoon starts: tape-looped thunder and a humid push of air as the downpour starts over the rectangular pool in the center of the place. She races ahead to watch the rain, threading through clutches of people with tiki drinks, and he follows her. They stand at the edge of the pool, just out of range of the splashing raindrops, and she turns and thumps him in the chest. "This is *so* cool," she says. "Ridiculous and cool."

"It's your night," he says.

"I've always wanted to come here."

"I know."

"How?"

"You told me."

"Huh," she says. "I don't remember."

"I do," he says. "I can do all the remembering for both of us." He regrets saying that last part—it sounds stupid, and it doesn't mean anything—but he's had a few drinks, and what the hell, not every line can be a winner. "Let's find a table," he says.

They pass through a pack of college kids in tuxes and dresses—it's a weeknight in January, what the fuck are they celebrating?—and another large, raucous group that he pegs as big-firm lawyers celebrating a verdict. Mia spots a couple leaving a table for two with high-backed wicker chairs and races toward it—he's impressed by how quick and agile she is, even after so many drinks—and she narrowly beats another couple, who shoot glares that she ignores.

*We are fast,* he thinks. *We are fast, and we get what we want.*

Toronto flags down a waiter and orders a scorpion bowl for the two of them, then tells Mia he's going to the bathroom. At the bar, he catches up to the waiter, an older Chinese man whose shining bald head reflects the overhead lights. He flashes the diamond at the waiter, asks if he'll float it in their drink.

"No float," the waiter says.

"What, you won't do it?"

The waiter shakes his head, smiles, reveals tobacco-browned teeth, and Toronto is thrown for a moment. He wonders if his own teeth are anywhere close to being that much of a horror show.

"No float," the waiter says again. "*Sink.*" He draws out the *s*, taking pleasure in the sound.

"Whatever. Of course it's going to sink."

"You say float."

"Are you going to do this," Toronto says, "or do I have to find someone else to tip well?"

The waiter smiles, nods. "Of course I do it. Drink come with umbrella, I put ring on umbrella. Easy." He holds out his hand.

Toronto glances around, then hands over the ring. "Don't lose it," he says. "Whatever you do, don't lose it. And hang on to the case. I'll need it back." He hands the guy two twenties, thanks him, and sits back down with Mia. He's glad he's half in the bag; his heart is racing, and he doesn't want to think of how much more nervous he'd be without a cushion of alcohol. *Get it together,* he tells himself. *Shut up and die like an aviator.* He doesn't remember feeling so skittery when he proposed to Jill or Cinda. Maybe it's a good sign. Mia must matter to him more.

The last drops of the monsoon trickle from the ceiling, and the two of them watch as the thatched bandstand floats back into the middle of the pool. The feathered-hair woman at the keyboard plunks out the intro to a midtempo Journey song; then the guitar and bass join in, along with a plastic-sounding drum program.

"This is high school, right here," he says.

"What do you mean?"

"This song. It was our prom theme."

"What is it?"

"What do you mean, *what is it?* You don't know this?"

"I've probably heard it," she says. "What band?"

"Journey."

"Wow. You guys were lame." She nudges him playfully with her foot and gives him her sweet smile—it's a little gummy, and one of her incisors is crooked, but it's shapely and beautiful all the same.

"All prom songs are lame. What was yours?"

"How would I know?" she says. "I had already left."

The waiter approaches them with the scorpion bowl as the song ends.

He holds his face expressionless as he sets the drink down, asks if there's anything else he can help them with, and leaves. Toronto gives the guy credit for knowing to not to intrude on their moment. He just earned himself another twenty.

Mia is examining the drink—the remarkable size of it, the harsh, ammoniacal smell of the liquors rising up in sheets like desert-highway heat—but she hasn't noticed the ring yet, even though it's there, under her nose, literally, hung over the tip of an orange paper umbrella.

"This is going to knock me on my ass," Mia says. She lifts her head and looks around the room, taking in all the rush and chatter and the drunk people chugging along on the crowded dance floor. He watches one of her eyes and sees the iris wobble. Nystagmus. Of course she's not seeing the ring; the drinks from dinner have hit her, and hard.

"Next time the monsoon starts," he says, "you can use your umbrella."

"What?"

"The *umbrella*," he says. "In your drink."

And she looks down, and finally Toronto gets the nine-thousand-one-hundred-dollar moment he's been waiting for: wide eyes, mouth dropping into an incredulous O and then spreading into a scrunch-lipped smile that raises her cheekbones into brilliant definition, and god*damn* he loves those cheekbones of hers.

"You didn't," she says.

"I did."

"You did?"

"Marry me," he says. "Will you?"

She doesn't respond. "Will you?" he asks again.

She bursts into tears.

At first he smiles, flattered at how moved she is, how intense her feelings are. The tears don't stop, though—he thinks they're going on longer than happy tears should—and when she gives a hiccupy little sob, it occurs to him that she could say no. That he might've misread her. Misread *them*. The bottom drops out from his stomach. How could she say no, when there's something so raw and passionate and alive between them? She couldn't. Could she? Her shoulders tremble, and he thinks, *she's really doing it, she's really saying no,* before he realizes that she's nodding, nodding, yes, yes, yes, each nod more enthusiastic. "Yes," she says. She takes a deep breath and wipes her eyes.

"I love you," he says.

She puts the ring on her finger and admires it, tilting it so the stone will catch the light. Toronto imagines hearing that high, clear glockenspiel note they use in movies when a diamond gleams. For ninety-one hundred dollars, they should give you a glockenspiel player for the night to play the note on cue.

They toast each other with their straws. "To us," he says.

"You know how to overwhelm a girl," she says.

He has another surprise for her: they're staying upstairs at the Fairmont tonight, and there's a bottle of Veuve waiting for them, chilled—although he should probably get her to drink some water first. He looks at her face, those cheekbones, those fading freckles on her nose, lets his gaze trail down the skin of her neck, down to her chest—she's wearing a bodysuit, paisleyed in two shades of dark green and snug over her athlete's breasts—and he goes rock-hard. He'll take her upstairs to the hotel room, strip her down and admire her body and maybe try out calling her *Mrs. Toronto,* and after they've thrashed and sweated and moaned together, maybe he'll take her across the street to the Top of the Mark and get the pianist to play Sinatra for her. "Witchcraft," maybe, or "Under My Skin." Then back to the room, and they'll spend the rest of the night tangled up in each other.

The floating band is playing the intro to "Safety Dance" when Toronto's straw slurps against the bottom of the bowl. "Let's get out of here," he says. "I can't stand this song." She's about to say something when he puts his hand over her mouth. "And don't tell me you've never heard it before."

There's a commotion as they're leaving: one of the laughing lawyers kicks off her shoes and dives into the water, white blouse and all. Waiters and security staff and chunky slick-haired Asian men in suits come running and shouting as more of the lawyers splash into the water: a cannonball, a jackknife, cries of *Marco* and *Polo.* The band keeps playing. Toronto's waiter leans against the bar with his arms crossed, watching, looking vaguely amused by the spectacle. As they pass near him, the waiter holds up the ring case, and Toronto motions for him to toss it, which he does. Toronto catches and pockets it in one motion.

"Smooth," Mia says.

"Damn straight," Toronto says, feeling like The Chairman of the Goddamned Board himself.

**M**ercer and Fiona are sitting at her kitchen table, sharing the newspaper and eating breakfast: coffee in pastel-blue ceramic mugs, scrambled eggs, nine-grain toast, orange juice, and huge umber-colored multivitamins that Fiona insists they both take. Cricket sits in Mercer's lap, placidly licking a front paw. A thin film of salt coats the windows, lending a soft-focus effect to the scene outside, where pelicans glide through the mist and bullet into the water.

Fiona flips through the Bay Area section, skimming the pages. "Are they ever going to write something about the DiMaio kid?" she asks.

"The parents haven't wanted to go public," Mercer says. "Funkhouser's trying to sell them on it so we can get some leads, but it's their call. We're going to try to get some more out of Jude in the next few days."

"How's he doing?"

"All right, as far as I know. I don't think he's back at school yet."

"He seems like a good kid to me," Fiona says. "I'm usually right about things like that. He has a sweet face. Like you."

Mercer smiles sheepishly and quickly raises his mug to his lips. He feels surprisingly good, even though he'd hit his head, even though he'd stayed awake for hours afterward, wondering what was wrong with him. He has a knot on the back of his head that's the size of a jawbreaker, but his hair covers it, so Fiona doesn't know to worry, and the headache isn't much worse than the ones he's had since Jude kicked him. No, he's feeling pretty lucky—relaxed and contented, lulled by the gray-sky morning and sea air and by the astonishing sex they had at sunrise, having freshly drifted up from sleep. They came together, and she cried afterward. That had surprised him—and concerned him, too—until she explained that it was good, that she'd simply been overwhelmed with *feeling*. Yes, he's lucky, he realizes, and he should be grateful.

"How's Moisés?" he asks her.

She looks up from the newspaper. She raises an eyebrow, which deepens the furrow in her forehead. "Moisés?"

"The orderly. Do you see him much?"

"He's long gone. He left around the time you did. Why?"

"I want to thank him." He scratches Cricket on the top of her head and behind her ears. He can feel her purring through his fingers.

"I'm surprised you didn't thank him before. He did a lot of groundwork for you."

"What are you talking about?" Mercer asks. The cat presses herself up into his hand, wanting more more more.

"Don't play dumb," she says, smiling. "I know you had a crush on me. You sent him to find out if I liked you. It was so eighth-grade of you."

"I didn't," Mercer says. "You've got it backwards."

"You don't have to be embarrassed about it."

"I'm not. You told him you thought I was cute."

"No, I didn't," she says.

"You did," he protests.

"If anyone knows what I said or didn't say, it's me."

A noise comes out of him—a staccato, nervous laugh—and he reaches out and rubs her knee under the table, but it feels like an empty gesture. Situation control. Cricket, as if sensing the change in his mood, springs from his lap and darts out of the room, skidding on the hallway hardwood as she rounds the corner. "You didn't say anything to Moisés? You weren't attracted to me?" he says.

"I was, when we were drinking coffee. You were inept, but in a sweet way." She closes the newspaper and sets it on the empty chair next to her. "You really didn't say anything to him, either? You didn't tell him you thought I was cute?"

"I did, after he asked."

"This is funny," Fiona says. "It's so strange."

"Why would he make it all up?"

"Who knows? Maybe he guessed we'd get along. Maybe he knew I'd been alone for a while. Maybe he's someone who travels the world getting people together. A wandering matchmaker."

"Still," Mercer says. "To make up something like that." He can feel the bump on the back of his head throbbing.

"We're here now, together, and that's what matters," she says. She reaches across the table, places her hand on his forearm, gives it an affectionate shake.

He wants to agree with her, but he feels foolish. Gullible. He's angry at Moisés for manipulating him, and at himself for making it so easy. He doesn't like the idea of doing anything he didn't necessarily decide to do.

"It's a good story, don't you think?" she says, scooping up eggs with her fork. "Kind of romantic and lucky and random and mysterious. Because it sounds like you wouldn't have had the balls to approach me without Moisés saying you should."

"It's not a question of balls."

"Would you have talked to me? Asked me for coffee?"

"Once I met you," he says, though he's not at all sure that's true. Sitting there now, his pulse thrumming in his head, he traces all the desire he's ever felt for her back to the moment Moisés said she liked him. Is he with her— with this middle-aged woman—just because it was a sure thing? Is he settling for watching DVDs and taking multivitamins with her instead of going out and hitting parties and bars and trying to find someone *he* wants?

He feels as if he's turned bright red, and there's a vertiginous twirl in his head. A tingle runs down the left side of his body, and he clenches and un- clenches his left hand under the table to make sure he still has motor control.

"So all Moisés did was speed things along," Fiona says, but he's having trouble listening to her. The tingling has stolen his attention. That, and his fall in the bathroom. He wonders if he might be dying after all. The worry is only half-serious, but half is enough.

He hears her asking if he's all right, and he nods, and then the spell passes, leaving him with a mild swimmy feeling in his head and fading prickles in his left leg and foot.

"I'm fine," he says, to her as well as to himself. He looks into his coffee mug. "Maybe I need decaf."

"You went away there for a second."

"It was nothing. I got distracted."

"Look at this," she says, holding up the newspaper and pointing to a photo of an exhausted-looking woman with five newborns. QUINTUPLETS FOR SAN RAFAEL WOMAN. "These IVF multiple births are out of control. Five babies? Count me out." She shakes the paper and flips the page. "Now, one," she says, as if she's speaking to the newsprint, "one would be great." She looks at him over the rims of her reading glasses. "You know why you'd be a good father? Because you're sensitive. You don't like to think so, but you are."

Mercer checks his watch without actually noting the time. "I have to go," he says. "I just remembered. I told Mrs. Featherstone I'd help her move in." It's not true, strictly speaking, but he needs to get home to his apartment as soon as possible, needs to give himself time to think. A long, hot shower, maybe, one where he turns the water as hot as The Willows' boiler can make it, sits down, and lets the spray drill him on the head and face and shoulders and chest as he steals himself thirty minutes of calm.

At the front door, she opens her mouth to say something, but nothing comes out.

"What?" he says.

"Nothing," she says. "Go. Do what you need to do."

Mercer drives east on Sharp Park Road, heading for home. The dense cloud cover is bunched over the coast; when he summits at Skyline Boulevard, he sees in front of him blue sky decorated with cumulus puffs. Splitting the blue is a vapor trail, and he follows it from its diffuse tail to its new and sharp-edged origin. It's a vertical line, a downward slash through the sky, and the plane looks like it's in free fall. An optical illusion, he tells himself; the plane isn't really crashing, it can't be—but a shiver runs through his neck and shoulders.

He sits up straighter and watches the plane continue to dive. Its apparent velocity depends on his perspective: when the mountain road curves left, the plane slows to motionless, and when the road curves right, the plane appears to dive faster. Hard to tell at this distance, but it looks like some old-time plane, some air-show relic that looks out of place in the sky. And it's falling. A shiver takes hold of him, and his heart rushes to a crazy speed as he hears road reflectors thunking under the tires.

He jerks the wheel. Crosses back into his own lane. No cars coming, no cars behind. All good. Okay. No problem.

But the plane keeps falling and falling and falling, he can feel his arms trembling as his hands hold tight to the wheel. The illusion before him is both horrifying and hypnotic, and he has to remind himself several more times to stay on the road and in his own damn lane.

. . .

Piloting the plane is Lincoln Beachey, aviation revolutionary and hero to millions; the wind roars in his ears, and the sun streams down around him like champagne. The sky tugs upward at his cheeks, as if saying *Come back! Come back!* as he plummets straight down in a death-drop, the green and stone-studded ground rushing toward him. His signature stunt: you cut the engine, drink in the moment of utter silence, then straight-shoot downward, into a rolling whitecap of cloud and out the other side, and everyone on the ground believes you're in mortal peril as you fall and fall. Then, just as they have begun to shiver and grow faint, you twist the wheel quickly and the motor roars back to life and you go sailing off over their heads, free as a man in love, and your laughter trails in your wake.

That's how it used to go, at any rate; now, in this place, the laws of physics are elusive, shifting as often as the wind. You must ignore everything you once knew about aerodynamics, about friction, wind shear, wind resistance; you must fly only by feel, react and improvise and accept that the ground will claim you sooner or later, and usually sooner. It doesn't make flying any less of a pleasure. No: you build, you fly, you crash, you suffer, you build, and you fly again. This is what it means to be alive. Even if, technically, you no longer are.

His gloved hands hold the wheel steady. He feels the air change around him, thickening, killing his speed. It might loosen again and fling him downward with a jolt; it might not. Who can say? He hears the complaint of over-stressed metal from the rear left. Through his oil-sprayed goggles, he watches the ground coming closer, sees dirt-covered people looking up from deep and wide Root-holes, can even make out the blank, abandoned looks on their faces, and he prepares to swoop out of the drop and bring the engine to life— not yet—not yet—and *turn.*

Then the spark and hum of the engine and the hot thrill of grappling with atmosphere and wind, of watching the ground skim past (his mind slows time; he can see every single blade of grass), of the ecstatic hope that he has done it, that for the first time he has cheated the physics of this place and flown the death-drop like Beachey-alive, like Beachey-the-envy-and-inspiration-of-millions, and he feels so full of *possibility* and of grace and gratitude that he cries out with joy and is—

—is grabbed—

—a fist, a cosmic fist—

—shaken—

—flung, and—

—impact and roar—

—bouncing and spinning —

—chest pressed empty—

—torn canvas, sprung wires—

—snap of wood, snap of bone—

—hell-hot smell of oil—

—then black—

— —

— —

— —

—and—

—slowly—

—awake again.

He lies still, studying the fickle sky. His body fires with pain. His feet dangle, ankles broken, and his shoulder feels shattered, his sternum crushed. His spine a riot of fractures. But he feels not a single twinge of regret. It is all worth it. All the effort and sweat and pain, all worth it for that warm flood of feeling, that sacred sensation of limitlessness, and he simply cannot *wait* to do it all over again.

As he waits for his bones to mend themselves, he breathes through the waves of pain and replays the last moments of the flight, taking careful note of what went wrong: a sudden flash-drop in air temperature just above the ground, a surprising aileron wobble, the engine one stroke too slow in chugging to life. All the other pilots he has met here have given up, chewed the Root and gone away. How the unpredictability of this new air offended them all! As if one is *entitled* to a world that works the way one thinks it ought to!

When at last he can move his neck, he turns his head and surveys the wreckage of his monoplane. It is crumpled and scorched, the fuselage split wide, the once-pyramidal supports splayed out in a frenzy of wire. He takes inventory of what is salvageable and what must be replaced. He hears his old friend and mechanician Warren Eaton's voice in his head: a calm, crooked half-smile of a voice. *Best get to work, Linc. Best get to it.*

*Yes, Warren,* he thinks, and he sits up slowly and shakes the dirt out of his shirt cuffs. *Best get to it.* He needs to fix this crippled plane and get back into the sky. As soon as his damaged body lets him, he hauls himself to his feet and sets about picking through the wreckage. He moves stiffly but quickly. Time is not to be wasted, ever. Particularly when you have an afternoon roller-skating date with the charming young Mrs. Ralston, a date that *cannot* be missed. After all, a man should never do without flying—or love—for too long.

Yes. Best get to work, Linc. Best get to it.

# A DEAD MAN'S BATHROBE

**M**ercer needs to get away. He hadn't expected that his visit to Lorna Featherstone's apartment would take hours, or that he'd be dumb enough to eat there. His stomach is rumbling angrily, and a full-on gastrointestinal meltdown feels imminent. He wants to be at home, alone, when it hits.

He'd walked over to her apartment to deliver a stack of her mail, feeling bad that he hadn't brought it to her sooner. A lot of it looked important: credit-card bills, letters from several attorneys and the funeral home, official-looking notices from the county and the state. There was also a bright-yellow envelope hand-addressed to the dead sergeant from something called the Order of the Sacred Ray of Kinesis, postmarked from Littleton, West Virginia.

The letter from the church—or whatever it was—was on top when he handed her the mail; her eyes went to it immediately, and she looked stricken. He watched her quickly tuck it into the center of the stack, as if he wouldn't already have seen it. Maybe she was one of those people who believed religion should be kept private. Or maybe she was embarrassed—he didn't want to judge, but the Order of the Sacred Ray of Kinesis did sound pretty goddamned weird.

Lorna apologized profusely for his trouble and promised she'd fill out new forwarding forms as soon as she could. Her voice was hurried and breathless, and she looked overwhelmed and exhausted standing there amid stacks of moving boxes and drifts of Styrofoam peanuts, and he decided it was time for him to start being a better neighbor and offer his help. And then he could feel better about the lie he'd told Fiona, too.

She accepted his offer enthusiastically, and he spent the next three hours unpacking boxes, moving furniture at her direction, and making small repairs with just his pocketknife and a rusted old hammer, the only tool she could find. She insisted on making lunch for him, and once she offered he didn't feel he could say no. Surrounded by the slowly resolving chaos of the apartment, they ate cold-cut sandwiches at her shaky kitchen table. She'd draped it with a lace tablecloth that held the ghost of a gravy stain in the middle. They exchanged small talk about some of the officers in the department, about development projects around town, about the weather; the conversation was pleasant, but halting; Mercer sensed that they were both expending a lot of effort searching for the next thing to say, and he wondered if she felt it, too. He'd nearly finished eating his sandwich and was contemplating having another when, during one of their lulls, he engrossed himself in reading the label on the mayonnaise jar. He quickly wished he hadn't. He stopped chewing and felt his stomach lurch. The expiration date had passed more than two years before.

"What's wrong, dear?" Mrs. Featherstone asked. He noticed how dark the circles under her eyes were.

"Nothing," he said. "Everything's great. Thank you." He eyed the remains of his sandwich. She would be offended if he didn't finish it; he'd made a point of telling her how hungry he was. She would feel like she'd failed at the simple task of putting out sandwich fixings. She would cry. She'd already gotten weepy twice since he'd been there. No: he was not going to make her feel like a failure. What he was going to do, he decided, was finish this goddamn sandwich and smile like there wasn't a thing wrong in the world and hope his system was tough enough to handle whatever colonies of things had grown in the jar. When he saw her looking at his empty plate with satisfaction, he felt he'd done the right thing.

Now, though, it's all he can do not to double over and howl.

"How's the boy from the cemetery?" Lorna asks him, placing their lunch dishes into the drying rack, cheerful and oblivious.

Mercer tries to look thoughtful as he waits for a cramp to subside. "He's out of danger. He was discharged the next day. We still don't know what really happened."

"He doesn't remember?"

Mercer shakes his head. "There may be substance-abuse issues. His parents just put him in rehab." Funkhouser had left him a message with the news; Jude would be unreachable for a few days as the staff doctors evaluated him, but after that, Mercer was to drive up to Napa to interview the kid on his own. *I'm pretty sure the family knows more than they're letting on,* the detective had said. *But they do seem to like you. Why they do is a mystery to me, but maybe anyone looks good next to Toronto.*

"Children," Lorna says. "They lose their way so easily."

"We don't know the whole story yet."

"Wes and I didn't have children," she says. "He didn't feel ready, and then I had—" She pauses and looks around, as if someone else might be in the room. "I had some female problems."

"I'm sorry," Mercer says. What else can you say to that? He feels like an intruder. "Are you all right now?"

"Ancient history," she says, waving the question off. "What's your family like? Are you close to your parents?"

He gets along with his mother, he explains, but he hasn't seen her in a year. She retired, got a pension from the county, fell hard for her extension-class art history professor, and followed him to Tahiti, where he's doing research on some forgotten Norwegian painter who lived there at the same time as Gauguin. His mother calls every month or two; mostly, he gets postcards. "I haven't been in touch with my father in a while." He does the math. "Nine years."

"That's a shame."

"Not really," Mercer says. "That's how I want it."

"Maybe someday," she says.

"Maybe," he says, because it's easier to agree. Another wave of stomach pain hits him and sends shivers through the rest of his body. Immediately after, though, he feels better. That might have been the worst of it.

Lorna takes a seat on the living-room couch with a small box labeled PHOTOS and sets to unwrapping picture frames. She arrays them on the tea table in front of her and sits still, studying them. "Is there someone special in your life?" she asks him.

"Sort of."

Lorna looks genuinely confused. "She's sort of special, or she's sort of in your life?"

"I don't know," he says. "We had a fight this morning. A misunderstanding, I guess."

"It's good to get things out in the open. I wish Wes and I had been better at it."

Mercer nods.

"So, does she have a name?"

"Fiona." He thinks about how uncomfortable he felt when he left her house earlier, and his stomach rolls again.

"Fiona. That's a nice name."

"It is," he says. "She's a nice person." He raises his arms above his head and stretches, hoping it'll uncoil his insides. "What's next on the to-do list?"

"Do you need any furniture? I have too much furniture."

"Thanks, but I don't need anything."

"What about your girlfriend?"

"She has plenty of furniture," he says. "Too much."

"I have too much, too, now that I'm here. This isn't even all of it. I'm paying for a storage space."

"You could have a garage sale," he suggests.

"Yes, that would be a smart thing to do, wouldn't it," she muses. "Do you think you'll marry her?"

"Fiona?"

"Yes, Fiona."

"I don't know. Things are complicated right now."

"You're just like Wes when he was your age. I had to twist his arm to get him to marry me. Hurry up, I told him, or else this ship's going to *sail*." She sweeps her hand through the air for emphasis. She holds her follow-through, and her expression turns distant. Her thoughts have gone somewhere else, he can tell, and she's not aware that she has frozen in midmotion. After a long moment, she lowers her arm; focus returns to her eyes, but she avoids his gaze. She glances down at the picture in her lap. He can't see it clearly, but he can tell it's old, black-and-white, a portrait of a couple. Her parents, maybe. "It's funny how life turns out," she says.

Mercer nods, not entirely sure what she means. He wonders if she really thinks he's like Featherstone. He hopes not. He doesn't like being told he's *like* anybody. Especially not a sad old guy with a bad comb-over.

She slaps her thighs theatrically. "All right. Enough of my prying. You can tell me more about her some other time. Promise you will?"

"Promise," he says. He glances at his watch. "What's next?"

She asks him to hang her cuckoo clock on the living-room wall. "My last request," she says, "and then you're free." She crosses the room, opens a box marked FRAGILE on every face, pulls out several handfuls of heavy brown packing paper, and removes another box. She lifts the clock out of the smaller box carefully. Strips of yellowed newspaper cling to the dangling chains. "Wes bought this in Germany when he was stationed there—1963, I think it was. He brought it home for me. He said he wanted to be reminded every hour of how lucky he was to have me. He was quite a romantic back then."

Mercer nods, hoping she won't start revealing secrets of their marriage. He gets up on a stepladder and measures a centered spot, darkens the spot with a pencil, and drives in a nail and bracket. She hands the clock to him carefully. He finds the hook after a few misses, then slowly takes his hands away, making sure the clock won't fall. As he straightens it, he admires its design—the detailed leaves and branches, the gold-leaf inlays, the grave-looking Roman numerals—and he appreciates the ingenuity of the network of weights and chains and the mystery of the shuttered bird. Something is missing, though. What is it?

"Children love that clock," Lorna says. "When my friends brought their children over, they'd stop whatever they were doing and stand in front of it, waiting for the bird to sing." She picks up a few of the framed pictures and redistributes them around the room.

"Where are the hands?" he asks.

"What?"

"The hands. They're not on the clock."

"They're not?"

"No, ma'am."

"Oh," she says. "I must have taken them off so they wouldn't get broken. They're very delicate, those hands." She searches through the box that held the clock, lifting out one scrap of newspaper at a time. "You know," she muses, "I think I remember putting them in a little envelope. Now I just have to remember where that would be."

She stands and looks around the apartment, back and forth, back and forth—looking, he guesses, at all the possible places in which the clock hands might be hiding from her, at all the unpacking left, all the settling in she'll have to do, all this *stuff* that's heavy with memories. "Well, I'll have to do without them for now," she says. She pulls a tissue out of the wrist of her blouse and dabs at her eyes. "I'm sorry. I don't mean to cry in front of you so often. But sometimes I feel a bit overwhelmed."

"I understand," Mercer says.

"Excuse me," she says. "I need to stop. Just for a few minutes. To clear my head." She sidesteps boxes and picks her way toward the bedroom, where she clears a space on the bed, sits down, and clicks on the TV. Mercer is visited with a sudden and shocking twist of pain in his bowels. He can't wait any longer. He walks to the bathroom as fast as he can without alarming her.

When he emerges, dizzy and sweating and fearing the relief he feels will be short-lived, he hears a familiar voice coming from her TV: the baritone rasp of Reverend Clifton Chase Whipple. Reverend Whipple is an institution on Bay Area television. His show runs at least three times a day on Channel 59. He preaches to the camera in close-up, so the screen is filled with his thick helmet of gray hair, his paper-white and wrinkled skin, his deep-set eyes under bushy pepper-shot eyebrows, his suntanned neck flesh overhanging a collar cinched tight with a bolo tie. His ministry owns a Greyhound-sized bus called *The Redemption Express,* and the name is painted on the bus's steel sides in hot-white letters that lean forward, as if the words themselves are in a hurry to get there. Mercer has seen the bus many times, in the city and down on the peninsula, and he has always thought it absurd, promising salvation as it chugs along in the slow lane and belches diesel fumes. What kind of people would ride in that thing? Who's behind those smoked-glass windows?

"I like him," Mrs. Featherstone says to him. "Do you ever watch?"

"I did once," he says, walking to the doorway and looking in at the screen. Years before, he and Owen had been late-night channel-surfing, drunk and stoned, when they came across Whipple's show. They'd watched the entire hour while Mollie softly snored, passed out on the couch with her head in Owen's lap. A prayer-line phone number crawled across the bottom of the screen, and they'd called it to goof on the old man and his followers, but all they got was a recording asking them politely to call during regular business hours, when prayer associates were available. They had assumed he was preaching live. His pallor made him seem nocturnal.

"Did you like him?" she asks.

"Religion's not really my thing," Mercer says.

"I've never been all that religious myself."

This surprises him. If she and the sergeant weren't religious, why were they getting hand-addressed mail from a faraway church?

"It makes more sense to me lately, though," she continues. "Since Wes passed. I like to think he's in a better place. And besides, when you get older, you want to have something to believe in." She has been worrying the tissue in her hands, and it's disintegrating, flecking her fingers with white. "I love the way he speaks. He's so calm, but he sounds like he believes what he's saying more than anything else in the world. He seems like a nice man. I think his voice sounds like Spencer Tracy's. I liked Spencer Tracy."

Whipple doesn't sound like a very good preacher, to Mercer's ear. His cadence isn't hypnotic or rousing or even very smooth—none of the things you'd expect. He sounds utterly ordinary, apart from being hoarse. *Friends,* he gravels, *this Saturday, our fearless driver Brother Dusty and I will be taking* The Redemption Express *down to Tanforan Shopping Center in San Bruno to support the Red Cross in their blood drive. Meet us there, or make a reservation to ride the* Express *with us by calling the number at the bottom of your screen. However you get there, friends, just get there, and give a little bit of yourself for the folks who need your help.*

"See?" Mrs. Featherstone says. "He's doing good things. Getting people out to give blood. Not like the ones who are out to steal your money."

Her expression hardens. Mercer wonders if the sergeant got fleeced by the Sacred Ray people—although he's never heard anyone describe Featherstone as devout, or foolish, or desperate. "You're right," he says benignly, "a blood drive's a good thing." He's pretty sure, though, that you should never trust anyone who calls you *friend* over and over. He has a vague sense that this is something his father taught him when he was little.

*And friends,* Whipple says, *remember that we'll be having an auction to benefit the ministry at the end of the month. So if you have an old car or boat, or any old furniture or clothing, even real estate—*

"Furniture!" Mrs. Featherstone says. "That's what I'll do. I'll donate it."

"You might want to find out exactly how they'll use the money. There are a lot of scams out there."

"Yes," she says. "Yes. That's very smart of you. I'll look into it. But I have a good feeling about him."

It's her life, Mercer reminds himself. Her decision.

"Maybe I'll give blood, too," she says.

"I should get going," Mercer says, "if there's nothing else you need me to do right now."

"You go right ahead, Officer Mercer. Thank you so much for helping. Carolyn Benzinger said you were a nice young man, and I'm going to tell her how right she is."

"I meant to ask you before: how's your shoulder feeling?"

"It hurts a little when I reach straight up," she says. "But it's a lot better. Aspirin and rest. I see your eye is getting better, too."

He nods. His cheekbone is still sore—sometimes it throbs—and the headaches still plague him from time to time, but the bruise is nearly gone.

"We're both healing right up, aren't we?" she says. "We're going to be good as new."

Mercer is putting on his jacket to leave when she tells him to wait. "There's something I want to give you," she says. He follows her to the bedroom closet. When she flicks on the light, the first thing he notices is a heavy-looking, pewter-colored metal box on the floor at the back. It looks like a fireproof safe, nearly the size of a steamer trunk. Why would she need something so big? Then he sees a stamped silver plate at the top, partially obscured by a dry-cleaning bag that drapes over it.

HERSTONE

Y 1, 2004

He's so surprised that he flinches when she hands him a cardboard copy-shop box, the size that holds a ream of paper. "Hang on," she says. "There are more." She stacks four of them in his arms, one by one.

"What are these?"

"Old paperwork. I found it all in the garage, behind his workbench. Shouldn't it be at the station?"

"Probably," he says. "A lot of people keep copies of their incident reports. But I'll take them in, make sure everything's logged into the system." He heads for the door, balancing the stack of boxes. "Take care, Mrs. Featherstone."

"Please," she says. "Lorna." She hustles ahead of him to open the door, then stops again. "Wait. One more thing."

Inwardly he cringes. The pressure in his stomach is building again. He'd better get home, fast.

She disappears into the bedroom again, and he can hear her searching through more boxes. She reemerges with a bathrobe, black-watch flannel, the plaid pattern blurred by wear. She shakes it out and refolds it. "Here," she says, placing it on top of the boxes, right under his nose. "It's my welcome present, like I promised," she explains. "You need a bathrobe. Everyone should have a bathrobe."

The robe has been washed, but it still smells like old man—that wet-paper-in-the-rain smell with an acid note of decay. He hopes she doesn't notice him turning his head slightly away so he can breathe neutral air. He doesn't want a dead man's bathrobe—just like no one wants a dead man's cruiser. Mercer doesn't want a dead man's *anything*. Especially Featherstone's. It *has* to be bad luck. "Really," he says. "I can't."

"Oh, go ahead," she says. "This way you won't have to answer the door in your shorts." She laughs, and Mercer realizes it's the first time he's ever heard her laugh. He decides to take the robe and to thank her for it. All he has to do is make her feel good about giving it to him. He doesn't ever have to wear it.

The moment he steps outside, his bowels twist. It's a race to get home, and he almost dumps the boxes all over the landing in his hurry to get the keys out of his pocket. He drops the keys twice trying to jam them into the lock, but he makes it inside in time. As he sits and suffers, he tells himself he should be grateful for small things like that.

At home, sweaty and spent, Mercer has two hours to kill before he meets Fiona but no energy to do anything more strenuous than lying down. He turns on KCSM in the living room and collapses onto the couch as big-band swing, sprightly and bouncy, fills the room. Between songs, the DJ announces that they're doing a daylong tribute to Glenn Miller.

He listens with his eyes closed, trying to clear his mind and relax completely, but his thoughts keep returning to Featherstone's incident reports. If they're just copies of reports, why did he keep them hidden? The boxes are in a stack next to the coffee table, within reach. The one on top is labeled with neat, black-markered numbers: 1999–2000.

Mercer could read through some of them. Never hurts to see how an experienced officer writes his reports. Besides, Toronto and Cambi have said that Featherstone was a gas-burner in his last years—wouldn't initiate stops, would be silent on the radio for long stretches of time—and it'd be interesting to see what he was up to. He could learn something about the man whose death opened a job for him. The man his new neighbor is grieving. The man whose ashes are in a ridiculously large nuclear-bomb-proof metal box in a closet a hundred yards away.

He sits up, lifts the top box off the stack, and shakes off the lid. The incident reports are faceup, and a quick riffle through shows that they're in chronological order, starting in June 1999. He hesitates before he starts reading. His eyes dart around the room guiltily, as if he's violating the sergeant's privacy. But that's ridiculous. Featherstone is dead. Besides, Mercer already gets the man's mail. And inherited his bathrobe. If that doesn't make them close, what does?

| COLMA POLICE DEPARTMENT CA0043479 | | 1. CASE NO. 99-0314-07 | |
|---|---|---|---|

| 2. CODE SECTION CPC 647(f) | 3. CRIME Public Intoxication | 4. CLASSIFICATION Misdemeanor | 5. REPORT AREA Beat One |
|---|---|---|---|

| 6. DATE & TIME OCCURRED —DAY 06-03-99 0253 Thu | 7. DATE & TIME REPORTED 06-03-99 0253 | 8. LOCATION OF OCCURRENCE 1500 block of Mission Road | |
|---|---|---|---|

| 9. VICTIM'S NAME—LAST, FIRST, MIDDLE (FIRM IF BUSINESS) | | 10. RESIDENCE ADDRESS | 11. RESIDENCE PHONE |
|---|---|---|---|

| 12. OCCUPATION | 13. RACE–SEX | 14. AGE | 15. DOB | 16. BUSINESS ADDRESS (SCHOOL IF JUVENILE) | 17. BUSINESS PHONE |
|---|---|---|---|---|---|

| 18. NAME—LAST, FIRST, MIDDLE | | 19. CODE | 20. RESIDENCE ADDRESS | 21. RESIDENCE PHONE |
|---|---|---|---|---|

| 22. OCCUPATION | 23. RACE–SEX | 24. AGE | 25. DOB | 26. BUSINESS ADDRESS (SCHOOL IF JUVENILE) | 27. BUSINESS PHONE |
|---|---|---|---|---|---|

28. DESCRIBE CHARACTERISTICS OF PREMISES AND AREA WHERE OCCURRED

Grassy area at side of road.

29. DESCRIBE BRIEFLY HOW OFFENSE WAS COMMITTED

Suspect was behaving in an erratic and violent manner, talking to himself and punching the air. Suspect appeared disoriented and fell over several times during interview.

30. DESCRIBE WEAPON, INSTRUMENT, TRICK, DEVICE, OR FORCE USED

Unknown intoxicant(s).

| 31. MOTIVE—TYPE OF PROPERTY TAKEN OR OTHER REASON FOR OFFENSE | 32. ESTIMATED LOSS VALUE AND/OR EXTENT OF INJURIES—MINOR, MAJOR |
|---|---|

**33. WHAT DID SUSPECTS SAY—NOTE PECULIARITIES**

Suspect (approx 19 y.o.) claimed DOB in 1889. Suspect said he was looking for the Athletic Club because he had a fight with a "Johnny Largo" to finish.

**34. VICTIM'S ACTIVITY JUST PRIOR TO AND/OR DURING OFFENSE**

**35. TRADEMARK—OTHER DISTINCTIVE ACTION OF SUSPECT/S**

**36. VEHICLE USED—LICENSE NO.—ID NO.—YEAR—MAKE—MODEL—COLOR (OTHER IDENTIFYING CHARACTERISTICS)**

N/A

| 37. SUSPECT NO. 1 (LAST, FIRST, MIDDLE) | 38. RACE–SEX | 39. AGE | 40. HT | 41. WT | 42. HAIR | 43. EYES | 44. SSN OR DOB | 45. ARRESTED |
|---|---|---|---|---|---|---|---|---|
| Bellano, Giovanni | W-M | 19 (app) | 6-01 | 140 | Blk | Bro | ? | No |

**46. ADDRESS, CLOTHING, AND OTHER IDENTIFYING MARKS OR CHARACTERISTICS**

Large contusion in center of chest. Suspect dressed as boxer. Suspect made reference to family in SF but gave no address.

| 47. SUSPECT NO. 2 (LAST, FIRST, MIDDLE) | 48. RACE–SEX | 49. AGE | 50. HT | 51. WT | 52. HAIR | 53. EYES | 54. SSN OR DOB | 55. ARRESTED |
|---|---|---|---|---|---|---|---|---|
| | | | | | | | | |

| 56. ADDRESS, CLOTHING, AND OTHER IDENTIFYING MARKS OR CHARACTERISTICS | 57. CHECK IF MORE NAMES IN CONTINUATION |
|---|---|
| | |

| REPORTING OFFICERS | RECORDING OFFICER | TYPED BY | DATE AND TIME |
|---|---|---|---|
| Featherstone | Featherstone | Featherstone | 06-03-99 0500 |

**OFFENSES INVESTIGATED AND RECOMMENDED CHARGES**

CPC 647(f) - Public Intoxication

CPC 415 - Disturbing the Peace

1) SUMMARY:

On 06-03-99, at approximately 0253 hours, S-Bellano was in a grassy area on the side of El Camino Real acting in an erratic and violent manner. S-Bellano appeared to have been injured in a fight and said he needed to find the other man in order to continue the fight. S-Bellano carried no identification and may have given false DOB. S-Bellano fled on foot.

2) VICTIMS AND WITNESSES:

None.

3) SUSPECTS:

Giovanni Bellano

4) VEHICLE:

N/A

5) STATEMENT OF REPORTING OFFICER:

On 06-03-99, at approximately 0253 hours, I was on patrol in full uniform in a marked patrol vehicle. I saw S-Bellano on the lawn in front of Holy Cross Cemetery, on the east side of the 1500 block of Mission Road. S-Bellano wore only boxing trunks, shoes, and thin padded gloves. He was weaving back and forth, punching the air, and muttering. His face was cut and there was a dark, fist-sized contusion in the center of his chest. I made contact, identifying myself as a peace officer. He claimed to have difficulty seeing me and asked me why I was "so blurry." I asked him if he had been drinking or taken any drugs. He did not respond to my question.

He asked me where had the rest of the crowd gone. I said they were probably asleep because it was the middle of the night. He put his hands to his chest and fell over. Before I could contact him physically to initiate CPR, he revived and stood again. I asked again if he had been drinking or taking drugs and he said no, but Johnny Largo had "socked him good" in the chest and his heart might not be working right anymore. I asked where Johnny Largo was and he said that was exactly what he was trying to figure out and hadn't I been listening. I asked him what they were fighting over. He said a "Mr. Almond" had promised the winner twenty dollars and the loser five.

Suspect said he lived in San Francisco but would not specify an address. He said he said he did not want his parents to find out he had been fighting. I asked him if I was supposed to believe he really was a boxer. He said yes so I told him to show me a 3-4 combo because I was a pretty fair boxer back when I was in the service. He said he didn't know what a 3-4 combo was. He threw some punches that had power but were not crisp. In my Army days I was twice the fighter he was. Col. Burke told me I should consider turning pro when I returned stateside, but I went to the Academy instead and Lorna didn't want me boxing in my spare time. Me being a police office was risky enough for her she said. Sometimes I thinkabout how that would have turned out. Or if I had started some kind ofg business like antiques or cabinet-making. It's hard to say. It would have been worth a try. If I had been boxing I would have stayed in shape, at least.

I asked S-Bellano if he was lying about the drinking or the drugs because he was worried about his parents finding out. He said "no". I asked him if I could search his trunks for contraband. He said "no". I asked if he felt he needed medical attention for his cardiac concerns. He said not until he finished the fight. I said there weren't going to be any fights tonight. I directed

S-Bellano to stand still while I performed a records
check. He did not cooperate. I was unable to determine
what direction he had fled in because it was dark. I
should not have lost him but I did.

6) EVIDENCE
None.

7) PROPERTY
N/A

8) STATUS
Case open.

9) OPINION
Send to County for 72-hour hold (5150) if observed
again behaving erratically. Suspect was agitated and
confused, possible danger to self and others.

---

**CPD MEMORANDUM**
To: Sgt. W. Featherstone
From: Cpt. E. McCandless
Date: 06-04-99
Re: Case #99-0314-07

As we discussed last month (05-08-99), incident
reports are not an appropriate place for personal
reflections (see underlined passages in report).
Eliminate and resubmit.
Also: see me to discuss your response to this
incident, which I believe was unsatisfactory and left
the citizen at risk.

*E. J. McC.*

| COLMA POLICE DEPARTMENT CA0043479 | 1. CASE NO.<br>99-0314-96 |
|---|---|

| 2. CODE SECTION<br>CPC 555, CPC 484 | 3. CRIME<br>Trespassing, Larceny | 4. CLASSIFICATION<br>Misdemeanor | 5. REPORT AREA<br>Beat One |
|---|---|---|---|

| 6. DATE & TIME OCCURRED —DAY<br>06-12-99<br>0230 Sat | 7. DATE & TIME REPORTED | 8. LOCATION OF OCCURRENCE<br>1 Stonehill Rd. [Colma landfill] | | |
|---|---|---|---|---|

| 9. VICTIM'S NAME—LAST, FIRST, MIDDLE (FIRM IF BUSINESS)<br>Colma Solid Waste Transfer, Inc. | 10. RESIDENCE ADDRESS<br>1 Stonehill Rd., Colma | 11. RESIDENCE PHONE<br>(650) 555-2727 |
|---|---|---|

| 12. OCCUPATION | 13. RACE–SEX | 14. AGE | 15. DOB | 16. BUSINESS ADDRESS (SCHOOL IF JUVENILE) | 17. BUSINESS PHONE |
|---|---|---|---|---|---|
| | | | | | |

| 18. NAME—LAST, FIRST, MIDDLE | 19. CODE | 20. RESIDENCE ADDRESS | 21. RESIDENCE PHONE |
|---|---|---|---|
| | | | |

| 22. OCCUPATION | 23. RACE–SEX | 24. AGE | 25. DOB | 26. BUSINESS ADDRESS (SCHOOL IF JUVENILE) | 27. BUSINESS PHONE |
|---|---|---|---|---|---|
| | | | | | |

28. DESCRIBE CHARACTERISTICS OF PREMISES AND AREA WHERE OCCURRED

In and among piles of junk at landfill. Upper level.

29. DESCRIBE BRIEFLY HOW OFFENSE WAS COMMITTED

Suspect entered landfill after hours without authorization. Suspect was collecting items with apparent intent to remove them from site.

30. DESCRIBE WEAPON, INSTRUMENT, TRICK, DEVICE, OR FORCE USED

Large wheelbarrow

| 31. MOTIVE—TYPE OF PROPERTY TAKEN OR OTHER REASON FOR OFFENSE<br>engine parts, lumber, automobile gasoline tank. | 32. ESTIMATED LOSS VALUE AND/OR EXTENT OF INJURIES—MINOR, MAJOR<br>$500 |
|---|---|

**33. WHAT DID SUSPECTS SAY—NOTE PECULIARITIES**

Suspect claimed DOB in 1887. Called me "friend" and "good fellow." Laughed often.

**34. VICTIM'S ACTIVITY JUST PRIOR TO AND/OR DURING OFFENSE**

**35. TRADEMARK—OTHER DISTINCTIVE ACTION OF SUSPECT/S**

Suspect was smoking cigar.

**36. VEHICLE USED—LICENSE NO.—ID NO.—YEAR—MAKE—MODEL—COLOR (OTHER IDENTIFYING CHARACTERISTICS)**

None observed. Except for wheelbarrow.

| 37. SUSPECT NO. 1 (LAST, FIRST, MIDDLE) | 38. RACE–SEX | 39. AGE | 40. HT | 41. WT | 42. HAIR | 43. EYES | 44. SSN OR DOB | 45. ARRESTED |
|---|---|---|---|---|---|---|---|---|
| Beachey, Lincoln | W–M | 25 (app) | 5-09 | 150 | Bro | Bro | ? | No |

**46. ADDRESS, CLOTHING, AND OTHER IDENTIFYING MARKS OR CHARACTERISTICS**

Clean gray flannel suit with necktie. Checkered wool cap, worn with brim backwards. Possibly a costume or disguise.

| 47. SUSPECT NO. 2 (LAST, FIRST, MIDDLE) | 48. RACE–SEX | 49. AGE | 50. HT | 51. WT | 52. HAIR | 53. EYES | 54. SSN OR DOB | 55. ARRESTED |
|---|---|---|---|---|---|---|---|---|
| | | | | | | | | |

| 56. ADDRESS, CLOTHING, AND OTHER IDENTIFYING MARKS OR CHARACTERISTICS | 57. CHECK IF MORE NAMES IN CONTINUATION |
|---|---|
| | |

| REPORTING OFFICERS | RECORDING OFFICER | TYPED BY | DATE AND TIME |
|---|---|---|---|
| | | | |

## OFFENSES INVESTIGATED AND RECOMMENDED CHARGES

CPC 555 – Trespassing

CPC 484 – Larceny


1) SUMMARY:

On 06-12-99, at approximately 0230 hours, S-Beachey was in the Colma landfill, collecting engine parts and other metals and wood in a wheelbarrow for the purpose of taking them away from the site. I contacted S-Beachey and informed him he was ~~comitting~~ committing illegal acts. S-Beachey fled on foot.


2) VICTIMS AND WITNESSES:

V-Colma Solid Waste Transfer, Inc.

W-none.


3) SUSPECTS:

Beachey, Lincoln.


4) VEHICLE:

N/A


5) STATEMENT OF REPORTING OFFICER:

On 06-12-99, at approximately 0230 hours, I was on patrol in full uniform in a marked patrol vehicle. I performed a passing check at the Colma Landfill per management's request of regular patrols (05-24-99). I heard sounds of someone in and among the piles of junk (upper level), picking up and throwing away pieces of metal. I discovered S-Beachey as he was loading an ~~auomobile~~ automobile gasoline tank into a large wheelbarrow. I contacted S-BEachey. He was cooperative and polite. He offered me a cigar. I declined. I asked what he was doing. S-Beachey said he was collecting materials for a project. S-Beachey said he could not

believe what people would throw away. I informed him
that he was trespassing and that landfill management
would likely want to press charges. I said he ought to
come during business hours like everyone else. He said
he couldn't do that but did not elborate. I told him the
home-improvement warehouse was open late if that would
fit his schedule. S-BEachey said he was unaware there was
such a thing as a home-improvement warehouse and asked
me to explain it. He then asked where it was. I gave him
diretcions. S-Beachey asked if they had high-quality
materials there. I said I was no expert but I thought
they did. S-BEachey seemed pleased.

I informed him that it was important not to be at
landfill in the dark because it would be easy to hurt
himself and the ~~landfll~~ landfill operator would then be
exposed to liablity. He laughed and asked how he could
possibly be hurt more than he was. He appeared in good
health and I told him I did not understand. I informed
him that this was serious business and not to joke. He
laughed and said he would not joke anymore if being
serious was so important to me. I asked him if he always
dressed so well for picking through trash. S-Beachey
said he always dressed wellbecause a man has to have
pride in himself. S-Beachey told me that my shoes could
use a good shine. S-BEachey had no ID but identified
himself verbally. S-Beachey asked if I had heard of him
and seemed surprised when I siad I had not. S-Beachey
claimed he was born in 1887. I informed S-Beachey that
he appeared closer to 25 years of age than to 115. I
reminded him that he had promised no more ~~jkeos~~ jokes.
S-Beachey said he was telling the truth. S-BEachey
otherwise appeared rational.

S-Beachey asked if I had ever flown in an airplane.
I said of course although not as often as Lorna has
wanted us to because I don't like to be away from home

for very long and plus I have sinus problems that make me fearful of being in a pressurized cabin. Its fair to say that between the two of us we have a lot of regrets. S-Beachey said that regrets are the most worthless currency in the world and that I should live as if I was already dead. I thanked S-Beachey for his clever advice and directed himto empty his wheelbarrow while I performed a records check. He did not coop]erate. I was unable to determine where direction he had fled. I was unable to locate the wheelbarrow or its contents either.

6) EVIDENCE

None.


7) PROPERTY

Gas tank, engine parts, wood scraps. Unknown whether wheelbarrow was stolen property also.


8) STATUS

Case open.


9) OPINION

Unsure. I am preparing this report at home so I can review it before I submit an official report to Cpt. McCandless. I think I should get some sleep first.


Reporting officers: Featherstone
Recording officer: Featherstone
Typed by: Featherstone
Date and Time: 06-12-99 0710

| COLMA POLICE DEPARTMENT CA0043479 | | 1. CASE NO. 99-0315-73 | |
|---|---|---|---|

| 2. CODE SECTION CPC 211, CPC 245, CPC 203 | 3. CRIME Armed Robbery, ADW, Mayhem | 4. CLASSIFICATION Felony | 5. REPORT AREA Beat One |
|---|---|---|---|

| 6. DATE & TIME OCCURRED —DAY 06-18-99 0230 Fri | 7. DATE & TIME REPORTED 06-18-99 0310 Fri | 8. LOCATION OF OCCURRENCE 1601 Hillside Blvd. (Olivet Memorial Park) | |
|---|---|---|---|

| 9. VICTIM'S NAME—LAST, FIRST, MIDDLE (FIRM IF BUSINESS) Bradford, Elias T. | | 10. RESIDENCE ADDRESS 1601 Hillside Blvd., Colma | 11. RESIDENCE PHONE none |
|---|---|---|---|

| 12. OCCUPATION Busi- nessman | 13. RACE–SEX W-M | 14. AGE 60 approx | 15. DOB 10-25- 1863 | 16. BUSINESS ADDRESS (SCHOOL IF JUVENILE) | 17. BUSINESS PHONE |
|---|---|---|---|---|---|

| 18. NAME—LAST, FIRST, MIDDLE Bradford, Winifred | | 19. CODE | 20. RESIDENCE ADDRESS 1601 Hillside Blvd., Colma | 21. RESIDENCE PHONE |
|---|---|---|---|---|

| 22. OCCUPATION Wife | 23. RACE–SEX W-M | 24. AGE 50 approx | 25. DOB 1-19- 1871 | 26. BUSINESS ADDRESS (SCHOOL IF JUVENILE) | 27. BUSINESS PHONE |
|---|---|---|---|---|---|

**28. DESCRIBE CHARACTERISTICS OF PREMISES AND AREA WHERE OCCURRED**

On Olivet cemetery grounds. 10 yds south of Bradford family plot (Sec. H-40)

**29. DESCRIBE BRIEFLY HOW OFFENSE WAS COMMITTED**

Suspects accosted victim in cemetary and demanded objects of value. Victim complied. Suspects then took and smashed his eyeglasses. S-Barker cut off victim's nose before fleeing scene with others.

**30. DESCRIBE WEAPON, INSTRUMENT, TRICK, DEVICE, OR FORCE USED**

knife

| 31. MOTIVE—TYPE OF PROPERTY TAKEN OR OTHER REASON FOR OFFENSE (1) Financial gain (gold coins, gold-handled walking stick, gold wedding band). (2) To inflict bodily injury, apparently for sport. | 32. ESTIMATED LOSS VALUE AND/OR EXTENT OF INJURIES—MINOR, MAJOR $17000 |
|---|---|

**33. WHAT DID SUSPECTS SAY—NOTE PECULIARITIES**

"We take what we want." Suspects laughed and spoke as if intoxicated. (I smelled spirits on the breath of all suspects.)

**34. VICTIM'S ACTIVITY JUST PRIOR TO AND/OR DURING OFFENSE**

Victim was tidying area around grave. Victim complied with suspects' demands but was assulted even after handing over valuables.

**35. TRADEMARK—OTHER DISTINCTIVE ACTION OF SUSPECT/S**

Acc. to V and W, suspects have committed many similar crimes: surround Victim when Victim is not paying attention, demand items of value, inflict injury for fun.

**36. VEHICLE USED—LICENSE NO.—ID NO.—YEAR—MAKE—MODEL—COLOR (OTHER IDENTIFYING CHARACTERISTICS)**

N/A

| 37. SUSPECT NO. 1 (LAST, FIRST, MIDDLE) | 38. RACE–SEX | 39. AGE | 40. HT | 41. WT | 42. HAIR | 43. EYES | 44. SSN OR DOB | 45. ARRESTED |
|---|---|---|---|---|---|---|---|---|
| Barker, Arthur ("Doc") | W–M | 40 (app) | 5–04 | 130 | Bro | Bro (Has only left eye) | 1899 | No |

**46. ADDRESS, CLOTHING, AND OTHER IDENTIFYING MARKS OR CHARACTERISTICS**

Address: former Sunset View Cemetery (<u>check address: same as Cypress Golf?</u>). White collarless shirt and gray trousers. Gunshot wound (face). Lacks nose & one eye.

| 47. SUSPECT NO. 2–4 (LAST, FIRST, MIDDLE) | 48. RACE–SEX | 49. AGE | 50. HT | 51. WT | 52. HAIR | 53. EYES | 54. SSN OR DOB | 55. ARRESTED |
|---|---|---|---|---|---|---|---|---|
| Unknown white males. Further physical details noted on obverse. | | | | | | | | |

| 56. ADDRESS, CLOTHING, AND OTHER IDENTIFYING MARKS OR CHARACTERISTICS | 57. CHECK IF MORE NAMES IN CONTINUATION |
|---|---|
| | |

| REPORTING OFFICERS | RECORDING OFFICER | TYPED BY | DATE AND TIME |
|---|---|---|---|
| | | | |

## OFFENSES INVESTIGATED AND RECOMMENDED CHARGES

CPC 211- Armed Robbery

1) SUMMARY:

On 06-18-99, at approximately 0330 hours, V-Bradford was cleaning the area ofhis grave when S-Barker and three unidentified male accomplices accosted him. Suspects brandished knives and demanded all of his items of value. V-Bradford complied. S-Barker cut off the tip of V-Bradford's nose. All suspects then fled on foot.

2) VICTIMS AND WITNESSES:

V-Bradford, Elias T.

W-Bradford, Winifred Gaines

3) SUSPECTS:

S-1: Arthur "Doc" Barker

S-2, S-3, S-4: Unknown white males

4) VEHICLE:

N/A

5) STATEMENT OF REPORTING OFFICER:

On 06-12-99, at approximately 0230 hours, I was on patrol in full uniform in a marked patrol vehicle. I performed a passing check through Olivet Memorial Park and saw V-Bradford in a bloodstained white suit. He was holding his hands to his face. W-Bradford (vioctim's wife) was next to him and noticeably upset.

I made contact, although both V and W Bradford appeared to have trouble seeing me. First I attempted to render aid, which V-Bradford refused. He told me his nose would grow back in a few days, it was just very painful right now. I told him I found that hard to believe and he said what I believe didn't matter one bit compared to that which is true.

According to their statements, V-Bradford was removing leaves and other debris from the gravesite he shares with W-Bradford when S-Barker and "his gang" accosted him. They brandished knives and demanded all of his items of value. V-Bradford complied and turned over itmes of value: gold coins, gold-handled walking stick, and gold wedding band. One of the unknown accomplices (wearing what V-Bradford called "eccentric attire") demanded and was given the victim's blue silk "pocket square". S-Barker then slashed V-Bradford in the face, cutting off the tip of his nose. Suspects laughed, then fled on foot.

V-Bradford told me that S-Barker has disfigured other individuals perhaps because he (S-Barker) is disfigured himself. V-Bradford told me that the suspects have been committing such attacks more often often. He said that the situation in the locality is one of increasing lawlessness. He described it as "not a place for decent people anymore" it was safe and orderly whuile Marshal Earp was here because no one wanted to challenge him. I asked where this Earp was and V-Bradford said "He took the route" and since then no one was keeping keep the peace. He asked if I was going to do something about it since I am an officer of the law. I informed him that I always perform my duties to the best of my ability. Which is something I have said for years and only recently wondered if it was true. How can you know what your abiliities are in the first place? How would you knw if what you're doing really is your best? What if you spend your whole life doing something and look back and see medicrty in every single thing you'v e touched or done or not done?

V-Bradford declined my repeated attempts to render aid. He said he was unwilling to let me touch him and didn't I know better than that. I said I guess I didn't.

I searhced the area around the site of the attack but did not locate the suspects or any evidemce. I also searched for but did not recover the tip of V-Bradford's nose/.

6) EVIDENCE

Evidence of incident: Victim and Witness statements.

Evidence of existence of Victim and Witness: officer's observation.

7) PROPERTY

Gold coins (value: $8000)

Gold-handled walking stick ($6000)

Gold wedding band (value: $3000)

Pocket square ($10?)

8) STATUS

Case open.

9) OPINION

Victim and witness accurately recounted events.

Will investigate related crimes committed by S-Barker et al.

Question: Why do V and W believe that noses grow back when, accordeing to them, S-Barker's nose has not?

Reporting officers: Featherstone

Recording officer: Featherstone

Typed by: Featherstone

Date and Time: 06-18-99 0725

Mercer flips through the rest of the reports in that first box, which run through December 2000. He traces his fingers over the pages, feels the impressions of typestruck letters, the rough pits of Featherstone's x-outs. Only the first report—the one about the boxer—is a computer printout. He might find a version of that one in the system, but the others? No way. Because someone would've had to read them. Someone would've known that Sergeant Wesley Featherstone had lost his mind. Seeing dead people. Talking to dead people. Policing dead people.

How could nobody notice? Mercer only met the guy once, but what about everyone else? They were responding to calls with him. Sitting through briefings with him. Depending on him for backup. How could Toronto not notice? Benzinger? With Cambi, it's maybe not so surprising. What about Mazzarella? How could they be around him day after day and not sense that anything was wrong?

And then there's Lorna. How can you not know when your *spouse* is cracking up? A drop of sweat falls on the report he's holding, and he watches the page shaking as his hand trembles. What's the point of being with someone if they can't save you from drifting alone into misery? Lorna and Featherstone. Mercer's mother and father. His throat dries, constricts.

How could nobody notice?

*Because when it gets right down to it, we are alone.*

Mercer keeps reading, eager to shut out his thoughts, and he finds himself unable to stop. The reports show Featherstone interacting with dead person after dead person, piecing together information about Doc Barker and his gang. Among them, three names appear most often: Ruczek, LoPresti, and Eastwick, all criminals when they were alive. Ruczek: a pickpocket with a taste for blackmail, low-rent pimping, and battery. LoPresti: bootlegger's enforcer. Eastwick, a bank robber known as the Yuma Kid. They shake down the wealthy, steal the meager possessions of the poor, bust up competing pruno stills, run kidnapping operations, inflict pain and injury simply because they can. Featherstone gathers tips from frightened and angry victims, tries to track the gang, tries to anticipate their moves, but he's always a step behind, and the population declines noticeably as more people get fed up, chew this "Root," and "go away" (whatever that means—Go away to *where*?).

Each report is interspersed with more revelations from Featherstone himself, a man looking back at his life with dissatisfaction, regret, and melancholy.

*Lorna and I don't know each other. We stopped trying before we started.*

*A child might have helped. Or made everything worse.*

*I have earned not much love, little money, and even less respect.*

*I have spent my entire life alone. So has Lorna, and it is my fault.*

*I even miss myself. Is there any way to be more alone than that?*

Mercer looks up when he notices the light draining out of the room. He checks his watch. 4:48. Fiona. He'll be late, and she'll be furious. Time got away from him. But if he hurries, drives like hell, maybe he can still make it. He picks two sweatshirts up off his bedroom floor, grabs his jacket and keys, races down to the garage, and fires up the Olds, gunning the engine to clear the cough out of its pipes. Across the aisle, a woman strapping a toddler into a car seat throws him a dirty look. He gives her a wave that alludes to an apology without actually being one, and he squeals up the driveway, leaving behind a thick blue fog of exhaust.

Lillie Coit, sitting on the rotting shingles of The Willows' roof, watches the young officer speed away in his automobile into the darkening western hills. *Slow down!* she calls. *Be careful! You're not going to a fire!* Of course, he doesn't hear her. They never listen closely enough. She sighs and picks at a patch of hardened sap on the elbow of her shirt, following his taillights until they disappear. Sometimes all you can do is let go and hope for the best.

**M**ercer drives aggressively over the hill, his progress impeded by a few slow drivers, including one who's playing bump-and-run with the lane markers. Mercer would take the guy down in a second if he were on duty; you don't have to be speeding to be a fucking menace. When he hits Highway One, his heart sinks: a line of brake lights all the way to the south. The traffic crawls through Pacifica and up over Devil's Slide, and he keeps up a steady stream of curses directed at the drivers in front of him. To his right, the sun is sinking into the ocean, accelerating as it nears the horizon, racing to meet the blue. *Relax,* he tells himself. *It's one sunset. There will be others. It's not life or death. She knows that.*

He should call Fiona, should have called before he left the apartment, but he'd let himself believe he could be a hero and make it to Moss Beach in time. He hadn't realized the fucking sun was going to *plummet*. He reaches into his pocket for his cell phone and comes up empty. Of course. You rush, you forget things.

He's still following red lights in Montara when the last drop of pure sun leaks away, but the sky is still lightish, a lilac color, and he thinks they'll have a nice view for at least a few minutes, but the darkness keeps coming in fast, and as he winds through the trees and pulls into The Distillery parking lot, the sky is smooth blue-black ink. There's an empty spot right next to Fiona's car, and he parks. He takes a few running steps toward the entrance, then sees the sky for what it is: night.

She'll be angry, she'll complain about how worried she gets when he's late, and he'll apologize over and over. But then he'll tell her about Featherstone's ghost reports, and she'll understand why he got so wrapped up in them. They'll relax on the deck, have drinks and nachos while huddling together under a pile of blankets, then drive back north to her place and settle in for a night of ghost stories. Everything will work out. How can it not? He speed-walks through the restaurant and jogs down the stairs to the back deck. As he stands in front of the sliding-glass door, waiting for the electric eye to open it for him, he sees that she's the only one outside, a lone figure bundled in gray wool blankets, shapeless and still.

The cold ocean wind hits him like a truck. She must be freezing. He hesitates in the doorway and watches as she reaches for her wineglass and knocks it over. It shatters on the deck. She doesn't turn to look, doesn't even flinch. He walks out to her and sits down on the end of her chaise longue. She ignores him. All he can see of her face is her eyes, which stare through him and over the water. Her shoulders are trembling.

"Hi," he says.

No answer.

"I'm sorry," he says. "I lost track of time."

"I'd tell you to quit blocking my view," she says, "but there's no view. On account of it being night."

"I'm sorry," he says again.

"We were supposed to watch the sunset."

"I know."

"Maybe you weren't aware that the sun sets at a particular *time*. That it doesn't wait for Michael Mercer. Or maybe your promises just don't mean anything."

"Hang on," he says, trying to slow her momentum. "I said I'm sorry, and I meant it."

"I'm wasting my time with you."

"I screwed up. I did. I should've gotten here on time."

"Did you want to?"

"Of course."

She considers this. After a moment, she asks, "What are you doing with me?"

"What do you mean?"

"I'm too old for you."

"You're not," he says. "Let me decide that."

"Or maybe," she says, "you're too young for me. I'm *forty-three*, for God's sake."

"I can't put the sun back in the sky," Mercer says. "If I could, I would."

"Don't try to be cute."

"I'm not trying to be cute. I'm *sorry*." He nudges a piece of broken glass around with the toe of his shoe. They're quiet for a moment, staring out into the blue. He thinks of the night they stood together outside the Ferry Building; the sharp wind off the water was invigorating, thrilling, even erotic. Tonight everything feels different, and the change seems as sudden as it is dramatic.

"Are you going to tell me what was more important than being with me?"

"I lost track of the time. I was helping Lorna, and then—"

"Stop. I don't want to know. I don't *care*. I don't even want to be talking to you."

"What's going on?" he asks. "What happened?"

"You couldn't wait to get away from me this morning. Do you think I couldn't tell? Do you think you're that clever? You're not."

They can hear muffled laughter from inside the restaurant, beaten back by the wind. Mercer buttons his jacket over the second sweatshirt. He sits there, cold and silent, not knowing what to say. Veils of mist flutter in the floodlights that brighten the grassy ledge in front of them. A lone flashlight swings tiny arcs on the beach far below, in the hand of an unseen walker. The waves slap the sand again and again.

"I was a catch, once," she says.

"Come on," he says. "Don't."

"You don't want me. You want someone else. Or maybe you don't want anyone."

"I don't know what you want me to say."

"Forget what I *want* you to say. How about saying what *you* think?" She pauses. "For once."

"What I think," he says, "is that I made a mistake. That I got distracted and that I was late."

"What I think is that you're afraid of love. Yes, you heard me: you're afraid of love."

"That's ridiculous."

"No shit," she says.

A busboy steps out onto the deck, crouches next to them, and sweeps the pieces of glass into a metal dustpan. Nobody says anything. All there is is the wind and the *swiff-swiff* of the busboy's little broom and the sharp sounds of glass skidding over wood and metal. Mercer thanks him when he's finished, and Fiona snorts as the busboy goes back inside. "Always the polite one," she says. "It's such a pose. You're not real."

He knows what he should do because he's been trained: defuse the situation. Listen. Reflect her words back, so she knows she's been heard. Calmly discuss the next steps. Build agreement. He knows the procedure, but he can't think of the words to use. His pulse speeds, and it's as if he can feel the pathways in his brain constricting, choking the flow of language.

A feral orange cat darts across the dark space between floodlights, like a prison escapee.

"How's Cricket?" he asks.

She ignores the question.

"I'm going to tell you why I was late," he says, and he suspects these words are the wrong ones, but they're the ones he has. "Trust me. It's amazing. Sergeant Featherstone was—"

"I don't give a *fuck* about Sergeant Featherstone," she snaps.

He pulls back as if slapped. He gets up off her chair. He leans on the deck railing and lets the wind rake his skin. His scalp tingles from the cold. He watches as the cat sprints back where she came from. A distant barge inches over the water, its running lights the closest things to stars in the fog-socked night. His limbs and head feel heavy and tired. The silence starts to fray his nerves. A shiver twists through his shoulders, neck, head.

"How can someone be afraid of love?" she asks. "What's *wrong* with you?"

He's had enough. He's tired, his head hurts, and his stomach is twisting again. "How much wine did you have?" he asks.

"Are you joking?"

"I'm not joking. I'm worried about whether you can drive home."

"So we're going home now?"

"Apparently there's no point in talking," he says. "Let's call it a bad night and cut our losses."

"*Cut our losses*?" she echoes. "What do you know about losses?"

"I'll follow you to your place, then head home."

"You don't need to follow me."

"You can follow me, then."

"No."

"You've had too much."

"I'm fine."

"You're over legal."

"How do you know?"

"It's what I do," he says. "It's my job to know."

"Don't follow me."

"It's on my way home."

"Take another way home. I don't want to see you. I don't want to see your face in my rearview. I don't want to see the headlights on that stupid car of yours."

"Tough," he says. "You're impaired, and I'm going to make sure you get home safe."

"I'm *impaired*? Fuck you. You're just as impaired as I am. You just don't know it."

"Let's go," he says, and he puts his hand out to help her up. He's a little surprised when she takes it and pulls herself to her feet. He was expecting more anger, more drama. She sheds four blankets, then heads for the glass door, hugging her shoulders.

They walk wordlessly back into the warmth of the restaurant, and Mercer's stomach seizes up. *Goddamn it,* he thinks. *Arguments. Arguments and bad mayonnaise. No wonder I'm a mess.* He excuses himself to use the bathroom. When he comes out a few minutes later, he's reassured to see she's still there, looking at the framed photos and newspaper articles on the wall. This isn't the end. She's calming down. He comes up behind her and sees she's reading a story from *USA Today* about the ghost of the Distillery. She rocks back and forth slightly as she reads. Impaired balance. No question.

"Who is it?" he asks.

"The Blue Lady," she says wistfully. "She had an affair with the piano player, when this place was a speakeasy. She was murdered down on the beach by her husband. She comes back here because it's where she met the man she really loved. She wears a torn blue dress. She likes to pull things off shelves and drop them. There's a light by the hostess's stand that she likes to turn on and off."

On their way to the exit, he stops them at the hostess's stand and watches the lights closely. "I don't see anything," he says, trying to make her laugh. "You see anything?"

"Stop," she says. "No jokes."

"Fine," he says.

"Do you think it's easy, dealing with men? Especially your age?"

He sighs, louder than he means to. "Let's go. Let's just go."

Outside, she says, "You're not following me home."

"What I should do is take your keys," he says. "Get you a cab."

"Don't try to control me."

"I'm trying to make sure you don't hurt yourself. Or someone else."

"Don't patronize me, either."

This is no-win. Whatever he says, she'll hurl it back at him. He's used to drunks and speed freaks and other knuckleheads doing that when he's in uniform, but he can't take it from her, can't take it now. "Fine," he says. "Go." He realizes he never got to tell her about Featherstone's ghosts, and he's tempted to offer up the story as a last-ditch effort not to leave on such a sour note. What's sticking in his head, though, is her accusation—*You're afraid of love*—

and the more he thinks about it, the more unfair and condescending it seems. It's always the guy's fault. Men are always afraid of something. Forget it, he decides, his head pounding, his chest tightening with anger. He's going home alone, and he's going to keep Featherstone's ghosts all to himself.

**B**ack in Colma, the Zes-T-Mart night clerk clocks in for his shift. He goes to the locked cigarette cabinet, counts the cartons of Chesterfields. He writes the number on a pad next to the register, because he's good and stoned and he doesn't trust himself to remember. He stands so he can see the cigarette cabinet reflected in one of the windows, because he read on some website that if there are going to be any *manifestations*—shadows, vapor, lights—he might not be able to see them if he looks straight on. The image is murky, though, because the window is streaked and dirty, and he figures he should probably clean it, only he doesn't feel like going back into the supply room to get the glass cleaner and a rag.

It's a quiet night. He flips through a hot-rod magazine. He drums along on the counter to preprogrammed lite-pop with two sticks of beef jerky. He buys himself a scratch-off lottery ticket and loses. He watches the hot dogs rotate, pink and iridescent with oil, turning and turning and turning and turning.

Shit, where did that pad go?

# TEN

# THE CHILDREN'S SECTION

**M**ovie Night comes twice a week at Seven Oaks. Tonight, it's a western called *Vinegarroon,* a vehicle for a boy-band heartthrob named R. J. Poirier that was panned when it came out a year ago. The movie is as bad as Jude expected: wooden line readings, expository dialogue, continuity problems, no sense of pacing. He's glad his father taught him how to spot flaws that most people miss. It makes him feel like he can't be taken advantage of.

Jude loves westerns—the good ones. His father owns prints of all the best—*High Noon, She Wore a Yellow Ribbon, Rio Grande, The Searchers*—and when his grandfather was alive, the three of them would go downstairs to the screening room after dinner and watch. They'd sit in the dark together, Jude's grandfather letting him steal sips of his Sambuca, his father sipping port and commenting on camera angles, and afterward they'd sit in the dim light and smile and talk about how they don't make them like that anymore, do they? His grandfather, who'd worked for years in Hollywood building sets, would say, *You should make a western sometime, Marco. I'd love to see what you could do.*

*I make the films I want to make,* his dad would say stiffly.

*Just think about it. We could all work on it together. Jude would like that. Wouldn't you, Jude?*

And Jude would say yes, he'd love it, it would be the best thing ever.

*It's my work,* his dad would say. *Don't tell me what I should do.* From his tone, Jude could tell this was part of a battle that had gone on for decades, one that his grandfather wished were over. If Jude could recognize that, why couldn't his dad? And as for the western, of course, now it's too late. Jude wants to yell at his dad: *Why didn't you do it? It would've made him so happy. It* would *have been the best thing ever.*

So maybe Jude shouldn't be surprised that westerns make him cry these days—even shitty, fake, plastic westerns like *Vinegarroon.* He wipes his eyes and nose with his sleeve and hopes no one has noticed. Good thing they're not watching *Unforgiven,* or he'd go completely to pieces. It's his all-time favorite; he's seen it thirteen times. Plus, he saw it the night he met Reyna. He might never have met her if he hadn't. It was a Friday night, his parents were out of town, and he was inching along Haight Street in traffic, headed home for another wasted night alone. Wilson had texted him: DANCING 2NITE. U IN? Wilson had new friends now that he'd come out: friends from the school district's LGBT Alliance, online friends, friends he'd met in clubs, friends he had so much in common with now that he'd *discovered who he was,* and they were all more important to him than the best friend he'd had since first grade. Which cut the total of Jude's close friends from one to zero.

No, he was not IN for dancing. He had tagged along with Wilson and his new friends once, a month before, and it was a night of loud, crappy, thumpy techno and stupid tight ribbed T-shirts and Jude being ignored, feeling childish and alone, and he had sworn never again, never again ever. When he got Wilson's text, he'd thought, *Fuck that. I hate dancing. I can be a nobody at home, for free. And with better music.*

He saw the marquee at the Red Vic. His favorite film, and here he was at the theater, twenty minutes before showtime. Perfect. The first good luck he'd had in a long time. How could he not stop? He lucked out even more and scored a parking spot half a block down from the Vic, in front of Villains Vault, a used-clothing store in the old bank building. He found a seat in the center of the half-sold house and settled in for one hundred and thirty-one minutes in the dark with Clint and a bowl of popcorn with real butter. When the closing credits rolled and the houselights came up, though, Jude realized he'd never seen this movie with his grandfather, and he never would. The feeling of loss hit him like a brick. All he could think about was the funeral. His grandfather, stiff and wrong-looking, a wax figure in his casket. He was still crying when he left the theater. He kept his head down so no one on the street would see.

The wind was whipping down Haight Street, wet with fog, so he walked quickly. He had just beeped the Prospector unlocked when he heard someone call his name. Four kids were sitting on the steps of the clothing store, sharing forties in paper bags. One waved and called his name. It was Trent Umbarger, who was a year ahead of him in school. They'd never talked much, and Jude was surprised Trent even knew his name. Two other guys slouched on the steps with him, along with a girl in a hoodie that she'd pulled snugly around her face. Her skin was so pale it looked blue in the streetlight. Jude responded with a half-wave, not wanting to look overeager in case Trent was going to make fun of him, but Trent surprised him, said come on over, have a drink. Jude was pretty sure his eyes were dry, but he wiped them quickly as he walked over, just to make sure.

They all looked older than Jude. Next to Trent sat Carlos, who looked at least twenty-five and reclined with his elbows on the step above. Above them were Bobby, who had an angular, mean face, and Reyna, the girl in the hood. They were sitting close to each other, but not quite touching. Jude relaxed when Trent said Bobby and Carlos were from Burlingame; they wouldn't be desperate and unpredictable.

He looked more closely at Reyna, hoping he wasn't being too obvious. He could tell she was hot, even if he couldn't see all of her face. Light-brown eyebrows; a small nose, slightly upturned; wolf-gray eyes; a silver ring through her lower lip. She had a pierced tongue, too. He heard her clacking it against her teeth.

"Jude's father is in the movies," Trent said.

"He directs," Jude said. He ran through the list of his dad's films, then quickly regretted it. He shouldn't have sounded so enthusiastic, so film-geeky. Anyway, *The Hallelujah Dogs* was the only one any of them had heard of.

"I saw that," Reyna said. "It was intense."

Jude nodded. "It is," he said. Was she impressed? She held his eyes a little longer than she had to.

"Nice vehicle," Bobby said. "Is it your dad's?"

"It's mine," Jude said.

"Sweet Sixteen present?"

They all laughed. Jude couldn't think of anything to say. Bobby was pretty much right, but he didn't want to admit it.

"I'm cold," Reyna said.

"Frigid, if you ask me," Bobby said.

"You didn't think that when I was blowing you this morning," Reyna said.

"Oh!" Trent shouted. "You're bad-ass, Reyna."

"Will you blow me, too?" Carlos asked.

"No way, bitch," she said, and then Bobby punched Carlos in the arm.

"Let's get out of here," Bobby said. "Let's go to Squid's."

"Who's Squid?" Jude asked.

"A guy we know," Trent said. "Has a warehouse in the Mission. Always a party. You want to go?"

"You could give us a ride," Bobby said. "Come on. It's not far. It's on Cesar Chavez, near the freeway."

Jude hesitated. The movie had left him feeling drained, he had a good book at home, and—Burlingame or no Burlingame—these guys still made him a little nervous.

"It's really not that far," Reyna said, and before Jude's worries had a chance to catch up with him, he had opened the SUV and they'd all climbed in, Trent riding shotgun, the other three in the back seat, with Reyna in the middle.

"You're riding bitch, bitch," Bobby said to her.

"We'll see who's riding bitch later," Reyna said, and they laughed, all of them, and Jude did too: first a little noise that he could pretend was just him clearing his throat, in case they weren't inviting him to laugh with them. No one seemed to mind, so he laughed for real. He didn't really want them to have open bottles while he was driving, but he didn't want to look like a tight-ass. *Life's too short,* he told himself. *Just go with it and quit worrying.* That's what Wilson was doing. That's what these four were doing. It's what everyone except Jude did.

He watched Reyna in the rearview as she pulled the hood back. As they passed under a streetlight he saw the nuclear-green tips of her spiky platinum hair. Jude decided that she might be the most beautiful girl he'd ever seen. Or the hottest. He'd never considered the difference before.

He stayed at the warehouse all night and woke up on a pile of old drop-cloths. A dozen other people were splayed over furniture and on the floor around him, but he didn't see Reyna. He wondered when she'd left and if she'd said good-bye to him. He felt terrible, right on the edge of puking. He remembered people pressing beer after beer into his hand. He remembered paying for at least two beer runs. He remembered talking to Reyna more about movies. He remembered tossing Trent a fifty to get some grass from a guy who delivered. He remembered someone taking up a collection to get two girls to take off their shirts and make out while everyone watched. He remembered some people calling him *Hollywood.*

He left without waking anyone up and found the SUV parked at a crazy angle with a fresh ticket under the wiper blade, and that triggered a wave of paralyzing guilt—the guilt he always felt on hungover mornings, the guilt over being a shitty, flawed person who'd lost control and maybe embarrassed himself. He drove home—his parents were out of town, thank God, and he parked down the street so Mrs. Hankin-Cherry wouldn't see him, in case she was watching—and he crawled into bed to hide from the day. Reyna stayed in his head, though, and even though he felt physically wrecked and crushed by guilt, he also felt alive, alive with lust and freedom and being the kind of kid his parents never dreamed he could be, and when Saturday rolled around, he called Trent at sundown and said, Hey, where's the party tonight? You guys need a ride?

And now here he is at Seven Oaks, all stressed out and pissed off from hours of therapy he doesn't need for a problem he doesn't have, sitting in a darkened room with a circus of teenage fuckups, crying at a crap movie like *Vinegarroon.*

Are you lonely? the therapists want to know. Sad? Of course he is. He has good reasons. The girl he loves is going out with a guy who humiliated him. He has no friends. His grandfather is dead. His parents don't trust him. Being perfect isn't enough anymore. No one understands that he doesn't belong here. And plus he just almost died, okay?

Do you think that changed you? they want to know. Do you see your life differently? I can't see my life, he says, because I'm stuck in this place with drunks and meth freaks and oxy addicts and self-mutilators and purgers and other emotional cripples, and my life is nowhere near here. But he knows the night in the cemetery *has* changed him, and not all for the worse. He feels tougher. Stronger. Less willing to take shit from people. Another good thing, then, about almost dying.

At the end of the movie, the night orderly, a bald, round-headed guy named Wally, turns on the lights. Jude blinks and rubs his eyes with the heels of his hands. All the kids are sprawled out on couches. Some of the boys and girls are casually touching—arms draped over shoulders, legs resting on legs—but that's against the rules, and the light makes them retreat into their own spaces. Jude is alone in the back, farthest from the screen. He raises himself so he's sitting on the back of his couch and tries to look cool and detached as he surveys the room. None of them have done anything to make him feel welcome. He tells himself that's a blessing in disguise.

"Feet off the cushions, Jude," Wally says. "Respect your environment."

When Wally turns his head, Jude flips him off. *Respect this, Wally, you douchebag.*

He overhears a couple of girls talking about R. J. Poirier. Jude has been in Group with both of them.

"He's so hot," one says. Her name is Rose. She's a seventeen-year-old blonde with a cocaine problem and arms crosshatched with thin white scars. "He's way hotter than Johnny Depp."

"I'd fuck him," her friend says. Megan. Brunette, alcoholic, has affairs with middle-aged men.

"You wouldn't want to," Jude says from across the room, and everyone looks at him.

"I would," Megan says. "I just said so."

"He's into weird stuff," Jude says. "Diapers. Feces. You wouldn't even want to shake this guy's hand."

"What the fuck are you talking about?" Rose says. "Don't go making up things like that about people."

"Could you be *more* jealous and desperate?" Megan says.

"I'm not making it up. Everyone in the industry knows."

Rose rolls her eyes. "Oh," she says. "The *industry*. You're in the *industry*, I suppose."

"My dad is," he says, and he immediately knows it was a mistake, he sounded insecure and show-offy even though he honestly didn't mean to. It's so hard to know what the rules are, to know what people want—although another part of him says the whole problem is him, that people just don't like him and he'll never quite understand why.

"You're so full of shit," Megan says.

"Easy," Wally the orderly says to no one in particular.

Jude flashes middle fingers to the room—to these addicts and losers in love with their damage who think *he's* the one who's fucked up. "Y'all can go ahead and ride those palominos straight to hell," he says. The laughter follows him down the hall, and with each step he gets angrier at himself. Of all the ways he could have told them to fuck off, why did he quote that poo-fiend's dumbest line from *Vinegarroon*? Why can't he even do the little things right? What's *wrong* with him?

The next morning, Jude is sawing his way through the Prelude and Allemande of Bach's First Cello Suite—it's hard, even harder than he'd thought, he can barely string two measures together at quarter-speed without breaking down—when Clinton-Like-the-President opens the door to the music room and tells him he has a visitor. He hands Jude a business card with a gold badge on it.

"Forget it," Jude says. He doesn't want to talk about himself with anyone else. That's all he does in Group after Group after Group.

"That's not one of your choices," Clinton says. "Let's go. You can leave your instrument here."

"It's called a cello," Jude says, "and I'm putting it back in my room so no one messes with it." The cello was his grandmother's. After she died, it sat in a closet for years before Jude's grandfather gave it to him on his ninth birthday. *I always thought I'd take some lessons, learn how to play,* his grandfather said. *Thought it would be a way to stay close to her. But these hands aren't good for much anymore. My fingers hurt, you know? Broke every one of them at least once. See how crooked? Anyway, I thought you should have it. It's a beautiful piece of wood, you know, and it deserves to be played.*

"You have to learn how to trust people, Jude," Clinton says.

"Uh-huh." Jude looks at the name on the business card: Mercer. From the hospital. The one who was less of a dick.

"You'll have to make it a short visit. It's almost time for Group."

"When isn't it?" Jude says.

Officer Mercer is waiting for him in the sunroom. Light streams in through a bay window, and dust motes drift through the beams. He's sitting on one of the pine-green couches, hunched forward, hands clasped like he's deep in thought, or praying. He's not in uniform this time. He's wearing jeans and a blue polo shirt with COLMA POLICE stitched over the breast in gold. Black sneakers, white socks.

Mercer stands up, reaches out to shake Jude's hand, and Jude lets him. They sit, the cop back in his place on the couch, Jude in a matching green chair, ninety degrees from him. A few sections of the newspaper are spread out over the table between them. Jude reminds himself not to let anything important slip.

"Thanks for your time," Mercer says.

Jude shrugs. "I'm not going anywhere."

"How are you feeling?"

"Fine."

"You look a lot better."

"So do you," Jude says, referring to his eye. The guy's face was a mess the last time Jude saw him; now there's just a faint yellow-green smudge.

"Thanks," Mercer says. "Jude, I'm here because I need to ask you more about what happened in the cemetery."

"I've already—"

"You're probably going to feel like you've answered a lot of these questions before, but we need to go through them. Anything that you can remember— even if it seems insignificant—will be a big help."

"Where's your partner?"

"Officer Toronto? He's not my partner. You don't really have partners in a department our size."

"No Bad Cop?"

"He's not a bad cop," Mercer says. "We weren't trying to pull anything on you."

"He's kind of a dick." Jude watches the officer carefully. Can he get away with saying that?

"He was upset about what happened to you. We both were. Are. No one's saying you did anything wrong. No one wants you to get in any trouble. You're dealing with enough right now."

Jude notices a spot on Mercer's knee, figures he was drinking coffee in the car on the drive up and dribbled on himself. He sees Mercer follow his gaze, then cover the spot by resting his hand on his thigh, as if it were a natural gesture. Then he moves his hand away, as if he's decided that there's no point in covering it up.

"Coffee," Mercer says. "Spilled in the car."

Jude is surprised. A lot of adults would pretend they hadn't noticed rather than admit that they were clumsy. Some would probably try to tell you there wasn't any stain. The therapists in this place might admit they spilled, but they'd immediately ask you how *you* felt about them spilling their coffee. *I feel fine. You're the one with the stained pants, moron.*

"Speaking of cars," Mercer says, "your vehicle was located in a parking lot in San Mateo. No significant damage. Stereo's gone, but everything else is intact. We're going to try to get some prints."

Jude tries to keep his face neutral, but he knows it would've been better for everyone if the Pioneer had disappeared. And if they were going to let it be found, why'd they have to take his killer stereo? Jerks. "Good," he says. "That's great."

Mercer goes through the same litany of questions—*How many people? Sex? Race? Facial hair? Distinctive clothing? Jewelry? Tattoos?*—and Jude tells him, again, that he doesn't remember anything. "You have to understand," Jude says, "I was pretty out of it. Somebody slipped me something. It's not like I'm going to suddenly have total recall."

"That's all right," Mercer says. "We can just talk."

Jude stays quiet.

"So how are things going here?" Mercer asks him.

"I don't belong here."

"Your parents think you do."

"I don't see how they can complain. I do everything they want."

"This whole thing has given them a pretty good scare."

"What if I said I didn't care who did it? If I'm sick of trying to relive it and just want to get on with my life?"

"It's not your call at this point."

"Sucks to be me."

"You getting visitors? People to keep you company?"

"Just you," Jude says. "And my mom."

"Any friends?"

"I don't really have a lot of friends."

"No?"

"No."

"I find that a little hard to believe."

"Like I said," Jude says. "Sucks to be me."

"What about Wilson?"

"Wilson and I don't hang out anymore."

"Why not?"

"It's not important."

"Was Wilson one of the people who did this?"

Jude laughs.

"What's funny?"

"If you met him, you'd know," Jude says. "Wilson and I didn't have a fight or anything. He just figured out he was gay and got new, cooler friends and totally left me behind. I just didn't want to talk about it in front of my mom."

"She'd be upset that he's gay?"

"Maybe," Jude says. "But it would make her ask me twice as often if I have a girlfriend yet, and isn't there anyone I like, et cetera, and it's like, Mom, I don't have the answer you want. Girls don't talk to me. So stop asking. I don't need the pressure. And I definitely don't need to talk to the fucking priest again."

Mercer nods slowly. "Makes sense to me," he says. There's a sharp knock on the door, and Jude sees the cop jump, then try to cover it. Clinton pushes the door open, leans in, and taps his watch, which has an enormous, oversized face. It's like armor. "Group in five minutes, Jude."

"Thanks, Clinton-Like-the-President."

He sees Clinton give Mercer an eyebrow raise: grown-up code for *This kid is such a pain in the ass*. Mercer doesn't acknowledge it, just looks at Clinton steady-eyed for a moment, not playing along, then returns his attention to Jude.

"That guy's an asshole," Jude says, once the orderly leaves. He studies Mercer's face for a reaction. There isn't one, as far as he can tell. Mercer has a square jaw and short black hair with a slight widow's peak, and it occurs to Jude that he looks a little like his father did when he was younger. Like in the early promo shots that line the wall along the staircase.

"So how do you spend your time here? Other than Group?"

"You do whatever's on your Goal Sheet."

"What's a Goal Sheet?"

"You make it with your therapist. You make a list of little things to achieve. It's supposed to teach us structure and self-reliance." He rolls his eyes.

Mercer scratches his head, then clasps his hands together again. Jude knows from speech class that this is a trick for people who don't know what to do with their hands when people are watching. "So what's on yours?" he asks.

"Two hours a day of practicing. I play the cello."

"That's right," Mercer says. "Your mom mentioned that."

"She brought my cello up here. They said it could be part of my therapy. I decided that since I'm stuck, I might as well practice. I'm teaching myself Bach's Cello Suites." He can tell from the blank look on Mercer's face that he has no idea what the Cello Suites are. He wonders if the cop will try to bullshit him.

"I don't know them," Mercer says.

"It's like the best music ever written for the instrument. There's six of them."

"They hard?"

Jude nods.

"Doesn't sound like a little goal. They let you put that on there?"

"Sticking to the Goal Sheet is for mediocrities," Jude says. "I'm not going to be mediocre."

"I can tell," Mercer says.

"Thanks," Jude says, and for a second, he's afraid he's going to start crying.

"Anyway, that's impressive, learning all those suites," Mercer says. "It'd be cool to hear you play, when you're ready." Mercer runs his hand through his hair, which Jude can see is getting thin on top.

"Have you met my dad?" Jude asks.

"Not yet. Just your mom."

"But you know who he is, right?"

Mercer nods.

"You ever see his movies?"

"One."

"Which one?"

"I forget the name. Snow. Sweden. Plutonium."

"*Stockholm Underground.*"

"That's it."

"You like it?"

"My girlfriend did."

"But did you?"

"It was fine," Mercer says. "I usually go for more action."

"That movie puts me to sleep," Jude says.

"I stayed awake, but I know what you mean."

"What's your girlfriend's name?"

Jude watches as the cop chews his lip, trying to decide how much he wants
to reveal. "Fiona," Mercer says, surprising him.

"What's she like?" Jude asks.

"She's smart. She's nice. She's a nurse at the hospital they took you to. She
looked in on you, before you woke up. I asked her to."

"What else?"

"She lives by the beach," Mercer says. "She has a cat named Cricket." He
pauses, longer this time, then adds, "She's a little older."

"You in love with her?"

"Hard to say."

"Why?"

"That's not always an easy thing to know."

"I think it is."

"Yeah?"

"I'm in love with someone. I knew it the first time I saw her. Literally."

"What's her name?" Mercer asks.

"Reyna." He meant to keep her a secret, but it feels great to say her name
out loud.

"Has she been here to visit you?"

"No," Jude says. "She's not my girlfriend. Not yet. We just made out once. She's with this other guy right now."

"That'll happen," Mercer says.

"It sucks."

"Sometimes you just have to be patient, and they'll come around."

"The worst part is that it's this guy Bobby, who's a complete loser. I mean, he sits on Haight Street and harasses people for change. And he's from *Burlingame.* Idiot."

"Bobby what?"

"I don't know," Jude says. "I've never asked."

"What's her last name? Reyna's?"

It startles him to hear the cop say her name. His face turns hot, and he gets nervous. He's said too much. Mercer was just working him all along. "I have to go," he says. "Group."

"You can't tell me her last name?"

"I have to go," Jude says. He sticks out his hand for a shake like he's seen his dad do when he wants to get rid of someone. Then he spins, and he's out the door.

"You have my number," Mercer calls after him. "Call me if you want to talk. Whenever."

Jude ignores him. *Don't hold your breath, dude,* he thinks.


Lorna marvels at the buzz of activity inside Lucky Chances, amazed that so many people are gambling on a weekday night. Insomnia was what brought her here, but she suspects the majority of the people around her have been playing cards for hours and hours. Maybe the entire day, or longer. She never knew this culture existed, and it's exciting to be in the middle of it.

When the plans to open the card room were first approved by the town, she'd been certain that it wouldn't ever get built, or if it did, it wouldn't survive for long. Wes had been dead set against it. It would bring a bad element, he said, and the owners seemed hostile to any oversight by the police. He'd declared that he'd die before either of them ever spent a dollar in the place.

Which, she realizes, is how it turned out.

"Winna winna winn-ah," the dealer says in a carnival voice. He slides a twenty-five-dollar chip to her and collects the house's cut from her stack of dollar bills. She's at the pai gow poker table, along with an old Chinese man who speaks no English and two beery young collegians who speak too loudly and too often.

Part of the thrill of being here, of sitting in a place Wes disliked, of gambling—which he'd never approved of—is getting back at him. For years of remoteness and secrecy. For years of having to adapt to his schedule. For their childlessness. For liquidating half of their investments and giving the money to a church of hillbilly freaks and swindlers. The attorney shook her head when Lorna asked if they could get any of it back. *Everything he gave away was his to give.*

*Twenty-seven thousand dollars for a fireproof box? A fireproof box for ashes?*

*I don't understand it either,* the attorney said, *but I don't see any actionable fraud.*

Actionable fraud? The actionable fraud is sitting there on the floor in her closet. She's had to put a bedsheet over it so she won't get angry every time she looks for something to wear. It took two movers to lift it. *What is this, lead?* one of them had asked.

*I think so,* she'd said. *At least partly.*

Her next hand: a pair of aces high, a pair of eights low. Not the strongest, but it could be good enough to win, and she feels her scalp tingle with excitement. And that's another part of the thrill of being here. The suspense, the anticipation, the competition, the payoff. Plus, it's all for a good cause.

Reverend Whipple was at the blood drive, just as he said he'd be, sitting at a folding table in front of *The Redemption Express,* meeting every donor personally and autographing copies of his book, *Pain to Change: Transforming Your Life by Transforming the World.* He'd shaken her hand firmly, asked her name and repeated it, thanked her sincerely. He kept having to clear his throat, which he apologized for, and she gave him a lozenge that she had in her purse. *You see?* he said with a hoarse laugh. *Once you start giving, it's hard to stop.*

*This is the best I've felt in a long time,* she said as she wrote a check for two copies of his book. She told him about her life since Wes died, and he listened, even though there were people in line behind her. He listened, and he treated her like she was a person, not like a fragile little widow, not like someone to be pitied for having been married to a man who'd lost his mind. *I want to do more,* she'd said.

He told her about the Sudanese children his church was sponsoring and showed her a pamphlet. Twenty-five dollars, he said, would feed three kids for a month. She knew that the photos were calculated to make her feel pity for these children with their lost and plaintive eyes and their bony frames and their dead-looking skin, but that didn't change the fact that these kids were out there and they needed help.

She wrote a check for two hundred fifty on the spot. *I'll be giving you more,* she said.

*Only what you can afford to give,* he said. *But every little bit is appreciated.*

*By the way,* she said as he was hugging her good-bye, *do you take furniture donations?*

The truck arrived at the storage space that afternoon and cleaned it out as she watched. When the loaded truck disappeared down the on-ramp to 280, she felt free. Free and clean and worthwhile and good.

The aces and eights win; the dealer has nothing. "Winn-ah," he says again, and he slides her another twenty-five-dollar chip. She decides to let this one ride. A fifty-dollar win means food for six. She can't wait to write another check.

*Only what you can afford.*

The drunk men leave, their supplies of chips exhausted. At the table now it's just her and the dealer and the white-haired, hunched Chinese man, who spins chips in long knotty-knuckled fingers and grumbles to himself. Employees push carts of food past her, wheels silent except for little *thwick*s when they hit seams in the carpet. If she listens through all the chatter and squeals and laughter, she can hear the white noise being pumped in. This is a very strange place.

Her next hand: a straight to the jack, and an ace-queen low. It should be a winner. It has to be.

Now that she's gotten used to living in the apartment, she figures she can get by for ten years on what she has banked, if she's frugal. She has everything she needs, and she's not interested in traveling alone. Why not give her extra money to the needy? It's a much better idea than handing it over to some redneck hustlers who spook foolish old men with ghost stories.

Yes, Wesley, you were a fool. An unhappy man, and a fool. And the wasted part of her life is *over.*

She's lost in the snowy white noise when the dealer asks if she needs help setting her hand again. "No, thank you," she says, "I just got distracted." She arranges her cards and sets them on the table. The dealer shows a straight to the seven and an ace-ten. The Chinese man grunts and pushes his cards back toward the dealer, disgusted, and the dealer collects his chips. He flips Lorna's cards, fans them out.

"Winn-ah," he announces. "The lady gets paid again."


Mercer knows he should be happy with what he got out of Jude up at Seven Oaks—Bobby from Burlingame, the mysterious Reyna, his own certainty that Jude knows more than he's letting on—but he's troubled by the way the interview ended. He pushed too hard, and the kid shut him out. He gets it—that's exactly what he does when he feels betrayed—but that just makes him feel worse.

Shortly after two A.M., when nothing is coming over the radio except for Toronto and Cambi needling each other, Mercer decides to run a check through Cypress Lawn. He pulls up to the Fern Grotto loop, radios his position, and advises that he's going on foot patrol. Sergeant Mazzarella asks why.

"Just want another look. In case there's something we missed."

Toronto's voice crackles through. "Go get 'em, Ghostbuster."

Before he leaves the cruiser, Mercer pops his sixth and seventh aspirins of the night. He's ruining his stomach, but this headache is a killer. Even his teeth hurt. Outside, it's in the high forties, but still the fog is hanging a heavy, damp chill over the town, so he zips up as he walks. On the gate hangs a bigger and more threatening sign that says UNSAFE CONDITIONS—DO NOT ENTER—TRESPASSERS WILL BE PROSECUTED. He shines his flashlight through the bars. The blackberries have grown in the last two weeks, creeping farther into the pathways. He sweeps the light across the upper level, then into the pit. Nothing. No sign that anything out of the ordinary ever happened here.

He walks the outside perimeter, shines his light up the vine-twined tower, looks into tangles of branches and leaves. He's wasting his time. The area was searched repeatedly. Now that he's lost the kid, though, he feels obligated to find *something* new. He pauses as he catches a whiff of something sharp and sour—a little like the sauerkraut smell of his apartment—but the wind quickly carries it off.

He decides to walk east, up the slope, still scanning the grounds carefully, but also admiring the shadows that the headstones throw in the glare of his light and through the mist: rounded and squared-off, cross-topped and angel-crowned, shapes changing with the angle of the beam. Every now and then there's a little give in the soft ground beneath his feet, which he finds unsettling. He passes a place where the ground has caved in, a three-by-three square, marked off with metal stakes and red caution flags. He shines his light into the hole, sees nothing but dirt.

The wind rustles leaves that tumble through the field of light and brush against stones before they tumble on, and Mercer hears a rhythm in the rustle. The rhythm gets steadier, more regular, and sharper, too, and the sound shades into a repeated *slap*. Then, a higher, more melodic tone, not much louder than the ringing in his ears. He continues through the cemetery as quietly as he can, and soon he recognizes the high part as a voice—no, *voices,* chanting in unison to the beat of the *slap-slap-slap.* He'd swear it sounds like kids jumping rope, only that would make no goddamn sense.

He douses his light. There's enough moon that he can move without it, as long as he steps carefully. He creeps closer, ducks behind a tree. Crosses quickly to the back side of a mausoleum. He's getting close; there's less echo in the sounds now, as if they're coming across open space instead of bouncing off stone.

He comes to a field of knee-high markers, lichen-covered and darkened by time. The rounded top of the stone is carved in an outline of a lamb. He scans the field: most of the stones have a lamb or mossy lamb-shaped bumps. BABY HANNAH, the one in front of him says. Next to it, BABY EDWARD. He feels the back of his neck prickling.

The voices seem to be coming from the dark southeast corner of the field, where trees and bushes overhang a fence that separates Cypress Lawn from Holy Cross. He closes his eyes—this is not going by The Book, not at all—but this way he can concentrate on the voices, hear some of the words—*dream, sheen, down, fell*—and he's sure of it now, it's a jump-rope rhyme, and he can hear the scuffs of shoes interspersed with rope-slaps, and the voices are the voices of little girls chanting a rhyme that spools over and over:

*Lincoln Beachey thought it was a dream*
*To go up to heaven in a flying machine.*
*The machine broke down, and down he fell.*
*Instead of going to heaven he went to—*
*Lincoln Beachey thought it was a dream . . .*

Then, suddenly: silence. The air around him turns cooler. He senses motion around him: insubstantial things, drifting and darting. But nothing is there. He's alone, and he's hearing little girls sing playground songs.

Jesus. He does *not* want to be hearing voices. It is a bad, bad sign, to be hearing voices.

It has happened once before. He was twenty-four or twenty-five, a pitch-dark time when he'd wake up most mornings and think, *Oh, shit. Another day.* He was walking down Dolores Street after a party where he'd felt alone and inept and unable to talk to anyone, and he'd left after fifteen minutes. As the palm fronds slapped and whispered in the median, he'd wondered if his dad had been this miserable. The voice came as he was unlocking his car, and it sounded like it was emanating from the very center of his head, more felt than heard. It was high-pitched and gluey, a "Stairway-to-Heaven"-backward voice, but he heard the words clearly: *Save your strength.* At home, he sat up most of the night, huddled into himself, stunned and trembling, wondering what was wrong with him, not wanting to admit that he'd heard a voice but also needing to ask: *For what? For what should I be saving my strength?*

Mercer blinks, shakes his head clear. He's alone in the children's cemetery. That's all. Sleep deprivation, stress, maybe post-concussion symptoms. Featherstone's ghost reports can't be helping, either. The thing to do is to stay cool. And Book or no Book, he won't be reporting this. No way.

Is this how it started for Featherstone?

The one person he can imagine talking to is Fiona. She'd catalog his symptoms and tell him what was wrong with him, or at least hold him and talk him down and help him keep his head together. If Mercer had his way, he'd drive the Crown Vic straight to her place right now. But he doesn't have his way; he has reality, in which she's not speaking to him. Even then, he dials six of her seven numbers on his cell before he thinks better of it and hangs up.

*No,* he tells himself. *I am not hearing dead people. I am not—*

His earpiece squawks, startling him, and he hears Toronto's voice requesting multiple backups on a traffic stop on Hillside, in front of Lucky Chances. A low-riding Chevy full of young males. He's waiting to make an approach. Mercer says he's en route, and before he even clicks off he is running, hurdling low stones, weaving around blocks of granite and marble. There's no need to sprint, but it feels good to quit thinking and be physical, all muscle and training and instinct. In the cruiser, he guns the engine, buzzing with adrenaline. Dispatch chatters as he races to the card house. All units are converging. Plates registered to a Hispanic male, 21, on parole, subject to search and seizure. The sky is a crash of flashing lights when Mercer arrives. A Fourth-of-July sky.

Toronto and Benzinger are approaching the low-rider from each side; Cambi, hanging back, waves Mercer over. "I have a feeling," Cambi says. "You ready?"

"Fuck yeah, I'm ready," Mercer says, and on cue the rear passenger-side door of the Chevy slings open and a wiry, dark-skinned kid bolts down a grassy slope toward Spagnola & Sons Monument Co. Benzinger sprints after him, and Mercer follows her down the hill, legs and lungs burning, and picks his way through the Spagnolas' tiny demo graveyard of display stones. Benzinger takes the south side of the building, Mercer the north. As he rounds the northeast corner, the subject is right there, heading straight for him. A dark goatee frames the kid's mouth, which is pink and surprised. His skin is sweat-shiny. He stops and tries to backpedal, but Mercer has already launched himself into the air.

The impact is glorious. He hears the air forced out of the kid's lungs as they hit the asphalt, and it's the sweetest sound he's ever heard. This is the real world, and he belongs in it, and he is grateful. Benzinger arrives just after the cuffs clack tight, and he smiles up at her.

"One for the highlight reel, huh?" she says.

He nods—only now catching his full breath—because goddamn, it doesn't get any better than this. It does not.

# NIGHTWALKING (I)

**H**ot, sudden sweat glazes Mercer's forehead, and he closes his eyes to shut out the glaring white lights, the cameras, the rows of people all expecting words from him. The reporter's question floats in the air like a fat summer bug, but he can't grab it. He strains to remember—he was asked only seconds ago—reaching for its tone, for its rhythm, for any of the words that composed it, and he comes up with nothing. Then it's gone, the question, as if it buzzed down the red-carpeted aisle and out the window and into the weakly lit sky, gone forever. It's tempting to give up, to just stand in this wash of hot light, sweaty and gape-mouthed, and wait for it all somehow to end. He hears the low thrumming of the ventilation system. He hears someone cough.

He remembers to breathe, then relaxes his eyelids, lets them hang closed for a moment and tells himself to calm down. Ignore the stretching silence. Be patient. If he can unclench his brain, even a little, maybe he'll remember.

But he doesn't. He opens his eyes again and looks at the people in the room—some with pens poised over notebooks, some holding out tape recorders, some behind video cameras—and he sees their faces turning to disbelief or, worse, pity. The wooden podium is slick under his sweating hands. He feels helpless. This is a nightmare of silence, and he's trapped in it. *This is your job, goddamnit,* he thinks. *Get it together.*

**H**e hadn't known he'd be the one speaking at the press conference until he arrived at the station. Funkhouser had called him and Toronto into work early to discuss the DiMaio case, and they'd met in the detective's office, going over the facts, preparing the statement, talking about the questions that might arise. When they were through, the detective had clapped him heavily on the shoulder and said, "Showtime, Boy Thirteen. You ready for the spotlight?" The tips of his sturdy white mustache curled upward as he smiled. Mercer said yes even before he figured out what Funkhouser meant.

"I'm not good at public speaking," he said to Toronto as they walked to the break room. "You sure you don't want to do it?"

"The family asked for you," Toronto said. "Mommy didn't like me."

"What about Funkhouser?"

"He hates doing shit like this."

"So do I," Mercer says.

"Shut up and die like an aviator, Boy Thirteen."

Toronto sat on the couch and turned on the TV, settling on college basketball. Mercer sat with him, pretending to watch but staring blindly, trying to beat back the dread that was stealing over him. "I don't want to fuck it up," he says. "I could forget to say something important."

Toronto kicked Mercer's foot. "Get over yourself, drama queen."

"I may need help," Mercer said.

"I swear," Toronto said, "that I will do everything in my power to fuck you up."

Mercer heard Mrs. Featherstone's chirpy voice from the front-desk area and got up to say hello, grateful for the distraction. He opened the door and saw her talking to the dispatcher through the Plexiglas window. In her hands was a plastic-wrapped plate stacked high with squares of coffee cake. An over-stuffed tote bag hung from her elbow. She was wearing her raincoat, even though the wind had chased out the clouds before noon. "Hello, Michael," she said when she saw him in the doorway.

"Hi, Mrs. Featherstone," he said. "How are things?"

"Things are wonderful," she said. "I got a job."

"Great. Doing what?"

"I'm going to be a docent for the Historical Society," she said. "They need someone to fill in while Ida Neely gets her new hip." She gestured out to the trailer in the City Hall parking lot, where the Society was housed. "I'll be right here in your backyard."

"If you're ever working night shift, we can carpool," Mercer said, holding the door for her. "Come on in. Nick and I are just killing time."

Toronto looked up from the couch, where he was packing a dip into his mouth. He snapped his fingers to shake off loose flakes. "Hi, Lorna," he said, picking up an empty paper cup someone had left on the floor. He pointed to the bulge in his lip and said, "Excuse me. Don't mean to be rude."

"I've seen people spit before, Officer Toronto," she said. "Don't worry." She set the coffee cake on the table and unwrapped it. Mercer eyed it warily. Nerves had his stomach knotted already. Toronto had an easy excuse with his mouth full of tobacco. Bastard.

"Michael? Would you like a piece?"

He almost said yes, just to avoid turning her down. For once, his good sense won out. "I'm too nervous to eat."

"Why are you nervous?"

"I'm doing a press conference at four. The DiMaio case. The boy in the cemetery. The family finally agreed to let us spread the word, get some more leads."

"Oh," she said. "That sounds exciting."

"Our young hero isn't keen on public speaking," Toronto said. He spit into the cup.

"You'll be fine," she said. "Nothing to worry about. Although we should do something about your face."

"I've been saying that for months," Toronto said.

"Get bent," Mercer told him.

"There's still some bruise around your eye," Lorna said. "But we can cover that up. Do you mind? You'll look a lot better."

"Makeup, you mean?"

"I have some foundation with me. We can take care of it in no time flat. And I don't want to hear anything about how it's not a masculine thing to do."

Mercer saw that Toronto was looking very interested in the basketball game and doing his best not to laugh.

"Your eyes look puffy," Lorna said. "You need more sleep, Michael."

"I'm aware," he said.

"It'll catch up to you. Trust me. Wes had a lot of trouble sleeping when he went back to the night shift. Now hang on—wait—I have something that'll get rid of those bags." She dug around in her purse and came out with a yellow tube. She uncapped it and squeezed a white cream onto her finger. "Hold still," she said, and she dabbed the cream under both of his eyes, then smoothed it into his skin.

"What is it?" he asked.

"Hemorrhoid cream," she said, still rubbing. "It works wonders."

Toronto snorted, then quickly—and not too subtly—turned his laugh into a cough. If Lorna noticed, she gave no indication.

"Thanks," Mercer said. He was uncomfortable about every part of this situation. Going on TV. Speaking in public. Having Mrs. Featherstone touch him so familiarly. Wearing an old woman's hemorrhoid medicine on his face.

She was rubbing a second layer into him when Sergeant Mazzarella walked in from the parking lot. His jacket was unzipped, and his belly draped over his waist. "Sergeant Mazzarella!" Lorna said happily. "Have some coffee cake. It's a new recipe. You'll be my guinea pig."

Mazzarella looked to Mercer, then Toronto. Mercer could tell he wanted one of them to take the first bullet.


*Shut up and die like an aviator.* That's exactly what he's doing. He can't talk, and he's crashing and burning in front of everyone.

Easier this way. Better to fall apart completely than to let people see you struggle and fail.

Around the back of the room, in the shadows against the dark wood-paneled walls of the meeting hall, he can see Chief McCandless, Detective Funkhouser, Sergeant Mazzarella, and a few of the day-shifters. They're all waiting for him, too, and they must be wondering what the hell is wrong with him that he can't answer a simple question. It *was* a simple question—that much he remembers. He looks around at the dark wood walls and the velvety red carpet. The great chamber of Colma City Hall looks like the inside of a coffin. Is that accidental? Or did the decorator have a dark sense of humor? But that's not what he should be thinking about. He needs to remember the question. Now.

Then he spots Toronto and Cambi and Benzinger, standing together in the far corner. Cambi is flipping him the bird with both hands, waving them around like he's shaking a pair of maracas to a mambo beat, and Toronto has his tongue out of his mouth, lapping zealously through the crotch of two extended fingers. Benzinger swats Toronto in the back of the head with an open palm, and Mercer feels the corner of his mouth curl into a smile. It calms him, their sophomoric fucking-around, and he feels himself unlock. He stifles a laugh, then leans in toward the microphone.

People cringe at the amplified collision when he bumps his front teeth on the mike. Someone laughs, but that doesn't feel as bad as he thought it would. "Can you repeat the question?" he says. He enjoys how his voice sounds through the PA: a resonant baritone, fattened with reverb.

The reporter, a jowly woman with hair a painful shade of magenta, obliges. "I asked you to spell your name for us."

"Oh," Mercer says. "It's Mary-Edward-Robert-Charles-Edward-Robert."

"That's, like, six names," someone says.

"His name's Mary?" someone else says.

He reads the statement that he drafted with Toronto and Funkhouser, laying out the facts of the assault in the cemetery: when and where it took place; the condition in which Jude was found; the description and tags of the SUV, in case anyone saw it that night. No suspects at present. He gives the number of the tip line and emphasizes how much the family would appreciate any information at all.

A redhead in the third row catches his eye. *No,* he tells himself. *Focus.*

A hand goes up. "Do you have any details on the boy's condition?"

"He's recovering well. He'll be back in school soon."

"And he doesn't know who did it?"

"He doesn't have a clear memory of the incident. He may or may not have known the assailants."

"Was there anything in the SUV?"

"Some evidence was retrieved from the vehicle, yes. It's still being evaluated." Which isn't exactly true. They got a few usable latents, but no matches in the database.

"Officer Mercer," a young Asian woman says. She has collagen-puffed lips and a trapezoidal hairdo. Mercer recognizes her from a local entertainment show that he has come across while channel-surfing in the afternoon. "Did this have to anything to do with Marco DiMaio?" she asks.

"We really don't know."

"Is it possible this was payback for his Mafia film?" she asks, and there are snickers around the room. One of the laughs sounds like Toronto's.

"That's not an angle we're pursuing actively," Mercer says, keeping his face straight.

"Any other thoughts as to motive?" the redhead in the third row asks. Her voice is a whiskey-scratched contralto. Mercer likes it. He can feel the blood rushing to his groin.

"We're looking at all the possibilities," he manages. "We do think robbery is unlikely."

"Hazing, maybe?"

"We haven't ruled it out. And as I said, the family is urging anyone who might have seen the victim or the vehicle on the night in question to call our information line as soon as possible. They're obviously very upset, and they would like to see the assailants in custody." He gives the number again and thanks them all for helping to get the word out.

As the room is clearing, the redhead approaches him at the podium. *White female, 26 to 28.* Her skin is tanned, and her hair is back in a loose ponytail. She's dressed more stylishly than the others: black slacks, a pink blouse that's snug at the chest. He reminds himself not to stare.

She thrusts out her hand. "Officer Mercer," she says. "Kelly Chaleski. I'm a writer. I'm doing a feature piece on Marco DiMaio for *Limn* magazine."

"*Limb?*" he says. "Like trees?"

"*Limn,*" she says. "Let's see. Lemon, Igloo, Murphy bed, Nectar."

"'Murphy bed' is two words."

"I'm new at cop-spelling."

"I guess you could hyphenate," Mercer says. He calls across the room to Toronto. "Nick, can you hyphenate 'Murphy bed'?"

"If you're illiterate," Toronto says.

She smiles. Mercer feels confident and quick. Getting through the press conference has given him a little swagger. "So, *Limn,*" he says. "It's a magazine?"

"Culture, ideas, criticism. I'll have them send you a copy."

"Sure. I'd like to see it."

"I was down in Belize with the DiMaios when they got the news. I asked if I could mention it in the article, and he agreed. You can check with him, if you like. I don't yet know how it fits in, or if I'll end up using it at all, but it could be interesting to show him responding. A different angle on him. As father, instead of filmmaker."

Mercer nods. He's looking at her nose, which is perfectly symmetrical, not too big or too small. He wonders if it's natural.

"I know you're the one who's had the most contact with Jude," she goes on. "Would you have some time to talk more about the case? Maybe take me out and show me where it happened?"

"I'm happy to talk. You'll need to talk to the sergeant about a ride-along. That's him right there." He points to Mazzarella, who is sipping coffee from a Styrofoam cup and talking to one of the city councilwomen. He's not showing any ill effects from Lorna's coffee cake yet. It's still early, though.

"Is it a big deal?" she asks.

"Not really. He'll make you sign a waiver."

She shrugs. "I'm not scared."

"You haven't met the guys I work with," Mercer says.


Tuesday. The 6:00 briefing.

"Gentlemen and lady," Mazzarella says to them, "as you may know, Officer Mercer has a rider tonight, so let's have some good behavior for a change."

Cambi whistles, and Toronto leans over to slap Mercer on the back. Mercer does his best to remain poised. Truth is, he has butterflies again, and bad. He keeps his hands in his lap because he's afraid they'll shake. What if Kelly finds out who he really is?

"The rider's name is, what, Mercer?" Mazzarella asks.

"Kelly Chaleski. She writes for a magazine."

"A redheaded Polack," Cambi says. "There's got to be a joke in there somewhere."

"You're not the man to find it," Benzinger says.

"What does that mean?"

"She means you couldn't locate your own ass if you were naked in the Hall of Mirrors," Toronto says. Even the sergeant laughs at that one.

Officer Landau, back in his civilian clothes, stands in the doorway, listening. He scratches the top of his bald head. "I can't believe Boy Thirteen's going to get laid out of this," he says, wrinkling his face in disbelief.

"I'm not getting laid," Mercer says. "I'm getting interviewed."

"She's hot," Landau says. "Work it, Mercer."

"Act your age, Dick," Benzinger tells him. "Get some support hose and move to Palm Springs."

"What? Don't you think the girl's hot?" Landau asks her.

"Not my type," Benzinger says. "But I can see why boys would like her. Dirty old men, too."

"She's got a nice rack," Cambi says.

"All right, people," Mazzarella says. "Let's focus here."

"Dick's right," Toronto says, ignoring him. "You'd better work it, Mercer. Or maybe I'll move in on you."

"I thought you were engaged," Benzinger says.

"It's been less than a week. There has to be a law that says you have a grace week to screw around. Especially if it means swiping a hot chick from Boy Thirteen."

"It's our duty, if you think about it," Cambi says. "To rescue her from him."

"I have some concerns about tonight, Sergeant," Toronto says. "What if I need backup and Mercer's off somewhere getting a hummer?"

Benzinger jumps in. "What if I need backup and you're off giving one?"

Mazzarella claps his hands sharply. "Enough. I have an eighth-grader at home. I don't need more of them here. Mercer, you know the drill. Rider stays in the vehicle until you confirm that the situation is secure."

"Check," Mercer says.

"Because the last thing I need is a dead citizen on my hands," Mazzarella says.

Everyone around the table groans. Toronto looks at his watch. "Six-fourteen," he says. "Benzinger, you're closest." He, Cambi, and Mercer all take out their wallets and toss dollar bills to her.

"What, there's a pool now?" Mazzarella says.

"You held out longer than usual, Sarge," Benzinger says, scooping up the money.

"Joke all you want," he tells them. "Just be safe out there."

Kelly arrives at the station on time at 6:30, when all the officers are leaving to go out on patrol. Mercer meets her at the front desk. She's wearing a fringed, dark-brown suede jacket over a tight black baby-doll T-shirt. There's glittery silver lettering across the chest—again, he doesn't want to stare, but it looks like it says BUTTERY.

Mazzarella has left the safety of the sergeants' office to put on a show for her. "All right, men," he says, as they're all gathered by the door.

Benzinger coughs loudly.

"And Officer Benzinger," he adds sheepishly. "Let's get home in one piece."

Mercer and Kelly walk together through the lot. The Crown Vics are lined up, clean and gleaming in the overhead light. Mercer opens up the door for her.

"Thanks for agreeing to this," she says, getting in.

"It'll be fun," Mercer says. "You're my first rider. Are you going to be warm enough?"

"I'm pretty tough."

"All right," he says. "Hang on just a sec." He closes her door and crosses to the other side of the lot, where Toronto, Cambi, and Benzinger are still talking.

Toronto pinches a dip out of his tin and loads up. "Be good tonight, Boy Thirteen," he says. "We'll have our eyes on you."

"Seriously," Cambi says. "That rack. Perfect. Just a handful, you know? Nothing wasted."

Toronto spits. "Make sure you tell her I'm a hero, too."

"I mean, she's a *weapon*," Cambi says. "Suspects won't be able to run. They'll trip over their hard-ons."

"Don't push it, Arthur," Benzinger says.

"Benz, why can't *you* be hotter?" Cambi asks her.

"I'll get hotter when you get smarter."

"See you," Mercer says, turning away. "I have a job to do." He takes deep breaths as he walks. *No ghosts,* he tells himself. *No ghosts and no voices. Not tonight. Tonight is for confidence. Confidence,* he whispers, and then he opens the door and gets behind the wheel.

Whoever gets the vehicle in the morning is going to flip him shit, because the interior already smells like Kelly's perfume—floral and woody. The scent seems familiar, actually. Maybe someone he dated wore it. Or a one-nighter, someone in and out of his life so quickly that all she left was a vague sense memory.

**M**ercer drives her slowly through Cypress Lawn. She reads off names that she recognizes: Steffens. Niebaum. Coit. DeYoung. Spreckels. Hearst. He avoids the children's section. There are no ghosts, and there are no voices in his head. There are no ghosts. There are no voices. There is only this car, this girl, him.

They turn around in one of the loops and head back down the hill, just as he and Toronto did the night they found Jude. "This is right about where we were when I first heard him," he says. He's happy to have a story to tell. It keeps his mind occupied.

"Was he calling out?"

"It was pretty soft. We almost missed it."

They get out of the car. He shows her where Jude's SUV was parked, then leads her across to the tower. When they get close, she stops. Her gaze travels up, following the knotted vines to the bushy green on top. "That is too weird," she says. "Creepy."

At the gate, he shines the light into the grotto: bottom level, top level, the clearing where the assailants—and probably Jude, too—were drinking and smoking. He spotlights the chamber in the far corner and recites the details for her: the duct tape, the vomit, the seizure. He leaves out the part where Jude kicks him in the head.

"Kids come here a lot?" she asks.

"Not a lot," he says. "Now and then. Party, make out, you know."

"Cemetery sex," she says. "It's great."

"Huh," he says.

"I grew up outside New York City. Babe Ruth is buried the next town over from us. And my high-school boyfriend was a *big* Yankee fan."

Mercer doesn't respond. He's pretty sure that going by The Book does not involve talking with a citizen about where one does or does not have sex.

"You're missing out," she says. "Don't worry. I won't write about how you're a cemetery virgin. I'm on a tight word count."

The next couple of hours bring them little action. Just one traffic stop, an older guy in a pickup who tried to beat the light at Serramonte and Hillside and failed. To Mercer's surprise, he's relaxing around Kelly, and the conversation is unforced, flowing easily. She traces her history for him: parents who both wrote for the *New York Times,* four years at Sarah Lawrence, a move to San Francisco to cover the boom, and then she found herself covering the bust instead. She's only twenty-five. Mercer tells her how he became a cop, and she slaps him on the arm, which startles him. "Get out," she says. "A mime? You're kidding."

"Serious," he says. "I got to meet him at a lunch, actually. Nice guy, but people thought he was too weird. He kind of got forced out. He tours grade schools now. You know, teaching kids how to cross the street and whatnot."

They're driving northbound on Hillside, and Mercer is trailing a red Acura. He runs the plates, just for the hell of it. They come back clean.

"So what do *you* think happened to Jude?" Kelly asks. "Was it hazing?"

"Something like that. I just can't believe he'd be dumb enough to cover for them."

"You saw him at Seven Oaks, right? What's his drug of choice?"

"I couldn't comment on something like that," he tells her. "Even if I knew."

There's silence in the car.

"Which I don't," Mercer says to fill the space. "He seems like a good kid to me. Lost, maybe."

"Most kids his age are lost. I was. Weren't you?"

"I don't know if we ever get found."

"Ooh," she says. "Philosopher Cop."

They ride through the lettered streets, pass the entrance to the Italian Cemetery, then go back down to Hillside, southbound.

"So," Kelly says. "What's next? How are you going to find who did it?"

"We have a couple of first names to go on. We may get some leads from going public. And an old friend of his, this kid Wilson, offered to come down and talk to us."

Mercer reaches back for the two-liter bottle of cola he keeps in the car, unscrews the cap with his free hand, and glugs down a few mouthfuls, feels the sugar make one of his back teeth howl. "Energy," he explains. He takes another swig before capping the bottle and tucking it back behind the seat.

Toronto's voice comes over the radio: Woodlawn Cemetery, Section F. Code 10-69X. Cambi responds, saying he's on his way. Benzinger says she'll let them handle it themselves.

"What's 10-69X?" Kelly asks.

"Hang on," Mercer says. He has the radio raised to his mouth, about to decline the call, when he looks over and sees her smiling eagerly. He changes his mind. "Thirty-three Boy Thirteen," he says. "We're on our way."

He guns the Vic and they shoot off. They fly down Serramonte, turn hard onto El Camino, and she's bracing herself with one hand on the door but still has that smile on her face and her eyes get wider as he hits sixty-five, seventy, then veers left into the Woodlawn driveway. He has to admit it: the Vic is one sweet vehicle.

He takes the passage through the gates faster than he should, probably, then hits the steep bank of the hill. The Vic's suspension is incredible; it eats up bumps and spits them out. He slows as they ascend, and he curls off onto a rightward loop, the headlights sweeping over the jagged bases of the smashed-up Snow-White-and-Seven-Dwarves figures that mark the boundary of yet another children's section. Three bends in the path later, they come upon the other two cruisers, both with their ambers on. Toronto and Cambi are standing on the grass fifty yards out, waving them forward. They're halfway to an eight-foot hedge of yews that boxes in a gravesite about ten yards square.

"Come on," Mercer tells Kelly.

"Shouldn't I wait?"

"Why?"

"Until you know it's safe?"

"No time. Come on. Be quiet, and keep your eyes open." He's not going by The Book, this is totally not going by The Book, but he's having too much fun. He's so attracted to this girl that it hurts. He hasn't felt like this in ten years.

Toronto's motioning for them to hurry up but to keep low. Mercer runs in a crouch, looks over his shoulder and sees she's doing the same. The fringes on her jacket flap softly as she follows him between the stones. She runs with her arms out, wrists cocked.

*No ghosts,* Mercer thinks. *No ghosts, no voices.*

The four of them meet, and Toronto makes the *ssh* sign, then points to the opening in the hedge. *The subject's in there.* They douse their lights and creep quietly toward it, single file, Toronto in the lead, Kelly last. At the hedge, Toronto motions *stop.* He points to Cambi, and the two of them slip in through the gap in the hedges, one on each side. Mercer waits for them to get in place, then waves Kelly forward. He leads her in to the center of the plot, where a huge glass case sits on a stone pedestal. A black shape hulks inside it.

Toronto shouts "Go!" and the three flashlight beams light up fierce yellow eyes and sharp white teeth in a gaping, snarling mouth. A terrible creature, lunging toward them, pouncing. Kelly screams and flings her arms around Mercer's chest. Toronto and Cambi burst out laughing. Mercer would laugh, too, but there's the matter of her arms around him. It's a moment he wants to focus on enjoying.

Cambi stops laughing long enough to mimic Kelly's shriek—high-pitched and hoarse—and cracks himself up all over again.

Kelly steps back, her weight on one leg, arms akimbo. "Okay," she says. "What the *fuck* is a panther doing here?"

"It's Myron Osterman's," Toronto says.

"Who's he?"

Toronto shrugs. "Some rich guy. Amateur taxidermist. Wanted to show off his work."

"Don't be embarrassed," Mercer says. "They did this to me last year. All the rookies get it."

"He screamed like a girl, too," Cambi says.

"I did not," Mercer says.

"Deny it all you want," Toronto says. "We've got witnesses we can call."

Cambi is in the middle of a story about a trainee who drew his weapon on the panther when Mazzarella calls over the radio, clears his throat, and suggests that there's only so long you can milk a 10-69X.

Back in the car, Mercer turns to Kelly. "Got to be serious for a minute. If anything goes down tonight, don't grab me. Duck, jump out of the way, take cover behind something, but don't grab me. I need to be free to react, okay?"

"Ten-four," she says. "Hands off."

Which is really too bad. But, The Book. He can't keep ignoring it.

He checks his watch. A little after eleven. "I'm supposed to bring you in now," he says. "You're only scheduled for four hours."

"I can't stay out longer?"

"You want to?" he asks.

"Damn straight," she says. "This is fun."

"All right. Off the record, I think we only have the four-hour rule so we can get rid of riders we don't like."

"So I pass the test?"

"Flying colors," Mercer says.


0200 hours. Eastbound on C Street. They're cruising up the hill when Mercer spots a woman in a white bathrobe walking on the sidewalk without shoes, her back to them. The untied sash trails behind her, and the robe hangs wide open, swinging as she walks. Her gray-black hair hangs nearly to her waist. Her legs are plump and bare.

"Is she—" Kelly asks.

"Yeah," Mercer says. "She is." He has encountered Cecilia Rao on her night walks before. She never has anything on under the robe. She is weaving—not in a drunken way, but smoothly, dreamily.

"Thirty-three Boy Thirteen," Mercer radios. "Eastbound on C. Mrs. Rao is out again. I'm making contact." He drives ahead slowly and pulls even with her. He doesn't light her up. She turns her head to look at them, then turns back. She keeps walking.

"Hi, Mrs. Rao," he says across Kelly, through the open window. "It's Officer Mercer."

"Hello," she says. "It's a beautiful night, isn't it?"

"Yes it is, ma'am. Can you stop walking, please? Can you stand still for me?"

"How can I stand still," she says, "when the world is spinning so perfectly? When my skin is tingling with love?"

"It's cold out, Mrs. Rao. You should have clothes on. Can you stop walking, please?"

Finally she stops, standing in a spill of bleaching streetlight. Mercer throws the cruiser into PARK and gets out. He pops the trunk and gets out the emergency blanket, the same one he used to cover Jude.

"I'm alive," she says, twirling in the streetlight, arms outstretched. "Tonight I'm alive."

"You'll catch cold, ma'am. It's not a good way to stay alive."

"Don't you worry about me, Officer. I'm just celebrating."

"It's my job to worry about you, ma'am. I know you're celebrating, but I need for you to celebrate in your own house if this is all you're going to wear. You'll be a lot warmer." He approaches her with the blanket, and she lets him drape it over her, as if she's a movie star and he's her costumer. He pulls the blanket closed and guides her hand so she can hold it in place herself. "I'm alive," she says. She tries to spin again, but Mercer holds her still.

"I'm going to take you home," he says. "Are you ready to walk back to the car with me? You can sit in the back seat, and I'll drive you home."

She hums as they walk to the cruiser together. Mercer opens the back door and eases her in. "There you go, ma'am. Are you comfortable?"

"Oh, yes," she says. "Thank you."

Mercer takes his place behind the wheel. "Mrs. Rao, this is Kelly," he says. "She's riding along with us tonight."

"Hello," Kelly says.

"Hello," Mrs. Rao says. "It's a beautiful night, isn't it? There's so much love in it. Everywhere. Can't you sense it? That's why I'm celebrating." She leans forward and whispers, "I've had a sexual event."

Kelly looks to Mercer, at a loss.

"That's nice, Mrs. Rao," Mercer says. "But you need to celebrate inside. I can take you home again tonight, but you can't keep doing this. It's not safe for you. You understand that, right?"

She sinks back into the seat, folds her arms over her belly.

"I don't want to ruin your night, Mrs. Rao. I'm glad you're happy. But I just want you to be safe, and that means not walking around without clothes on."

"I know," she says, with sadness in her voice now. "I know."

"I need you to understand something, ma'am. When we see you outside like this, it makes us wonder if you can take care of yourself. If it keeps happening, we're going to have to take you to a hospital for a seventy-two-hour hold. You know what a seventy-two-hour hold is, right?"

"I'm not stupid," she says. "And I'm not insane. I'm just happy. I was, anyway."

"I just want to make sure you understand."

He takes her to her house on A Street and walks her up to the front door, which, fortunately, she has left unlocked. She shakes herself out of the blanket, pulls her robe closed, and steps inside.

"Thanks for cooperating, Mrs. Rao," he says. "You take care, now."

"What was that all about?" Kelly asks him, back in the car. "A sexual event?"

Mercer shrugs. "We don't know. She lives alone, and there's never anyone else in the house. Every now and then, she goes out for walks like this. Could be a kind of sleepwalking. Could be early dementia. She's a good friend of the mayor's wife, so he's just asked us to take care of her when it happens. All we can do is send an officer to talk to her tomorrow, maybe talk to the mayor and his wife, try to convince them that it's a problem that needs to be addressed. It's sad. She's a nice lady. She sends us thank-you notes."

"You were kind to her," she says.

"It's my job," he says. He's glad the car is dark so she can't see him blushing.


As 0300 approaches, their conversation slows, and Kelly rides with her head leaning against the window glass, slumped in her seat. Her yawns are contagious, and Mercer grabs the soda bottle and drains it, needing the sugar push. The streets are quiet, have been for hours, and he takes her back to the station.

They're standing outside the cruiser in the parking lot when Toronto and Cambi pull in. Mazzarella steps out of the station and joins them all. This is not the good-bye Mercer was hoping for. She gives him her business card from the magazine, and they agree to talk again as the DiMaio case develops. He hopes it'll develop soon.

"Good night!" Mazzarella says, pumping her hand. "It was great to meet you!" he calls as she walks to her car. "I hope you got everything you need! I hope Toronto wasn't too much of a jerk! He usually is! Call us if we can help any more!"

"Jesus, Sarge, keep it in your pants," Toronto says, under his breath.

"Besides, you've got competition," Cambi says. "Boy Thirteen's hot for her, too."

Mazzarella scratches his head, looking uncomfortable. "I was just doing some PR," he says. "Mercer, how'd it go?"

"Great," Mercer says. "She's great."

"Smoking hot," Cambi says. He packs a dip into his mouth, then tosses the tin to Toronto, who does the same. "You talk about the rest of us?"

"A lot. Nothing complimentary."

"What's going on with you and your nurse?" Toronto asks.

"She's not talking to me," Mercer says. "It's over, I think."

Toronto spits, wipes his chin. "Your rider's unattached. Dating, but unattached."

"How do you know?"

"I asked her when we stopped for coffee," he says. "I knew you wouldn't have the sack to do it yourself."

"Thanks, Nick," Mercer says. For once, he's not saying those words sarcastically.

"Yeah," Toronto muses. "She's buttery, all right."

◉

# TWELVE

# THE UGLIEST GODDAMN FISH IN THE WORLD

Three messages are on Mercer's machine when he gets home the next morning.

7:30 P.M.: *Hola, Miguel. It's Owen. Haven't heard from you in a while. Saw you on the news. Who did your makeup? You looked like the practice head at a beauty school. Huh? Say again? Okay, according to Mollie, that was rude and I should apologize. Anyway, I'm heading north to look at some land, so I'll miss Neptune this week. Give a shout when you can.*

7:52 P.M.: *Officer Mercer. Susan DiMaio calling. Jude's father and I just want to express our thanks for all your kindness and effort. We're having a get-together at the house Saturday evening, and we'd be delighted if you could join us. It'll be an interesting group. Feel free to bring a guest. Oh, and Marco would like to meet Officer Toronto, too, so please pass along the invitation.*

12:02 A.M.: *It's me. It's midnight. [Exhale.] We should talk. Can you meet me for lunch tomorrow? I hope so. [Sigh.] I've had some wine. I'm not sleeping very well. [Sigh.] I hope you are.*

He sips his wine as he listens, staring at a spot on the floor. Even though his mind is buzzing with thoughts of Kelly, he's exhausted. He feels seriously impaired. He just hit a concrete support pole down in the garage while maneuvering the Olds into a narrow space. It left a deep gray gouge along both passenger doors.

He could call her now, and there's a part of him that feels obliged to. The other part of him is too tired to speak, let alone to confront any of the bad feelings from the other night. This is the part that wins. He drops himself into bed and, instead of staring at the shapes on the ceiling as he waits for sleep, he thinks about Kelly, hears her throaty laugh, sees her red hair lit in the moonlight, feels her arms around his chest.

Fiona calls him at noon. He jumps out of bed when the phone rings, crazy-alert. It takes him a few rings to find the phone, which is on the couch, under yesterday's Sports section. "I meant to call," he tells her.

"You always do," she says.

"I fell asleep."

"Don't worry about it. It's all right."

"I haven't been sleeping much, either. I'm getting a little weird."

"Getting?"

"Ha," he says, and she laughs. It's a nervous laugh, but it makes him feel more at ease. Just the thought of more conflict with her has been knotting his insides.

"So," she says. "Lunch?"

He squints at the clock in his kitchen. "Give me half an hour."

They meet at Huber's, a hofbrau in Daly City, because she's craving comfort food. Huber's is right across the street from Death's Door—which, Mercer thinks as he approaches, is probably not a phrase the restaurant would want to use in their advertising.

Fiona is already there, sitting at a dark-wood table in the dim light. Dense, proteiny aromas fill the wood-paneled room, and a poster on the wall announces that Huber's is celebrating the Festival of Meats for the entire month of January. He sits across from her, and there's an awkward moment before they both decide to stand and hug. She looks as tired as she sounded over the phone, with dark and heavy-looking eyes. She's wearing lipstick, which is unusual; it's bright pink, and it makes her look like a different person to him.

They're both fine, they inform each other. Tired and stressed out, but getting by. They miss each other. Moss Beach was a disappointment, and neither of them was at their best. She says, "I saw you on the news. You did well."

"Thanks. I was nervous."

"You looked pale. And your face was shiny."

"Bright lights," he says. "Plus makeup and stuff."

They're interrupted by their waitress, a big-boned Teutonic grandmother in a blue dirndl. She takes their drink orders and tromps off to fill them. The restaurant is about half full, mostly blue-collar men on lunch break. Plates clatter and glasses clink; jokes are told, their punch lines swallowed by laughter; meat glistens, and starchy side-orders congeal as they lose heat to the room. Fiona is about to say something, but the waitress shows up with their drinks—iced tea in a quart-sized cup for her, a frosted mug of beer for him—and Fiona stops herself, waiting for the woman to go away.

Mercer sips his beer. It tastes good, even though this is breakfast time for him. His plan is to lay the foundation for another nap, "You were going to say something," he says. He senses that she wants another apology from him, but he's not sure what it would be for.

She shrugs. "I forget," she says.

They sip their drinks. They're the only two people in the place not talking. Something has happened to them, Mercer thinks; something fundamental between them has shifted. To fill the silence, he tells her more about the DiMaio investigation; he knows he's rambling, but he's afraid to stop. She watches him closely, in a way that looks full of effort, as if he's speaking in a language that she's just learning. "We're pretty sure he knows who it was, and he's covering for them," he concludes. "It's surprising. He doesn't seem like that kind of kid."

"Haven't you ever done that?" she asks. "Hung out with people who aren't good for you?"

"Not really. I've had the same friends since grade school. Owen and those guys."

"You're lucky," she says. She looks at her watch. "Shall we?"

They get up to fill their plates along the buffet line. Mercer loads up on ham and potatoes and knockwurst. And carrots, too. Night vision. He passes on the sauerkraut because it smells too much like his apartment.

Back at their table, Fiona says, "I'm going to visit my cousin this weekend. I'm leaving tomorrow afternoon. Taking Friday off."

"Weren't you just there?" Mercer asks. Every time Fiona goes to Reno to visit her cousin Perri, she comes back feeling miserable. Perri is about fifty and has some kind of personality disorder. Mercer can't remember what the disorder is called, but it might as well be a diagnosis for *being a mean person who is particularly cruel to people who try to help her*. According to Fiona, it's gotten much worse in the last few years, since her husband left her for a Vegas cocktail waitress. Mercer doesn't know what Perri says that gets so deeply under Fiona's skin, but it has to be bad to rattle her like that.

"It's been three months," Fiona says. "I don't have much family left."

"Just be be careful," he tells her.

"Be careful? What's that supposed to mean?"

"She makes you cry. She doesn't appreciate you."

"It's not about appreciation, Mike. The way I was raised, you don't keep family at arm's length. You embrace them. Even if it hurts."

Mercer shovels up some potatoes. "My family doesn't work that way," he says.

"I know. You just cut each other loose." She stares at him for an uncomfortable moment. "It scares me," she says, "that you'll do for strangers what you won't do for people you love."

He drops his fork onto his plate. The noise it makes is louder than he intended, but still, he's angry. "Go ahead," he says. "Tell me more about what I don't do."

"You're not trying to help your dad."

"Don't bring my dad into this."

"You don't even know where he is."

"*He* doesn't know where he is," Mercer says. "And he probably doesn't know where I am. So we're even."

"No one's keeping score, Mike."

"I am."

"See?" she says. "It's things like this that make me worry about being with you. When things go wrong, are you going to try to work them out, or are you going to use it as an excuse to cut and run?"

"I'm not like my dad." *I could stick around for someone,* he thinks. *It just might not be you.*

"Maybe you won't mean to run, and you'll do it anyway. Maybe that's how you're wired." She sets her fork on the table. "Remember what you told me about Minnesota?"

Minnesota. Early in the relationship; they had lain in bed together, a little drunk and postcoitally dreamy, and they'd taken turns revealing things they'd never told anyone else. When he was little, he confessed, eight years old at most, he decided that when he grew up, if he wasn't happy about the way his life was going, he would just leave it. He would move to Minnesota, live in a cabin in the remote woods, and feed himself with fish that he'd catch every day. Mercer still doesn't understand how he got the idea; he was a surburban kid from California, he didn't much like the woods or the cold, he wasn't interested in fishing, and he couldn't have found Minnesota on a map. He was so confident of his plan, though, and of its rightness, that he'd announced it to his parents over dinner. He'd believed it was an important thing for them to understand about the world.

It must have been a good plan, because his father stole it. A year later, Rudy Mercer came home early from work one day, took the Pinto, and disappeared. Three months later, Mercer got a postcard from his father. On the front: a color photo of the Hull-Rust mine of Hibbing, Minnesota. On the back: *Got a job here at the mine to make ends meet. You'll be happy to hear I'm doing a lot of fishing, just like we talked about. Caught a big nothern pike yesterday! They're ugly SOBs. Just like your old man. —Rudy.* It had taken him a moment to figure out who "Rudy" was.

He went to the encyclopedia in the school library the next day and looked up the northern pike. He thought it was the ugliest goddamned fish in the world, and his father could go on catching those ugly fish and mining his goddamned rust forever, for all he cared. Three weeks later, a heavy envelope from Hibbing arrived for Mercer. Inside was a souvenir packet of six little iron balls. They looked like the old musket ammunition that a costumed actor had shown them in school. Mercer took the balls out to the creek that ran behind their house and dropped them in, one by one. He liked the insignificant *bloop* sound they made when they hit the water. He liked watching them roll along the creekbed in the light current. He liked watching them go away.

"I was *eight*," Mercer says. "I was a kid. It doesn't matter now what I thought then."

"It shows how your mind works. You don't consider what other people need from you."

"My whole job is to consider what other people need from me," he says. "I do that forty-eight hours a week."

"But you don't do it for the people you love. You don't have the impulse. And that makes me worried."

"Well, don't let it," he says.

She pokes at the ice in her cup with her straw. "What are we doing? What's the point?"

This is his chance, he knows. To say, *there is no point*. To say, *let's end this*. But he can't bring himself to. Instead he says, "Why do we need to have a point?"

Her response stuns him. "Are we having kids or not?" she asks, a look of determination on her face. "I need to try now, if I'm going to try at all. I need an answer from you, so I can decide whether to look somewhere else or just give up on the idea of being a mother."

He pushes a piece of ham around his plate while he thinks. "You said you were okay with not having them."

"I did. But I've been thinking a lot about family, and I've seen the way you've connected with the DiMaio kid. You could do this, if you let yourself."

"So we're back to me being afraid."

"That's not what I meant. Not really."

"What are *you* afraid of?"

"I'm afraid that I've wasted my life so far. And that I'm in danger of wasting the rest of it." She looks down at her plate distastefully, then at her watch. "Speaking of which," she says. "I'm short on time." They finish the meal in silence, neither of them eating much.

He holds the door for her as they walk outside. Someone is tarring a roof nearby, and the air smells pungent and wrong. Their cars are parked in different directions, so they stand in front of the restaurant.

"I'm telling you," she says. "I used to be a catch. I don't think you understand."

"Come on," he says, because again, it's the best he can do.

"I'm older than you are," she says. "You need to deal with that sometime. Really *understand* it and put yourself in my shoes."

"I know," he says. "I know."

"So. I'm going up to Reno. We'll take a few days off. I'll think about what I want, you think about what you want, and we'll talk when I get back? Fair?"

He nods.

Later that afternoon, while lying on his couch, roused from a nap by a squalling baby next door, he realizes he forgot to tell her about the DiMaios' party. If she knew, she might want to pick another weekend to spend with her bitter old cousin.

The phone is on his nightstand. All he has to do is call her.

Toronto surveys the apartment. It looks a lot better—less cluttered, less chaotic—now that he's moved in. He brought hardly anything with him—he can transport his entire life in two boxes and a garment bag, and he's proud of it—and Mia finally realized how much she was overcrowding her life. The afternoon before she hit the road with the circus, they loaded all her extra stuff into his car and headed up to Haight Street. She sold clothes to Waste-land and Villains, CDs to Amoeba. She still had three big boxes of crap to do-nate to Goodwill. *See?* he said. *Don't you feel lighter?* She had blown the hair out of her face and nodded. *Don't worry,* he said. *You're not going to float away.*

He misses her already, but it's exciting to be in the apartment alone. He's letting go of his old life, embracing a new one. Open road ahead. It's a hell of a rush, all that possibility. "This is home now, buddy," he says to the Toronto in the mirror. "This is where the rest of your life begins." He's thirty-eight, getting the first bristles of gray at his temples and around the back of his head, and here he is, sitting on the floor in a dumpy underground apartment, and it's all just fine with him. It doesn't matter if most of the guys he knows have wives, kids, houses. This is where he wants to be. He and Mia can gut it out here for a year or two, save up some cash.

He's taking the opportunity to enjoy his first smoke of the day inside the apartment instead of out on the street, since Mia's not here to crab about it. He sits cross-legged on the mattress on the floor, wearing workout shorts and a tank top, his ceramic ashtray on the floor in front of him. He's looking at himself in a mirror that rests on the floor, leaning against the far wall of the bedroom. The mirror has been through several moves with him. It's a good one—four feet by five feet, heavy glass, real glass, not that shitty reflective metal. He enjoys this simple pleasure: to sit and smoke and talk to his reflec-tion. It's calming. *You're like a parakeet,* Mia said. He told her not to knock it; there's no problem he can't deal with by talking it through with himself.

Yes, the mirror is visible from the bed, and that can make for some nice views of Mia, but that's just an added bonus. A lot of the time he keeps it covered, draped with a piece of satiny blue cloth with a pattern like waves.

A printout of Mia's show schedule is on the bed next to him. By now, the circus has worked its way south through California: Santa Barbara, Claremont, Riverside, San Diego. He figures they're at this very moment on the way to Arizona for a run of shows in Phoenix and Tucson. He imagines her reclining across a seat on the touring bus, watching the dry landscape flash past, every now and then holding up her hand and looking at her engagement ring, watching the sun play off at different angles, and thinking of him. And at the same time, she'd be doing those isometric exercises, keeping her calves and thighs and glutes strong, even as she's traveling. She's compulsive about staying toned, and it shows.

He checks out his mirror self. It's amazing, really—he's an odd-looking guy, with his deep-set eyes and his big ears and his planet-sized Adam's apple, but he's always gotten amazing women. "And this one's the best of the bunch," he says to his reflection, gesturing with his cigarette for emphasis. He knows that she is because of the fight. It was their first big one, and it was a knockdown, drag-out, but it showed him that Mia can handle conflict, can fight and make up and let bad feelings go. She is wise beyond her years.

The fight came out of nowhere. It started two days after he gave her the ring. She'd been packing for the tour, and he'd been sitting there on the narrow counter of their tiny kitchen, watching her move, striding purposefully over the fake-wood floor, every movement balanced and purposeful. He thought of how much he'd enjoy watching her move ten, twenty, thirty, forty years from now. Which—like nearly everything in the last few days—got him to thinking about the wedding. "We should keep the wedding small," he said.

"Small's good," she said, without pausing. She unfolded a pair of jeans, snapped the wrinkles out with a *thwack,* then refolded them and laid them into her duffel bag.

"Just friends and family, right?" he said. "Well, family for me, anyway."

She paused as she was selecting socks from an open drawer. "I called my parents last night. Told them the news."

"That's great," he said. It was a pleasant surprise. He's always admired her independence, but never the ferocity with which she's clung to her estrangement from her parents. Family's important. Got to have some connection with your family, even if they drive you batshit. "How did it go?"

"Good enough. It's been a long time. So, a little weird."

"I'm glad you called," he said again. "You're getting *married*, babe. Your parents should be there."

"We'll see," she said. "Don't push."

"It's traditional. I'm a traditional guy."

"Whatever. It's not about you."

He thought she might be tearing up when she said this, so he hurried the talk along. "What about friends? For me, a bunch of people from work. Maybe ten. A few guys from college, plus some of the regulars at the Door. You want circus people?"

She nods. "Maybe ten. Ten sounds good."

"Who else?"

"Some girlfriends from high school," she said. "My friends here in the city. So maybe ten, fifteen more. Plus Mathias."

"I thought he was back in Denmark." He's never met Mathias, but he's heard a lot about him, and he's seen pictures: a skinny Danish guy with a head of fluffy brown hair, usually with his arm around her. He was her first friend in San Francisco, a grad student she'd served while bartending at the Hemlock. He showed her the city, gave her the sympathetic ear, ended up sleeping with her. Oldest move in The Book. Toronto had answered the phone once when Mathias called from overseas. He'd gone down on Mia while she was speaking to him, even though she kept swatting at him, as if she wanted him to stop. It was fun to watch her struggle to maintain.

"He is in Denmark. But he'll fly in for this."

"No, he won't."

"Of course he will. He's my friend."

"He won't come because we're not inviting him."

"What are you talking about?"

"You slept with him," Toronto said. "End of story."

"So what if I did?"

"So, no way. No exes at the wedding."

"He's not an ex."

"You fucked him."

"Those are totally separate things."

"I'm not inviting anyone I slept with."

"You can," she said.

"I don't *want* to," he said.

"You probably don't even know who half of them are."

"I know at least half," he said, trying to joke. "Look, there's a way to do things and a way not to do things. Having exes at the wedding is the latter. You can bet my parents didn't have any exes at their wedding."

"I don't care about your parents' wedding. Mathias is the closest friend I have."

"In Denmark."

"He's coming."

"He came," Toronto said. "I assume, anyway."

"Fuck off," she said.

The fight went on at least an hour, full of insults and tears, full of ultimatums, full of insinuations and attacks and accusations. A percussive hour of stamped feet and slapped tabletops and smacked walls. Finally, she spun around and threw her duffel bag at him. It missed, and her clothes scatted around the room. He did his best not to laugh; she'd missed so badly. He watched her breathing heavily, in and out, in and out, her face reddened to the color of a volcanic-ash sunset.

"What are you laughing at?" she said.

"I'm not laughing," he said.

"You're about to. So fuck you in advance."

"Come here," he said.

"No."

"Then I'll come to you." He walked toward her, his arms outstretched. "This is stupid. This isn't worth it. You're going away. Let's have a good night. Besides, you know you want me." He'd gotten her backed up to the wall, and he planted a kiss on her. It was pure Hollywood—old, sexist noir Hollywood—but that stuff *works.* Those guys understood smooth. They understood tough.

Sex. Intense, urgent, frantic sex. Her nails digging into him, her face contorted. Make-up sex with some leftover anger for fuel, and he'd taken her four, five different ways, and they'd both shouted when they came. And after that, he'd spent at least another half hour down on her, through orgasm after orgasm, until she pushed him away with such force that it hurt his neck, and as he rolled over onto his back, he said, "You don't need Mathias anymore. You've got me." And she'd been too spent to respond, had just lain still. She might have cried a little. But in the end, she'd slept tucked under his arm, her head against his chest.

First the friction, then the flame. Friction, flame. The metal wheel has grown hot, and the skin on her thumb is sending her crazy messages of pain, but Lillie Coit flicks the lighter again and again, again, watching each flame leap up from a tiny spark. Flick. Flick. Flick. When the gas runs out, she unwraps another lighter and flicks some more. Their crinkly red wrappers litter the wooden floor, and she still has three unused ones on the pew. Fire has always helped steady her nerves, and she is thankful that the little store— Zestmart, is it?—was so well-stocked. Flick.

Tonight, her nerves need steadying. She'd been taking a stroll at dusk— always a risk, with those horrible men out there, but one has to stroll sometimes, one can't just *hide away*—and she'd been having a not-unpleasant time clomping on the daisies with her big brown boots when she stopped to join a small crowd gathered around a group of little girls playing jump-rope games. She marveled at the girls' timing, at their lightness on their feet. As a child, she had avoided such pastimes; she was large and clumsy and terrified of setting herself up for ridicule. Flick. Flick. The girls' rhymes were morbid and bloody and dark—such an odd sight, these little things in neat Sunday dresses and hair ribbons, skipping rope and singing songs of drowning and dismemberment, nooses and bullets. Still, it was all quite harmless and enjoyable until one of the girls noticed her, and then they stopped dead in midverse. The jumper landed, the twirlers stopped twirling, the rope lay silent and limp on the packed dirt. Everyone in the crowd turned to face her.

"Hello, girls," she said, unable to think of anything else.

There was a painfully long silence before the girls holding the rope began to spin it again, slowly at first, then faster, and the rope slapped on the hard ground more loudly than before, each beat nearly violent in its crispness. Two girls leapt in and skipped with expert flair. To the eye, nothing would have seemed odd—except that not one of them was watching what she was doing.

They all stared straight at her, wide-eyed and vacant. The chant began, a dozen little-girl voices intoning as one:

*Over, under, sideways, down*
*A man in blue is coming to town*
*Mountain, valley, hill and dale*
*Old Doc Barker's on his trail*

*Fat man, skinny man, short man, tall*
*The blue man thinks he'll save us all*
*But Old Doc's knives go snicker-snack*
*Once you cross you can't go back.*

After the second verse, their postures softened, they turned their heads away, and they twirled and jumped like normal little girls again, singing a song of poisoned ice cream. The whispers started, and Lillie fled, needing solitude and fire. Her boots eventually carried her to this chapel. A safe, quiet place to think. Flick. Her toe taps against the kneeler, and the sound echoes through the room. Flick.

Her policeman is going to cross. She had wondered. Flick.

The last one—Featherman, was it? Futterston?—he had meant well, but he was no match for Barker. He was slow, weighed down with the sadness he carried. Those men had toyed with him, and since then they've only gotten bolder and crueler. Flick.

Is this Mercer up to the challenge? She is not sure. Flick. One thing she does know: the whispers have started, and all whispers reach Doc Barker before long. They'll be waiting for him. He might not even have a chance to prove himself. Flick. Flick.

If only she could warn him. Flick.

Flick.

Flick.

The sky is still dark when Jude wakes up. The glowing hands on his travel alarm clock point to 4:10. He feels wide awake, his brain rushing, his blood surging. It's strange to be so out of sync with the day, but it's also exciting to feel this much concentration, intensity, energy, and strength in himself. He had resisted when Dr. Hoff prescribed the antidepressants a few days ago. He was *so* wrong. He feels alert, confident, alive. He feels fucking *propelled.* If he keeps on feeling like he does now, even in the middle of the night, god-damn, there won't be anything he can't accomplish. How did his parents let him go so long without meds? He's been living his life slowly, sadly, spine-lessly, and altogether half-assedly. And they've watched him, stupidly. All that time, wasted. He wants to have it back—these last few years in particular.

He turns on his light and tries to read a book—*Turn of the Screw,* which is what his English class was reading before all this happened to him—but his brain is racing too fast. The book can't keep up with him. He puts it away, thinks about what to do next. He does a few sit-ups on the industrial gray carpet. He does some push-ups, which are harder; upper body's not his thing, never has been. He sits down at the little desk in this room and decides to write a letter to Reyna. He writes *Dear,* then stops because his hand won't be able to keep up. Plus he doesn't know her address. Waste of time. He'll talk to her when he gets out. He'll tell her straight-up how he feels about her, and she'll see the confidence in him. So. That can wait. It'll be better in person.

He wants to play his cello, but the soundproof music room is locked for the night. If he plays here, he'll wake everyone up. But fingering. He can work on his fingering silently. So he takes his grandmother's cello out of its case and sits down with it and lets his fingers stretch and crawl and leap up and down the neck, hearing the notes—all with perfect intonation—in his head. He starts with warm-up exercises, Brahms, then Beethoven, then Nirvana: "Where Did You Sleep Last Night?" from *Unplugged,* so simple and beautiful and raw and sinister. He hums the vocal line softly as he plays. And then it's back to the Bach Suites, working through the fingering on the Courante and Sarabande, focused on being quicker, more precise, and he pushes through the pieces, measure by measure, again and again, until he notices the room has bright-ened around him and the sun is flaming over the hills and his jaw is pleasantly sore after hours of clenching tight. It's a new day at Seven Oaks, a day full of possibility, a day he can do whatever he puts his mind to, a day he can be whatever he wants to be.

He gets a chance to try out this last idea in his AM group. Sondra the group leader has them go around in a circle talking about things they've done that were destructive or hurtful to others and their reasons why. When his turn comes, Jude decides to have some fun and imagine that he's Bobby. *I like to pressure my girlfriend to do things she doesn't want to do. I like to see how much she'll let me get away with. I want to keep her down so she'll have to stay with me. I like to pick on guys who are weaker than me. Survival of the goddamn fittest, right?* He gets caught up in his act, imagines that he must be feeling a little of what Bobby feels, the will without guilt, the power without any sense of consequences, and he's sure that he's playing the role convincingly until Rose raises her razor-scarred arm and says, *Sondra? How long do we have to listen to his bullshit?*

Later, Jude gets permission to call home. He expects to speak to his mother, but his dad answers the phone. He launches the same speech he was going to give her: that everything's changed now with the meds, he feels great, this was the problem all along, and he's ready to come home, he doesn't need to be here anymore, he can go back to school, get on with his life, start looking seriously at colleges, get ready to go with them to the film festival in Barcelona, which he's always—

"I hope you don't think you're going to Barcelona," his father says. "You've missed too much school already. And I'm not ready to trust you in a situation like that."

There's a hissed exchange on the other end—he thinks he hears his mom saying, *Are you crazy? Not now!*—and then his mother is on the line talking to him. "I'm glad you're feeling better," she says, "but you need to be patient. Make sure you get yourself straightened out. I know it's hard for you to be away. Try to make productive use of your time. You've been practicing, right?"

It's all he can do to keep from telling her to fuck off, that he'll practice when he wants to and *because* he wants to, because he *loves* playing—not so he can be *productive* and have a better performance tape to send out for college admissions.

"Wilson has called a few times," she tells him. "He asked me to tell you that you're in his thoughts."

"He doesn't care," Jude says. "He just pretends to care."

He can hear his mom's quick intake of breath. After a pause, she says, "I think you two have some things to work out."

"Whatever. Did anyone else call?"

"No. Are you expecting someone?"

"I guess not," he says.

By eleven, he feels the lack of sleep catching up with him. He's agitated and sweaty and his hands are shaking and there's a strange pressure around his eyes, but he's still fully revved. He stamps up the stairs to his room, then grabs his cello and speed-walks down the hall. He hears Rose's mean laughter from inside a room, so he leans in and says, "Rose? By the way? You're a colossal bitch." And he's off again before she can say anything, off to the music room, where he closes the door behind him and breathes in the still, chalky air. It tickles his sinuses, but he loves it. It's the smell of music and hard work and success.

He sits, tunes up—why don't they do something about how goddamned dry the air in this place is?—and sets the music in front of him, all of Bach's notes on their staves beneath a blackening cloud of Jude's penciled reminders and admonitions to himself. He starts with the Courante, thinking it'll be easy after all that practice with the fingering this last night, but it's not. He can't coordinate his two hands, and he's just hacking his way through the goddamn thing, and he can't even get through eight measures at quarter-speed without stumbling and fucking up and overall sucking, over and over and over on parts he thought he knew. It should be easier than this, he has *earned* a little ease, goddamnit, and every single mistake just makes him madder and madder and he keeps going back to the top, determined to try to play it through smoothly *just fucking once* but he can't, and every return to the top is a failure and every measure is a failure, even, somehow, the ones he doesn't manage to butcher, and he can hear the voice of his cello teacher, Monsieur Tellier, quietly suggesting that the suites might be beyond his ability right now. But he's good enough, he's got the abilities, he does, only it's just mistake after mistake after fucking mistake and finally he can't take it anymore and he screams *Motherfucker!* as loud as he can. There's no echo. His voice is sucked into the acoustic tile and deadened.

He stands up and whips the bow against the white wall, cracking it in half. One piece is in his hand, the other dangling from slack horsehair, and he's overwhelmed by a flood of emotion: he's the wonder boy, he's not supposed to behave like this, but he's also supposed to be able to do whatever he sets his mind to—they've been telling him that for sixteen years, and he's finally fucking started to believe it—and the cello suites shouldn't be an exception, but fucking A it feels really *really* good to break something. Great. It feels *great*. It does. He imagines his dad yelling when Jude shows him the broken bow, and before he really knows what he's doing, he dumps the cello onto the floor. The echoey sound it makes is pretty satisfying, and then he kicks it, and that feels pretty good too, only it hurts his foot, so this time—and he's sweating now, there's a buzzy hot ferocity in him, maybe the most intense thing he's ever felt, and it's scary in a way, but goddamn, he feels alive. His face burns, he hears a high-pitched buzz in his head, his vision is fuzzed and starry, he picks up the cello and swings it into the wall with all his weight behind it, BOOM once, BOOM twice, and he hears himself shouting mother*fuck*er mother*fuck*er and he hears wood cracking and strings going *sprang* and he keeps swinging and swinging and then he looks down and sees that all he's holding is the neck with strings hanging off like whip lashes.

He's ruined it. Destroyed it.

He looks at what used to be his grandmother's cello and realizes he has just fucked up worse than he has ever fucked up before, and there are going to be consequences. He feels like his grandfather has just died all over again, died from shame, from his grandson letting him down. He drops to the ground, knocking the chair on its side, and he is breathing heavily, gasping out strange animal noises, now suddenly crying, now retching, now sobbing and shouting, and now Clinton-Like-the-President is flinging open the door and looking down at him with wide eyes and saying *Jesus, kid. Jesus.* Jude has never felt so small or so ugly or so wrong.

The white sand is still warm from the afternoon sun, and Reyna carves trails in it with her bare feet, enjoying the feel of the fine grains against her soles, between her toes. She doesn't dig her feet in, because the sand underneath is cold; it's winter here, and even though the temperature must've hit seventy-five today, there's something delicate about the warmth, something insubstantial, it doesn't have the heavy crush of summer heat. She's sitting in a nylon-backed collapsible camping chair that Bobby stole out of the back of a VW bus full of college girls from Irvine. *If you take what you like, then you have what you like,* Bobby says, every time they swipe something good.

The college girls are gone now, with their chatters and shrieks and their coconut rum and their squeaky nylon athletic shorts, and the crescent-shaped beach is quiet. Apart from Reyna and Bobby, there's just a gray-haired hippie couple with twin ponytails and matching balloony Guatemalan knit pants, and a shark-eyed, greasy-looking Russian named Ilya who claims he winters here in Baja and runs drugs up to Alaska in the spring and summer but who seems like the kind of guy who's full of lies and boasts and bullshit. They've spaced themselves evenly around the wide swing of shore: the hippies at the north end, Reyna and Bobby at the south, Ilya in between. Bobby's over talking to Ilya right now, probably checking into whether the Russian is holding.

Thirty pesos for a night on the beach under one of the thatched huts. Thirty pesos for paradise. A full moon on the rise in the new dusk. A cold can of Azteca in her hand, and she's superdreamyhigh because she and Bobby just shared a ball of oily black hash that they picked up in Tijuana. A breeze that's stroking her scalp and keeping the bugs away too. A bird in the reeds behind the beach— at least, she thinks it's a bird—makes a funny gulping noise that makes the whole world absurdly alive. *Ga-gulmmm, ga-gulmmm, ga-gulmmm.*

They're on Playa Coyote, near a town called Mulegé. They're a long way from San Francisco, two full days on the road due south. Nobody's expecting her anywhere, because she told her housemates she was taking off for a couple of weeks, and she quit her waitressing job from a pay phone in Kettleman City. She learned early on that you'd better have fun while you're young, because she doesn't know a single adult who's happy. Not her dad, coming home late every night for a dinner of scotch and Ativan. Not her mom, erratic and bitter and fond of throwing things. As soon as she left home, they split up. They should've done it a long time before.

Reyna sips her beer, feels warmth prickling her skin down her arms, down her legs, around her ears. She may be just as fucked up as her mom, but at least she has the good sense to be fucked up on a warm beach, where the moon is ghosting through the black-orange sky and sandpipers are scooting across the wet sand and tiny ripply waves are lapping up on the shore. She's showing bare arms and legs to the dropping night and the thing in the reeds is going *ga-gulmmm* and she's just noticed the water a few yards out from the beach taking on a vague and shimmery green glow.

Thirty pesos for paradise.

Bobby drops into the sand next to her. He pulls a beer from the Styrofoam cooler they bought on the road and cracks it open. Melted ice runs in rivulets down the red can, and it's beautiful. The carbonated misty puff when he opens it, the sound of peeling aluminum as the pop-top opens, beautiful. She empties her beer with a too-big swig—*ga-gulmmm*—just so she can grab a fresh one and hear it all again.

"Shit, you must be on fire," he says.

She can't make any sense of this.

"Sunburn," he says. "You're totally burned."

She looks down at herself and sees even in the failing light how her arms and legs have reddened. As she notices, the heat prickles sharpen into pinches, and she's aware of too much heat coming off her body.

"You're so pale," he says. "Pale as milk."

"You're lucky," she says. Bobby's dark, has some Indian or Mexican in him. He doesn't know which.

"Does it hurt much?"

She shakes her head, slowly. The green in the water shimmers more brightly when she moves her head, so she does it again.

He presses his thumb into the skin of her thigh, and she watches as his thumbprint lingers in yellow for forever before the pink fills it back in. "It's going to. Should've covered up."

She holds up her hand. "Listen," she says. *Ga-gulmmm.*

He listens, nods, dismisses. Maybe he doesn't even know she was talking about the bird. "Ilya's got good shit," he says.

"He was staring at my tits before."

"I don't blame him," Bobby says. "I was, too."

"The water's glowing," she says. "It's green."

"Creatures," he says. "They glow. Like fireflies."

She thinks of a summer she spent with her aunt's family in Wisconsin, and of the hot nights she and her cousins spent running through a field with a glass jar, catching the glowing insects. "We called them lightning bugs," she says.

"Same thing."

"So these are bugs? Or fish?"

"I don't know. Not fish. Smaller than fish. Microscopic things."

"It hurts," she says. She's thoroughly pinked. She should've known. She burns so easily. Always has. "You don't think Jude died, do you?"

"No way," he says. "Don't worry so much."

They probably would've heard if he was dead. She checked the newspapers whenever they stopped on the drive down. But she can't be sure. "He's not as tough as you, Bobby," she says. Jude had nearly cried, telling them about his grandfather who'd died a few months before. Sure, he was just drunk and blabbering, but she felt bad for him, even as Bobby and Carlos and Trent were nearly laughing in his face.

*You guys ever think about death?* he'd asked them.

*Why?* Bobby said.

*I do. Since he died, I do a lot.*

*Poor baby,* Bobby said.

Reyna told him not to be such a dick. Carlos and Trent laughed some more. She couldn't see Jude's eyes in the dark, but she'd bet they held a puppy look of gratitude.

*So many shitty people in the world, and it's my grandfather who had to die.* Jude, saying this as if they would really listen to him, as if any of them might care.

*Old people are supposed to die,* Bobby said. *The sooner the better, usually.*

*They drive too fucking slow,* Carlos said.

*I have to take a leak,* Jude said, and he got up so quickly he almost fell. He steadied himself and waited for the guys to stop laughing. *I'm going to go piss on Death.* He shuffled out through the gate and into the cemetery, singing *piss on Death* over and over like it was the chorus of a song.

*So, you're his protector now?* Bobby said to her.

*Don't be an idiot, Bobby.*

*He looooves you.*

*No, he doesn't.*

*You know he does,* Bobby said. *You should kiss him. His head will fucking explode.*

Okay, so she did know it. There's something about looking a boy in the eye and seeing how much control you have over him, how much power he's *giving* you, and you feel sexy and strong and you have to play with it and see what happens, because it's his own fault, isn't it? If he's so weak that he gives you all his power? For a moment she'd thought it'd be fun to fuck him. Then she'd own him completely.

*Ga-gulmmm.*

The gulping bird brings her back to the beach. She sips her beer, then holds the cold can to her forehead, to her cheeks, to her neck. She holds it to her shoulder, then wipes cold condensation down the length of her arm. A mosquito whines in her ear but is carried off by the breeze.

The hippies at the other end of the beach are skinny-dipping. Slack skin and paunches. She doesn't want them in the water. The glowing things should be able to glow without hippies churning up all kinds of shit around them.

She has the vague sense that her skin is oozing fluid that will crisp when it dries. She might wake up in the morning covered in crust. She's pale as milk. It's her own goddamned fault. Bobby scrapes more hash into the pipe and takes a hit, passes it to her. She takes a hit, too, and things get better; the heat from her skin flies inward, into her lungs, and the green creatures in the water glow brighter as the sky drops black over them all.

"So, what, you miss him?" Bobby says.

"No."

"What, is he your new boyfriend?"

His hand is on her thigh, stroking. She pushes it away. "Shut up," she says.

He puts his hand back, higher up on her thigh, and his fingers worm their way through the leg of her cutoffs. "You want to fuck him?" He's touching her now, and she shivers inside her fried skin.

"Fuck you," she says, but what he's doing feels really, really good.

"You want to fuck me?" he says.

She nods. She does. "Just don't touch my burn," she says.

She loses track of the orgasms—she always comes when she's high—and afterward her head is humming. Just one low note, continuous and smooth. She sits up and watches the green glow in the water ripple and pulse, and it seems like maybe the humming is coming from the water. Maybe the green things in the sea have started humming to her.

Bobby's behind her, in the hut, and she can hear him rummaging through their bags. He finds what he's looking for and comes back, stands in front of her. He's put his shorts back on, and she can see the outline of his dick, still puffed-up, and a stain in the fabric where the tip is. It's funny, but it's sexy, too. *You were just inside me,* she thinks.

He's holding something out to her. It's his kit.

"I got some," he says. "From Ilya."

She doesn't want to shoot up. She'll chip every once in a while, but, tell the truth, it's not her thing. It scares her a little. She shakes her head no.

"Come on," he says.

"I don't want to."

"Why not?"

"I feel good. I like how the water looks."

"You'll feel even better."

"I want to keep feeling like I'm feeling now."

"Come on, let's fly," he sings. "Let's fly let's fly let's fly."

"What's with you?"

"I'm just saying, let's fly."

"I don't want to. You fly. Go ahead."

He opens the kit. "Fly fly fly," he says. The length of rubber falls to the sand.

"Fuck off," she says.

"Come on, little birdie," he says. "Fly," and maybe it's the way he says *little birdie* or maybe it's the glowing creatures humming *yes* to her, but soon they're cooking up over a Coleman that they stole from some Trustafarian campers near Rosarito, and in the flame light Bobby's face looks like the face of an angel, and when he ties her off she watches her vein rise up from nothing and it quivers with her pulse as the creatures hum and the bird *ga-gulmmms.* She holds her arm out to him and he takes it in his hands and she feels the needle punch through her burning skin, hears a whip-crack sound as he snaps the rubber halo off her arm.

"Love," she says, and she is flooded, she floods.

◎

# THIRTEEN

# HARD TEN ON THE HOP

At noon on the day of the DiMaios' party, Toronto leaves a message on Mercer's cell in a hangover-slowed voice, punctuated by deep exhales of smoke. He'll be late, he says, because he's going to haul his miserable ass up to Sacramento to see his sister's family, and he doesn't feel like rushing back. Mercer hits the delete key and curses. He doesn't want to go alone. These people have lives that are completely different from his, and he needs to know that someone has his back. Who can he invite? Not Kelly. He'll be nervous, and he doesn't want her to see him like that. He walks circles around his apartment until he comes up with the answer: Mollie. He's completely comfortable with her, and people love her the moment they meet her. He can't help but look better if he's with her, and that's important, because the DiMaios need to know that Jude's case is in the hands of someone capable.

Mollie says yes immediately. With Owen out of town, she was just going to settle in for an evening of me-time with a bottle of wine and a couple of DVDs. Why watch movies at home when she could have dinner with people who make them? She wants to catch up with him, too, and hear more about Fiona. There's not much to hear, he says, because things aren't going so well. "Then you need me to fix it," she says. "Or fix you, anyway. Did you even tell her about the party?"

"Not really."

"Oh, Mike," she says, "that's not good."

When he picks her up at the Seacliff house, she insists that they have a drink first. "We've got time, and Owen would be furious if he found out you came here and didn't get a cocktail." She mixes up two small glasses of rum and mango juice, and they sip their drinks while walking through the backyard together. She points out where everything will go for Owen's birthday party. Heat lamps here. Lighting rigs here, here, and here. The band, the dance floor, the bar, the food stations. Bocce in the side yard. Croquet along the far edge of the lawn, bounded by the fence. There are patchy spots in the lawn because the grass seed hasn't taken, so they're going to resod.

It's a foggy evening, and cool, but they're sheltered from the wind by the west-facing house. The cloud cover is low and thick, and fog pools in the ravine where the land falls away beyond their fence. Crows perched in trees above the ravine hack away in a darkening sky. Mercer hears a distant and comforting mechanical hum; he guesses it's a neighbor's hot tub. Once she finishes the tour, they sit at the redwood table on the patio. Her flame-streaked hair is down, and she's dressed smartly all in black—black slacks, black blouse, black boots, a black leather jacket with white stitching. Mollie, he realizes, is the most striking woman he knows; it's only because he's so comfortable with her that he rarely notices. "You look great," he says.

"Got to make the most of the opportunity," she says. "Maybe DiMaio will fall for me and make me a star."

"Better hurry. Fiona wants a role herself."

"You really should've told her about the party."

"I'm aware," Mercer says. "I don't want to talk about it now."

"Fair enough," she says. "I'll wait until you're liquored up. Speaking of, do you want another drink?"

"I'm fine," he says. "When's Owen getting back?"

"Tomorrow night," she says. "He and Heath are going to hike around up there in the afternoon."

So Owen and Kinnicutt went on a road trip without him. He's not surprised—when you're buying land to grow bud on, you don't invite a cop—but it still hurts. "So he's buying the land?" he asks.

"I don't know," she says. "Don't ask, don't tell."

Mercer nods. He's surprised she puts up with Owen's growing at all. The seizure laws are tough. The feds could take this house, the cars, everything. Owen doesn't need the money. He just likes being a lawbreaker and a connoisseur at the same time.

"Anyway, he's got a more important decision to make," she goes on.

Mercer wrinkles his brow, tries to think of what she could mean. She looks at him closely, her jaw set, her head tilted to the side. "He hasn't said anything to you? About us?"

Mercer shakes his head. "I haven't talked to him lately. I've been deep underground."

Her eyes narrow, just enough that squint lines form at their corners, then disappear when she relaxes. She runs both hands through her hair, leans back on her bench, and exhales deeply into the pinpoints of fog that are drifting around them. "It comes down to this," she says. "We've been together ten years. It's time to get married, and if he's not ready to commit, I'm willing to walk. And I won't marry him while he's growing. It's stupid, it's self-indulgent, and I don't want the risk."

"You're not supposed to tell me he's growing," Mercer says.

She smiles. "Turnips," she says. "He's growing turnips."

He's surprised. He's not used to seeing tension between them, other than the routine stuff, like who misplaced the car keys, who forgot to make dinner reservations, whose turn it is to clean the bathroom. "This is an ultimatum, then."

"We're not getting any younger. He didn't say anything to you?"

Mercer shakes his head. He feels shut out. A decision this important, Owen should be confiding in him.

"I'm surprised," she says.

Mercer shrugs, not wanting to admit to the injury. He sips from his glass, but all he gets is rum-tinged ice melt and a stringy piece of mango pulp.

"I just think it's time for him to decide if he wants to live a life or just a pose," she says. "The pose is getting old."

Mercer nods. He doesn't like when women try to change men into becoming people they aren't, but he understands her point. It's hard to think of Owen choosing to be more ordinary, though.

"Let's go," she says. "I want to start hobnobbing with the glitterati."

They walk up the steps to the house. At the back door, she stops him, pointing at his feet. "What's with the sneakers?" she says.

"I couldn't find my dress shoes."

"You only have one pair?"

Mercer shrugs.

"You can't go there wearing sneakers."

"They're black," he says. "No one will notice."

"This is why you need a girlfriend," she says. "Come on upstairs. You can borrow a pair of Owen's."

With Mollie in the passenger seat smelling like rose geranium and Owen's narrow black wingtips pinching his feet, Mercer pilots the Olds in from the Avenues along Geary, then Stanyan to Haight, past the hooded kids clustered in front of Chabela, Escape from New York, Villains Vault, then up around the curve of Buena Vista Park. He snags a lucky parking spot on the first pass.

"Thanks for coming," he says as they clomp down the hill together. He feels relaxed, lighter, somehow, than usual. Maybe it's being back in the city and away from Colma. Maybe it's that he's not anxious when he's around Mollie. Maybe both.

"Are you kidding?" Mollie says. "This is going to be fun."

The DiMaios' house is an immaculately restored Victorian. It looks newly painted: rich and flawless burgundy and white and gold. The house is set back from the street, with a straight path of stones leading to the front door through a California native garden.

A maid takes their coats and the gifts Mercer has brought, a bottle of wine and Kinnicutt's book—Kinnicutt's going to owe him big for this one. The maid ushers them through a set of French doors into a long and deep living room with shining blond polished floors. The room extends all the way to the back of the house, which is much larger than it looks from the street. There are fifteen to twenty people there, drinks in hand, chatting in small groups. Piano music tinkles from hidden speakers. Susan DiMaio, holding a glass of champagne, spots them from across the room and hurries toward them. Mercer introduces Mollie, who effortlessly says all the right things about the home being stunning and what a thrill it is to be there.

"Officer Mercer's been a big help to us," Susan says to Mollie. "But you probably know that already."

Mollie nods. "It's terrible, what happened to your son."

"You probably see worse, in your line of work," Susan says.

Mercer sees a look of confusion flash over Mollie's face, one that she quickly conceals, a trial attorney's practiced response to surprise. "I see a lot of things I'd rather not see," she says. "That doesn't make it easier to hear about kids getting hurt."

Susan looks close to tears, but she straightens, takes a deep breath, and collects herself. She looks strained, tired, and already a little red in the cheeks. "You have to meet Marco," she says. "Come with me."

She leads them across the room, pausing to give instructions to one of the young women carrying trays of hors d'oeuvres. While she's occupied, Mollie leans in and whispers, "My line of work? Did you tell her what I do?"

"No," he says. He's confused, too.

Following Susan, they approach a group of well-dressed, middle-aged people standing beneath a large and gilt-framed still life of winter vegetables and shotgunned game birds. Mercer has no trouble picking out Jude's father: the man to whom everyone else is listening. Like Jude, he's short and olive-skinned, with the same Roman nose and heavy eyebrows. Marco is much broader, sturdier, and his eyes are severe where Jude's are soft, like his mother's. The little hair he does have is black-going-gray and cut as short as Mercer's.

"Marco," Susan says, stilling his arm with a light hand. Jude's father cuts off midsentence and turns to them. "Honey, this is Michael Mercer. Officer Mercer."

"Marco," he says, extending his hand.

"Mike," Mercer says. They shake.

DiMaio hands his glass to another man and pulls Mercer into a sudden and surprising hug. He's wearing cologne. Sandalwood, maybe. "Thank you," he says. "I don't know how we'll ever be able to thank you. And don't say you're just doing your job. I don't care *why* you did it. I care *that* you did it." He addresses the guests around them. "This is the officer who saved my boy."

"And this is Mollie," Susan says. "His companion."

It's a funny choice of words, and Mercer and Mollie share a look with each other. Well, she is his companion tonight, he thinks; she is accompanying him.

"Your partner's coming too, right?" DiMaio says. "Officer Canada?"

"Toronto. Yes, sir, he's coming."

"There's no *sir* about it. Don't you call me *sir* ever again. You're not arresting me, you're an honored guest in my home."

"Sorry," Mercer says. "But yes, Officer Toronto's coming. He'll be late, but he'll be here."

"My wife says he's a pain in the ass," Marco says, and smiles are raised around the circle, along with glasses to lips, to conceal them.

"He's an excellent officer."

"But a pain in the ass."

Mercer shrugs. *Of course* Toronto's a pain in the ass, but you don't say something like that in front of a citizen, ever. No matter who.

DiMaio calls over one of the servers to get drinks for the two of them. "How about some wine?" he says. He points to a man in an aloha shirt across the room. "It's a cab franc. That guy made it."

While they're waiting for their drinks, Marco makes introductions around the circle. One man is a city supervisor; one is a local stage actor; a few others are in the film business. There's also the round next-door neighbor, an odd-looking woman in green-framed glasses who introduces herself so enthusiastically that she's a little frightening. There's an attorney, a youngish partner with a downtown firm, and he and Mollie quickly establish that they know some of the same people and spin off into a satellite conversation.

The neighbor, who is short and round, with white Prince Valiant hair, looks at Mercer through her enormous glasses. "She's a lawyer?" she says, motioning to Mollie with her downy chin.

Mercer nods, confused as to why this woman looks confused.

"Will your partner be bringing his girlfriend?"

"Fiancée, actually," Mercer says, unsure of why she's asking. "They just got engaged."

"That's wonderful. She's lovely. Very professional."

He wonders how this woman knows Mia. "She won't be here," he tells her. "She's on tour with the circus."

Her forehead furrows, and her white eyebrows crimp together. "In what capacity?"

"I'm not sure," Mercer says. "Tightrope, maybe?"

They're interrupted when one of the older men—tall, stooped, flakes of shed skin flecking his ascot—asks Mercer if any arrests have been made yet, if they've found out who attacked Jude.

"We have some leads," Mercer says, "but it's probably not appropriate for me to go into detail. Mr. and Mrs. DiMaio are aware of the investigation's progress, and I'll let them share it with you."

DiMaio slaps him on the back. "Good man," he says. "By The Book. I like that."

Mercer replays his own words in his head, and he realizes how stiff his words sound in a social setting like this. He drinks his wine quickly, hopes he'll start feeling looser soon.

Everyone in the group is eager to talk about Colma. One of them has parents buried at Olivet, another at Holy Cross, and another has relatives at both Hills of Eternity and Woodlawn. The man with the ascot has a plot reserved at Cypress Lawn; one of the film people has a family mausoleum at Greenlawn. The neighbor knows someone who buried her chow chow at Pet's Rest. Mercer is used to hearing this, the recitations of who's buried where. Seems like most people who live around San Francisco have a loved one planted somewhere on Mercer's beat.

Later, Mercer is standing quietly in a small group as the winemaker in the aloha shirt talks about last fall's crush. Mollie sweeps past him, fresh from another conversation with the attorney. "His firm does white-collar defense," she whispers to him. "They've been running a search for a lateral."

"I thought you liked your job," he says.

"Never hurts to network." She smiles. "Are you all right without me for now?"

Mercer tells her yes, although he's at least one more glass of wine away from feeling at ease. He stands still and listens to the winemaker for a few more minutes, until he feels a tap on his shoulder. He turns to find Kelly Chaleski smiling at him, her arms open for a hug. She's decked out all in blue—a short velvet jacket in sapphire, something sheeny and sky-blue underneath—and her skin is newly honeyed with a light tan. Excitement hits him like a truck. Then panic hits him like a truck coming from the other direction.

"It's great to see you," Kelly says. "You look a lot different out of uniform."

Before he can think of anything to say, a tall, sandy-haired guy walks up behind her and wraps his thick arms around her shoulders. He's younger than Mercer, by a few years at least. His hair has been labored over—curled and crisped with gel—and there's no sign that he'll be losing it anytime soon. He's wearing a charcoal-colored, tight-fitting button-down and a look of practiced boredom. Mercer hates him immediately.

"Mike's a police officer," Kelly says to her date. "He's the one who took me on the ride-along." The date nods, and Mercer is reminded of the condescension he saw from the jack-off in the Lexus the morning they found Jude. He catches Mollie's eye. *Come back. I need you.* She gets it; within moments, she's at his side.

Kelly introduces her date as Booth; it's unclear whether that's his first name or his last. He doesn't say much; he scarfs hors d'oeuvres, drains glasses of champagne, and ogles the college-aged women serving them. Mollie and Kelly carry the discussion, which is interrupted when Booth's cell phone rings with the bass line to Pink Floyd's "Money." Kelly rolls her eyes as Booth goes out to the balcony to take the call.

"How long have you two been together?" Mollie asks.

"We're not *together* together," Kelly says. "Neither of us wants anything serious. What about you two?"

"Our hostess says I'm his companion," Mollie says.

"What do you say?"

"I say I've known this guy way too long to ever *think* about being his companion."

"Hey," Mercer says. "I'm not that bad."

Susan DiMaio, finishing a circuit around the room, puts a hand on Mercer's shoulder and leans into their circle. "Excuse me, ladies," she says with a joviality that sounds strained to him. "Officer Mercer," she says, "can I have a minute with you?" She has switched from champagne to martinis, and her glass is empty.

"Sure," he says. He's disappointed to be pulled away from Kelly, but he has responsibilities. He reminds himself that Mollie will look for ways to talk him up to Kelly; she'll make him look better than he could himself.

He follows Mrs. DiMaio's brisk walk through the dining room, where a long table is set for dinner, and into the kitchen, where the catering staff is reloading trays with shrimp, stuffed artichoke hearts and mushroom caps, crab cakes with mango and avocado. Susan sets her glass on the countertop and eyes the trays that are about to be brought out. With a toothpick, she pokes some of the mushrooms around so they sit in a more pleasing formation. Mercer can't tell what the difference is, but it seems to matter to her.

"Drink?" she says.

Mercer holds up his wineglass, which is still half full. He means this to be a gesture of *no, thanks,* but she locates an open bottle on the kitchen table and fills his glass to the top.

"We've had a setback," she says.

"With Jude?"

She nods. "His cello. He smashed it," she says. "Pieces. Into pieces."

"God," Mercer says. He notices the silver cross around her neck and immediately corrects himself. "I mean, I can't believe it."

"It was his grandmother's," she says, slapping the counter for emphasis. "It's worth ten thousand dollars."

"He loves his cello," Mercer says. "He went out of his way to tell me."

"Loved it. Past tense."

"He's had a traumatic experience. Maybe it's good that he's getting it out."

"Not like that, it isn't," she says. "You don't smash things that are precious." She looks down at the floor, then up into the bright-white recessed lights. Her eyes, wet again, gleam. She blinks, once, twice, and a few tears spill. "I think they broke him," she says. "Whoever these people are."

"We're trying our best to find them," Mercer says. "I know things are going slowly, but we're working as hard as we can."

"He's on antidepressants now. The psychiatrist suggested right away, but Marco and I said no. I mean, what mother wants to medicate her son?"

Mercer nods, chooses to keep quiet, to let her talk.

"We finally said yes. I know you don't have children, Officer Mercer, but when you do, I hope you don't have to go through this. All you want is for your child to be happy. And when he's not—" She breaks off her sentence, swallows, and now she's crying, now her voice is wavering, and she says, "And when he's not, you feel like you've failed."

"You haven't failed," Mercer says.

"But you feel like you have."

"He's been through a lot. This could all be temporary."

She pokes a finger into his shoulder; it's not aggressive, but it's not soft, either. "I want you to find them," she says. "You have to find them."

"We will," he says. He immediately regrets it, remembers one of his Academy instructors warning them, *Don't promise anything you can't deliver. Don't pretend to control anything you don't control. When you're talking to a citizen, these are the worst things you can do.*

At dinner, DiMaio raises a toast to Mercer. He thanks everyone for coming, says with glass raised that they're going through a hard time as a family, and nothing gets you through hard times like good friends. "Thank you, Officer Mercer," Marco repeats, "and to your colleagues."

The seat with Toronto's place-card in front of it is empty. Mercer thinks it's rude of him to be so late. Not that Toronto isn't capable of rudeness—he often seems to cultivate it carefully—but Mercer's still surprised, because he's making the department look bad. Between courses, he goes out to the balcony and tries calling Toronto's cell. It immediately punts to voice mail. He tries twice more, with the same result.

Where the fuck is he?

Mercer stays quiet through the meal, instead listening to the conversations sparkling around the table. He is between the old man in the ascot and the stage actor; both have given up on him and turned away to speak with their other neighbors. Mollie is seated next to the attorney, and the two of them are chatting animatedly. The next-door neighbor preaches confidence in the city's real-estate values. The most social energy is around Marco, as he talks about the projects he's considering: an adaptation of a novel by a Czech writer Mercer's never heard of, the story of the Haymarket Square Riot, a love story centered around the Dunkirk evacuation. "I'll need extras," DiMaio calls down the table. "Officer Mercer, if you want to be in pictures, just let me know."

Mercer smiles and murmurs thanks. He's embarrassed at the moment of attention that Marco has brought to his silence, he's crushed that Kelly is here with Booth, he's pissed at Toronto, he's worried about Jude, and all he wants to do now is get through the meal and go home. He saws at his lamb shank, trying to get the last shreds of meat off the bone. There's little reward for his efforts, but it beats trying to talk. The one good thing: through it all, he can sneak looks at Kelly. And every time she notices and meets his eyes, it feels like a gift, Booth or no Booth.

After dinner, there's another round of cocktails, dessert wine, port. Some of the men go outside to smoke cigars; Marco leads a group downstairs to show them the screening room. Mercer heads out to the balcony to try Toronto's number again: still no luck. He snaps his phone shut and looks out over the DiMaios' backyard. People are gathered out on the stone patio, and Mercer catches snippets of conversation about business and movies and the business of movies. Smoke drifts up to him, sweet and rich. Moonlight pushes through a gauze of fog. The highest limbs of the trees above him are waving gently as the ocean breeze sweeps across.

A tap on his shoulder, and again it's Kelly. "We didn't get to talk much at dinner," she says.

"You were far away," he says. "You wouldn't have heard me if I shouted."

"Anything new in the case?"

"Not really, no. How's the article coming?"

"It got bumped, so I have another two weeks. If anything breaks, right up to the last moment, you call me, okay?"

"Sure," he says, though he immediately wonders if he should've said no, if he should insist that she get her information through Jude's parents, not through him. He knows that's what he should say, but he doesn't say it.

"Are you staying around for a while?" she asks.

"Not sure," he says. "You?"

"Booth is going to catch up with some guys from work who are out for a bachelor party. I said I'd leave with him if I wasn't having fun here."

"Are you?"

"I'd like to talk to you."

"There's not a lot more I can tell you about the case."

"That's fine," she says. "I'm just saying I want to talk to you some more. You shouldn't worry about Booth. We're totally casual. We don't even really like each other that much. He's got a whole scene, and it's fun to tag along. He just keeps me from getting bored."

He takes this in, feels his excitement build.

"So, are you staying?" she asks, and when he nods, she says, "Good. Then we'll stay together."

Mercer watches the two of them as Booth prepares to leave. He gives her a quick kiss—short in duration, but with some tongue—and Mercer hears her tell him to keep his hands off the strippers. They're both laughing when he heads out the door.

Mollie, who's been off talking to a group of older men about the city's homeless policy, approaches him on a crooked line, throws her arm around his shoulders, and tells him she's going to leave, too. "I'm not going to be the third wheel."

"Come on," Mercer says. "Stay. No one's counting wheels."

"You like her, don't you?"

Mercer nods.

"I think she likes you."

"What about—?"

"Booth?" She wrinkles her face like there's a bad smell. "Who knows? But she does like you."

"How do you know?"

"Girls have their ways," she says. First Toronto, now Mollie, talking to Kelly on the sly, gathering information, maybe talking him up. Outside forces, pushing the two of them together.

"I'll call you a cab," Mercer says, reaching for his phone.

"Please," Mollie says. "Don't chivalry me. I know how to use a phone." She kisses him on the cheek, then gives him a poke in the stomach. "Have fun. Don't think too much."


Late. Kelly takes Mercer's hand and leads him out the back door. Each carrying a glass of port, they cross the wide stone patio and follow a curling mulched path. Rosebushes line the garden, along with Italian cypresses that are lit dramatically from below. Outdoor speakers purr classical guitar music into the night. They pass by people they've spoken to before with nods of acknowledgment, not wanting to get drawn into anyone else's conversation.

The path leads to a set of moss-slicked wooden steps pressed into the hillside that wind down through hydrangeas and bear's breech to another flat area below. In the shadowy far corner of this lower yard is a gazebo; the cool yellow footlights that line the steps throw their shadows long as they cross the grass toward it. Inside the gazebo is a glass-topped, wrought-iron table with four chairs fitted with thick cushions. They sit, clink a wordless toast of port, and sip.

"Where's your friend?" she asks. "Officer Toronto?"

"He should've been here by now. I tried calling, but his phone's off."

"Tell me this," Kelly says. "There's really nothing going on with you two?"

"Me and Toronto?"

She laughs. "Sorry," she says. "Too much wine. I mean you and Mollie."

It's his turn to laugh. "She's a good friend, that's all."

"How good?"

"She's my best friend's girl."

"That's where the best affairs start."

He thinks she might just be trying to be provocative, but there's also something in her tone that suggests she believes it. He tells her Owen and Mollie are about to get engaged. He feels a sense of certainty as he says this. He can't imagine Owen being dumb enough to let her go.

"That's a long way from married," she says.

"I just called her because I didn't want to come alone."

"Why not?"

"I get nervous," he says without thinking. He regrets it immediately. An admission of weakness. He can imagine her walking away.

"I know," she says. "I was at the press conference."

He smiles, relieved. "Yeah," he says, "I do better at parties if I'm with someone I know."

"Well, now you know me."

"Getting there," he says.

She leans toward him, and it might be meaningful or she might just be shifting her weight, but he's feeling more confident now. The thatchy shadows from the gazebo's roof play across her face, and she gets close enough that he can smell her hair—the clean scent of rosemary—so he leans toward her, toward this woman who's made him amped and jangly since his first glimpse of her, leans toward her before she can pull back, before he starts thinking too much, and he meets her with a kiss. Her lips are soft and port-sticky and they taste red and sweet and then their tongues are touching, chasing, and he puts his arms around her and pulls her in close. He runs a hand up one of her sleeves and finds soft, smooth, night-cooled skin. This is a rare moment—he has everything he wants; he is doing exactly what he wants. It thrills him. This is the kind of attraction he felt when he was eighteen, when everything was new and vital and unfathomable and nakedly carnal, only now there's a liquid calm running through him, too.

She's a great kisser, sometimes leading, sometimes responding. He's not sure how much time goes by—time is meaningless when you feel like this—and then he feels her hand warm over his groin. He presses into her—this is *urgent,* this connection, this contact—and then her hands are undoing his belt and sliding down his zipper and reaching in. The shock of her cold fingers almost makes him shout. It's a good thing he doesn't, because two women are coming down the steps into the lower yard, talking about the landscaping, and Mercer glimpses white hair and bright-green glasses on one of them. The neighbor. He grabs Kelly's wrist, whispers *wait.* There's a gap in the women's conversation as the neighbor looks across the yard right at the shadows that hide them while the other woman fingers the leaves of a plant. The moment is painful, watching her and wondering if she is watching them, and then Kelly rubs him softly and slyly, teasing, playing with his inability to respond. He wants to tell her he doesn't want to be seen, that the DiMaios will be upset to know the man responsible for their son's well-being is scrumping away in their gazebo, but instead he holds her hand tighter and says *wait* again, but she doesn't, and he hears a giggle escape from her.

Finally the two women clup back up the hill with careful steps—and is that one last look thrown over the shoulder at them?—and once they're out of sight, he kisses Kelly with all the force he's been holding back, and his hands go under her shirt, up and down her sides and over her breasts, firm, nipples hard in the cool air.

This is when the cell phone in his front pocket vibrates. She pulls her hand away in surprise, then reaches back for him. "You're not getting that," she says.

"I have to see," he says, and he struggles to get the phone from his pocket. TORONTO flashes over the bright-green background. "Shit," he says. He wants to ignore it, but the hairs on the back of his neck are telling him to take this call, take this call, ignore everything else your body's telling you and take this call. She says something as he puts the phone to his ear, but he can't hear what it is because in his ear now is a blare of background noise: distorted music, raised and exuberant voices.

"Boy Thirteen," Toronto says, and his voice sounds sludgy. He's wasted.

"Where the fuck are you?"

"I'm at that fag bar where you used to work."

"It's not—"

"Not a fag bar, I know. I should know because this place is full of women and I am buying them all many drinks and myself too of course. So get your ass down here and have some drinks with us."

Kelly takes his free hand and puts it under her shirt again.

"I'm busy," Mercer says. "I'll call you later, okay?"

Toronto exhales a raspberry, slow, long, and from the sound of it, sloppy. "Nothing is okay," he says. "Okay is exactly *not* what anything is, young Boy Thirteen. I am fucked up. I am all fucked up. I am a broken man. But what the fuck, right? Tell me if I'm not right when I say what the fuck."

Mercer holds up a *wait* finger to Kelly, and she puts up one of her own, mocking him, then sticks her tongue in his ear. "What happened?" he asks Toronto. "Stop talking shit and tell me what happened."

"Mia's gone," he says.

"Of course she's gone. She's on tour. You know that."

"Listen to this," Toronto says, and before Mercer can pull the phone away from his head, three sharp raps crack into his ear. "Hear that? That's ten-thousand-dollar percussion, you fucking fuck. I got a funny thing in the mail today. It was very funny because it's a ring. It's very funny because I remem- ber very recently giving it to her. Which I take to mean that I should find myself a new wife. Even if Mercer's old fag bar isn't probably the best place to find one."

"Shit," Mercer says. Kelly's hand is in his pants again, and though he can't believe he's doing this, he puts his own hand over hers, stills it, lifts it away. "Nick, don't move, all right? I'm close. I'll come get you. Don't move, and don't give the goddamned ring to anyone, all right?" He snaps the phone shut, zips up his pants. "I'm sorry," he says to Kelly. "You have no idea how sorry. I'd give anything to stay here with you."

"Then give it," she says. "Stay."

"I can't," he says, buckling up. "I'm sorry."

"You should be," she says. "You have no idea what you're going to miss."


The Hard Ten smells like old, spilled beer. It's dark inside, lit mostly in dim red, with neon glows haloing the beer signs in the window. Mercer doesn't recognize the bartender, a tough-looking Brit with a shaved head, two gold-hoop earrings, and a tattoo on his neck. Two old guys on the stools closest to the door look up from their drinks. One nods, and the other shouts, "Mikey!"

"I'm looking for my friend," Mercer says. "Tall guy. Drunk. Probably shouting." Both of them point toward the far end of the bar, where Mercer sees Toronto with a woman who outweighs him by a good fifty. He's trying to spin the ring between his thumb and forefinger but fumbles it onto the bar. He snatches it back up—his reflexes are quick, even in this state—and he tries to spin it again.

Mercer makes his way through the narrow place, pushing through the four-deep line at the bar. It's a young crowd, and the people are more Cow Hollow than Haight Street. He doesn't recognize anyone else. It's only been a year. Amazing, he thinks, how quickly a place can come to not feel like home anymore. He's a ghost here.

Toronto waves when he sees Mercer approaching. "Boy Thirteen," he shouts above the music. He points to the woman next to him. "Meet this girl. I don't know what the fuck her name is, but I'm about to propose to her."

"No, you're not," Mercer says.

"Hi," the woman says to him. "You know this guy?"

"I have this ring, see," Toronto says. "It came in today's mail."

"Put that away," Mercer tells him. "That's worth a lot of money."

"Ah, fuck. I don't care."

"Give it." Mercer holds out an open palm, and Toronto drops the ring into it.

"Good. Good, you hang on to it," Toronto says. "I'll need it when Mia comes back." He pats the woman on the shoulder. "Sorry, honey," he says to her. "I'm engaged."

"Come on," Mercer says. "I'm taking you home." He's about to lift Toronto off the barstool when he feels a hard knock against his back. He barely keeps himself from turning with a cocked fist.

It's Bonnie, the girl with the off-center eyes, the one he slept with after his last shift and never called back. She's holding a full cocktail and pointing at it emphatically with her free hand. "If I were a lesser person, I'd throw this drink in your face," she says. She's clearly drunk, and Mercer's not surprised; this is a woman who can put it away.

"People don't throw drinks at each other," Toronto opines. "That's a fucking Hollywood contrivance."

"I should've called you," Mercer says to her. "I know. I'm sorry."

"I should throw this fucking drink at you," Bonnie says, and Mercer can tell that she's absorbed what Toronto said and is now thinking of herself as a character in a movie. When people start doing that, bad things usually happen.

"You know what?" Mercer says. "I don't have time for this. If you're going to throw the drink on me, go the fuck ahead and do it." He holds her gaze, and then she lets fly. There's a cold splash across his face. An ice cube pings off the bridge of his nose. The liquid stings his eyes, feels sticky against his lips—*a seabreeze,* he thinks, *she always drank seabreezes.* "Great," he tells her. "Thank you. We're done now." He grabs Toronto by the elbow and pushes him through the crowd, toward the door.

"Later, Mikey," one of the old guys says calmly, the same way he did a year ago, when Mercer would be back the next night for another shift, and they'd be waiting there for him, as usual.

It's only a few blocks to the apartment on Grove Street, and Mercer walks with Toronto leaning onto his shoulder as they cross Oak and Fell and Hayes and turn west onto Grove. They pass a big group of young black men in fat parkas and football jerseys and sideways caps, loudly talking smack to each other in the parking lot of the barbecue joint. They whistle as Mercer and Toronto go by on the other side of the street. "Get it on," one of them calls out.

Toronto spins, about to retort, but Mercer tugs him forward. "Let it go, Nick," he says. They trudge against the cold wind that's blasting in from the ocean, straight into their faces. "Let it go."

"Butt-lovin' tonight," one of the kids shouts after them.

Mercer helps Toronto down the stairs to the apartment's door. Toronto manages to fit the keys in on his own. Inside, it's a wreck. Empty beer bottles are scattered across the floor, and shards of brown glass sparkle in one corner, where one must have exploded against the wall. The air is dead-close, smelling of cigarette smoke and spilled beer and sweat. The phone is on the floor amid the bottles and the butts, switched on, a faint red light showing that its charge is nearly gone. Toronto staggers ahead, kicks away a few bottles that spin on the parquet, then flops down onto the mattress. Lying on his back, Toronto turns his head and looks at himself in a mirror that's set on the floor.

"You want to talk?" Mercer asks, but Toronto waves him away. "It's going to be all right, Nick. Whatever happened. Whatever's going on."

"No one knows where she is," he says. "I've called and called and called, and I've been calling everyone. No one will tell me anything except for one of them that said it's over and she needs space and I should quit trying to find her because she's scared, scared of me, and I had my ring back and wasn't that what really mattered. And I said no, not at all, not the fuck at all, but she wouldn't listen." Toronto coughs mightily, and the coughs turn into the kind of crying that a tough man does when alcohol gives him the narrow opening he needs.

Mercer says nothing, sits down cross-legged on the floor across from his friend, who's now patting his pockets, looking for smokes. Finding none, Toronto sits up, elbows on knees, head in hands. There's a long silence, during which Mercer hears laughter from the street and everyone calling everyone else *bitch* and then more silence.

Slowly, Toronto raises his head, takes in the room around him. His eyes are puffy and his face is red. The dark shadow of his beard ages him. He lifts his hand, sweeps an arc through the air, left to right. At first, Mercer's not sure if Toronto's showing him what is there or what is gone.

"How the fuck?" Toronto says.

"How the fuck what?" Mercer asks.

"How the fuck," Toronto says, "can I live here?"

# FOURTEEN

# DEATH'S DOOR (I)

The sun is rising on Wednesday morning, and the Colma night crew has just finished a night that demands full attendance at The Door for drinks. The pursuit and apprehension of J. Mitchell McElheney will enter the lore of the department, a story to be told again and again.

The call comes at 0200 hours, summoning available units to the golf course: a streaker has been spotted wiggle-dicking his way up and down the course for the sixth time this month. The course owners have been on them to nail this guy, because he's been relieving himself in the holes, and the greens-keeper is threatening to quit.

The four patrol officers—Mercer, Toronto, Benzinger, and Cambi—converge in the parking lot at the clubhouse with their light bars lit, their rear decks and corner strobes and spots and alley lights all illuminating the fairways. The sounds of police work: squawks of matched static from cruiser radios, the creak of duty-belt leather, rubber soles crunching over bits of gravel in the parking lot as they plan their approach.

"We are having a plague of nakedness in this town," Toronto says wearily. "Boy Thirteen's kid, Mrs. Rao, this guy. Does *anybody* fucking wear clothes anymore?"

"Let's spread out," Benzinger says. "Look around, close the net when we find him."

"Just so you know," Toronto says, "I'm not running after this motherfucker. If he wants to go around crapping in the pin placements, that's fine by me."

Normally someone would give him grief for this, but they all know that Toronto's not sleeping and that he's spending his off-duty hours as drunk as possible. He's been cleaning himself up for his shifts and not making mistakes, but they've all smelled the fumes rising from his pores, and they've taken pains to shield him from the higher-ups when the fumes are too sharp. His emotions are on a hair trigger, and they're all keeping close watch.

"There," Benzinger says softly. Their eyes follow the beam of her flashlight out to a cypress tree that doesn't completely hide the naked man crouching behind it. "Mine," she says, and she takes off down the fairway in long, balanced strides as the streaker darts back into the trees. Mercer runs to the left and up the parallel fairway, hoping to head off the subject, while Cambi moves his bulk into a position on the right flank. Toronto stays in the parking lot with the cruisers. "Just bring him right to me, guys," he calls.

Sleep-deprived and clumsy, Mercer slips and falls on the damp grass, but he hauls himself up and resumes the chase. His pulse is pumping. It doesn't get much more fun than this—taking down a knucklehead in a low-risk situation. (*There's always risk,* his inner Mazzarella points out.) Benzinger's voice comes into his earpiece: "At the third hole," she says. "I'm fifty yards behind." She's not even breathing hard. "He's wearing shoes, so he can go through the scrub." Then: "He's coming back to you, Mercer."

Mercer stops and listens. He hears the streaker's feet approaching over dry leaves and twigs. He sets his feet wide but stays on his toes. The running feet come closer, closer, and he's expecting to see a naked running man appear from the dark in front of him when he catches a glint of light a few yards to his left. Light catching glass. He freezes when he sees a small, rat-faced man holding a monocle up to the moonlight, as if checking for smudges. His clothing is absurd: powder-blue tux over a ruffled yellow shirt, blue silk handkerchief in the breast pocket, top hat with a ring of wilted daisies around the brim. Rings on every finger: gold on one hand, silver on the other. *Ghost,* Mercer thinks. *Dead man.* "Police?" Mercer says. "Don't move?"

The man turns and squints at him. A long, still moment passes before a dangerous smile creeps across his face. "We heard you might be coming," he says in a sandpaper voice that Mercer feels more than hears.

Up the slope to Mercer's right, the streaker sprints past him, a blur of pink. When he turns back, the little man is gone. He shines his light around him in a full circle. Nothing. He'd be embarrassed about missing the streaker if he weren't terrified that he was losing his mind. Or had already lost it.

The Book. Go by The Book. Mercer hits his mike. "He got by me. Art, Nick, he's heading between you two."

A misfiring neuron, maybe? A sleep-starved brain playing tricks on him? He gets his body moving again and scrambles to the top of the slope. Benzinger powers past him, her arms pumping, chasing the naked man back toward the clubhouse. Approaching the first tee, she puts on a burst of speed and dives for his ankles; there's something feline and beautiful about her body as she extends, grabs, and brings him down in the first cut of rough. Before Mercer can get there to help, the naked guy somehow wriggles away from her and veers toward a line of golf carts on the grass near the maintenance shed. He reaches into a cart and removes something from the area of the steering wheel. "Weapon," Mercer shouts to Toronto, who's closest.

"For fuck's sake," Toronto says. "It's a fucking pencil." He shouts to the runner. "Stop! Drop the pencil, and stop running now!"

The naked man, using the cart as a shield, brandishes the scoring pencil. Mercer approaches him from the front, Toronto from the near side, Benzinger—covered in grass clippings—from the far. The guy spins and runs smack into Cambi, who has come up quietly behind him. Cambi spins him into a rear-arm finger-flex, then kicks out the back of his knee and drops him. Mercer hears the *clack-sprick* of cuffs closing over wrists.

"Hey, Toronto," Cambi says. "Little help?"

Toronto goes behind the cart and holds the streaker as Cambi stands up and straightens his clothes. "Fuck," Cambi says. "He got me." He pulls out the golf pencil that's sticking out of his abdomen and drops it onto the cart path. "Sonofabitch tore my shirt," he says, after checking between his buttons to see if he's bleeding. Benzinger and Mercer burst out laughing, and Cambi gives a little snort once he's confident he's not mortally wounded.

"Mercer, how'd you miss him?" Benzinger asks.

"Got distracted," he says. "A squirrel or something." Now that the action is over, unwelcome thoughts are filling up his mind. *I am not Featherstone,* he tells himself sternly. *I am not delusional. I am not insane.* He leans against his cruiser and shivers.

**W**ith the shift completed and the streaker, a 5150, safely down at County on a seventy-two-hour hold, they're in the mood to have a few drinks and laugh it up. Mercer is grateful for the distraction of company and the dulling of his senses. The only exception is Toronto, who's drinking at twice their pace and has already sunk into surliness. They're joined at the table by Jerry Fahey, the old fireman, who's been putting it away pretty good himself. Mercer wonders if Jerry even took a break between closing time at Molloy's and the first draw off The Door's tap at six.

Cambi has been showing everyone he can the small, graphite-stained puncture. Right now, it's Jerry's turn. He has his reading glasses on, and he's inspecting Cambi's belly from inches away. He whistles. "You took some lead, son," he says, poking at the tiny wound with a thick, callused finger.

"Don't be so dramatic," Benzinger says. "It's graphite."

"Really?" Cambi says. "I wanted it to be lead. It sounds better."

There's one thing they're not talking about, and they're not going to: Cambi was holding J. Mitchell McElheney—at that point, covered up with a blanket—while Toronto was trying to take down his information. Toronto got frustrated because the detainee was squirming and singing to himself instead of responding to questions. "Hey," Toronto snapped at him, "knock it off." When McElheney didn't, Toronto bopped him on the head with his posse box. Not too hard—a love tap, really—but definitely not by The Book. Instant liability. Cambi moved in and grabbed the streaker, then told Toronto firmly that he'd take it from there. Mercer watched, stunned, as Toronto plodded back to his cruiser and sat behind the wheel with his eyes closed.

No, they won't be talking about that. Toronto knows he fucked up. The sooner everyone forgets about the bump on J. Mitchell McElheney's head— especially J. Mitchell McElheney—the better.

Jerry waddles up to the bar and returns with two double bourbons. He puts one in front of Toronto, sips the other one himself. As bad as Toronto looks, Jerry is far worse—his eyes sunken and tired, his hair mussed, his face bloated.

"Hey, Jerry," Mercer says. "Are you getting enough sleep?"

"I'm an old man. I can't sleep anymore. Don't have time for it, anyway. Got to study."

"What the fuck are you studying," Toronto declares, "and why."

Jerry reaches into a dirty canvas tote bag under his chair and drops a book on the table, right into a puddle of beer. The book looks like it's already seen its share of barroom spills; it doesn't sit flat on the table because the cover and all the pages run in wavelike ripples. The cover, formerly white and now a riot of yellow, brown, and orange stains, reads: *A Practical Guide to Estate Planning.*

"Jesus, Jerry," Benzinger says. "Did you puke on that thing?"

"Maybe you should laminate it," Mercer says.

"What the fuck, anyway?" Cambi says. "Estate planning?"

"I'm an old man," Jerry says.

"Yeah, but you don't have a fucking *estate,*" Cambi says.

Jerry flips him the bird. "It's good stuff to know," he says. "I should've been a lawyer. That's what I should've done with my life. My wasted fucking life."

"For what it's worth," Benzinger says, "we like you, Jerry."

Jerry tugs on his beard, looks at Benzinger with his glassy eyes and droopy lids. "Benzinger, when are you going to fall in love with me? I've been waiting a long time."

"Sorry, Jer," she says. "You got the wrong parts."

Toronto, who's been looking at his nearly empty glass as if he'd be too sad to make the last sip go away, looks up. "She was chasing dick tonight, Jer. Maybe you have a chance."

Jerry leans back in his chair, sips his drink. "Another thing I gotta learn," he says.

They wait.

"Is what?" Cambi asks.

"Is how to patent my inventions."

"You have inventions?"

"I just now got one."

"You just invented something?"

"I just now invented something, by myself," Jerry says. He's looking at the baseball cap on Cambi's head, black, with a silver Ford Mustang logo stitched into it. "It's the sleeveless hat."

"I don't get it," Cambi says. He takes off his hat, looks at it from several angles.

"Think about it. The *sleeveless* hat. The sleeveless *hat*."

Toronto laughs, and a fine mist of whiskey sprays over the table. "That makes no fucking sense, Jerry," he says, between coughs.

"Ah," Fahey says, waving an instructive finger, his wide, cracked lips spittle-gleamy in the bar light. "That's the genius of it, you little bastards." He folds his arms on the table and rests his head on them.

"All right," Benzinger says. "Who's got Jerry duty?"

"Don't talk like I'm not here, Benzinger," Jerry says. "I love you."

"Mercer and I got him last time," Toronto says. Together, they'd lifted the older man into the back seat of the Olds and delivered him back to his house. Fahey had left lamps turned on in every room. The place shined with loss, an island of still and empty incandescence in the sleeping neighborhood.

"I can do it again," Mercer says. "No big deal."

"I'll take him," Cambi says. "I have to head out soon, anyway. If I have another, I'm no good to drive. Plus I'm beat."

"Boy Thirteen," Toronto says. "How about you close this out by telling everyone about your big Hollywood party?"

"Did you meet movie chicks?" Cambi asks. "Can you hook me up?"

"I didn't meet any movie chicks," Mercer says.

"Tell them who you did meet," Toronto says.

"What are you talking about?" Mercer wants to shut this down, doesn't want to get into talking about Kelly in front of everyone.

"You remember Mercer's rider from last week?" Toronto says to the table.

"Hot," Cambi says. "Smoking hot."

"She was at the party," Toronto says. "They hit it off."

"Holy shit," Cambi says. "Did you stuff her, Boy Thirteen?"

Jerry raises his head. "Mercer stuffed someone?"

"You guys are pathetic," Benzinger says.

"I didn't stuff anyone," Mercer says. *I might have*, he thinks, *if a certain someone who shares a name with a major Canadian city hadn't fallen right the fuck apart. Someone who hasn't even thanked me yet, by the way.* "Nick, you're not driving home, are you?"

"I have no home," Toronto says. "I have a shitty space that's not mine where I happen to be sleeping."

"Well, you're not driving *there*, are you?" Benzinger asks.

"Fuck it," Toronto says. "I'll crash at Jerry's."

"There was a time," Jerry says.

"A time when what?" Toronto says.

"A time when I took *women* home from bars."

"You're no prize yourself."

"Now that you're single again," Jerry says, "you can call up some of your old students. They're probably of age now."

"That's the best goddamned idea you've ever had, Jerry. That's a trillion times better than a sleeveless fucking hat."

"You know what I want to do right now?" Jerry says. "I'll tell you what I want to do."

"What's that?" Mercer asks.

"What?"

"What do you want to do?"

"Right," Jerry says. "I want to play a goddamned game of pool. Who's with me?"

"Come on, Jer," Cambi says. "It's time to go."

"One goddamned game. Have a Coke and sit down. I'll run the table."

"I'm in," Mercer says. He and Jerry walk over to the pool table in the back of the bar and select the least-warped cues from the rack on the wall. Mercer feeds quarters into the table, racks the balls, lets Jerry break. Jerry knocks in a stripe and keeps shooting, circling the table, checking his sight lines, stalking his shot. He keeps opening and closing one eye. He probably can't see straight.

There's a sign on the wall that says *No massé shots You will be 86'd, the Mgmt.*, but Jerry lines up to take one anyway. Mercer says Jerry's name, interrupts him, nods toward the sign. "Son," Jerry says. "You don't get to be my age reading signs." He calls out to the bartender. "Mae," he says. "I been coming here thirty years. I'm an old man. You got a problem if I fuck up Chicko's table taking the goddamn shot I want to take?"

Mae, a haggard-looking woman with yellow-gray hair, smoke-creased skin, and a long cigarette dangling from her mouth, waves him on. "Be my guest, Jer."

Jerry raises his cue high, coming at the ball from a steep angle, and Mercer watches with the rapt attention of someone watching a car blow through a stop sign and headed for impact. But Jerry makes perfect contact, and the cue ball takes a tight turn around the solid in front of it, sideswipes the thir-teen, dumping it into the corner pocket. The old man's hands might be shaky and his eyes may be whiskey-blind, but he has years and years of muscle memory.

"Ran into Lorna Featherstone at the store," Jerry says, sizing up his pros-pects on the table. "Heard she's your neighbor."

"I'm just getting to know her. She's nice."

Jerry nods. "Always thought so," he says, and he seems more lucid now that he's engaged in the game, moving, thinking. "Got some advice for you, Boy Thirteen. Marry a good woman, and die before she does." He drops the nine into the side pocket, leaves himself an easy shot on the twelve.

A thought strikes Mercer: Sure, Jerry's a mess, but he's still grieving. Maybe he and Lorna could help each other move on. He's contemplating how he could get them together when the door to the bar creaks open and a shaft of gray morning light intrudes on the gloom. The woman who steps in off the street is backlit, and only after the door closes behind her does Mercer see that it's Fiona. She peers around into the depths of the bar, as if her eyes are hav-ing trouble adjusting to the dim red light, and then she spots him. "Mike," she says.

"Hey," he says, approaching her and thinking, *Should have called her. Should have called her.*

At the cop table, Cambi nudges Toronto. When Toronto raises up, Cambi motions toward Mercer and Fiona with his hatchet-head. "Watch this," he whispers.

"Can I see you outside?" Fiona says.

Toronto twists in his chair to face Mercer, in the process emptying half his drink onto the floor. *That's her?* he says with his eyes.

Mercer ignores him. He leaves his glass on the bar and approaches Fiona, a knot of dread forming in his stomach. Nothing good ever comes of *Can I see you outside.*

"Somebody's in dutch with the missus," Toronto says, behind him.

"Mercer's married?" Cambi says.

"No, just whipped," Toronto says.

"What about Buttery?" Cambi says, and Mercer thinks he hears Toronto kick him under the table.

He follows Fiona out. His eyes adjust slowly from the red safety light of the bar to the bright-gray morning, sending little jolts of pain into the back of his head. Fiona's eyes are puffy; her hair is limp. Her breath smells like last night's wine. On the sidewalk, she wobbles a little as she sets herself into a defiant stance. They face each other, a few feet apart, next to a trash can and a row of yellow and black and red newspaper dispensers.

"Nice place," Fiona says, her tone acid.

"I know it's a dump," Mercer says. "It's just where we go."

They watch each other, saying nothing. A bus rumbles by, fouling the air with diesel.

"Are you all right?" he asks her.

"No."

"You look like you haven't slept."

"I haven't. I'm too angry."

"What's wrong?"

"You haven't called."

"It's only been a couple of days," he says. "You haven't called me either."

"How come you didn't?"

"I just told you."

"Tell me," she says. "How was the party?"

He locks up. This is a moment he's been trying to avoid. He opens his mouth, and the ignorance that emerges—"What party?"—is a reflex, a stall.

"Fuck you," she says. She points a finger at him. "Fuck. You. You knew I wanted to meet DiMaio. You knew I would've wanted to go, and you hid it from me."

"I'm sorry," he says. "I fucked up. You said you were going out of town, and—"

"You're ashamed of me."

"I'm not."

"Just say it," she says, as close to yelling as he's ever heard her. "Stop wasting my time."

"I won't. It's not true."

"Do you have any idea what happened to me last night? Let me tell you. I get a call from a near-stranger, asking me if I want to sell my house. So I tell her no, and she says, okay, just checking in. And I'm about to hang up—I'm already pissed that she called me—and she says, *I was surprised not to see you and your boyfriend at the party. Your boyfriend's partner, Officer Mercer, was there.* I say, first, *What party?* and second, *You're wrong, Officer Mercer is my boyfriend.* She says, *Really? That's so strange.* I ask her why, and she tells me Officer Mercer brought a woman with him, and by the end of the night, he was getting frisky with another woman entirely."

The neighbor. The stare across the lower yard.

"Her exact words," Fiona says. "I'm not kidding. So why don't you tell me, Mr. Frisky, who you were getting frisky with and what the friskyfuck is going on?"

"I went to the party with Mollie," he says. "It's no big deal."

"And it was Mollie that you were fucking outside?"

"There wasn't any fucking."

"But it was Mollie?"

"Not really," he says. "No."

"Something is wrong," she says, "when I have to find out from a stranger that you were fucking someone in a *gazebo.*"

"I wasn't fucking anyone. Did you hear me?"

She steps closer to him, and he folds his arms across his chest, closing himself off. "Say it," she says. "Say you're ashamed of me because I'm too old and not your perfect ideal fucking fantasy."

"No," he says. "Stop it."

"Say you want someone better and prettier and younger. Say you want someone you can show off to your friends." She waits, and his silence only fuels her. "I deserve so much better than you," she shouts.

He looks down at the gum-dotted sidewalk. This is the end. He can't tell if he's relieved or miserable. Which, he realizes, was the problem all along. "Yes," he says. "You do."

An engine revs, and he looks up to watch a silver BMW racing to beat the changing light. It's at that moment—when he's distracted, rattled, searching for words in his sloshy mind—that Fiona lets loose a wordless cry of frustration, then steps toward him and pushes him in the chest, two hands, her full weight behind the shove. He staggers back, loses his balance, and feels himself dropping like a rock. He sees a flash of bright yellow, hears a sharp, bony *crack* as his temple catches the corner of the newspaper dispenser. There is a blast of pain, and then warmth spreads over the right side of his face. The world goes grainy, and a metallic smell fills his nose. He may or may not hear her yelp something like *oh* or *god* or *sorr*—and she may or may not be leaning over him when Benzinger's voice cuts through the air, shouting, *Step away. Step away from him* now.

He puts his hand to his head and comes away with a palmful of red. He tries to roll over and thunks the back of his head on the concrete. He wants to lie still. It's safer. He even pushes away Benzinger when she tries to lift him up.

**H**e remembers Mae the bartender finding rags they could use to wipe his face and stop the bleeding. He remembers Benzinger and Cambi trying to figure out how the two of them were going to deal with three incapacitated friends. He remembers refusing again and again to go to the hospital. He remembers flipping his keys to Benzinger and saying in a voice he meant to sound like Batman's: "To the Oldsmobile!" He doesn't remember the car ride, but he remembers walking up the stairs at The Willows under his own power, taking the keys from her, and unlocking the door to his apartment. He remembers apologizing to her for the smell, which is the strongest it's ever been.

"What smell?" she says. "It smells like a guy's apartment," she says. "Dirty laundry. Armpit. So what?"

"You don't smell the sauerkraut?"

"Sauerkraut?"

"Sauerkraut," he says. "It's awful."

"Mercer," she says. "It does not smell like sauerkraut. Let's get back in the car. I should take you to the ER."

"No," he says. "I'm fine. Just have to sleep it off."

"That's one thing you're not going to do," she says. "No way. I'm going to sit here and keep your sorry cheating-on-your-girlfriend ass awake."

"I'll be fine," he says.

"And I'm going to wait, to be sure."

He remembers walking into the apartment and collapsing onto his couch. He remembers Benzinger picking up some of the newspapers and clothes on it and pitching them to the floor, and he remembers Benzinger holding him and keeping pressure on the wound. He remembers trying to explain that none of this was Fiona's fault. He remembers Benzinger talking to him in a voice that was so kind, you could die happy as long as it was in your ear.

Today is a good day to fly. The sun is shining overhead; the air is clear; and the cool currents rushing over the hills are steady and predictable. Instead of the crash-prone monoplane, Beachey is flying a replica of his beloved Little Looper, and it feels like a carefree conversation with a long-missed friend. The spruce and ash from the sprawling warehouse on the hill are of excellent quality. The rotary engine—twice the power of the old Looper's Gnôme, and discarded wholesale by some living fool—sings to him in a sturdy, steady tenor. The bouncy melody of "Too Much Mustard" runs through his head, and he taps out its rhythm on the wheel even as he steers the biplane through a loop. He has not felt so capable, so intuitive, so deft of touch in ages.

He turns loop after loop. He weaves through power lines. He flies low to the ground at Pet's Rest and races the dead horses along the fence line. He wonders if the lovely Mrs. Ralston is out roller-skating, and he flies over her favorite pathways in the hope of spotting her. It is thrilling to fly for a crowd of fifty thousand, but it is *sublime* to perform for one beautiful young woman.

He spies the archway at the entrance of Cypress Lawn, and he feels the old excitement, the tingling throughout his body. Yes: he shall fly *through* it. A quick estimation suggests there is just enough clearance, and on this lovely afternoon he and his machine are in perfect harmony. He lets out a whoop as he dives.

But then he pulls up, distracted by a commotion near the duck pond: four men punching and kicking a fifth, who lies supine in the mud. Beachey circles, watches as one of the attackers—a short, balding man with a disfigured face—grabs the victim by the neck, drags him to the edge of the pond, and forces his head underwater. The others gather closely around, cheering on the torture; one of them, wearing mismatched clothes of impossibly bright colors, literally doubles over with laughter. After a disconcertingly long time, the disfigured man lifts the drowning man's head out of the muddy water, allows him to breathe, then plunges him back in. Beachey circles again, unable to look away as the poor fellow is dunked, and dunked, and dunked. This violence is deplorable, gut-wrenching, but Beachey long ago swore off interfering in other men's affairs. He chooses simplicity: flying, women, a good cigar. Still, without quite intending to, he circles the melee again, lower. One of the men waves him away, as if he were a nettlesome bug.

The attackers lift the man out of the water and set him on his feet; a powerful kick from the disfigured man sends him tumbling over the grass. Miraculously, he has enough strength to begin crawling away, which prompts even more strenuous laughter. What Beachey sees next chills him: Bright Clothes hands Wounded Face a thick, gnarled piece of Root, and the four men advance on their prey. Immediately, Beachey conceives of another stunt, one even more challenging than the archway, and he swoops toward the ground. He has a powerful engine, a sturdy frame, and boundless confidence, and that is all he has ever needed for an air trick.

He comes in over the pond, rippling the surface and scattering the ducks, and in one smooth curl, he clips each of the four thugs with the tip of his wing. He circles back and dives again, nearly kissing the ground at the staggering man's feet. With a deft rudder flick and the subtlest of weight shifts, he scoops the man off the ground and catches him in the frame to his right. The sharp jolt nearly drives the Looper into the ground, but Beachey steadies her and pulls up. He shouts over the engine to his bloodied and wide-eyed passenger, "Hold on," and just for good measure, he tilts a wing, speeds through the stone archway, and leaves bewildered onlookers gaping in his wake.

"You took my side," his passenger says after they touch down in a field to the south.

Beachey watches the long grass waving in the breeze; it would be unseemly to admit this, but he imagines the grass is waving to him in admiration of his aerobatic feats. He claps the man on the shoulder—causing him to wince, unfortunately—and says, "I don't take sides, my friend. I simply fly."

The man shakes his head, and Beachey notices that he has a structural deformity in his face as well—a dent of sorts, where the cheekbone should be. Also a flat spot on the pate. "No," the man says. "You took a side." He extends his hand. "The name is Gage," he says.

The feeling that steals over Beachey then is one he hardly remembers. It is an exile coming home to sow rebellion. While Gage stands with his arm out-stretched, Beachey listens to his pulse accelerating as he locates the word for this feeling. It is *doubt*.

R eyna and Bobby are riding along Highway 152, the winding road through the hills between Los Banos and Gilroy. The cooler on the seat be-tween them is filled with ice-cold cans of Azteca, and they have open beers in the cup holders. The inland sun is warm and the windows are down, although Reyna has a sweatshirt draped over herself so she doesn't get burnt any worse. Bobby's at the wheel, accelerating into every turn, glancing over to gauge her reactions—she knows he wants to see fear in her, that this is a game they play. He wants to see the fear, but she's not going to give it to him, she's going to keep a look on her face that says, *Fuck yeah, push it harder.*

They sailed through the border crossing. She was driving, and the guards waved them right through. There's something about her face that inspires trust. She cannot believe what good luck this is.

They pass roadkill: squirrels, skunk, deer, something that might have been a cat. *How did a cat get all the way out here?* she wants to know.

She has to pee, so they stop at Casa de Fruta, the tourist trap outside Hol-lister. Bobby gets out along with her, says he's going to take a look around. When she comes back out, he's in the truck with the engine running.

"What'd you get?" she asks after they peel away.

"Look behind the seat."

On the floor behind him is a camera bag. "Excellent," she says, and she laughs.

"It was sitting on the front seat. Doors unlocked. Some people are so fuck-ing stupid."

She nods. Sure, they could buy a camera if they wanted one, but Bobby likes doing it this way. He likes rearranging the world the way he wants.

"Go ahead and open it up," he says. "See what it is."

It's a digital camera, a Nikon, pretty high-end. "Nice one," she tells him. "Score." She powers it on, and spins the dial to PLAY so she can see the images on it.

Disneyland. A little Asian girl, chubby-cheeked and pigtailed, smiling and holding hands with Donald Duck on one side and a Disney princess on the other. She's not sure which one. There are too damn many to keep track.

She's reminded of a time she went to the county fairgrounds as a kid, back when her parents were still together, and she got her picture taken with a blond woman whose silk sash read *Miss Nevada County*. There were 4-H cows and hogs, vegetable art, clog dancers, horses. In one tent were costumed bunnies being shown by girls not much older than her. One girl had been dressed as Alice, from the storybook—blue dress, white blouse, white gloves—and her bunny was the White Rabbit, with a red vest and a black top hat. Next year, little Reyna decided, she would have a bunny and dress it up and win the bunny prize. And then she'd walked around thinking about her bunny (she liked the kind with the long floppy ears) and thinking of ways to dress it up, and in all the color and noise and movement around her, she lost her parents. She remembers wandering around and crying and desperately looking for Dad, Dad, Dad. Then there was a hand on her shoulder and she looked up to see a gaunt man with a scruffy half-beard and a nose that wasn't all there and a sour smell she didn't like. He told her he saw her dad go into the Funhouse and they should go in there and look for him. She had the sense to run the hell away from him, thank god. She ran until her little-girl legs burned and she lost her breath and someone led her, crying, to the Lost Children Tent. Her parents found her, after a while, so nothing terrible happened, really, but that was the year that her parents really started hating each other, and she never got a bunny, never went back to the fair, ever, and all she has is that memory of the girl who got to be Alice in Wonderland.

"Fuck Disneyland," she says. "And fuck everyone who goes there." She hits a button. DELETE.

The little girl, arms up on the Flying Dumbo ride, sitting with a white woman. Adoptive mother? Probably. Fortyish with gray in her long, straight hair. Saving the goddamned world. DELETE.

The little girl being held by her father, her fingers in her mouth as they look off to the side, her hand and sleeve stained pink and no doubt sticky and sweet. Dusk. The parade going by. DELETE.

DELETE. DELETE. DELETE.

"Who are they?"

"How should I know?" she says. "Just some family." DELETE. DELETE. "Now they're no one."

"Where are the pictures from?"

"Disneyland."

"All Disneyland?"

"So far." DELETE. DELETE.

"No naked shots of Mom?"

"God, I hope not," she says.

He motions for her to give him the camera, tells her to hold the steering wheel. He looks at the camera, switches the dial to RECORD. He doesn't ease off the gas, and she has to take the truck around a tight turn. He takes the wheel back with one hand, holds the camera in the other. Has that Bobby grin on his face.

"Lift up your shirt," he says.

"What?"

"Lift up your shirt. Show me your tits and say cheese. What good's a camera without naked pictures on it?"

She laughs and yanks her T-shirt up. The wind whipping through the truck is cool on her breasts. "Cheese," she says, and he clicks and the flash goes off and the camera beeps. He has to stomp the brake and swerve to make the next turn. "Close one," he says. She laughs again as he speeds up on the straightaway, but this time it feels fake; she listens to it die in her throat with a strange sense of remove. Why did she just do that? She just says *Cheese* and flashes her tits because he tells her to? Just does what he wants, whenever? How long has she been doing that without even noticing? It reminds her of the way Jude was with her; she could make him do whatever she wants, and that just makes him seem pathetic, doesn't it? She bites down on her lower lip as she thinks, hard enough to take her past where the pain starts. Is that what she is? Bobby's Jude?

Bobby lays on the gas, and the forward lurch makes her feel like she might throw up. He looks at her, waiting for her to react, and anger flashes in her. "What the fuck?" she says.

"What?" he asks. A confused look bunches his features.

"You always need *attention*," she says.

"What's wrong with you?"

Stop, she tells herself. Stupid. Quit thinking. Have *fun*. "Nothing," she says. "It's nothing." Because what more could she ask for? They're flying and the wind is in her hair, and now the nausea is gone and the tingle of sex is rising in her. Yes. She can't wait until they get up to Carlos's place—the first thing they're going to do when they get out of the truck is fuck, and maybe she'll take a picture or two of him while they're at it. They're flying and they're alive, and they've got pictures to prove it. Right? Maybe some people think they're bad kids, but you know what? She and Bobby, they're youth and sex and good times on four spinning wheels. And fuck anyone who thinks otherwise.

# FIFTEEN

# DEATH'S DOOR (II)

**M**ercer, still on the couch, shakes off the blanket that Benzinger laid on him and rolls onto his back. The kitchen clock reads 3:30, and the afternoon sky is a dark, murky gray. He looks at the clock again to remind himself what time it is, then does math: Benzinger has been gone for an hour, and it'll be another two hours before she calls him to check in.

He hasn't slept. Benzinger wouldn't let him for the first few hours, and now he feels too exhausted to sleep, anyway. His head is throbbing, and he hears the sound of the impact over and over. Worse, both of his ears are ringing, which makes quiet feel like an assault. He had Benzinger turn on the jazz station and tell him stories from her first years on the force. He asked what it feels like to run in those races when you know someone on the starting line might go home feetfirst. He's needed these distractions: her voice, soothing but croaky from lack of sleep; tinkling piano and honking trumpet and rumbly sax and slap-slide bass; the ticks and puffs of the heat vents; and now the double-time footsteps and carelessly slammed doors and shouts-for-the-sake-of-shouting of kids home from school.

His face is swollen again, this time on the other side. The laceration isn't as bad as they'd thought at first; Benzinger closed it up with a butterfly bandage. He's lucky, he knows; if he'd hit the newspaper dispenser just a few inches to the left, he might have seriously damaged an eye. When he replays the fall in his head, he gets shivers.

He reaches his arm out, and after a few misses, manages to pull a box of Featherstone's reports closer to him. His head hurts and his eyes are swimmy, but he forces himself to read, partly to prove to himself that he can, that all things considered he's doing just fine. He skims through a stack of Featherstone's reports, and he feels like he is watching the sergeant change, watching him steadily losing his grip. He sees Featherstone piecing together the strange logic of this other side; sees him withdrawing his hope from real life and pouring it into the dead world; sees him believing—or *wanting* to believe— that he is the only one who can stop these gangsters. He runs his fingers over the pages as he reads, taking pleasure in the tactility of the letters, even as it depresses him to think of the sergeant clacking away behind a locked door, alone and losing his mind.

```
    I asked W-Sambito what he meant by "killing", as
I believed V-Klinefelter to already have been dead.
W-Sambito explained what the Root does. (See Appendix
A.) I expressed disbelief. W-Sambito said that I was
already talking to a dead person so what was so hard to
believe?
    I asked W-Sambito why if it's so easy to get rid of
a person (i.e. forcing Root on them) it has been such a
rare occurence before now. W-Sambito said he didn't know
& maybe it was just because no one wanted to.
    Am aware how this all sounds now that I am typing it.

    I admonished W-Kim to use more respectful language
toward me. W-Kim said he would as soon as I "got off
[my] worthless ass" and "did somehting about this
Goddamned Barker problem." W-Kim said, "It's the
wild [expletive] West out here these dyas" and told
me Wyatt Earp could have "taught [me] a [expletive]
thing or two about law and order." I advised him that
I did not know Mr. Earp and that while I would listen
to any suggestions he might have, I am the one who is
empowered to act in a law-enforcement capacity in this
jurisdiction. W-Kim confirmed that Earp is no longer
present within city limits.
```

Witnesses all alleged that S-Barker et al. are the primary perpetrators of theft, violence, Rooting, etc. Witnesses advised that criminal activity has increased sharply in recent months. Witnesses said in their opinion lack of effective law enforcement since Marshal Earp's departure had emboldened S-Barker et al.

Deep-breathing excercises don't help much when dead people are threatening you.

The juvenile witnesses were cooperative and volunteered that S-Barker et al often stored stolen property at the abandoned Farragut mausoleum (100 yds to the southwest). I thanked them and sent them back to their baseball game and asked if I could watch an inning or two. Now I think Lorna and I made a mistake not trying to have any children. Which is my fault no matter what story she tells people to make it hers.

Interviewees expressed gratitude for my presence and great hope in my ability to remove Barker et al from the locality. Attempted to ascertain exactly what I could do here that they couldn't. No one is sure, especially not me. But its nice to be relied on.

Information from W.Va. group (OSRK) verifies that I am not alo0ne in having experiences like these. No evidencve that anyone has atte4mpted to function in a law-enforcement capacity though.

Another memo from chief. Must be more careful. Stay on radio whenever possible.

When I announced my presnce and ordered them to surrender, one of the individuals (S-Barker) made a hand gesture in the shape of a gun and mimed shooting me. S-Barker made an accompanying sound effect and laughed. Suspects fled on foot. Did not call for

backup. Presnece of other officers would compromise
the investigation.

Deceased kittens are particularly affectionate. Goats
can be aggressive.

Stolen bicycle was not recovered. I believe I heard
a bicycle horn honk when S-Ruczek rode away on it. I
believe S-Ruczek was mocking me.

It is hard to keep this secret from Lorna but I don't
want to have her have to not believe me.

After I finished collecting information from the
witnsses, I returned to my patrol car and drove to the
chapel at Holy Cross. Doors were locked. I sat outside
on a bench to think and stayed there until Officer Landau
parked next to me in his marked partol vehicle. He
informed me that my shift was over and that I should go
home already and was I or was I not the most useless
sack of crap on the planet. I told him there was no need
to be so hurtful about it. Offcer Landau laughed and
told me to "lighten the [exlpetive] up."

Passed psych eval.!

Appropriate course of action is unclear to me. No
surprise.

Haqve decided to type/file reports in the garage and
not inside anymore. Lorna is easily upset. This morning
she said it makes her sad that I am the man she spent her
life with. I don't blame her. But I don't know what has
been missing. Which makes you wonder what is the point?

Reminder: track shipment from OSRK.

Reminder: update will with specific procedures to be
followed re storing ashes in OSRK box.

Carried the juvenile over mys houlder from the hiking trail to his family plot. Parents assured me that his compound fracture would "take care of itself" but also expressed gratitude. I advised that that is what I am here fgor.

S-Barker et al were no longer present by the time I arrived. I suspect they are taunting me.

Seven more victims of Rooting. Residue/scorch marks found on grass in Serbian Cem confirm this. Suspects are Barker et al. Motive not apparent. These people don't appear to need motives.

V-Flood reports kidnapping of son (W-M, 9) from vicinity of Pet's Rest. S-Barker et al observed nearby (see Statement of W-Gund). V-Flood later received unsigned ransom note. V-Flood delivered jewelry to drop point in Hoy Sun but the juvenile was not there as promised. New scorch mark on steps of Farragut mausoleum. Suspicious. V-Flood is distraught.

Barker causes so much suffering. Taking him down would the most worhtwhile thing I've ever done

Having skimmed his way through each of the boxes of documents, Mercer reads Featherstone's last report in full:

| | | 1. CASE NO. |
|---|---|---|
| **COLMA POLICE DEPARTMENT CA0043479** | | 99-0314-63 |

| 2. CODE SECTION | 3. CRIME | 4. CLASSIFICATION | 5. REPORT AREA |
|---|---|---|---|
| 241, 243 | Assault / Battery upon a Peace Officer | Felony | Beat One |

| 6. DATE & TIME OCCURRED —DAY | 7. DATE & TIME REPORTED | 8. LOCATION OF OCCURRENCE |
|---|---|---|
| 07-27-02 0330 Wed | 07-27-02 0330 Wed | Cypress Lawn Cemetary, 1370 El Camino Real, Colma |

| 9. VICTIM'S NAME—LAST, FIRST, MIDDLE (FIRM IF BUSINESS) | 10. RESIDENCE ADDRESS | 11. RESIDENCE PHONE |
|---|---|---|
| Featherstone, Wesley B. | 609 Clark Ave., Colma | (650) 555-4013 |

| 12. OCCUPATION | 13. RACE–SEX | 14. AGE | 15. DOB | 16. BUSINESS ADDRESS (SCHOOL IF JUVENILE) | 17. BUSINESS PHONE |
|---|---|---|---|---|---|
| Peace Officer | W-M | 61 | 11-04-1937 | 1198 El Camino Real, Colma | (650) 555-8321 |

| 18. NAME—LAST, FIRST, MIDDLE | 19. CODE | 20. RESIDENCE ADDRESS | 21. RESIDENCE PHONE |
|---|---|---|---|
| | | | |

| 22. OCCUPATION | 23. RACE–SEX | 24. AGE | 25. DOB | 26. BUSINESS ADDRESS (SCHOOL IF JUVENILE) | 27. BUSINESS PHONE |
|---|---|---|---|---|---|
| | | | | | |

**28. DESCRIBE CHARACTERISTICS OF PREMISES AND AREA WHERE OCCURRED**

Children's section, Cypress Lawn Cemetery (east side). Flat grassy area.

**29. DESCRIBE BRIEFLY HOW OFFENSE WAS COMMITTED**

Verbal threats were made. Suspects advanced upon Victim in a menacing manner.

**30. DESCRIBE WEAPON, INSTRUMENT, TRICK, DEVICE, OR FORCE USED**

Fists, knives

| 31. MOTIVE—TYPE OF PROPERTY TAKEN OR OTHER REASON FOR OFFENSE | 32. ESTIMATED LOSS VALUE AND/OR EXTENT OF INJURIES—MINOR, MAJOR |
|---|---|
| Intimidation of peace officer; attempt to prevent Victim from pursuing investigations of Suspects. | Apprehension of imminent bodily harm and/or death. Sensation of intense cold, resulting in shivering for a prolonged period. |

33. WHAT DID SUSPECTS SAY—NOTE PECULIARITIES

S-Barker stated that I "did not belong" there and "would be got rid of."

34. VICTIM'S ACTIVITY JUST PRIOR TO AND/OR DURING OFFENSE

Watching children play.

35. TRADEMARK—OTHER DISTINCTIVE ACTION OF SUSPECT/S

see earlier cases involving Barker Gang.

36. VEHICLE USED—LICENSE NO.—ID NO.—YEAR—MAKE—MODEL—COLOR (OTHER IDENTIFYING CHARACTERISTICS)

N/A

| 37. SUSPECT NO. 1 (LAST, FIRST, MIDDLE) | 38. RACE–SEX | 39. AGE | 40. HT | 41. WT | 42. HAIR | 43. EYES | 44. SSN OR DOB | 45. ARRESTED |
|---|---|---|---|---|---|---|---|---|
| Barker, Arthur ("Doc") | | | | | | | un-known | |

46. ADDRESS, CLOTHING, AND OTHER IDENTIFYING MARKS OR CHARACTERISTICTS

| 47. SUSPECT NO. 2 (LAST, FIRST, MIDDLE) | 48. RACE–SEX | 49. AGE | 50. HT | 51. WT | 52. HAIR | 53. EYES | 54. SSN OR DOB | 55. ARRESTED |
|---|---|---|---|---|---|---|---|---|
| Ruczek | | | | | | | | |

56. ADDRESS, CLOTHING, AND OTHER IDENTIFYING MARKS OR CHARACTERISTICS

57. CHECK IF MORE NAMES IN CONTINUATION

X

| REPORTING OFFICERS | RECORDING OFFICER | TYPED BY | DATE AND TIME |
|---|---|---|---|
| | | | |

Additional suspects:

Suspect #3: LoPresti (first name unknown)

Suspect #4: Eastwick (first name unknown)

**OFFENSES INVESTIGATED AND RECOMMENDED CHARGES**

CPC 241—Assault committed upon a peace officer

CPC 243—Battery committed upon a peace officer

1) SUMMARY:

On 07-27-02, at approximately 0330 hours, I, the victim, was on foot patrol in full uniform inside Cypress Lawn cemetery. S-Barker et al emerged from behind tombstones and threatened me with physical harm if I did not discontinue my investigations. When I declined, I was assaulted. I defended myself.

2) VICTIMS AND WITNESSES:

V-Featherstone, Wesley B.

3) SUSPECTS:

S-Barker, Arthur "Doc"

S-Ruczek

S-LoPresti

S-Eastwick

4) VEHICLE:

N/A

5) STATEMENT OF REPORTING OFFICER:

On 07-27-02, at approximately 0330 hours, I was on patrol in full uniform in a marked patrol vehicle. I performed a passing check through Cypress Lawn Cemetery (east side). I heard children's voices and investigated on foot. I discovered three boys and two girls kicking a soccer ball in in the Children's section of the cemetery. Various animals (cats & dogs — presumably pets) were present.

Suspects emerged from behnid me (north). Children and animals fled.

S-Barker addressed me by name and said I should go away because I had no business interfering in his affairs and that he hated peace officers & did not want them in his presece. I informed him that I had lawful jurisdiction in this area and was investigating many crimes in which he and his associates were suspects. (Suspected offenses include but are not limited to ninety-five robberies, thirteen arsons, eight instances of cruelty to animals, the Flood and Fair kidnappings, the Hotaling homicide, the Flamburis homicide, the Showfolks of America gang-killings.) [See Appendices.] I told the suspects I wanted to question each of them individually and would not tolerate any further attempts at intimidation.

All of the suspects advacned closer to me. I ordered them to stop and drew my weapon. All four suspects were observed to possess knives (5-7" blades). S-Ruczek laughed. It is a distinctive screechy and v. irritatig laugh. S-Barker was close to me and raised his hands in a threatening manner. His fingers were bloody as usual.

I drew my weapon in self-defense. I aimed it at S-Barker and ordered him to stop. S-Barker did not comply. S-Barker kicked my wrist I dropped my weapon. I was hit by 8-10 more punches in the head, neck, and abdomen. Punches caused pain & also intense cold wherever contact was made.

I located my weapon and discharged it at S-Barker. S-Barker was was struck in the chest and fell. Other suspects discontinued their advance and expressed surprise. They all laughed. While they were distracted, I retreated, proceeding west and then circling around to

where my patrol vehicle was parked. I apporached the car
just ahead of Suspects Ruczek, LoPresti, and Eastwick.
S-Ruczek said that Barker would be "fine by tomorrow" and
next time they would "chill me off once and for all"
and I was "Doc's meat now." I drove my patrl vehicle
to the chapel at Holy Cross which was locked & sat on
the bench. Was v. cold. Am home now but shaking has not
stopped. I cant get warm

   6) EVIDENCE
N/A

   7) PROPERTY
N/A

   8) STATUS
Case open.

   9) OPINIONS
   While I am requred to file a weapons discharge report,
I will not do so.
   Longer I wait ==> worse my chances. Must neutralize
S-Barker ASAP. Everything depends on this, everything
depends on me.


At five o'clock, Mercer awakens from a shallow doze. Benzinger phoned the captain from his apartment that morning, so he's not expected at work, but he decides to get ready anyway. If he shows up, he'll score some points for toughness and dedication. He takes a hot shower, careful to keep his head wound dry; pours a bowl of cereal but can only finish half. He hunts for his keys for ten minutes before finding them on the coffee table, where they'd been within arm's reach.

Outside his front door is a package: a book, wrapped in brown paper. The

note that accompanies it is from Mrs. Featherstone, handwritten on Colma
Historical Society letterhead:

*Dear Michael,*

> *I found this in our stockroom. Isn't this the fellow you asked about?*
> *Last copy! Enjoy!*
> *I think it's wonderful that you're taking an interest in our history. I'm*
> *having fun learning about it myself! So much to know! So little time!*
> *Fondly,*
> *Your friend,*
> *Lorna* ☺

The book is a thin paperback called *Lincoln Beachey: The Original Bird-
man.* Staring up at him from the cover is a young man in a black-and-white
photograph, grasping the controls of an early airplane. He's wearing a checkered cap and a three-piece wool suit, and he looks fearless and jovial, rugged
but polished. Lincoln Beachey. The dead girls sang about him. Featherstone
reported several encounters with him. He doesn't remember asking Lorna for
any information about Beachey, but his memory is pretty sketchy these days.
He has *got* to get some sleep. He should call Owen and ask for some pills.
Owen has all that stuff in quantity.

He wonders: did Owen decide he was ready to marry Mollie? He hasn't
heard from either of them, but he can't decide if this is a good or a bad sign.

Down in the garage, he slides into the Olds, drops the book into the passenger seat, and notices a smudge of his blood on the passenger-side window.
He leans over and scrapes away the stain with a spit-moistened finger, checks
for stains on the beige leather, and is relieved to see that he didn't bleed all
over everything. He doesn't care so much about the stains; he just doesn't
want reminders of what happened this morning.

The moment he walks into the break room, Benzinger pushes him gently
but firmly back into the doorway. "Whoa," she says. "What in hell are you doing here?"

Toronto's with her, and he looks pale and ragged. He hasn't shaved, and his
heavy, dark stubble makes his skin tone look even less healthy. "Boy Thirteen,"
he says, "you look like shit."

"I'm aware," Mercer says. "You look pretty crappy yourself."

"Nah, I'm fine," Toronto says. "Slept it off. Water, coffee, bacon and eggs and hash browns, aspirin, a couple hundred sit-ups, and now I feel like a champ."

"You shouldn't be here, Mike," Benzinger says. "We've got a per-diem coming in. The young guy. Gomez."

"It's all right. I want to be here."

Benzinger flicks his earlobe, hard. "Tough shit. You're sitting this one out."

"Go home," Toronto says. "Relax."

"I'll just sit here and catch up," Mercer says. "I have a lot of paper to get through." Which is true, pretty much, and while he's at it, he'll go over Jude's case again. Maybe brainstorm some locations to check out in Burlingame; a little legwork might turn up something about the mysterious Bobby. What's at home, anyway? A silent phone and a box of ghosts. He needs to be here, with the midnighters. If the headaches get too bad, he can sit in the break room and drowse in front of the TV. He can stay out of the way.

When Mazzarella spots him, he drags Mercer into the sergeants' office for a sit-down about how important it is for a law-enforcement officer to take care of himself, his own beer gut notwithstanding. After surviving the harangue, though, Mercer is left alone with the DiMaio files and his paperwork on two DUIs, a misdemeanor possession of cocaine, a residential burglary. He monitors the radio traffic between Toronto, Cambi, Benzinger, and Gomez. Not much is happening—the usual traffic stops, an argument between neighbors—but he wishes he were out there.

Taking a break, he gets the Beachey book out of his locker and takes it into the men's room so no one will see him reading. On the back cover he finds the basic facts of Beachey's life: daredevil pilot in the first days of aviation; a household name across the country; a legendary showman and unrepentant rake. Was the first American to loop-the-loop. Buzzed Congress when it was in session, and bombed a Navy ship with sacks of flour, all to show skeptics that airplanes, derided as frivolous toys, had enormous military potential. Died at twenty-eight in front of a hundred thousand people at the Pan-Pacific Expo; during his "death-drop," the wings sheared off, and he plunged into San Francisco Bay. Even then, he controlled the plane well enough to survive the impact, but he drowned because he was belted into his seat.

Mercer opens the book to a page in the middle and skims through a newspaper reporter's account of an interview with the pilot:

> Finally this reporter mustered up sufficient courage to speak. "Well, Mr. Beachey, our readers would like to know how it feels to soar up into the clouds."
>
> "Well, it is a pleasing sensation that I cannot describe. You know when a man's in love? A feeling something like that."
>
> "Is it that pleasing?" we exclaimed. And right then and there we decided that flying must be all right.
>
> "You see, there is always a chance that you might fall; you are always in some danger, just the same as when you are in love. That's why I make the comparison. Many an aviator has taken a hard fall, never to recover—and so has many a lover.
>
> "As you go up, up, up, you seem to be standing still with the earth rapidly moving away from you. And as you mount higher the air becomes cooler. Far below you can see the world stretched beneath, and the cities look like toy houses, the people look like midgets. It is a pleasing sensation; makes one feel free and happy and helps to drive away your earthly troubles.
>
> "After all, it is simply the dancing along life's icy brink and the attendant excitement that makes life worthwhile."

His eyes quickly grow tired; the words swim on the page and the flicker of the fluorescents becomes intolerable. Worse, once his focus drifts, the ghost-girls' Beachey song starts to loop through his head. *Stop,* he tells himself. *You're just making it worse for yourself.* He washes his sweaty face in the bathroom sink, blots himself dry, then tucks the book under his shirt and returns to his desk. He slips it into a drawer when he's sure no one's looking. Whenever the dead girls' voices rise up again, he drowns them out by humming the theme to *Hawaii Five-O.*

At nine-thirty, Mercer's stomach growls and he decides to go for a burrito. Mazzarella wants one, too, and so does the dispatcher, because the only things to eat in the station are some lemon bars that Lorna made. The dispatcher gets on the radio and takes orders from everyone out on patrol, then phones in the order to Flaco's in South City so Mercer can just zip down, pick up, zip back.

As Mercer crosses the parking lot, the thick evening mist turns to drizzle; once he's inside the cruiser, it turns to rain, fat drops plocking on the windshield. He flicks on the wipers and leaves the parking lot eastbound on Serramonte. The pavement glistens under his headlights; the double yellow line seems unusually bright.

Ahead of him, a vehicle takes the illegal right-on-red from Serramonte onto Hillside. Mercer pounds the gas pedal, and the Vic shoots ahead, closing the gap within seconds. He hits the mike to call in the plates, but he stops himself because he recognizes the car—a light-blue, late-model Chevy sedan. It's Lorna's, and as it turns into the Lucky Chances parking lot, Mercer sees her behind the wheel. His mind is slow to make sense of this—why would she be *here*?

Southbound on Hillside, just past the landfill, he notices a flicker of firelight from a grassy strip on the other side of the road. He shoots by without seeing clearly—right then, the rain picks up, obscuring the windshield—but it looked like—and he's not at all sure of this, but it *looked* like—someone in a fire helmet waving his arms with a lighter in one hand. In the rain? "What the *fuck*?" he says aloud. He turns his attention back to the road, where headlights glow from around a curve, and he switches the wipers onto high. He is about to swing a U-turn when the radio bursts alive.

"All units," the dispatcher says. "Check your radios. We've got an open mike."

Mercer looks down at his radio. Shit—it's his mike that's open. He's reaching to flick it off when the sound of shrieking tires sends a jolt of fear through him. When he looks up, the oncoming car is spinning across both lanes. He stomps the brake, but there's no time. He hits broadside.

Then more sound, blasting through him. Mercer feels pain slash his shoulder, feels his body whip, feels as if he's been twisted apart at the waist and flung in different directions. His head hits something hard that ought to be the airbag, and there's an echo in his ears, twinkly and metallic. The voices on the radio become the voices of the people standing over him. The wet pavement captures reflections of flashing lights. Carnival lights. His mind drifts to bumper cars and midway games and fudge puppies. He tries to tell the people around him that he hasn't been to a carnival in years and he regrets that, but no one answers and everything goes black.

When his eyes reopen, he sees a kid sitting in the back seat of one of the cruisers. Not much older than Jude. Holding a cold-pack to the side of his head. Toronto's voice rises out of the hum and the spatter of raindrops. Yelling. "Stupid kid. Stupid goddamn kid. Slam on your brakes just because you see a cop? Because you get *scared*? And driving too fast for the conditions? Stupid kid. Stupid, fucking kid. That's my *friend* in that car, you little—"

Then Benzinger, but not her angel voice. "Nick! Shut up and get away from him, now! Gomez, get him out of here. Go!" She is one of the blurred figures above him. He guesses from the size of the other person's head that it's Cambi. They stay blurry, though, and rain comes down from everywhere.

"Probational," Mercer hears himself say, though the syllables feel gummy and wrong. "I'm still pro—"

"Don't worry about that," Cambi says. "Not now. Wasn't your fault. Not your fault, Boy Thirteen."

He should be in agony, he figures. There is pain, but it feels distant and not quite his. Can he move? He tries arms hands fingers. Yes. Legs feet toes. Yes. Benzinger leans in and says, "Don't move. Don't try to move."

In the distance, he hears what might be a fist punching metal, then Toronto's voice again. "Goddamn kid. Twitchy motherfuckers shouldn't be *driving*, is the problem."

"Don't let them fire me," Mercer says. He must not have said it loud enough, because Benzinger's face leans in close and whispers *what?*

"Don't let them fire me," he says, but he's drowned out by sirens shredding the wet night.

"Yes," she says. "Fire's here. Paramedics, too."

Then a voice close to his ear, telling him to hold still and relax and hang in there, and it's Jerry the fireman, that big dumb drunk sonofabitch, and someone's now holding his hand, and he realizes that's Jerry, too. Benzinger holding his head this morning, now Jerry holding his hand, it's too much goddamn kindness, it's more than he can handle, and he cries. He's not sure if he's crying in a way that anyone else can see, but he is crying, crying, crying, and then he's out.

Sitting on the hillside above the flashing lights and the shouting and the twisted metal and the spray of shattered glass, Lillie Coit hunches forward, hugging herself as she rocks back and forth. She was only trying to warn him. She was only trying to help.

◉

PART TWO

◉

DIE LIKE AN AVIATOR

◉

# SIXTEEN

# HAVE YOU SEEN ME?

The grass is wet with morning dew, and Mercer hopes he won't slip as he walks away from the chapel at Holy Cross. The last notes from the bagpiper at the top of the slope have fallen away. Damp clippings collect around the toes of his shoes. Most everyone is driving from the chapel to the gravesite, but Toronto suggested they walk, for Mercer's sake. As long as he keeps walking, he's fine. The pain that burns at the base of his spine and shoots down his right leg only hits him if he stands still, or if he sits, or if he stands up again after sitting. Lying down, he's good for an hour or so, depending on his position. But walking, he's great. Just great.

Toronto, striding next to him, hands him a flask. Mercer takes a discreet sip, and the cheap-bourbon burn feels good in the back of his throat.

"More fucking bagpipes," Toronto says. "I could go my whole life."

"You said it," Mercer says.

Mercer had stood alone at the back of the chapel, shifting his weight and changing his stance often. It was a Catholic Mass, so it was long; twice he had to go outside and walk a lap around the building because his leg muscles had locked up and the pain was awful. There were eulogies from an out-of-town nephew and from a fellow firefighter, who recalled feats not of heroism but of sturdy, matter-of-fact courage. The mayor spoke, praising the generosity of Jerry Fahey, who'd lived simply and left a generous sum to the fire department and to several scholarship programs, and who would soon be laid to rest alongside his beloved Edith. *He never got used to a world that didn't have Edith in it.*

Fahey. Dead. His abused body finally quit. They found him in his recliner with his estate-planning book in his lap, and with every light in the house switched on.

"How are you holding up?" Toronto asks. "Long time to stand."

"Better than sitting," Mercer says.

"Let me know if the hill's too steep."

"What are you going to do, carry me?"

"If I need to."

"Like hell you are," Mercer says.

They each have another sip from the flask before Toronto slips it back into the pocket of his dress blues. "Fucking Jerry," Toronto says.

"Fucking Jerry," Mercer says. "Yup."

"Fucker would drink and drink and then take a half-rack home with him. I can't remember him *not* drinking."

"It served a purpose," Mercer says.

"Speaking of," Toronto says. "Are you still on the painkillers, too?"

"Takes two just to get out of bed."

"Be careful combining. I don't want to have to come and pick up your dead blue respiratory-arrested ass."

"I don't breathe out of my ass."

"You talk out of it a lot."

"All I want," Mercer says, "is for things not to hurt so much. I'm only twenty-nine. Twenty-nine. You'd think that wouldn't be too much to ask."

"You can ask," Toronto says, "but don't count on getting. Welcome to life."

They walk past the cars parked near the gravesite, past the hearse at the front of the line, and they fall in with the other mourners around Jerry's grave. Apart from the nieces and nephews, whom Jerry never mentioned, Mercer knows just about everyone. Fire and police from Colma, Daly City, Broadmoor, South City. Colma city employees. Chicko and Mae from Death's Door. Mercer's never seen Chicko with his hair combed, or with an unstained shirt, and he's never seen Mae in sunlight. Behind them all, San Bruno Mountain looms like a vast worried forehead, with deep shadows furrowing its slopes.

There's a white-noise *schuss* from cars on the freeway, and gas-powered edgers and leaf blowers buzz in the distance. From among these mechanical sounds rises another one that catches his attention: the sound of an old prop plane starting up, the *sput-sput-sput,* the propeller whine, the choppy, Dopplered grind as it flies. He glances around, but he doesn't see anything in the air. The sound isn't directional; it seems to be everywhere. It's drowning out the priest's somber tenor, but no one else seems to hear.

Then there is a *chup-chup-bang,* and there is the wrenching crack of wood being split, like a thick limb being torn from a tree in a storm, and he feels a heavy impact with the earth vibrating through his feet. And still no one else is reacting. Hands raise tissues to dab at eyes. The white-bearded priest continues on solemnly, but his voice sounds like it's coming from underwater. There is a burble of *Amen.*

Relax, he tells himself. Maintain. It must be the pills and pain and whiskey messing with a sleep-bled brain. He closes his eyes—a pose that he hopes looks like grieving—and concentrates on the beating of his heart and the sour-mash aura that envelops him and Toronto.


Ishi, the last Yahi Indian, kneels alone under a willow tree, chanting a tribal song of mourning.


After the burial, everyone drifts back to the parking lot, family with family, police with police, fire with fire. A limousine takes the family members away. Chicko invites everyone in uniform to Death's Door for drinks on the house, and Mercer is the only one who begs off. He expects the other cops to pressure him into going, but no one does. Consciously or not, they're keeping their distance from him; injured cops are the last people healthy cops want to be around. There but for the grace of God, and all that.

Mercer limps to the Oldsmobile. He stands there with the door open and fusses with his key ring, stalling so he won't have to lower himself in while anyone's watching. (*Slowly,* the doctor told him. *No twisting. Get in like you're wearing a skirt.*) He flips his cell phone open and plays a few hands of blackjack, but he keeps busting and gets fed up quickly. The guys are really lollygagging in the parking lot, so Mercer decides to make a call or two.

First, Kelly. They've been playing phone tag since the accident, although she did visit him in the hospital. Most of his visitors brought flowers, books, magazines; she brought a bottle of vodka and a box of condoms, STUDDED FOR HER PLEASURE. An incentive, she said, to get well soon. She couldn't stay long because she was on a deadline—a short piece, not the DiMaio feature, which she was still fine-tuning.

He punches up her number on speed dial. The line rings and rings, then goes to voice mail. He hears her voice—cool and professional, but still with the sexy rasp that tinges everything she says, no matter how mundane, with something raw and unrestrained. *You've reached Kelly Chaleski at* Limn *magazine. I can't take your call right now, but . . .* At the tone, he says, "Kelly, it's Mike." He gets nervous and pauses, suddenly afraid he might be slurring. "I'm just leaving my friend Jerry's funeral. I could use a little cheering up. Call back when you can, okay? It'd be great to hear your voice. I miss you." He regrets those last words. Needy. But there's truth in that: his back is fucked up, he has headaches that don't quit, and he can't go to work because he's been put on leave. He has nothing but free time. He'd like to spend some of it with her, see where this thing goes.

He calls Owen, but Owen gets no answer there, either. Owen and Mollie came to the hospital, too, with Kinnicutt and the two Johnnys. Mollie was sporting a big diamond on her finger. When he noticed it, she winked at him, and Owen flashed a sheepish but cool smile and said, "What else could I do? She's been putting up with me for years." Mercer wondered if Owen was going to ask him to be his best man, and even though he decided he didn't care about ceremonial stuff like that, he was disappointed when they all left without the subject ever coming up.

When the parking lot clears, he eases himself into the car. Instead of going home, though, he gets on 280 heading south. He's feeling wistful, but sharper, more alert than usual. *Maybe loss wakes you up,* he thinks. Long drives hurt like hell, but it feels like a good day to be out on the road. He can tough out the pain. Plus he has a couple of Vicodins loose in his pocket that he can suck on if he needs to. They're dry and bitter, but he's grown to like the taste.

When he sees the sandstone Father Serra, who's still pointing, always pointing, he follows the missionary's advice by heading toward the water on Highway 92, winding through the hills, past nurseries, past goats, past farmers' stands. When he reaches the coast and Highway 1, he turns north, figures he'll make a loop and head home. By now, though, the pain has crept along his leg; the muscles have seized up, the nerve is burning, and he keeps having to tell himself to unclench his teeth. He's got to get out and walk around.

He turns left onto the first beach-access road he finds. It's a beach with no name, or no sign, anyway. The narrow, rutted road ends in a semicircular gravel-and-dirt parking lot on a bluff. There's a guy in a pickup truck reading a newspaper, facing out at the waves. Mercer parks so the guy won't be able to see him easily, then opens the door, swings both legs outside, and uses the door frame to pull himself up. The pain goes supernova, and he leans all his weight on the door, afraid he'll crumple to the gravel if he doesn't. He lets his right leg dangle and waits for the muscles to unclench. His eyes water, and he pounds a fist down on the roof of the car. He looks over and sees the guy in the truck staring at him. Mercer gives him a thanks-for-caring wave and limps off toward the dirt trail that winds along the bluff. There's a salt smell in the cool wind, openness and relief in the coastal air. He watches a steamer disappear into the white clouds draping the horizon, watches a few wet-suited surfers ride small waves off a stretch of sandy beach to the south. After a few minutes, he hikes back to the car, vows to find a new way to clear his head that doesn't involve so much driving.

Stopped at a light on the north side of Half Moon Bay, a man (W-M, 40) and a girl (W-F, 10) cross the highway in front of him. The girl has a round face and a snubby nose and long, wavy brown hair; she wears a floppy bucket hat that hides her eyes. He feels a spark of recognition: she looks like the girl on a *Have You Seen Me?* mailer he got recently. He'd taken the time to remember the blue-inked, age-progressed face—if he can't be on active duty, the least he can do is be alert.

A truck behind him honks because the light has turned, and the girl, startled, looks back at the road. It's not her after all. She is the not-lost daughter of the man who has his hand on her shoulder, and Mercer is a damaged man whose mind is playing tricks on him.

Up over Devil's Slide and through Pacifica, he wrestles with the idea of stopping at Fiona's. He turns off the highway at her exit and does a drive-by, even though he knows he shouldn't. She's not there—of course she's not, she's at work, which he guesses he knew all along. The outside of the house looks the same as always, except that bright-yellow oxalis is invading the spaces between the rosebushes. He expected to feel regret or sadness looking at a place where he's not welcome, but he doesn't. Instead he feels only flatness; it's just a house, it's there in front of him, and it feels familiar in a distant, beige kind of way. He sees a flutter in the curtains—Cricket, probably, about to leap up to the window seat—and he stops the car, waiting, but the cat does not appear. When his leg starts to burn again, he turns the car around and heads for home.

He approaches the driveway to The Willows just as Lorna's Chevy is turning in, and he follows her down the incline to the parking garage. At the base of the ramp, they split up; Mercer's spot is to the left, hers is to the right. He hopes he can avoid her—he doesn't want to talk, doesn't want her to see him like this—but he knows he can't jump out of the car and get upstairs quickly enough. He hauls himself up, hangs on the door, and waits, teeth clenched again, tight, tighter. He imagines a tooth shattering from the pressure, spreading jagged bits of enamel.

Her shoes clap across the concrete toward him. "Officer Mercer!" she calls out. "Let me help you!"

"I'm fine," he says, but it comes out in a strangled tone that doesn't project across the echoey space. He tests his weight on his leg and immediately jerks it back into the air, wincing. He stands there on one leg, feeling like the world's stupidest stork.

"I didn't realize it was so bad," she says. "Please let me help. You can hold my hand. Lean on my shoulder."

"Lorna," he says, "I don't want any help."

She smiles at him. "You're just like Wes. He had trouble asking for help, too."

He's suddenly furious. "I am not like Sergeant Featherstone!" he shouts. The force of his voice makes her step back. He can't tell if she's frightened or wounded, but right now he can take pleasure in either. He wants to keep shouting at her. He wants to tell her that her husband was completely out of his fucking mind, in case she hadn't noticed. He gimps over to the staircase, leaving her in silence. He grabs the railing and pulls himself up the first step. Second. Third. He knows she's watching him struggle. Fine. Whatever.

There's a new *Have You Seen Me?* card in his mailbox: a sweet-looking Hispanic boy with wild puffs of curly black hair. He tacks the card up on his wall, next to the girl's and the dozen others he has put up, and studies these faces, trying to remember them all. Jesus. So many kids, just *gone*.

Jude checks the piece of paper, trying to decipher his own writing. The directions are approximate; the girl at the warehouse in the Mission either hadn't known precisely, or had been too trashed to be precise, or had held back at the last minute because she wasn't sure she should be giving the information out.

There's a notebook attached to the dashboard on a suction-held platform. His parents are checking the mileage on the Prospector every day, and he's supposed to log all of his trips in the book like some cabdriver. He figures he can do it retroactively, see how many miles he goes, then concoct an itinerary that'll satisfy them. They're down in L.A. for the weekend, anyway, and he doubts Mrs. Hankin-Cherry, who's supposed to watch him, is going to bother totting up his miles, even as nosy as she is. Fuck all of them, anyway. This is something he has to do.

He stops in front of a run-down-looking house with paint that has faded to a urinary yellow. In the driveway is the matte-black pickup the girl said Bobby was driving these days. In the yard are a couple of empty plastic bags, an old tire, and a puke-green couch with no legs. He can hear music playing inside. There are a few other cars parked on the street in front: a rusted El Camino; a shined-up VW Fastback; a sensible newer Honda; and a brown Pinto with a BOYS SUCK bumper sticker and a gash in the hood, around which white spray paint declares the car CUNTMOBILE.

Jude gets out and walks slowly up the driveway. Through the passenger-side window of the truck he sees a few empty devil-red cans of Azteca—Reyna's favorite—along with her gray hooded sweatshirt. He follows the weedy path of cracked stones from the driveway to the front door. He hasn't planned this, doesn't know what he's going to say. He rings the bell, but it's broken, so he knocks. No answer. He knocks again. And again. And there's something about having a closed door between him and Reyna that makes him brave and a little crazy, and he kicks the door and pounds it with his fist and shouts, "Let me the fuck in!" A heavy-lidded girl opens the door. She has a half-dozen metal hoops through each eyebrow and in each nostril, more piercings through her eyebrows and lips. He met her at the warehouse. She's younger, maybe fifteen. Her name is Lynn, but Bobby calls her Ratgirl because of her skinny face and pointed nose. Another girl from the peninsula who's fallen off the achievement track, if she was ever on it.

"Hey," she says. "Who are you?"

"We met at the warehouse. Squid's."

"Huh," she says, opening the door wider.

The house smells like bongwater and smoke and sweat and neglect. What he's seeing is the damage from a party that has been going on for weeks. Fist- and foot-sized holes gape in the drywall. Empty bottles and cans are on the floor, kicked or tossed to the perimeter of the room. The rug is thin and fraying and Rorschached with black stains. A ponytailed guy has nodded off on a ripped-up recliner that leaks yellow foam. He recognizes another girl from the warehouse, Yolanda; she's sitting against the wall, drumming on her thighs out of sync with the music. Her boyfriend, whose name Jude can't remember, sits next to her. He looks vacant.

The plastic beads strung over a doorway rattle and part, and Carlos appears.

"Hey, Carlos," Jude says, feeling proud, feeling tough, and he expects Carlos to goggle at him, expects him to be blown away that Jude would show his face after what happened.

Instead Carlos takes a pull on an Azteca, then belches and tosses the empty can into the corner. "Word," he says. "Long time no."

Jude doesn't know what to say.

"*Mi casa es,* and whatnot," Carlos says. "Grab a beer."

"Is Trent around?" Jude wants to play it cool, not sound too psycho about needing to see Reyna.

"Nah, man," Carlos says. "Trent's in rehab. Some fucking boot-camp kind of rehab. In, like, Guam or some fucking place."

"No way," Jude says. "I was, too."

"In Guam?"

"Not exactly."

"Trent ODed, dude."

"Wow," Jude says. "That's intense."

"It was pretty fucked up."

"But he's all right?"

"Well," Carlos says, "he's in Guam."

"Is Reyna around?" Jude asks. "And Bobby?"

"Kitchen." Carlos points a thumb over his shoulder, down a gloomy hall-way. There are more ragged holes in the wall and, beneath them, fine white dust and chunks of drywall on the floor, on the baseboards. The tiny kitchen is at the rear of the house, and Jude stands in the doorway, looking in. Reyna is in there alone, with her back to him. She's fumbling to fit two slices of white bread into an old metal toaster.

He's been wondering what it would be like to see her again. One of the kids at Seven Oaks had told him the meds would kill his libido, make him a zombie, but seeing her again is an electric jolt, even just this view from the back. Faded boys' jeans hang off her narrow hips, and she's wearing a loose tank top that might offer a glimpse of her tits if she moves the right way. It's even cute that she's too fucked up to make toast. He's instantly hard, meds or no meds, and he's sure he was right to come here.

She pushes down the toaster lever and stands there; he can tell she's look-ing into the glowing wires, feeling the heat waft across her face.

"Reyna," he says. He says it again, and then a third time before she re-sponds. She turns to face him and a slow smile spreads across her face. Her forehead and nose and shoulders are a new-new pink.

"Whoa," she says. "Jude."

He stays in the doorway, slouching against the frame in a way that feels cool. "Found you," he says.

"I'm making toast," she says.

Jude nods. "I saw."

"So, you're all right?" She stuffs her hands into her front pockets, which pushes the jeans even lower on her waist.

"Sure," he says.

"I've been feeling bad. It wasn't supposed to go that far."

"It's cool," he says. "Whatever doesn't kill me, and whatnot."

"So, yeah," she says, "what have you been up to?"

He almost says *I've been thinking a lot about you.* That's what he's been imag-ining saying to her. His nerve fails him, though, and instead he says, "Rehab."

"You? That's crazy."

"That's my parents," he says.

She approaches him and folds him into a bony hug. "I'm glad you're all right," she says. It's a quick hug, friendly and nothing more, but this is what he's needed, this moment of connection, this soft brush of her breasts against him, this warmth, and it doesn't matter that they're in a kitchen where silverware is rusting in the sink and mold is growing in the seams of the linoleum and the air smells of stale beer and leaky freezer and burnt-black toast crumbs.

"There were cops," he says. "I didn't tell them anything."

"I knew you wouldn't," she says, and right there is all the justification he'll ever need for feeling like he did the right thing in not ratting her out. "Things sometimes get out of control, right?" she says.

"Right," he says. "Whose place is this, anyway? It's a dump."

"Carlos rents it. Yolanda and her boyfriend kind of live here, too. Mostly it's a place for everyone to party and crash."

Footsteps approach from down the hallway, and Reyna peers out under his arm to see who's coming. Bobby, followed by Carlos and Ratgirl. Then they're all in the kitchen together.

Jude has spent a lot of time imagining what Bobby's reaction to seeing him would be—in the best daydreams, Bobby looks like the bad guys in *Unforgiven* when they realize Clint has come back to kick their amoral asses—and again, he's disappointed. Bobby ignores him. He wraps his arms around Reyna, sways her back and forth, smiles at her. Jude hates him more than ever.

"Look who's here, Bob," Reyna says.

"My man," Bobby says to him. "How's it hanging?"

"I'm doing all right," he says.

"That shit wasn't supposed to happen," Bobby says. "Ask anyone."

"We're cool," Jude says. "Don't worry."

"Did I say I was worried?"

"There were cops," Reyna says, looking up at Bobby. "He didn't say anything."

"Good man," Bobby says.

Ratgirl squeezes past them and opens the fridge. "We're out of beer," she says.

Bobby turns to Jude. "Beer run? Can you drive? We're all pretty fucked up."

"All right," Jude says. "I can drive."

"You buying?" Bobby says.

Jude looks at Reyna and she rolls her eyes at him. "How about you buy, Bobby, for fucking once?" he says.

Bobby laughs. He holds his hand out to Carlos, to Ratgirl. "Come on," he says. "Give till it hurts." Then they all walk back to the living room, and Bobby makes the rounds. When he has a fistful of ones and fives, he and Reyna and Jude head outside to the Prospector. Jude hopes Reyna will ride shotgun, but she gets in back, and Bobby plunks himself down in the passenger seat. He scratches at his scraggly beard. He smells like armpit.

"Onward," Bobby says, and Jude looks in the rearview at Reyna, who's running her hand over the seat leather. She meets his eyes and smiles at him, a smile that feels honest and maybe even welcoming. Onward they go.

It's late at night, who knows what time it is, and the speed freaks are still awake and jabbering at each other somewhere in the back of the house, but most people are on couches, on chairs, on the floor. Jude wakes up because he has to pee, and even with the lights on in the place he's tripping over himself and bumping into walls. He doesn't know what was in that bud of Carlos's that he smoked, but it knocked him on his ass. He's so groggy he can't remember where the bathroom is. He pushes open each door when he comes to it. Sooner or later he'll find a toilet.

First room: a boom box plays some slow, tripped-out grooves, and Carlos is lying on the bed, on top of the covers, with a girl who showed up at the house with a bunch of friends sometime around sunset. They're a tangle of limbs, and the room smells like vomit. The scene screams out heroin, and Jude doesn't want any part of that. Shit'll kill you. It almost killed Trent. Carlos is even dumber than he thought.

He turns and leaves, cracking his shoulder on the door frame as he passes through. The next door leads to a linen closet, empty. Next one: a room with a mattress on the floor and two naked people in a twist of sheets. Even before he recognizes them as Reyna and Bobby, he watches them, fascinated. His gaze follows the path of her exposed skin: up one leg, across her flat stomach. It's dark, but he thinks he can see a curve of breast. He should turn around and leave, but he doesn't. He's just watching her as she breathes, and then his hand is running over the front of his jeans in the same rhythm. He's standing in a hallway touching himself, this is a bad, bad idea, anyone could see him, but now he's imagining what it would be like to be in Bobby's place now, and then his hand is undoing a button and slipping inside his jeans, gripping, rubbing. He should be ashamed to be doing this, ashamed, but—

He feels a hand on his back, and he wheels, yanking his hand out of his pants, and there is Ratgirl, holding a plastic jug of vodka. "Dirty," she whispers to him, and giggles.

She leads him down the hall and into the bathroom, where they're surrounded by a sour, eye-watering smell. She hands him the vodka, and while he's drinking, she tugs his unbuttoned jeans down. She kneels on the tile and gives him a few licks and a tickle with the bar in her tongue, then rises and gestures for the bottle again. She stands on tiptoes and says with wet lips into his ear, "You're cute," and Jude's impulse is to say, *Yeah? You're not, everyone thinks you look like a rat, and there's a pound of metal in your face,* but instead he stops at "Yeah?" And then he thinks of Reyna with Bobby, of seeing them together, and suddenly it doesn't matter if he lies and says, "So are you," and the next thing he knows they're squeezed together in the cold bathtub, and his mouth is bumping metal everywhere as they kiss. He tugs off her shirt and sees her tiny, slack tits in the moonlight that drops through the dirty window. Yanks down her jeans. Then he's on top of her, inside her, thrusting wildly but without leverage, sliding, falling out, going in again. After a while she starts making little rat-cries, and he hates her for not being Reyna. It goes on forever, and he wonders if he's too wasted to come. All he wants to do is *feel* something, goddamnit, just get there and get this over with, so he slams himself into her harder and harder and harder, and they're both sliding around and banging heads and elbows on the wall, the faucet, the soap holder.

"I'm sorry," he says to her, after.

"Huh?" she says.

He can feel the disgust settling over him, weighing him down, crushing. The thick fog in his head clears enough for him to understand that he has to get out of that house now, right now. Maybe he can't drive home, but he can stumble out to the street and sleep in the Prospector, under the blanket that his mom put there in case of emergency.

He grabs his jacket off a chair in the front room, not walking quietly, not caring if he wakes anyone up. A digital camera on the floor catches his eye, and without thinking beyond *I want that,* he kneels and grabs it. Outside, he sets off the Prospector's piercing alarm trying to get in, but he jumps into the driver's seat and jams the key into the ignition to turn it off before the entire goddamned neighborhood wakes up. When quiet settles back in, he notices that he's shaking, his hands, then his shoulders, and suddenly it's like his whole body is convulsing. He pounds the dashboard, then presses his fists into his eyes so tears won't get out, but his face is getting wet and he can feel drops falling from his chin.

The SUV goes nowhere when he steps on the gas, again and again. It's a while before he dully realizes he's still in park. He cuts the engine, because a voice inside him is saying he will definitely, absolutely not make it home alive if he tries to drive. He climbs into the back seat and curls up under the blanket, trying to quit shaking, trying to get his goddamned body to lie still.

Toronto wakes up to the sound of sirens. It happens a lot in this neighborhood: the fire station is a block away, and right next to that is the old folks' home, which gets daily visits from ambulances. He closes his eyes and listens: these are the fire engines. He hears them whoosh by, speeding east toward Alamo Square.

He looks at the clock. It's not even seven yet. He guesses he went to bed at four. This is going to be some fucking day. His head feels like it's in a vise.

Gray light leaks through the blinds, which he didn't close all the way. The place looks emptier than he remembers, and a fuzzy memory emerges: being out on Grove Street in the late-late night, too late even for the homeboys in the barbecue lot, and dumping Mia's shit onto the curb. Clothes, CDs, makeup, shoes, blankets, the bulky papasan chair he's always hated. Everything he could pick up while lurching around the apartment out-of-his-head drunk. All she took with her was a duffel bag of clothes, her Rollerblades, a few magazines: enough for a long trip, not enough to look like she was going for good.

He still can't decide if she knew she'd abandon him all along, or if she decided spontaneously somewhere out in America, on an empty stretch of southwest highway, maybe, or in a motel bed with some stank hippie juggler. Another mystery: why she sent back the ring. Guilt, maybe? Did she think it would absolve her? It won't. She should've kept the goddamn thing.

He finds his cigarettes on the floor and shakes one out. His hand shakes badly as he lights it. The taste of bourbon is metal in his mouth, and that won't go away for hours, no matter what he eats or drinks or how much he brushes or gargles or smokes. He's also soaked in sweat, though he can't figure why; the apartment isn't warm, and the blankets are thin. He sniffs. The air around him smells sour and foul. His shorts are way too damp. He checks the sheets: damp. He pissed the bed. So wasted that he pissed the bed. God*damn*it.

Okay. Shit happens when you drink, and worse shit happens when you drink angry. But a shallow, fickle little bitch like Mia shouldn't make him lose control like this. She's not worth it. *But what would you do if she showed up this afternoon, said it was all a mistake, she wants you, loves you so much that it scares her, and can't you please understand that?* Answer: he doesn't know. He doesn't fucking know. That's love right there. Love fucks you *up*.

He takes a long shower and puts on clean clothes: jeans, T-shirt, sweat-shirt. He opens the apartment's lone window an inch or two, which is as far as the safety locks let it go. As he tears the soiled sheets from the bed, one corner of the fitted sheet doesn't come off, and he gives it a furious yank that blows out the elastic and the seam, and goddamn, that felt good. He drops the sheets into a laundry basket, grabs a box of detergent from the closet, and walks into the miserable gray light outside.

Just outside his door, at the base of the steps that lead up to the sidewalk, the Grove Street Cowboy is sleeping on a piece of dirty cardboard. Toronto sees him around a lot: an old black guy with a wiry white coil of beard. Walks around in a filthy, fake-buckskin jacket with fringes on the chest and sleeves. The Cowboy's mouth is moving a little, making little chewy noises, and the air around him stinks to high hell. Toronto feels a sudden, intense anger at him, at this broken fucking person sleeping in the doorway of the shitty apartment that Toronto shouldn't have to be living in, and he's about to nudge the guy with his foot, or shout him awake, or maybe even kick him—yes, he could kick the motherfucker, because he wants to bring down the full weight of his misery on some other human being, imagines the flood of release he'd feel.

But he doesn't. The muscles in his right leg are tensed, ready to explode with force, but he just doesn't do it. He can't. He relaxes his leg and watches the man sleep and chew and stink as the anger fades and leaves him ashamed of the state he's in. Jesus. He just almost kicked the shit out of the Grove Street Cowboy.

He steps around the Cowboy and climbs the steps, holding the basket over his head. Halfway up the stairs, he turns back and sees the old man looking at him. "Find somewhere else, buddy," Toronto says. "Let's move it along." The old guy nods, smiles an egg-toothed smile at him, mutters something Toronto can't understand.

Most of Mia's stuff has disappeared from the sidewalk—in this neighborhood, discarded things get picked over pretty quickly. All that's left are a few T-shirts and books. He's pretty sure he dumped all of her panties, but they're gone. Who the hell took those?

He walks the block and a half to the Laundromat on Divisadero. It's open but empty. He gets change for a five from the dispenser and starts the load, then collapses into a plastic chair, feeling dizzy and a little nauseous. *How could he have fallen for someone who'd just leave and not say anything? What the fuck is wrong with people that they disappear on you?*

He burps up bile, and the taste nearly starts him retching. He drops his head in his hands and bounces his knee, trying to get rid of all the jitters that are running through him. Mia's gone. He loved her, fiercely and intensely, and it was *real,* and that's not some melodramatic bullshit, that is stone-cold truth. He has lost what he's spent his whole life looking for. How could he ever feel worse? How could this *not* be the bottom? It's moments like these, he knows, that make people do stupid shit like find Jesus and turn themselves into Bible-thumping, twelve-stepping zombies. Fuck that. That's not for him. He may want to slash his goddamn wrists, but that's just another feeling he can tough out, goddamnit.

He looks for something to kill time with. There's a *Chronicle* on the table next to him, but it's three days old. Underneath it is a magazine devoted to black women's hair, and tucked into that is a Jehovah's Witness pamphlet that promises a glorious new world in which, apparently, happy little pigtailed girls can safely hug lions. Fucking *please*. On the bulletin board are the usual flyers for lost pets (GRAY TABBY: "SCUPPER") and guitar lessons and roommates wanted and junk hauling and life coaching. Someone has also pinned a bookmark up there, a plain green bookmark with the name and address of the San Francisco Zen Center on it, a nice little graphic of an ink-stroked circle. At the bottom, in a small, simple font: BEGINNERS' ZAZEN, 8:45 A.M., SATURDAYS. *Zazen*. Fucked if he knows what it means, but he likes the sound of it as a word, and something appeals to him about that circle that doesn't quite close on itself. He doesn't know much about Zen, but he's pretty sure they don't promise a glorious new world with cuddly wolves and horns of plenty, and he likes that, too. It's Saturday. It's eight-fifteen. And the place is on Page Street, ten minutes away.

Okay. This is not a rock-bottom epiphany. Rock-bottom epiphanies are for assholes. But he could use some more walking to clear his head. He'll grab a coffee and have a smoke along the way. He can always turn right around— and you can bet he will if anyone even *thinks* about asking him for his money.

Back on Grove, the Cowboy is swerving along the sidewalk in his direction. Toronto gets ready to hold his breath, but he decides no, if the world brings him the stink of an old man with a body full of booze and crap-loaded pants, so be it. Toronto nods as they pass. The Cowboy looks past him with unfocused eyes, as if they hadn't just interacted, as if Toronto weren't even there on the street.

It's as he's walking east along Fell Street, against the traffic, coffee in one hand and a cigarette between his lips, that he admits he misses Mia. He misses her so bad it hurts, and it might even make him puke here on the street. He stops and doubles over and waits. Eventually the nausea passes, and he starts to walk faster, because it feels like he's doing the right thing, checking out this place. He just has a sense, a sense that today's as good a day as any to try to believe in something besides other people.

When he arrives at the brick building at Page and Laguna, he realizes his wash cycle is finished, that the Laundromat is probably getting crowded and someone will take his sheets out and do fuck-knows-what with them. It's a good reason to head home—no, to head back to *that apartment*—but instead he says *Fuck it.* He drops his butt on the sidewalk, grinds it with his toe, wipes his eyes on his sleeve, and marches up the steps. Whatever will happen to his sheets will happen to his sheets. That's fucking Zennish right there, isn't it?

The front door is open, and there's a soft-looking, middle-aged woman in a russet-colored robe standing there. Her head is mostly shaved, just a dome of whitish fuzz over it, and she has a double chin and juggy ears. She bows to him as he reaches the top step, and that stops him. She watches him watch her, calm and still. There is kindness in her face.

He opens his mouth. "I—" he says, but he can't get further.

She nods slowly, like she understands anyway. And goddamn if he doesn't start crying his eyes out when she steps toward him and holds out her hand.

# SEVENTEEN

# SMYTHED

The day of Owen's party, Mercer drives out to the airport and rents a gleaming-white convertible. There's too much riding on this night for him to pick up Kelly in the Olds, with its dents and scrapes and broken antenna and blue smoke.

He also buys new clothes. He'd been irritated by Owen's insistence that everyone wear white, but when he looks into the fitting-room mirrors at Billingham's, he sees a good-looking young man in a white linen suit and a collarless white dress shirt, put-together and capable, not a sleep-deprived cop on disability leave. He'll have to thank Owen for giving him the excuse to splurge.

He picks Kelly up at her Cow Hollow apartment at eight. He has the top down, and the cool twinkly mist feels invigorating. He pulls into her building's driveway, climbs out, hangs, stretches, shakes out his leg, and walks up to the door. He's limping, but not badly, especially considering that he's laid off the Vicodin for most of the day to keep a clear head. He punches the buzzer for her apartment, and when he hears her voice in the speaker—*I'll be right down!*—he notices that his hands are in fists, as if they're trying to keep all the good feeling in him from getting away.

She comes through the door, throws an arm around him, and plants a kiss on his cheek, and then she turns a spin in front of him. She's wearing white go-go boots, a short white skirt that stretches over her hips, a white leather jacket, and white barrettes shaped like daisies in her red hair.

"You look amazing," he says.

"I feel totally Nancy Sinatra. I should have a bass line that plays when I walk." She smiles, and he notices that her teeth seem even whiter than the last time he saw her. "You're looking sharp yourself," she says.

"Thanks," he says. "I don't do a lot of dressing up."

"Is that an apology?"

"Just information."

"It's not information you need to give me. You look great. Deal with it." He holds out his arm. "Walk you to your carriage?"

"Why, thank you, sir," she says. She eyes the car. "This is yours?"

"Tonight it is."

She looks up at the gray sky, zips her jacket. "Let's put the top up," she says. "I'll freeze."

He's pretty sure he conceals his disappointment. "You got it," he says.

"You're in a better mood," she says.

"Better than when?"

"Last time you left a message. You sounded like you were having a near-death experience."

"The funeral," he says. "Plus, I was in pain."

"You're not in pain now?"

"I am, a little," he says. "But I'm in a good mood."

"Brilliant," she says. "Nothing but fun for us tonight. No games, no expectations, no apologies, just fun. The night takes us where it wants to."

"Count me in," he says. Crossing to the driver's side, he pretends to have trouble digging the keys from his pocket. When she bends over to wipe away a spot on her boot with a licked finger, he drops himself into his seat, keeping his face turned outward so she won't see him grimace.

Mercer points out the glow from Owen's backyard as they drive through the Presidio. "That's where we're going," he says.

"It's certainly bright," she says.

The house is a two-story, sand-colored Spanish-style that sits close to the street. Flickering lanterns line the steps up to the front door; flanking the steps, green and gold ornamental grasses flutter in the breeze. Laughter and violins rise from the backyard.

"Nice," Kelly breathes when she sees the interior: high ceilings, a sprawling open living area, immaculate hardwood and art-lined walls. Several dozen people—all in white—mill around, drinks in hand. Voices and laughter and clinked glasses ring through the generous space. Sitting on a couch are three girls from Mercer's high-school class, all visibly in different stages of pregnancy, all wearing shapeless white maternity dresses.

Mollie sees them come in and waves excitedly, then holds up a finger: *wait—watch this.* She finishes her drink, then takes a deep breath, gets herself into character—upper crust, all primness and decorum in a long, vintage white dress and elbow-length white gloves—and glides toward them. "What do you think?" she says. "I've been practicing my hostess walk." Her cheeks are reddening; Mercer guesses that drink wasn't her first. She hugs Kelly. "It's good to see you again. Are you taking good care of our friend here?"

"He doesn't need me to take care of him. He's pretty rugged."

"Where's the birthday boy?" Mercer says.

Mollie waves her finger at him. "No, no," she says. "Birthday *man*. We'll have none of this *boy* business. He's thirty now. You'll probably find him out back, trying desperately to be the center of attention." She offers to get them their first drinks; Mercer thanks her, but says they'll fend for themselves, and she should get back to enjoying the party.

Mollie catches his arm as they're moving on. "One thing, Mike. There are a few trays of spanakopita that we're keeping in the kitchen. You shouldn't eat it."

"Why's that?"

"Owen made it himself," she says. "It's special."

Mercer nods. "Thanks," he says.

He leads Kelly out to the deck, where a string quintet is playing. It's warmer than usual for this time of year, and the musicians seem uncomfortable. Mercer estimates the crowd on the wide swath of grass at close to a hundred, with people lined up at least five deep at each of the cocktail tables and food stations. Guests have spilled over into the next-door neighbor's yard, which is divided from Owen's only by some squat green shrubs. The neighbor's house is dark. Good, Mercer thinks; one less opportunity for a noise complaint.

"What did she mean about the spanakopita?" Kelly asks.

"There's marijuana in it."

"Yummy," she says. "I might just have to sample some."

"Be my guest," Mercer says.

"I am. And will continue to be. What about you?"

"I can't."

"Sure, you can."

"The job," Mercer says.

"What, they're going to drug-test you?"

"They could. But that's not the issue. I don't feel comfortable. I took an oath."

"Well," she says, "that's fine. I respect that. But you need to keep up with me somehow, so start drinking." She goes inside, returns with a paper plate with one small square of spanakopita on it.

"I'm pacing myself," she says. She holds the plate in front of him. "A nibble?"

He's momentarily tempted. He wants to stay on the same wavelength with her. But he can't. An oath is an oath. He shakes his head no.

"More for me," she says.

A lean white Samoyed jingles across the yard from one food station to another, wearing a white polo shirt that's knotted at its belly so as not to trail on the ground. On the croquet course, under the white glow of portable lights and the waning gibbous moon, a blond girl in white Capri pants and a fluffy white sweater swings her mallet and misses her ball completely; she and her companions shriek with laughter, the laughter of accomplished people un-used to—and deeply amused by—their own failure. Mercer looks down into the side yard, where Johnny G and Johnny K are playing bocce with two guys from Owen's dot-com days. They shout his name when they see him. He no-tices with some satisfaction that they let their gazes linger on Kelly.

"High-school friends," he tells her. "Good guys. I'll introduce you. Just want to find Owen first."

"That's him," she says, pointing. "It has to be."

She's right. Owen is in the center of the yard and at the center of a clutch of people who are hanging on his words. Even in this sea of white, his blond-blond hair and pale skin stand out.

"Looks like he's busy," Kelly says. "Bar first?"

As they wait in line for drinks, the Samoyed wanders over, nosing through the grass for bits of dropped food, sniffing shoes and legs. When the dog gets to Mercer, it looks up and barks once, which startles him—he's glad he doesn't have his drink in his hand yet. "Hello to you, too," he says, trying to cover. The dog fixes its steel-blue eyes on him, then yawns and wanders away.

With their glasses full, they pick their way through the crowded yard and catch Owen as he's moving from one group to another. He greets them with a wide grin and outstretched arms. He's wearing a suit that he had custom-made the last time he went to Thailand—white silk with a jacquard pattern ghosted onto it. A pince-nez sits on his nose. It must have plain-glass lenses, because Owen's vision is perfect.

"My dear Mr. Mercer," Owen says. "A hearty welcome to you and your lovely friend."

When Mercer introduces Kelly, Owen takes her hand and kisses it; she responds with an exaggerated curtsy.

"Happy birthday, amigo," Mercer says, and he doesn't object when Owen pulls him into a hug.

"I've heard much about you, Kelly," Owen says. "I'd be slack-jawed and dumbstruck at your beauty if my friend hadn't prepared me for it so thoroughly."

"Is he always so full of shit?" Kelly asks Mercer.

"Usually," Mercer says.

"What's it like being thirty?" Kelly asks him "Are you feeling old?"

"Are you kidding? Surrounded by lovely young ladies such as yourself? How could I?"

"Wow," Kelly says. "It doesn't stop."

Owen asks how Mercer's back is feeling. "I'm doing my best," Mercer says. He takes a big swallow of bourbon.

"That should help," Owen says.

A bulky man in a white three-piece suit and hat lumbers toward them, and Mercer is slow to recognize that it's Kinnicutt. He had expected that Kinnicutt would be one of the people who assembled their white outfits in intentionally clownish ways, but instead he looks suave, polished, comfortable.

Owen handles the introduction to Kelly, then excuses himself. "I have to go be hostly," he tells her. "I have a demanding public." And then he's off into the yard, the pattern on his suit flashing and fading as he passes under the lights.

"Let me guess," Kelly says to Kinnicutt. "Tom Wolfe."

"You got it," he says. "It's last year's Halloween costume."

Mercer's not sure who Tom Wolfe is. A writer, he guesses. "Heath's a writer," he says, working the transition. "I just gave a copy of his book to DiMaio."

"Did you talk it up?" Kinnicutt asks him.

He hadn't realized he was supposed to, and he's not sure how he'd do it anyway. "I wanted to give him a little time," he says.

"Michael," Kinnicutt says, "you disappoint."

"Kelly's a writer, too," Mercer says. "It's how we met. She works for a magazine."

"Which one?" Kinnicutt asks.

"*Limn*," she says.

He nods. "I like it," he says. "It's smart."

"What about you?" she asks.

"I'm smart, too."

She laughs, and Mercer feels a stab of jealousy. "What do you write?" she asks.

"Novels," he says. "I'm working on my second."

"Have I read your first?"

"Probably not," he says. "*The Shenanigan Tapes.* I wrote it, it came out, it went away."

"I've heard of it," she says.

"I'm hoping it'll get a second wind in Hollywood. That's why Mike was supposed to talk it up."

"Hey, I gave it to him," Mercer says. "That's a start."

"Don't you have an agent?" Kelly asks.

"Every contact helps," Kinnicutt says.

"I'm having coffee with Marco next week," Kelly says. "I can put in a word, too." She pulls a business card out of a silver holder and hands it to him. "Send me a copy."

"It's really good," Mercer says, because it's the kind of thing you should say when your friend writes a book, even if you don't believe it.

"I hope so," she says. "If it sucks, I won't bring it up."

Kinnicutt smiles. "That's all I can ask for," he says, and he winks, an affectation that Mercer thinks he picked up during his teaching stint in New York.

Two couples walk onto the dance floor and begin waltzing flawlessly. "Wow," Kelly says. "I wasn't expecting people to get all Merchant Ivory at this thing."

Mercer is lost in the music and the swirling, spinning dance when Kinnicutt says something to him. "What's that?" he asks.

"I said, is your dad living in Santa Cruz? I was down there the other day, and I thought I saw him."

Mercer throws a quick glance at Kelly. He doesn't want to be talking about his father in front of her. Or at all. "I don't know," he says. "We haven't been in touch."

"He was just kind of shuffling along down the sidewalk. It looked like him, anyway. He had a beard. White. He had a Hemingway look going on." A smile crosses his face, as if it's amusing to him, a damaged man who looks like Hemingway, and Mercer wants to throw him up against the sandstone wall and shake him. He's not sure if he's more upset at Kinnicutt, though, or at the idea that his father might be in the area, stumbling around.

Mercer uses his command voice. "I said, we're not in touch."

The waltz ends, and the dancers get an enthusiastic ovation. They take florid bows and move on. Kelly finishes her drink just as a server passes by, and she smoothly hands the empty glass off. "Are you ready for another one?" she asks Mercer.

He has a few sips left. "Still working," he says.

"Work harder." She smiles. Really, her teeth are astonishingly white.

"Have you tried the spanakopita?" Kinnicutt asks her.

"I have," Kelly says. "It hasn't hit yet."

"It will," he says. "It's good."

Once Kelly leaves for the bar, Kinnicutt moves in closer, like he doesn't want to be overheard. "Dude," he says, "I thought your girlfriend was—"

"Was what?"

"You know. Old."

"That was someone else."

"No shit," he says. "So what's up with you and this one?"

"We're getting started."

"You met her through the DiMaio thing?"

Mercer nods. "She came on a ride-along."

"You dog," Kinnicutt says. "A man in uniform."

As the night goes on, conversations buzz, peter out, recirculate. The crowd is divided roughly in half: those who've become their parents, and those who are living the same lives they did in college, only now without the college. From the former, Mercer hears about mortgages and birth coaches, about ecotourism and oil prices, about hedge funds and dog-walkers, about 401(k)'s and 403(b)'s, about case law and sales channels. From the latter, conversations about bands coming to Slim's, about the surf at Ocean Beach, about hookups and hangovers, about Vegas strippers and Vancouver bud, about sky-high rents and psychotic roommates. In both groups, though, are stunned-looking people who wobble and stare and muse about how the spanakopita must be catching up to them.

Mercer circulates freely, talking, listening, sometimes with Kelly but other times alone. In the crowd she has found old friends, colleagues, interview subjects. He has vowed not to cling, and he is being rewarded; each time she spins away, she returns before long, usually with full glasses and a toast to whatever the night will bring.

The string quartet packs away their instruments, surrendering their space to a DJ, a tan-skinned kid with dreadlocks and sunglasses that cover most of his face. He calls people out to dance in an unplaceable accent and spins music that sounds Brazilian, African, Middle Eastern, flowing seamlessly from one groove to the next. Mollie appears by his side and pulls him to the dance floor; he moves stiffly, careful not to twist at the waist, but it feels good to move. She puts her hands on his shoulders and leans in close to his ear. "How's it going with Kelly?" she asks.

"All right, I think. We're both having fun."

"She's cute."

"I like her a lot," he says. "I haven't felt like this in a long time." He spins her, then pulls her back into him.

"It's good to see you letting go," she says.

He dances with Rae, Johnny G's girlfriend, who's wearing a white sailor suit; he dances with a friend of Mollie's from work; he dances with a tall, athletic woman, who owns the Samoyed. He's feeling loose, his back isn't bothering him too much, goes in search of Kelly, finding her in a small group with some magazine writers. Without saying anything, he takes her hand and walks her back to the dance floor, in time to the music, and he even spins her a few times as they go. As soon as they get there, though, the DJ fades out the music and hands a microphone to Mollie.

Her voice fills the yard, echoes back from the gully. She thanks everyone for coming, tells them how much it means to Owen that they're here and how long he's been looking forward to this party. "Some people get upset when they turn thirty," she says. "Owen's excited. He says it's going to give him gravitas. We'll see about that.

"Thank you also, most of you, for observing the no-gift policy," she continues. "Some people brought booze, which means that we'll have to have another party to drink whatever we don't get to tonight. And one of you wiseasses—and I assume it's one of the doctors in the house—brought us a rainbow assortment of erectile-dysfunction drugs. We'll be making those available tonight for anyone who needs them."

"Save a few, honey," Owen calls out. "I'm an old man."

She laughs into the mike, which produces a soft ring of feedback. "Please be advised," she says, "that your hosts accept no responsibility for any prolonged, painful erections."

"You're responsible for mine, Mollie," Johnny K shouts out, and a ripple of laughter flows across the lawn. Mercer also sees a few people rolling their eyes, in a *Can you believe these people?* way, and he wants to grab them, sit them down, and defend his friends. Yes, Owen is pretentious. Yes, they all try too hard to be clever. But they're his friends, and they're good people, and that is something altogether too fucking rare. On both counts.

"Be that as it may, Johnny," Mollie says, "I'd like to raise a toast to Owen, my partner and my best friend. And to that gravitas he's promised me."

Glasses are raised, and drinks are drunk. Owen strides up to Mollie and kisses her deeply. Mercer watches him, expecting him to undercut the moment somehow—a joke, a pinched ass, a melodramatic gesture—but it doesn't come. He kisses her, plain and honest. He takes the mike and tucks his pince-nez into the pocket of his jacket. He thanks everyone, too. He says he is not just grateful but humbled, and that every day with Mollie has been the luckiest day of his life. There's a hush as he gives the mike back to the DJ. Mercer thinks it's because no one expects Owen to be plainspoken, succinct, ordinary, completely sincere and humble.

The air quickly fills with music again—a loungey groove with a flute melody and a bass drum urging it along—and Mercer is thinking about asking Kelly to dance when the two Johnnys and their girlfriends, Rae and April, approach them. "We're going exploring," Johnny K says. Code for: smoking out, maybe doing a few lines. "You guys want to come along?"

"I'm in," she says. She touches Mercer's arm and says, "You don't mind?"

"Go," Mercer says. "We're having fun, remember? We can dance later." She kisses him on the cheek, and they disappear around the side of the house. He hears the gate open, then close behind them.

A little while later, he finds himself alone in the kitchen, looking at four trays that are empty except for scatters of phyllo flakes. The trays are finger-streaked where spilled filling has been scooped up. The oven is on, and he opens the door to peek inside, enjoying the bank of sweet hot air, buttery and green, as it rushes out to him and warms his face. He's not so drunk that he'll ignore his oath; he's proud of his resolve, but sad to be missing out on the fun. He's on his way out the door when a crying woman pushes past him, followed by a man hissing at her to calm down, she's just making a scene. She slams out the front door; he mutters an exasperated *fuck* and follows. Mercer notices a smudge of her runny black mascara on his lapel, where she bumped him. That's his luck, he thinks; a couple gets loaded and implodes, and his new suit is collateral damage.

He gets another glass of bourbon outside, opting this time for a hundred proof instead of just eighty-six. He wants that burn. He also bites off and swallows half a Vicodin, which is dumb, he knows, but the synergy will be awfully nice, liquid and calm. He stands close to the bar trying not to look alone and watches as the dance floor writhes in white, and people on the lawn are swaying to the beats, too. He lets his eyes lose focus and watches all this white, all this motion, all these people blurring together in the stark blue-white light shining down on them.

**W**hen he sees Kelly return to the party with the Johnnys and their girls, he checks his watch. She's been gone fifty-two minutes. He watches her walk down the steps from the deck into the yard, watches her scan the crowd for him. At least, he hopes it's for him. She comes within ten yards but doesn't see him, and he has to call out to her.

She's wiping her nose. "We went down to the beach," she says. "You should've come."

"I can't do that," he says. "Like I said."

"That was okay, right?" she says. "We're still friends?" She hip-bumps him, and pain shoots down his leg. A cry of surprise escapes him. "Shit," she says. "I'm sorry. I forgot. I'm a little tweaked."

Mercer nods. He's not about to contradict her.

"If you pulled me over," she says, "and I was like this, would you arrest me?"

"Absolutely," he says.

"How would you know, though?" she says, putting her hands on her hips. "How would you test me?"

He rattles off the list of field-sobriety tests he likes to use: Walk a straight line and turn. One-leg stand. Horizontal-gaze nystagmus. Pupil evaluation. And so on.

"I'd be good at some of those," she says. "I bet I could beat them."

"I don't think so," he says. "I'd get you."

"Do me," she says. "Test me."

"Are you really interested?" Usually, when people ask him to do this at parties, he ends up feeling like a novelty. Like a monkey doing tricks for their amusement.

"Sure," she says. "It'll be fun *and* educational."

A small crowd gathers around them as he gives her a battery of tests. She fails every one of them, and afterward, he explains to her where she went wrong. On the walk-and-turn, she had started walking before he'd finished giving the instructions, had taken eleven steps instead of nine, had held her arms out for balance, had stopped once and wobbled. Her tiny, constricted pupils were also a giveaway. And with her eyes closed, she'd estimated that fifteen seconds were thirty. "There's no way you'd be driving home," he tells her.

She beckons him closer with a finger, then whispers in his ear. "What if I gave you a blow job?"

"You would?"

"I might."

"I'd have to check the rule book," he says. Suddenly he's hopeful again, excited to have her attention. Maybe they will take Owen up on his offer of a guest bedroom tonight.

"Let me know what it says. And don't take too long."

That voice, those words. He feels flushed, and heat races to his groin. He's exactly where he wants to be, here at this party with Kelly, free of obligation and responsibility, intoxicated enough that the pain feels distant. He pulls her in close to him. "You look great tonight," he says, into her rosemary-scented hair. "I love the boots."

She upends her drink, works an ice cube around in her mouth. "I'm going through a boot phase," she says. Her tone turns detached, as if she's delivering a soliloquy. "It's very fetishistic, I think. I just bought a pair of black knee-high boots, patent leather, and I wore them when I went clubbing with Booth the other night. You remember Booth. We did some X. Does that bother you? We did some X, and in the limo at the end of the night, I was feeling sexy and he was horny, and I said we shouldn't wait to get home. I hiked up my skirt and got on top of him. I came, like, seven times in the car."

Mercer is stunned. Silent.

"What?" she says.

"Nothing."

She's knocking her empty glass against her thigh, and it's making Mercer nervous. He fights the urge to grab it away from her, or to hold her arm still.

"You think what I said was inappropriate," she says. "You're upset."

"I didn't say that."

"You're not saying anything."

"I guess not," he says.

"I'm not in a monogamous place right now."

"I know." He should have known before, he realizes. She'd gone to the DiMaios' with Booth and ended up in the gazebo with him. He'd just chosen to believe that meant something more than it did. He feels presumptuous. Foolish.

"Just making everything clear, okay?" she says. "So we can enjoy the night. Are you upset?"

Mercer shrugs, drinks. His right leg is aching, and he shifts his weight to rest it. Of course he's upset. He's been miserable since the accident, and his only relief has been thinking about her. He doesn't want to share her, not with Booth, not with anybody. But he also doesn't want to pass up the chance that the two of them might start something new and good and intense and passionate tonight—with none of the doubt or guilt that he lugged around for all that time with Fiona. If Kelly would give him a shot, they'd be great together. This is a truth as thick and real as the lump that's risen in his throat.

"Don't be upset," she says. "We can still have fun, if you let us."

"Of course we can," he says, with as much conviction as he can summon. "We can have a lot of fun."

"Good," she says. "You'll just have to keep up with me."

He loses her in the crowd a few minutes later. He scans the lawn for her. All this white. So much fucking white.

He finds himself standing alone with a gin-and-tonic in his hand that he doesn't remember asking for. He doesn't see any of his friends, either. He wanders over to the croquet course, where the tall, goateed husband of one of the pregnant women is swinging a mallet through the air. He's wearing a white flannel suit that's pinched at the shoulders, tight through the hips, riding ankle-high, and the effect is to make him look comically elongated, Lincolnesque. Mercer wanders over and asks if he wants a game. There's another mallet lying in the grass nearby, and Mercer gets his toe under the shaft and flips it up to himself smoothly. He's gotten to be a pro at not bending over. "You know the rules?" he asks. "Because I don't."

Mercer has blue-black-green; the other guy—Jason something—has red-yellow-orange. Neither of them plays well; it takes a long time to get through the first couple of wickets. While Jason is lining up a shot, Mercer stares at his own shadow on the floodlit grass and realizes he's wobbling. There's a soft *plack,* and Mercer looks up to see Jason smiling; his ball bumped Mercer's green one. "I get to knock yours away now," he says. "It's not personal. It's the fun part of the game."

"Whatever," Mercer says.

Jason swings and sends Mercer's ball skidding across the grass, through a group of women who are laughing so hard they don't even notice. Mercer has to wade into their circle to hit back onto the course. On his next turn, he hits his ball into the red one. "Payback's a bitch," he tells Jason. He steadies his foot on his own ball and takes a mighty backswing. Pain shoots down his leg, and the *thwock* of mallet and ball is loud enough to stop several conversations nearby. The red ball goes sailing into the back fence. There's a splintering sound as the ball goes right on through the thin wood. "Shit," Mercer says, "I'm sorry."

"Dude," Jason says. "It's a fucking *game.*" He drops his mallet and walks away, shaking his head.

Well, whatever. Mercer walks toward the splintery hole in the fence, hoping the red ball didn't sail all the way into the gully. Shielding his eyes from the glare of the lights, he spots it, two feet away from the drop-off, resting on a bed of stripped eucalyptus bark. Mercer reaches over the fence, tries to use the mallet head to pull the ball back to him, but he can't do it, and he's afraid to stretch farther because his back and his leg are on fire. He's about to look for Jason—or anyone taller than he is, anyway—when he hears a scratching sound coming from beyond the fence. It's the polo-shirted Samoyed, clawing the ground, sending up a spray of dirt and pine needles and bark. The dog's nails scrape against something hard, and it yips, springs away startled, then returns, sniffing at what it's found.

Mercer walks along the fence line and finds a narrow gap where the dog got through. He squeezes himself in, leaving another dirty streak on his suit, and he cautiously approaches the dog, who is scrabbling away at something in the ground and growling quietly.

It's gray, Mercer sees, and flat. Marble? When he crouches for a closer look, the dog backs away from him, ears down. He sweeps away dirt with his palm and sees an *H.* Next to it, an *E.* Next to that, the curved, age-smoothed edge of the stone.

The dog sniffs at his hands, yawns with a high-pitched squeak, and trots away.

. . .

The gravestone is smooth, rounded at the top, three feet high, two feet wide, a few inches thick. Just a surname carved into it: SMYTHE. No first name, no dates, no epitaph.

It is photographed in the ground by a *Chronicle* photographer who's a guest at the party, then lifted out of the ground and displayed on the deck. People kiss it for luck, pose with it in cell-phone photos. Two guys in horn-rims make a game of using the name in movie titles: *Smythed Poets Society, Smythe on the Nile, Smythed Man Walking, Kiss Me Smythely, Smythe of a Salesman, Evil Smythe,* and *Evil Smythed II.* A woman with a lemon-sucking look on her face loudly asks if there's a body out there, too, and is told no, stones just got scattered around when the cemeteries were dug up. Johnny K pours a beer on the deck in front of the stone and says a prayer for all his Smythed homeys.

It's midnight, or one, or two, and the crowd has thinned. Johnny G bounces up to Mercer at the bar. He's full of energy, but his eyes are glass. "Mike, dude," he says. "What's with you and that girl?"

"What do you mean?"

"Nothing. It's just."

"Just what?"

"She's a funny chick, man."

"What are you talking about?" Mercer says. "What the fuck?"

"She found a hot tub. Went in search of. Found it. Chick knows a good time."

"She's in the neighbor's hot tub?"

Johnny laughs. "Yeah, man."

Mercer spikes a plastic beer cup into the grass. What is she thinking? She'll piss off the neighbor, and she'll get the party shut down. Selfish. Irresponsible. But as he's tromping across Owen's yard, past empty wine bottles and soiled napkins, past a couple making out in the shadows under a cypress, past groups of people laughing wildly and shouting, through the steady thump of the DJ's beats, he starts thinking about how he went on commando hot-tub raids when he was a kid, scaled fences for midnight swims, snuck into the walk-in beer fridges at bars and hotels, and his anger shades into excitement. This is exactly the kind of fun he hasn't allowed himself to have in years.

And a hot tub would be good for his back, wouldn't it?

He scrapes his way through one bank of shrubs, crosses two more lawns bounded by shrubs—these sickly-looking and twiggy, compared to Owen's— and as the party music grows muted and indistinct in the distance, he can hear the hot-tub motor pumping, the water churning and bubbling. He follows the sound to the far corner of the yard, where a redwood tub sits on a plateau overlooking the gully.

He sees Kelly from behind, sitting on the edge of the tub—it has to be her, there's no mistaking her, slim and white in the night, a tapered waist that flares into a heart-shaped ass. White clothes litter the decking, along with her boots, which slump over without legs inside. There's a splash and some motion in the tub that he can't immediately account for, and he sees shadows crawl over her back, only they're not shadows, they're hands, hands that are moving up and down her, and there's a writhe and a wiggle in her moon-pale shape and a male laugh that breaks through the sonic wake of the water jets. It's a laugh that Mercer recognizes, a burly laugh he's been hearing since high school. Heath Kinnicutt's laugh. He moves closer, and when Kelly twists to the side, he sees his friend there in front of her, bare-chested but still wearing his stupid Tom Wolfe hat.

Mercer halts. A reflex: his hand goes to his hip, expecting the brush of metal against his palm, comes up with air. He watches these two people, these naked figures groping in a haze of drifting steam, and he feels like a clown in his ridiculous and too-expensive white suit. He is alone in the night, alone and unseen, and goddamnit he is going to make himself seen. He approaches the tub with determined strides, keeping his center of gravity low, for stability. The damp heat from the tub weights the air. He can smell the chemical vapor of chlorine and salts, can smell the wet of the redwood, can hear the sound of lips coming together and pulling apart.

The voice that comes out of him is his command voice, and it says her name. He expects them to jump, to be startled or stunned, but Kelly wears a heavy-eyed look and a dreamy smile of entitlement. The only thing Mercer can read in her expression is disappointment that he didn't show up with a drink for her.

"I'm leaving, Kelly," he says. "You can come with me or not." He expects her to respond to the force in his voice. Confident enough to call her out, not so insecure that he has to pound Kinnicutt into pulp.

She doesn't answer, except to make a sound that might be a hiccup or a giggle.

"Mike," Kinnicutt says. "Dude, we're all friends here. We're all adults." He's smiling too now, a dopey caught-stealing-cookies smile.

Mercer glares at him, hard. Fucking *citizen*. Fat, lazy, spoiled *citizen*. He should have laid into him hours ago, just for bringing up his father. When he speaks, his voice is cold steel. "Do you realize," he says, "how easily I could break your neck?"

He turns, knowing neither of them will try to follow him, or stop him from leaving.

He's pounding through Owen's yard, drawing stares from the partygoers who are left, when he rolls his ankle on a croquet mallet in the grass. He picks it up and flings it into the trees over the gully, as hard as he can, pain be damned.

On the deck, he runs into Owen, who stops him with an outstretched hand. "Whoa," he says. "Easy."

"Did you know?" Mercer says.

"Know what?"

"Fucking Kinnicutt."

"Mike," Owen says. "Relax. Breathe."

"I'm leaving."

"No, you're not. You're sleeping here. We've got a room for you. Don't be dumb."

"Fuck off," Mercer says loudly, and even though he can't see the heads turning, he knows they are. "Everything comes so goddamned *easy* for you. And by the way, half the people here think you're a fucking *cartoon*."

He shoulders Owen out of the way and heads for the door. When he flings it open, it hits the wall with a satisfying bang. He's down the steps and down the path when he hears a window slide open. Mollie, calling to him from the upstairs bathroom. "Mike," she says. "Stay here. I don't want you driving. Stay here and sleep. We love you."

He stops, but he can't bring himself to turn and face her. Her *We love you* has him on the verge of tears. He holds out his hands, palms up: *what can I do?* She calls his name again, but he walks off down the dark street. The car chirps when he unlocks the door, and he hates it for sounding so cheerful.

# EIGHTEEN

# NIGHTWALKING (II)

—And push, and glide, and push, and glide, and left, and right, and left, and right, and how lucky she is to reside in a place with so many smooth, scenic pathways for skating, and you simply could not *ask* for a prettier moonlit evening, the sort of evening a young lady ought to make the most of—regardless of what that Lincoln's new friend Mr. Gage thinks. *Too dangerous!* Gage said when she left the hangar with her Plimptons under her arm. And he was so emphatic about it—quite mad, really, waving a wrench in the air, his face streaked with engine grease! How Lincoln manages to calm that man when his temper flares, she'll never understand. *Go,* Lincoln said. *No one is out to harm you. Enjoy yourself. One can't simply stop enjoying oneself.* Amen, Mr. Beachey! Amen, because the path is straight and clear in front of her, and push, and glide, and she closes her eyes, feels the cool lunar glow on her eyelids, smells the sweet jasmine on the night breeze.

Flowers. She has always adored flowers, and she certainly misses her roses in the garden at Belmont, but a pleasant evening ought not to be *wasted* missing things one no longer has, *n'est-ce pas?* A pleasant, moonlit evening is meant for a young lady to push, and glide, and push, and glide on the springy rockers that her delightful and handy suitor has constructed for her (along with a matching pair for himself). Lincoln! More dashing than in any of the old newspaper photographs, with his jaunty cap and his crooked smile and his twinkling adventurer's eyes. And not the sort of man to feel *threatened* if you choose to go for a skate while he works on his engines and such. (Unlike her husband, who would rail on about her *behavior* and thump the table to punctuate his silly point that he was a man of *wealth* and *stature* and her *behavior* was *scandalous* and couldn't she imagine what people would say about *him* with all this *skating*? Oh, that William—a man of that regrettable sort who fancy themselves indispensable to the world when really they are simply to be endured and, on a fine evening such as this, forgotten.)

Push, and glide, and spin! and left, and right. She clasps her hands behind her back, keeping a sleek profile in the breeze. Her eyelids are warm and the paths are smooth and her thoughts are pleasant. She counts out her strokes in waltz time, imagines a quintet playing along with her, each bow stroke of cello capturing the swing of a leg, violins playing a melody of the moon, violas the scent of the vespertine blooms. This surely is an evening to skate along with music in your head and allow all of these men—men, men in suits, men in dirt-crusted denims, men in all manner of odd "modern" dress, men who doff hats and men who lack them, all these men, from the gawky boys to the juddering old men whose cataracted eyes gleam as she sails by, trailing a swirl of jasmine breeze in her wake. Push, and glide, and left, and right, and spin!, and the next time Lincoln joins her, she will hum to him this delightful skating song that is running through her head and they will skate to it, matching strides.

How lucky she is! How could she fail to be happy, racing under the moon at exhilarating speed along a smooth path? How? It's a shame to slow down, she'd really prefer not to, but that man up ahead is waving his arms frantically and he looks in dire need of help—there's certainly something amiss about him, even apart from his garishly colored evening wear—*Hello! Do you need assistance, sir? Why, I haven't thought of it quite that way, but I suppose you could say I'm Mr. Beachey's "gal," yes. How do you—? What are—?* All the air is pushed out of her chest as he throws his shoulder into her, and her Plimptons leave the path, and the world inverts, sky is path and path is sky, she tries to stand but her arms are pinned, legs are pinned, and a horrible grinning half-face appears above her, and the last whiff of jasmine is gone, overwhelmed by the rank, earthy stink of the Root. She opens her mouth and screams, realizing her mistake only as her teeth graze the ghoul's knuckles and she tastes the dirt and the Root and the blood on his fingers, and she sees all those men who were admiring her before now turning away, timid and cold, willfully oblivious, and it's a horrible, deadening sight and please, oh God, please, don't let that be the last thing she—

**W**ednesday, 0400 hours. Mercer parks the Olds in the station lot, face-to-face with the cruiser he should be driving on patrol. He's here to escape his apartment and kill the stay-awake hours with the overnight crew. Full doses of painkillers, anti-inflammatories, and antihistamines bought him three hours of sleep, and then he was nerve-burned back into consciousness.

The dispatcher, Cristina, greets him from behind her bulletproof window. She's young, maybe twenty, with a heavy build, dark lipstick, and drawn-in eyebrows of purplish brown. "Hey, Mike," she says. Her tone is friendly, but she's not smiling; smiles are hard to come by at this time of night. "Your back's still pretty messed up, huh?"

Mercer nods.

She taps the security monitor display. "I saw you getting out of your car."

The next time he comes, he'll park farther away. Or maybe he'll just walk. He's supposed to be getting as much exercise as possible.

Toronto, Cambi, and Mazzarella are in the break room; Benzinger is out at First Chance with a DUI. Cambi slumps on the couch, a soda can in his hand. Toronto and Mazzarella sit at the table, each with a bottle of water. They all stare at him when he walks in. He understands why. He thinks of an old Warren Zevon song: he looks like something Death brought with him in a suitcase.

"Can't sleep," Mercer says.

Cambi extends a leg from his place on the couch, hooks an empty chair, and kicks it over to him. "Take a load off."

"I'll stand."

"What the fuck?" Cambi says.

"He can't sit, you ass-cramp," Toronto says. "It hurts him."

"Ass-cramp?" Mercer asks.

Toronto shrugs. "It just came out. It's not very good. I don't think it'll stick."

Cambi spits into his can. "How do you take a dump, Mercer?" he asks.

"What?"

"A dump. If it hurts to sit."

"I hurt," Mercer says, "is how."

"Grow up, Cambi," Mazzarella says.

"You guys aren't fun anymore," Cambi says. "Ever since Toronto started kung fu and truth-talking, or whatever the fuck it's called."

"It's called *Right Speech,*" Toronto says. "It means you don't use words maliciously."

"You called me an ass-cramp," Cambi points out.

"Good point," Toronto says. "That was a mistake."

"There've been some changes around here, Mercer," Mazzarella says. He points to Toronto. "Exhibit A."

"Kung fu?" Mercer asks.

"Zen practice," Toronto says.

"Whatever," Cambi says.

"In my day we didn't talk about religion on the job," Mazzarella says.

"It's a *practice,*" Toronto says.

Mazzarella rolls his eyes. "So what does the doctor say?" he asks Mercer.

Mercer tells them: the doctor says surgery. Two disks blown to hell, one lumbar, one sacral. The cortisone shots haven't done anything. He has a date with the knife next week.

"Have you even tried exercises?" Cambi asks him.

"I stretch," Mercer says. "They gave me stretches. Some yoga kind of shit, too."

"Oh, great," Mazzarella says to the ceiling. "Toronto finally cleans up his act, and Boy Thirteen turns foulmouthed."

"Yoga's good," Toronto says. "I just started. Clears your mind. Meditation, too. So, you're going to do it?"

"Meditate?"

"Have the surgery."

Mercer nods. "This shit is killing me." He doesn't mention the headaches, which aren't getting any better. Even the opiates don't help much; all they do is blur the pain. The pinpricks of light in his vision and the ringing in his ears, he's learning to live with those. But it's all wearing him down.

"You keeping busy?" Mazzarella asks. "It's important to keep busy."

"Reading a lot," Mercer says. He's been through Featherstone's reports four, five times. He's read the Beachey biography and a few other books Lorna brought over from the Historical Society, including one on Doc Barker. Interesting guy: sociopath and mama's boy. If he's going to get sucked into Featherstone's ghost world, he should at least know what he's up against. *If*, he emphasizes to himself. *If.*

Cambi groans. "Great. Another reader. Just what we need."

"Been helping out Lorna, too," Mercer says. "Little things around the apartment that won't get fixed otherwise."

"Good for you," Mazzarella says.

"Are you helping her bake?" Toronto says. "Because, and I mean no offense, the last batch of cookies—" He pauses, as if searching for a diplomatic phrase.

"Just say it," Cambi says. "Talk truth."

Toronto shakes his head. "They sucked worse than ever."

"I'm not cooking with her," Mercer says.

"If you start, let me know," Mazzarella says, joining in. "I'll stay twice as far away from the stuff."

"Mostly I listen," Mercer says. "Sometimes she talks about Sergeant Featherstone."

"Old Stoney," Cambi says. "I miss him."

"How well did you guys know him?" Mercer asks.

"As well as anyone did, probably," Mazzarella says. "He was a quiet guy, though."

Cambi shakes his head, then spits. "That fucking comb-over," he says. "What was he thinking?"

"We tried to tell him," Toronto says.

"You made fun of him," Mazzarella points out.

"That was how we tried to tell him."

"Did he have any hobbies?" Mercer asks. "Did you guys know anything he liked to do?"

"He liked being a cop," Cambi says. "Until the last couple of years, anyway."

"I don't have any idea what he did off duty," Mazzarella says. "He and Lorna never had kids, so it wasn't family stuff."

Cambi pushes himself up so he's sitting straight. "He told me to hurry up and have kids. Said I'd regret it otherwise. I said I'd have to get laid first. But he didn't seem to think that was very funny."

"Neither should you," Toronto says.

"He told me once that he wished he'd done more with his life," Cambi says.

"Really?" Mazzarella says.

"Jesus, Cambi," Toronto says. "I didn't know you were his little protégé."

Cambi shrugs. "He was wasting his time, then. I don't take instruction real well."

"No kidding," Mazzarella says.

"What did you mean about the last couple of years?" Mercer asks Cambi.

There's a silence, until Cambi breaks it by spitting. "He got weirder," Cambi says.

"Withdrawn," Mazzarella says. "That's the word."

"And weird," Cambi says.

"He'd go off the radio for long stretches of time," Toronto says. "Mostly, you didn't think about him. He'd still be there to back you up when you needed him."

"That's right," Cambi says. "So whenever you *didn't* need him, it was like, okay, Stoney, go and do what you need to do, and we'll just see you whenever."

"It wasn't a shift wife," Toronto says. "We knew that."

Cambi shakes his head *no,* agreeing. "No way. Not him."

"He could've gotten out with a full pension years ago," Mazzarella says. "He was pretty much working for free."

"He was scared," Toronto says. "I don't think he knew what he'd do with himself."

Mazzarella nods. "He even asked for nights again. Guys his age *never* ask for nights. It was like he dug himself deeper into the job, instead of trying to get out." He strokes his mustache and looks out the window. "He might've gotten religion at the end. I don't know—like I said, we never talked about it, and it's not like he started looking any happier—but you know how people start talking differently when they start believing in something?"

"Like Toronto over here, with his Right Speech," Cambi says.

"Keep it up, ass-cramp," Toronto says.

Cambi flips him off. "Stoney and I were on a call in the Italian Cemetery once," he says, "and he asked me where I thought we go when we die. I said, shit, Stoney, we're meat, that's the end of it. We're alive, we're a pile of meat, they put us in the ground, and then whoosh, we're dust."

"Whoosh?" Toronto says.

"Yeah. Whoosh."

"That's the sound dust makes?"

"If it's windy, sure."

"But there's no wind underground."

"Oh, fuck off," Cambi says. His face tightens and his eyes squinch shut, and Mercer can tell he's trying to think of a new insult. "Cock-biter?" he says, testing it out.

"No good, Arthur," Mazzarella says. "Anyone hears that, we'll get sued."

Cambi salutes him. "I'll keep working on it, Sarge."

Mercer asks if there's any news on the DiMaio case. Mazzarella says he doesn't know all the details, but he thinks Detective Funkhouser and Officer St. Cyr from the day shift have been working Burlingame, and they're looking into a couple of leads that the queer kid gave them. There's a place in the Mission that they want to have SFPD check out, but there's nowhere near enough for a warrant. Progress, but slow.

"Thanks, guys," Mercer says. "Thanks for letting me hang out."

"You'll notice we didn't send you to pick up burritos," Cambi says.

"Hey," Toronto says. "That was probably hurtful to him."

"I'm not the one doing Right Speech."

Mercer flips Cambi off and steps toward the door. "I'm going to head out. Tell Benz I said hey."

"Get well soon, man," Cambi says. "I need someone to have fun with. These guys are stiffs."

Toronto congratulates him on the joke, and Cambi looks bewildered.

"Take care of yourself, Thirteen," Mazzarella says.

Toronto follows Mercer outside, calls to him to wait. They stand in a corner of the parking lot, out of the glare of the light. Toronto lights a cigarette, sends a stream of smoke skyward. "So, really," he says, "you all right?"

"Getting by," Mercer says. "That's pretty much it."

"Any word from the nurse? Fiona?"

"Some hang-up calls, right after. Those were probably her. Nothing lately. I think she's pretty much forgotten about me."

"You miss her?"

"I miss everyone," Mercer says. "I miss myself."

"Take that mope-rock shit somewhere else. It's not that bad. What about Buttergirl?"

"That blew up. I'll tell you sometime when I have a few drinks in me."

"Bad?"

"Bad as it gets."

"What?" Toronto says. "You couldn't perform?"

"Never got a chance," Mercer says. "She screwed my friend." He doesn't know that for sure, but come on.

Toronto inhales deeply, nodding as he does. "That's cold," he says.

"Hot. There was a hot tub involved. She—" Mercer stops, realizing suddenly how disconnected he's been, how isolated, how deeply stuck in his own world of pain and crazy. "How are you doing?" he asks. "You hear anything from Mia?"

"Made some more calls. Friends, parents. They won't tell me anything. I know she was with the circus as far as Santa Fe. Then, whoosh. Disappeared. Only she can't *really* have disappeared, because no one is worried about her but me."

"They know, and you don't."

"Bravo. Sharp as ever."

"That's a fucked-up situation."

"Yep," Toronto says. "It is truly all fucked-up." He tosses the butt to the pavement, stubs it out with his toe. "Here's an idea," he says. "You know I gave up my old apartment. So I'm stuck in Mia's place until I can find something good and cheap. I haven't had time to start looking, and I need to get the fuck out of there. Too many ghosts, you know?"

"I hear you," Mercer says.

"So how about I stay at your place for a while? A couple of weeks. You need the company, I need a place to crash."

"Are you kidding?"

"I'll help you out after the surgery. Make sure you get out and walk, do your stretches, the whole nine. I'll be Mickey to your Rocky."

Mercer isn't sure what to say. Toronto's idea makes sense, in a way, but he has a hard time imagining himself being around anyone else that much.

"I travel light. I'll pay my way. If by some miracle you have a girl coming over and you need me to clear out, hey, it's done, I'm out of there."

"I need to think about that," Mercer says. "But thanks." He spoke to his mother a few nights before, and she offered to fly in from Tahiti to help him. He said no, he'd be fine on his own. He doesn't want his mom to see him like this. Who wants to see their kid all broken?

Toronto uses thumb and forefinger to point back and forth between them. "Helps me, helps you, is all I'm saying."

"I appreciate it. Seriously."

"A little company. If nothing else, it'll help you stay sane."

And that flips a switch inside Mercer; he suddenly realizes how terrified he is of *not* staying sane and how desperately grateful he is for Toronto's offer. Again he's on the verge of crying. Why the hell does kindness always make him cry? "Let me think," he says, turning away.

Toronto tells him to take care, cuffs him one lightly on the shoulder, and heads back into the station. Mercer looks at the Olds and decides to go for a walk. He's nowhere close to sleep, anyway. His feet turn him left down Serramonte, away from home, then south on El Camino. They take him all the way to the gates of Cypress Lawn. He understands that he's there for a reason, even though he can't quite put that reason into words.

He leans against the tower at Fern Grotto. The cemetery is silent; it is dark and green and peaceful. He remembers the night they found Jude— remembers hearing the boy's voice, remembers the rush of responding to the emergency, remembers feeling like he'd done everything right and a boy was alive because of it. He was happy that night—he was a *hero* that night—and since then, everything's gone straight to hell. He still doesn't understand how, or why. He's a nobody to Kelly. He was a nobody at Owen's party. He's a nobody to Fiona. He's not even allowed to do his job right now.

He sighs deeply, pushes himself away from the stone. He doesn't want to see any ghosts, he tells himself, no crazy ladies in firefighter gear, no ghost planes with ghost pilots; no jump-rope rhymes or backwards angel-voices giving him cryptic advice. He walks through the cemetery, up to the children's section and back, walks figure eights among the stones, daring the dead to come out. He's going to prove he's sane, or he's going to lose it completely. He walks until he realizes that he's cold, his skin is cold, his nose and ears are cold, and maybe the extra drugs are finally kicking in, because he's suddenly exhausted. *Dead on my feet,* he thinks. *Ha.* He heads back down the hill toward the gates, hoping he'll have the energy to make it back to his car at the station.

He's nearly at the archway when something whizzes past his face—it's so close that he feels a breeze—and he hears it plack against the arch somewhere to his left, then fall to the pavement and skid away on the pavement. *Knife,* his brain shouts as he stands there, stunned. He hears something that sounds like a laugh, high-pitched but whispery and insubstantial, an abrasion against the nighttime quiet. "Colma police," Mercer says, turning a dizzy 360. There's no response. "Hello?" he says, and his voice is smaller.

The laugh comes again, louder this time, and thicker, pushing air instead of riding on it. The malice in it is unmistakable. Mercer reaches for the pick mike that he isn't wearing; when he grabs nothing but air, his brain shouts *Run!* so he does. He runs, a limpy, wheeling, clownish run, as far as he can, and then he walks in a daze along El Camino. He can feel the opiate waves rolling inside him, but they only lap at the edges of the pain. When he comes upon Mrs. Rao walking in the opposite direction, her fingers holding her bathrobe closed, her bedroom slippers on her feet, and she waves hello, he waves right back and keeps on walking.

◉

# NINETEEN

# THE REDEMPTION EXPRESS (1)

Toronto is at morning Zazen, sitting with about fifty other people. The air around him is clean and open, with just hints of bodies and breath, clean wood floors, and, distantly, chamomile tea. It takes him a while to get comfortable on his cushion and in his head, to get his thoughts flowing smoothly; he came straight from work, and it was a busy night. A midnight domestic violence call loops through his mind now: the filthy kitchen of a run-down house, the air sharp with shouting, the floor spiked with broken glass, the shirtless man bitter-drunk and built like a truck. The guy made a run at Benzinger, and Toronto put him down hard. Knucklehead landed in the glass, got his back sliced open in a dozen places. Not what Toronto wanted to do, but what he had to do. Blood on the filthy ripped-up linoleum, and the woman shouting nonsense.

*Let it go,* he tells himself, *let the thoughts flow,* but the loop is persistent—shout, impact, blood—and he opens his eyes to reset.

He looks at the faces around him. A few cushions away is a girl he hasn't seen before: hair the saturated brown-black of coffee grounds, tied back in a long ponytail; long legs in shiny blue track pants; sharp cheekbones; peace on her button-nosed face. He forces his eyes away from her, because it's bad form to scope out girls when you're sitting. He closes his eyes, tries to nudge his thoughts into a gentle drift.

What he gets instead is another straight line of them—thoughts marching, not drifting. About Mercer. Toronto moved into The Willows two days ago, and he's glad he did, because Mercer needs his help far worse than he'd thought. The apartment was a disaster—clothes and newspapers and dirty plates everywhere, silverware rusted in the sink—and Mercer had on a ratty plaid bathrobe that smelled like it was rotting away. He was stoned on painkillers—slow of speech, a glassy opiated look in his eyes, hardly present at all. The wall next to the front door was covered with blue Lost Kid cards taped up in neat rows. You have to worry for your friend's sanity when he starts decorating with missing children.

The phone rang while Toronto was unpacking, and Mercer made no move to pick it up, just listened to the message as it came through the speaker. It was his old friend, that jack-off from the hot tub, apologizing half-assedly— *Everyone was wasted, Mike. No one knew what they were doing. We've been friends too long for something stupid like this to get in the way.* And that's the trouble with citizens, right there. You *think* you can trust them, you *tell* yourself you can trust them, but they will dick you right-the-fuck-over if it's in their best interest, every time. And they think they can get out of it by apologizing, when what they should've done was not dick you in the first place. Cops are different. A cop won't do that. Being a cop is all about honoring the trust you've been given. Citizens have no goddamn idea.

*He's not the one I want to hear from,* Mercer said. *He's dead to me.* Toronto agreed: better to pink-slip the bastard before he jams you again. But stand up and tell him, for fuck's sake. And then Mercer started on a moaning jag about Buttergirl, wallowing in his self-pity. Toronto gave him some advice: Figure out what you want. If you don't like where you are, change the shit you can change. If you want to get with the rider, do what you need to do—swallow your pride, put some stones in your sack, and call her to have it out. And if you don't want to, then stop making yourself miserable by pretending you do.

"Zen says that?" Mercer asked.

"I say that," Toronto said.

He laid down rules. First, Mercer would get dressed. Every day. And that meant wearing fucking *pants*. Second, he would drag his ass out of bed or up off the floor and exercise at least three times a day. Third, he would answer his phone when it rang. Someone calls, you answer. It is a process, and you honor it, and you deal with what comes your way.

The abbot rings the bell, Toronto opens his eyes, startled. He doesn't feel calm and focused like he usually does—too much thought, not enough drift.

Happens sometimes, he reminds himself. Not the end of the goddamned world. He exhales deeply and stands up. While he's stretching out the stiffness in his legs, he watches the girl in the track pants. She sees him, gives him a friendly-stranger nod, holds eye contact for a beat or two—which is enough. He hopes she'll stay for tea in the courtyard. He visualizes himself approaching her, introducing himself, coolly guiding the conversation wherever it needs to go—and now he knows, he can feel it, she will wait, she'll be waiting for him. Warmth races through his body; suddenly he's alert, charismatic, unstoppable. Everything inside him feels unified and purposeful, and everything outside him feels poised to go his way. What Mia stole, he has gotten back. He feels like Toronto again.

Mercer hesitates before picking up the phone. He's tired, so tired he can't see straight, how can he possibly have an interaction with someone? But he hears Toronto's voice—*you pick up the phone when it rings*—and something tells him that if he lets this call go, Toronto will somehow find out. He lifts the handset, punches the TALK button.

"It's Cricket," Fiona's voice says. "She's dying."

"What?" he says. It's the only word he has.

"She's dying." He can tell from her voice that she's been crying and that she's deep into a bottle of wine. "Her liver. The vet said she doesn't have long. Said it might be better to—" She breaks off.

What's the right thing to say? Why can't he just feel it and do it?

"I thought you'd want to know." Her voice winds even tighter, and she sniffles loudly. "She always liked you."

"Oh," he says. "God. I'm sorry."

Silence.

"And that's all you can say," Fiona says. "Of course. I should've known." She pauses, then shouts, "Why can't you *speak*?"

He wants to explain it, starts searching for words, but then comes the beep, the silence, the dial tone. He puts the phone down and curses out loud. Toronto may think he has all the answers, but when it comes to the phone, when it comes to all this business of *communicating,* his advice is worse than worthless.

Cricket. He pictures her, a little gray furball rolling on her back, crazy over a catnip mouse. He feels terrible. He really loves that cat.

**R**eyna wonders what's taking Bobby so long upstairs. The plan was to get in, get cash, get out. The plan was *not* for him to abandon her in the living room with his parents, who are friendly in a plastic way that makes her want to scream, and clueless in a way that makes her want to slap them while she's screaming.

The room is white, white, white. White walls, white rug, white curtains, white Scandinavian furniture. The three of them are sipping tea from white ceramic mugs. Bobby's father is tall and trim, with a henna-colored hairpiece. He's still in his work clothes—white shirt, loosened red tie, tan slacks. Bobby's mother is sitting forward on the white couch, watching Reyna closely with tiny rodent eyes. Her tight black curls splay out like a Halloween wig. When she smiles, the rest of her broad, square face stays still. Reyna's feeling extremely creeped out, and it's not because of the hash.

They've already gone through everything they could possibly talk about: where she and Bobby met, how long he's been *dating* her (their word), where she grew up, where she went to high school. Has she thought about college? Does Bobby ever talk about college? Does Bobby like his job at the import/export company? Do they work him too hard? Not hard enough? Where is the office, anyway? Is his apartment nice? What are his friends like? Could she encourage him to visit home, or at least call, a little more often? They know he's a private person—he always has been, even when he was tiny—but they'd like to be reassured that he's leading a productive life. Maybe Reyna could call them sometimes herself, if he's not going to? Bobby prepped her on some of the lies in advance, while they were idling in the driveway. Others, Reyna's making up as she goes.

Mrs. Park blows away curls of steam from her mug with a pursed-lip toot of breath. Again, only her mouth moves.

"You've got a good head on your shoulders," Mr. Park says. "I'm good at reading people. You could be a good influence on him."

"He needs that," Mrs. Park says. "He hasn't always made the best choices."

"Keep an eye on him for us, will you?" his father asks.

"He won't let us look out for him," his mother says. "We worry."

"We both worry."

"We can't help but worry."

"But we have to give him his space. He's made that clear. He's an adult."

"So will you?" his mother asks.

"Watch out for him?" his father asks.

"Make sure he's on the right track?"

"Making good decisions?"

*Stop,* she wants to yell at them. *Shut the fuck up.* But instead she puts on a soothing face and tells them he's doing fine. Bobby doesn't need looking after. Everything about him is confident, swaggering, in charge. He looks after *her.* She's the one who needs him. Needs him to fold his arms around her, needs him to fuck her senseless, needs him to be the life of the party and to score whatever needs to be scored and to make her feel like she's the hottest and most dangerous thing on two legs. He's Bobby, goddamnit, cool as smoke. He lives in the moment. Fun at any cost. He doesn't worry, doesn't take shit from anyone. Look after *him*?

Or is that the whole problem? Maybe the hash is making her paranoid, but she feels like the universe has shifted a few degrees, that things are changing right in front of her. Important things. Maybe he *is* the small and needy thing these white-white people in this white-white room have just told her he is. Maybe *she's* the one who's given him all the power.

He's been acting weird for a few days, now that she thinks about it. Moody and jittery. Ever since the night he dosed with Yolanda and Ratgirl. She'd sat that one out, smoked herself stupid with Carlos instead. Forget acid. A dumb goddamn drug. She doesn't need any Technicolor carnies coming after her. And on their way to his parents' house tonight, he'd driven them to his old middle school and looped through the parking lot. *I hate this school,* he'd said. *Fucking hate it.*

*So what?* she'd said. *It's middle school. Of course you do.*

*No, I really fucking hate it.*

*Then why are we here going around in circles?*

*My parents, too. I mean, fuck them. Who let them be parents?*

*What's up your ass?*

He'd stopped short, with the headlights shining on the flagpole. The flag was up there, drooping in the dead air. *Aren't you supposed to take those down at night?* she'd wondered.

Bobby had tossed his empty out the window, grabbed a fresh one, swigged. Looked unhappily at the can. *I should've bought some fucking limes.*

And she'd thought, What is that supposed to mean? I mean, really *mean?*

Mr. Park shifts in his seat. "He's taking a long time."

"He must be having his stomach troubles again," Mrs. Park says. "Has he told you about those, Reyna? They used to—"

"I'll check on him," Reyna says, on her feet and heading for the stairs before they can move. He might be having trouble finding the cash. Maybe he's trying to figure out what'll sell for the most. He doesn't have the best head for value. His bedroom is dark and empty, and so is the guest bedroom and the bathroom in the hall. She opens the door to the darkened master bedroom. "Bobby?" she whispers before stepping in. The light is on in the bathroom, behind a closed door. She knocks gently, says his name again. No answer. She tries the knob; she expects it to be locked, but it isn't.

Bobby is slumped in the corner, across from the toilet. His legs are twitching. His head lolls to one side, resting on his shoulder. His eyes are slits. Next to him, on the tile, a needle, his belt. Vomit covers the toilet seat and is still dripping onto the floor. It smells like stomach and beer. Are his lips blue? She can't tell. Blu*ish,* maybe. Blue would be a bad sign, she's pretty sure, but how blue is blue?

His legs jerk again, and Reyna jumps back. Is this normal? Is he dying? His parents? 911? *Fuck.*

She slaps him, trying to bring him around, says his name into his expressionless face as loudly as she dares. She yanks on the long black hair that flops over his forehead. Nothing. She starts running the cold water in the tub; she remembers Carlos saying he did that for Trent. She grabs him around the arm with one hand, grabs the waistband of his jeans with the other, and tugs. There's another spasm in his legs, and that is seriously creeping her shit out. She accidentally knocks his head against the wall, and she thinks, Bobby, you asshole, why did you have to do this? Are you testing me?

Fuck him for putting her through this. She never wanted to meet his parents. She never wanted to have to save him. Fuck that. She can't be anyone's savior. God, even Jude has never asked her to *save* him. But she gets her grip again and tugs, tugs again, tugs once more, and his twitching legs are making her nuts, and it's not until she has him hanging over the side of the tub that she realizes what a dead-end situation this is. He won't be able to walk out of here anytime soon, she can't carry him, and she can't stall his parents long enough to wait for this to pass. Think, she tells herself, as drops of cold water splash her skin. *Think.*

Bobby makes a sound that might be a breath and his legs stiffen and the tub faucet roars. Reyna reaches into his back pocket and takes his keys. Bobby, you may have shit to deal with, but it's *your* shit. If she's going to save anybody, it'll be herself. That, Bobby, is what we call Life.

The Willows, 0300 hours. Mercer creeps out of his bedroom with his softball bat hidden under his jacket. No way is he going out there unarmed. He pads across the thin carpet to the front door. Toronto, on a night off from work, is stretched out on the couch under a white sheet, snoring lightly, the remote still in his hand; the TV is on, sending bluish light and faint, fricative whispers over the living room. Mercer glances at the screen and sees Reverend Whipple sitting around a table with three other men in the garb of other religions. It looks like the setup to a joke. He undoes the chain lock and the deadbolt on the door, glances back to make sure Toronto hasn't stirred, and slips outside.

The night is cool, but Mercer is comfortable in his canvas jacket and his sweatpants, and he'll stay plenty warm if he keeps moving. He crunches another Vicodin between his teeth, lets the chalky bitterness spread over his tongue—and he walks. Slowly at first, but the farther he goes, the looser his leg and his back get. By the time he reaches the rear gate to the west side of Cypress Lawn, he's walking comfortably enough to pass for a normal person. He stops at the gate, and as the tip of the crescent moon peeks out from behind scudding clouds, a memory flashes through his head: Mercer, young, pausing in the doorway to the backyard, unsure if he really wants to play outside on his own. His father's voice, thick and slow, is behind him. *In or out,* the voice says. *Don't be a middleman.* This, from his father, who left and came back, left and came back, before finally he just left.

The phrase repeats itself as Mercer walks through fields of the dead: *In or out, don't be a middleman* as he circles the obelisk marking the Laurel Hill Mound—thirty-five thousand people right under there, Lorna said, exhumed from San Francisco. Thirty-five thousand people under his feet. *In or out* as he crosses through another children's section. *In or out* through a memorial grove of dead Armenians. *In or out* as he passes row after row of stones. Are you *in* or are you *out?*

# FIELD INTERVIEW CARD

| NAME Gage, Phineas B. | | | | NICKNAME | |
|---|---|---|---|---|---|

| ADDRESS 1370 El Camino, Colma (CypLawn W/ Laurel Hill Mound) | | | | PHONE N/A | |
|---|---|---|---|---|---|

| AGE 35 (appr) | RACE W | HEIGHT 5'6" | WEIGHT 145 | BUILD Med | COMPLEXION Med |
|---|---|---|---|---|---|

| DOB 7/9/1823 | POB New Hampshire | HAIR Br | EYES Br | MARKS/SCARS Apparent damage to facial struct. (depressions in R cheek, top of head); skin intact. | |
|---|---|---|---|---|---|

| SOCIAL SECURITY NO. Unknown | DRIVERS LICENSE NO. N/A | | STATE | TYPE | |
|---|---|---|---|---|---|

**DRESS**
Gray shirt, gray trousers. Suspenders.

| MAKE OF CAR N/A | YEAR | TYPE | COLOR | LICENSE NO. | STATE |
|---|---|---|---|---|---|

**OCCUPATION, OR SCHOOL ATTENDED AND GRADE**

Railroad crew foreman (VT); Street curiosity (New England/NY); Stagecoach driver (Chile); Farm worker (Santa Clara, CA); Aeroplane mechanician (Colma, CA)

**LOCAL REFERENCE/RELATIONSHIP**

Beachey, Lincoln (res.: CypLawn E; work: hangar, CypLawn West) / Employer, friend.
Ralston, Elizabeth Fry (res. CypLawn E) / friend (possibly ~~dec'd~~ Rooted)

| LOCATION OF INCIDENT 1370 El Camino, Colma | DATE/TIME OF INCIDENT 3/22/05  0240 |
|---|---|

**ASSOCIATES WITH SUSPECT**
None

**REASON FOR INTERROGATION**

Subject was wandering premises in a threatening manner, calling in agitated voice for (alternately) associate Ralston and Barker, "Doc," a suspect in numerous violent crimes (see Featherstone files). Subject was brandishing a steel rod. When I told him to stop, he waved pipe at me and shouted epithets.

After some discussion, Subject calmed down enough to
explain that he suspected Barker and three other
individuals of having kidnapped and/or killed Mrs.
Ralston while she was out roller-skating. I suggested
that he go get some rest. He said he could not rest
until he found what was stolen from him long ago. I
said that sounded like a separate issue from Mrs.
Ralston's disappearance and he agreed. He is looking
for a particular piece of iron bar (used for tamping
explosive charges), which is the isntrument that
caused his cranial/facial injuries. Said the steel
rod was a poor substitute but it was the best option
he had for arming himself. He expressed anger at
Barker and frustration with his employer/friend
Beachey, who had not yet acknowledged that Mrs.
Ralston might be in peril because "he thinks only
good things happen." I advised him to be careful, as
I had reason to believe Barker and his accomplices
are dangerous people. I volunteered to accompany him.
We walked to the northeast.

Shortly after (0250), we were surrounded and
assaulted by Barker and his associates (likely
Ruczek, LoPresti, and Eastwick). [Incident Report to
be typed and logged as Case No. 03-0104-05.]
Assailants expressed surprise at finding me with Gage.
I was surprised to hear that they knew who I was, but
now I know they do. I attempted to defend myself with
the bat but could not swing well due to my injured
condition and dropped it. Gage picked it up and used
it to beat all four assailants into unconsciousness.
(He was very agile and extremely angry.) He told me
to run and I did, as fast as my injured condition
allowed. As I left, I heard Barker shout "We'll see
you later, cupcake. You know we will." I believe Gage
hit him again at that point and he did not speak
anymore.

| DATE AND TIME OF CONTACT | | |
|---|---|---|
| 03/22/05   0240 | | |
| OFFICERS REPORTING | SIGNATURE | DATE/TIME |
| Mercer | *M. Mercer* | 03/22/05   1400 |

# FIELD INTERVIEW CARD

| NAME | NICKNAME |
|---|---|
| Coit, Lillie Hitchcock | |

| ADDRESS | PHONE |
|---|---|
| 1370 El Camino, Colma (CypLawn East) | N/A |

| AGE | RACE | HEIGHT | WEIGHT | BUILD | COMPLEXION |
|---|---|---|---|---|---|
| 45 (appr) | W | 5'6" | 145 | Med | Med |

| DOB | POB | HAIR | EYES | MARKS/SCARS | |
|---|---|---|---|---|---|
| 1842 | SF CA | Br | Br | None Visible | |

| SOCIAL SECURITY NO. | DRIVERS LICENSE NO. | STATE | TYPE |
|---|---|---|---|
| Unknown | N/A | | |

**DRESS**
Firefighter's coat, trousers, boots, helmet

| MAKE OF CAR | YEAR | TYPE | COLOR | LICENSE NO. | STATE |
|---|---|---|---|---|---|
| N/A | | | | | |

**OCCUPATION, OR SCHOOL ATTENDED AND GRADE**
Honorary firefighter and philanthropist (SF, CA)

**LOCAL REFERENCE/RELATIONSHIP**
None given

| LOCATION OF INCIDENT | DATE/TIME OF INCIDENT |
|---|---|
| 1370 El Camino, Colma (CypLawn W) | 3/22/05  0255 |

**ASSOCIATES WITH SUSPECT**
None

**REASON FOR INTERROGATION**
Subject appeared next to me and called for my attention.

DEPOSITION

I encountered the subject while approaching the rear gate
of Cypress Lawn West. She called me by name and said she
had been trying to contact me for some time. She told me
to "save my strength" and to return when I was physically
well enough to defend myself from the Barker gang. She
advised that she would keep watch over me.

DATE AND TIME OF CONTACT
03/22/05 0250

| OFFICERS REPORTING | SIGNATURE | DATE/TIME |
|---|---|---|
| Mercer | *M. Mercer* | 03/22/05   1430 |

He lies awake for a long time with Lillie Coit's words looping through his mind, and it feels like he's only been asleep for a few minutes before Toronto shakes him awake again. The sky has turned a shade or two lighter than pitch, but it's still night. He tells Toronto to go away and gingerly turns himself onto his other side, huddled under his covers.

"Lorna's at the door," Toronto says. "She says you're supposed to do a charity walk with her. With her church."

"She's out of her fucking mind," Mercer says.

"She says you promised her."

"I don't remember that." Painkillers or no painkillers, he'd remember committing to something so stupid.

"You're getting up," Toronto says. "I'm not going to renege on your behalf."

"Everything hurts," Mercer says.

Toronto looks down at Mercer's nightstand, sees the loose Vicodins that Mercer keeps there for nighttime emergencies. He picks up two and pushes them at Mercer. "Take these, then," Toronto says. "Numb what you need to numb. But you're going to keep your promise and go with her. You need water?"

"No," Mercer says.

"You're supposed to walk as much as possible. Remember?"

"I should really just sleep. The doctor says I need sleep."

"Sleep when you're dead," Toronto says.

*Doesn't work that way,* Mercer wants to tell him.

Lorna drives them into the city while Mercer lies on his back in the back seat of the Chevy. She narrates as if she's a tour guide. *We're getting off the freeway now. We're on Ocean Avenue. The church is in the Ingleside District. Reverend Whipple wanted to have less expensive land so there'd be more money for good works.*

The car slows, then comes to a stop, and Lorna turns off the engine. "Here we are," she says, in a voice that's far too chirpy and energetic. Mercer pushes himself upright, opens the door, and does his skirt-spin out into a potholed parking lot surrounded by a metal fence topped with razor wire. The church is a low-slung building with peeling gray paint. Around the edge of the parking lot are twenty or so cars, and in the center, with its engine idling, is *The Redemption Express,* its corrugated-steel sides taking on the cast of the weak pink sunlight that smears the eastern sky. A hand-drawn sign is in the destination display on the front of the bus. HEAVEN, it says, simple black capital letters on a white background, all wreathed in twining rose vines.

Reverend Clifton Chase Whipple stands next to the bus, shaking his congregants' hands as they board and smiling, smiling, smiling. He wears a cream-colored suit with his customary bolo tie, along with new blindingly bright-white running shoes that are slashed with stripes of reflective green and red.

Lorna asks Mercer if he's ready to walk, and he nods yes, releases his grip on the open car door, and puts his full weight on his leg. He limps alongside her through the parking lot, watching out for ruts and undulations in cracked pavement. He can smell the diesel fumes from the rumbling bus.

The Reverend folds Mrs. Featherstone into a hug. "Lorna," he says. "Lovely to see you, as always."

"I wouldn't miss it for the world, Reverend. People need our help." The charity walk is a benefit for cystic fibrosis research, Lorna told him in the car. *It's not our church's event,* she'd said. *Most of them aren't. He just gets people to participate.*

"They certainly do need our help," Reverend Whipple says to her. "You're an angel."

She introduces Mercer to the minister as "the young man I was telling you about." Whipple takes Mercer's hand and shakes. The older man's skin is thickly callused; Mercer can feel cracks running through it. "What's your name again, son?"

"Mercer. Mike Mercer. Nice to meet you. I've seen your show." He wonders if Whipple can tell that Mercer was one of those kids who'd get loaded and prank-call the prayer line.

"Police officer, right?"

Mercer nods.

"Lorna told me about the boy in the cemetery. How's he doing?"

"I'm not sure," Mercer says. "I'm not working right now, so I'm out of the loop."

Lorna jumps in. "That may be, but he's taken a lot of his time and energy to help the boy. He's been wonderful."

"I don't know how much good I'm doing," Mercer says.

"If the boy knows you're trying, then you're doing good," Whipple says. "Sometimes that's just what people need."

"He's helped me, too," Lorna says. "He's a giving and selfless young man."

Mercer says nothing. He wants her to stop talking about him, though.

"Don't embarrass him, Lorna," Whipple says. "Well, go on up and find yourselves some seats. The *Express* leaves the station in about five minutes."

Lorna goes up the stairs first, slowly but steadily, using the handrail to help lift her bulky frame. She says hello to the driver, Brother Dusty, a tank of a man with reddish-blond hair and a scraggly red beard. Mercer looks up at him and wonders if he's met him before. He's about to step up when the Reverend puts a hand on his shoulder.

"You're in some pain, huh, son?"

"How'd you know?"

"Lorna told me about the accident. And I saw how much trouble you had getting out of the car. You sure you want to walk with us?"

"I'm sure," Mercer says. "I promised. Doctor says exercise helps, anyway."

"You start having any trouble, you tell me. If you need to stop, we can find a place for you to rest and pick you up on the way back. Or we'll get you a cab home, on me. I've also got a wheelchair stowed under the bus, for emergencies. We could get that baby rolling for you."

"Thanks," Mercer says again. "But I'll be fine." There is no goddamn way he's riding in a wheelchair.

"I don't know how much Lorna has told you about the church, and I don't know what you do or don't believe in, but what I believe in is helping people. I don't heal people, none of that laying hands or anything, which is a load of horseflop, if you want my opinion, excuse the François—but if I can help you, you just let me know. Same goes for the boy, too, if you want to pass that along."

Mercer nods. "I should go sit down," he says. It still seems unreal to him that he's speaking with Reverend Whipple, even more unreal that he's boarding *The Redemption Express*. The bus is nearly full, a sea of white hair. It could easily be a senior center outing or a package tour to Reno. The rearmost seats are taken up with video gear. Whipple knows that if anything's worth doing, it's worth capturing on video and showing on television.

Lorna is in a window seat in the front row, and Mercer lowers himself next to her. The seats are upholstered with a busy pattern of gold and red that's worn nearly threadbare in a pattern of ass-and-thighs.

"He's a nice man, isn't he?" Lorna says.

"Seems like it," Mercer says, though his inner voice is saying, *I don't trust him.*

A few more people trickle in, and then Whipple mounts the bus. He thanks everyone for coming together to do the Lord's work, then sits down in the seat right behind Dusty the driver. Mercer's almost certain he's met the driver before. He wonders if Dusty is one of the bikers he cited the last time the Hell's Angels roared through town to visit Harry Flamburis's grave.

"Onward, Dusty," the Reverend says. Dusty drops the bus into gear, and they leave the parking lot, heading for the freeway on-ramp.

Whipple leans across the aisle. "How's your pledge card, Lorna?"

"Full to the brim," she says. "People really came through in the last couple of days." She opens her purse and takes out a folded piece of card stock. She hands it to him, proudly; Mercer sees a long list of names and pledges, dollars per mile, in a rainbow of different inks.

"This one," Whipple says to Mercer, nodding toward Lorna. "I've never seen anyone so dedicated to raising money. She's been our top fund-raiser ever since she joined us." He smiles, revealing perfect white teeth.

Mercer's surprised. Lorna's friendly, no doubt—he's heard that visitors to the Historical Society love her—but he can't imagine her being adept at separating people from their money. She doesn't have the self-confidence or the tenacity, and she doesn't have an iota of hucksterish slickness in her. But maybe having the wrong personality for the work is exactly what makes her good at it. Maybe people like that she's not what they expect. Whatever the explanation, it's a good sign that she's overcoming her grief, reinventing herself as someone new. He sees her reflection in the window as the bus rumbles into the city along the 280 extension. She's watching the smokestacks puff question marks into the gray morning with a distant, peaceful smile. To him it looks like an expression of relief.

S̲everal hundred people mill about at the starting line, which is in the field across from the Ferry Building; the route has them walking along the Embarcadero and westward all the way to Fort Point, by the Golden Gate. Waving in an onshore breeze is a huge banner with the charity's name and logo, and smooth jazz plays over a sound system. Tea and cider and donuts and muffins have been set out on folding tables. Everyone walking gets a purple ribbon to pin on when they turn in their pledge cards. The woman who takes Lorna's card whistles when she sees the pledges. "Fantastic," she says. Lorna tells her it's Reverend Whipple's inspiration that makes it possible.

When Lorna walks away from the table, Mercer gets her attention. "Who do the checks get made out to?" he asks in a discreet voice.

"What?"

"When you collect the pledges. Who do people make the checks out to? Is it the church?"

"No," she says. "To the CF Foundation."

"So Whipple doesn't see any of the money?"

"No," she says.

"Does he get a cut for bringing you all here?"

"He does it because he wants to. Because it's part of his mission."

"What's the angle?"

"He's not like that, Michael. Don't tell me you're as cynical as Wes was."

"I just want you to be careful. You can't trust everyone."

"I can take care of myself, Michael. I'm nobody's fool."

She selects a bran muffin, holds it up to the light, then sniffs it warily. Mercer sips his cider, thinking about how to ask what he wants to ask next. "So," he says finally, "Sergeant Featherstone didn't believe in things? Spiritual things?"

She pauses as she's peeling the paper off the muffin. "That wasn't part of our lives," she says. "I've only gotten interested recently. Wes was a cynic. A cynic's cynic."

"Even when—" Mercer says, and here he pauses, hoping that an appropriate phrase will occur to him. "Even at the end?"

"Between you and me, Michael," she says, "I understand now that Wes was a little, well, *dotty* in his last few years. He joined a church, but it wasn't a proper one. It was foolishness, pure and simple. No basis in reality." She takes a tiny bite of the muffin, then wrinkles her face and drops it discreetly into a trash bin. "I can do better," she whispers to him, with a conspiratorial grin.

He wants to ask her more, but the music fades out and the event organizer addresses the crowd over the squawky PA. She thanks everyone for coming, talks about the seriousness of the disease and the importance of funding the search for a cure. At seven o'clock on the dot, the walk begins. Lorna and Mercer and the rest of the congregation gather around Reverend Whipple, who reties the laces on his running shoes, then leads them out into the flow of walkers. The pace he sets is faster than Mercer expected, especially for such an old crew. Traffic along the Embarcadero has been blocked off, and people fill the bay-side lanes, heading northwest as the rising sun throws their shadows alongside them. The palm trees that line the road flutter and wave. Seagulls wheel and cry and bullet into the choppy waters. Boat engines thrumble and churn.

They reach The Waterfront restaurant—where, Mercer remembers, he took a girl from one doomed short-term relationship or another—and his leg still feels locked-down; he can't work the clamped muscles loose. He can ease the pain by keeping his right leg straight and swinging it around with each stride, but he can't do it subtly. Lorna is watching him.

"How is it?" she asks.

"Stiff."

"Do you need to rest?"

"Better to keep walking. It'll loosen up."

Lorna stays with him, and the two of them fall behind. They watch as Reverend Whipple works the scene, talking to everybody in the church group, speeding up and falling back, keeping up a stream of chatter. He's at ease with everyone, cheerful and charismatic and obviously well liked. Mercer still doesn't trust the man. He's a TV preacher, for fuck's sake. With each step, Mercer dislikes him more. *Somebody* has to. It's infuriating that some people get to breeze through life like this.

He's so busy watching the Reverend that he forgets to pay attention to walking. While swinging his leg out, he catches the high curb with his foot, and it brings him up short. Agony. Yet another blast of fire down his leg, hot needles through his foot and toes. He's aware that a shout may have escaped from him, and he hopes it didn't sound as much like *fuck* as he thinks it did. Lorna immediately puts her arm around him, just below the shoulders. She helps him stand as he points his grimacing face skyward and holds his leg off the ground, afraid to put any weight on it.

Reverend Whipple power-walks back to them. "You all right, son?"

Mercer holds up a finger. *Wait.* He can't talk yet.

"Hang on," Whipple says. He blows a sharp, two-fingered whistle, and shouts to his people to stop and come back to them.

Mercer is past the point of caring that he's a spectacle. Nothing matters except the pain, and getting it to end. The entire congregation, with their white hair and Easy Spirits and purple ribbons, clusters around them, wide-eyed and quizzical, dumb as goats.

"Michael's having a tough time," Lorna explains. "He was in a car accident. He's having surgery in a few days." There are murmurs of sympathy.

"Do you want to stop?" Lorna asks him.

Mercer shakes his head.

"Now's not the time for pride," Whipple says. "If you're hurt, you're hurt."

"I can do it," Mercer says through his teeth. He wipes sweat off his forehead with the back of his hand. In the same motion, he tries to dry his leaking eyes.

"There's a long way to go," Lorna says.

"I'm good," he says, and he takes a few steps forward. Just when he thinks he's found a groove with his short, careful steps, the next stride brings pain. "Fuck *me*," he says, his voice strained. He closes his eyes and waits.

He feels his arms lifted and wrapped around other people's shoulders. He feels his weight supported. He keeps his eyes squeezed tight. "I'm not stopping," he says to whoever owns those arms.

"We know," a man's voice says. "We know."

And through the rest of the charity walk, Reverend Whipple's congregation brings up the rear, dropping farther and farther behind the other groups until they're on their own, every other group out of sight, the laughter and songs and whistles blown away by the bay wind. They all putt along at Mercer's speed, no faster, and men and women alike take turns offering their shoulders to him. The sun rises higher, the day grows older, and the streets are reopened to traffic, so the walkers have to take to the sidewalks as cars rush past. When they reach the finish line below the Golden Gate, the tables and chairs are being folded up and loaded onto a rental truck, and the caterers have packed up the food and carted it away. No one seems to mind. Sipping a sports drink that someone handed him, Mercer watches as they take in the view of the bridge and the green hills of Marin, watch the boats heading out to open water, congratulate themselves on a job well done. When *The Redemption Express* chugs to life and opens its door, they file on board. Dusty the driver and the Reverend himself lift Mercer into the bus and ease him down into that front-row seat, and Mercer turns to the window, closes his eyes, utterly exhausted, too tired to be embarrassed, too tired to appreciate the kindness they've shown him, but too tired to resent it, either.

The cool metal grating at the base of the window breathes sweet-smelling air-conditioning onto his clammy skin, and thank God, he falls asleep.

◉

# TWENTY

# MERCER, AWAKE

Black ink on his skin, marking the incision site. Paper gown on his body, mask on his face, intravenous calm in his blood. White haze and bright lights and blue figures and a chance to start over clean and free. Ten nine eight, a countdown to nothing, seven six five and drift.

A low-pitched hum, pure tones ringing, and a voice—*good as new*—and drift.

Then he's in a new room. Wake, sleep, and repeat. Wake, sleep, and repeat. The sky outside his window darkens, and visitors appear and disappear. Mollie, with soft words and hair that brushes his face when she kisses his forehead—*but why not Owen? Where's Owen?* Toronto, who carries the smells of a smoky bar. Lorna, with her cheer and purple chrysanthemums. Then: a figure in the doorway, washed in a chemical pink light. Fiona. Fiona, but a Fiona from a different life, a Fiona with black hair and severe bangs, a Fiona come down from a fifties movie screen. Or maybe an echo of her mother on the day the music died. *Ghost Fiona,* he thinks. She steps into the room, crossing to him slowly and stiffly. He closes his eyes as her hand extends, and he braces himself for a jolt of ice from her dead hands, but her touch on his cheek is warm. *Sleep tight,* she says, just like she used to.

Then she is gone, just as everything goes, just as everyone leaves, here then gone. His skin loses her heat to the sterile chill of the room, here then gone. Here then gone, like the redness in the sky; here then gone, like the moon arcing across the window and beyond. Voices here then gone, himself here then gone, the night here and here and still here, then gone.

His eyelids flutter open to the new morning just as the nurse, a heavyset black woman with a crispy blond halo of a perm, struts into his room with a sunlit smile, a gold front tooth, and a sweet stranger's drawl. *Chile, how you sleep? How that night treat you? You on your way home 'fore too long, so rise and shine, chile, rise and shine.*

Fiona's first thought, seeing Mike in the hospital bed, is that he doesn't look like himself. His face is strikingly pale in the near-dark. He's put on a lot of weight, too—his face has rounded out, his neck has thickened—and it makes him seem puffy and strange.

The procedure went well, she was told. He'll have a week of incisional pain, and he'll need to rebuild strength and flexibility in his back and legs and core, but he'll soon be getting on with the rest of his life—a life that won't intersect with hers anymore. This moment, quiet, dimly lit in sick parking-lot-pink, feels like good-bye.

She regrets having called him with the news about Cricket. She'd been crazy-sad and a little drunk with the cat in her lap, and she'd wanted to hear his voice, wondered if she'd hear any sadness or longing in him. What she heard in his hello, though—in his *hello*, his *what?* his *oh, God I'm sorry*—was frightening to her, numb and defeated and hopeless-sounding. It had thrown her off guard, and the call didn't go anything like she'd wanted. That was the afternoon that she went out and got her hair done, to give her something to feel good about.

Is she feeling anything for him? She doesn't think so, no. But then, she's not feeling much about anything, so how can she say for sure? The only things she's truly feeling right now are grief and guilt, and both are connected to little Cricket: grief, because she knows she doesn't have long with this cat that she loves, that her father loved; guilt, because she knows Cricket is in pain, and she can't bring herself to put her down. She doesn't want to *think* about being in the vet's office, watching her friend IV'd into darkness. Maybe she's wrong for feeling so strongly about a cat, compared to everything else around her, but when she imagines going home and not seeing Cricket hop down from the windowsill to greet her at the door, well, it just feels empty and wrong.

Riding down in the elevator alone, she wrinkles her nose. Her hair is still holding the chemical smell of the black dye, and in this enclosed space, she becomes keenly aware of it stinging her nose. The patients can't be happy about that. She's gotten some looks.

She checks her reflection in the shiny metal of the button panel. The image is distorted, but she can see what she needs to: the newly black hair, the severe Bettie Page bangs, this retro-rockabilly look that she'd thought would make her feel new and glamorous and a little dangerous, too. Now, a week later, she sees herself and feels like a stranger, wonders where her old self went. Except for that goddamn furrow—it's a reminder that she'll never be able to reinvent herself completely. Her experience, her history, her years—they're not going away.

**M**ercer finds Jude standing in front of the clinic, his hands jammed into the pockets of his windbreaker, staring straight ahead into the street. Jude doesn't look him in the eye, doesn't say hello. The air around them is hazy and acrid; a balloon factory in Visitacion Valley is burning, spreading a stink for miles.

"Let's go on in, bud," Mercer says. "We'll find out what's wrong. We'll deal with it. You want to talk about what to expect?"

Jude shakes his head. He makes no motion to go inside.

"It happens to a lot of people," Mercer says.

"I'm not a lot of people," Jude says.

"Nobody is," Mercer says, but Jude won't walk, won't even turn to face the glass-door entrance, until Mercer puts his hands on his shoulders and steers him in the right direction. "You're going to be fine," Mercer says. "I've got your back." And together they step forward into the austere, low-ceilinged room, where the pine scent doesn't cover up the weightier smells of nervous sweat and mildew.

When the phone had rung in the apartment, Mercer had let himself believe it might be Kelly. He'd been feeling better since the surgery, but not any less alone or any less hungry for some word from her. So he'd been disappointed when, instead of hearing her voice, smoky-sweet and full of apology, he'd heard Jude's, shaky and halting, adolescent and anxious. "You told me I could call you for anything," Jude said. "I think I'm sick." Mercer had pulled out his San Francisco phone book and found the address of the free clinic for him, and when Jude asked if he'd come, Mercer quickly agreed. Jude's breathing was rapid, his voice panicked. Mercer felt guilty: he'd had his own stuff to deal with, sure, but he'd been inattentive to the case, inattentive to Jude himself. The kid probably felt abandoned.

He decided to wear what he had on: T-shirt and jeans, no indicia of authority—he would be Mike, not Officer Mercer. He found his jacket and keys, then knocked on the door of the hall closet, where Toronto was meditating, and announced that he was going out for a while. "I'm not your mom," Toronto said through the closed door. "You don't have to tell me every damn thing."

Jude signs the intake list and sits down in a plastic chair to fill out a questionnaire on a clipboard. Mercer doesn't sit—he doesn't want to strain his surgical staples, and anyway, he's gotten used to a life of standing whenever possible. He senses that Jude wants space as he fills out the form, so Mercer walks the perimeter of the room, reading the health alerts and PSA flyers on the walls, most of which feature photographs of serious-featured young people of many races, some alone, some with same- or opposite-sex partners. The room is quiet, except for a phone that rings regularly but softly, the intake clerk who murmurs into it, and the ventilation system, which whirs and clicks. Even when Jude has finished filling out the forms, he doesn't talk to Mercer; he opens up a book and reads, looking up at Mercer every minute or so, as if for reassurance, then turning back to the words. He's not turning pages very frequently; Mercer guesses he's too scared to absorb much. Mercer sees the cover clearly, and it still takes him a few seconds to recognize it as *The Shenanigan Tapes*. He's not at his best either, obviously. He just started titrating off the painkillers, and his brain feels a little foggy.

The other patients in the room are a male bike messenger with weight-stretched earlobes, a bearded guy about Mercer's age in a stained overcoat, and a boy and a girl, sitting together, each with loose blond curls and hoop earrings and threadbare tank tops under flannel. He can't tell if they're stylishly ratty honor-roll students or a pair of runaways who turn tricks under the freeway.

After forty-five minutes, Jude is called in. Before he disappears through the door, he glances back at Mercer, looking scared and sallow under the yellow light. Mercer nods, just a quick down-and-up, a fraction of an inch in each direction. Jude responds in kind, and it reminds Mercer of a moment in a western, a silent acknowledgment between gunslingers.

Afterward, Mercer takes Jude through the burnt-rubber air to The Neptune Café, just a short walk away. He orders two sodas and a plate of onion rings for them to share. Jude sits stiffly in his chair; he still hasn't said anything about what happened with the doctor.

"The book you're reading," Mercer says, to break the silence. "You like it?"

"So far. Just started it this morning."

"You get that at your folks' house?"

"Yeah. It was out. How'd you know?"

"I gave it to your dad. The guy who wrote it asked me to."

"He's a friend of yours?"

Mercer thinks of Toronto and his Right Speech, and he decides not to say anything negative, no matter how much Kinnicutt might deserve it. "We grew up together," he says instead. "How's school going?"

"Sucks," Jude says. "I'm way behind. And everyone stares. Or ignores me." He rolls the straw wrapper into a tiny ball, then pushes it around the table with a thumbnail. "Yesterday I was in a bathroom stall, and I heard a couple of guys laughing about me. They think I got butt-raped. Apparently that's funny."

"That's tough," Mercer says. "Trouble is, no matter how old you are, no matter what you do, there's always going to be some jerk-off laughing at you."

The waitress brings the onion rings, and once the two of them start eating together, Jude relaxes. He looks around the room, as if reassuring himself that there's enough activity and background noise to give him cover, then leans toward Mercer and says in a low voice, "I don't just have one."

"One what?"

"Disease," Jude says. "The doctor said I have a *cocktail* of them. Then he said, *no pun intended.*"

"Funny," Mercer says.

"Hilarious."

"They give you antibiotics?"

Jude nods. He swirls his straw around his glass. "I really fucked up," he says.

"Yeah, you did," Mercer says. "But you're not the first."

"Did this ever happen to you?"

Mercer is taken aback at first; then he realizes it's a good sign that Jude felt he could ask. "No," he says. "Could've. I did some dumb things. Got lucky, I guess."

"They stick a swab *inside*," Jude says. "It hurts like hell."

"I know. I've been a waiting-room buddy before." He'd done it twice. Once for his freshman roommate, a home-schooled Catholic who was going to pieces with fear and shame, and once for Johnny K, during a college summer at home. Johnny K was tighter with Kinnicutt, Owen, and Johnny G, but he'd chosen Mercer. *I know I can trust you,* he'd said.

Jude drags a strip of bare onion through a pool of ketchup, over and over, in figure eights. "I'm one of *them* now," he says. "I'm diseased."

"You've got an infection, is all. Doesn't mean anything about you as a person."

"I'm one of them," Jude says, and there's certainty in his tone. He won't be moved off this.

"It's not that big a deal," Mercer insists. "You'll take some pills. You'll make a better decision next time."

"Plus I have to wait a week to find out about the HIV test."

"Try not to worry."

"How can I not worry?"

"Won't do you any good. What's done is done. The odds are in your favor, anyway."

"I'm supposed to be exceptional," Jude says. "I'm supposed to be the one who does things right. I'm supposed to be the one who succeeds and has his shit together."

"You still are. You made a mistake. Everyone does."

"I'm not everyone."

"So I heard," Mercer says. "It hasn't gotten any truer in the last hour."

"You don't know what it's like," Jude says.

"You're right," Mercer says. "I don't." If anything, he's been expected to be unexceptional. Even by himself. "I've only ever gotten to feel exceptional once. One night. You know when that was?"

Jude looks down, studies something on his shoe.

"It was the night I found you."

Jude sips the last of his soda, the straw slurping loudly around the bottom. "That's sad," he says.

"It's true," Mercer says. He looks at his soda, wishes he had a beer instead.

There's a siren outside, and it quiets them. They both watch as an ambulance careens down the street, throwing flashing reds into the café.

"Have you told the girl?" Mercer asks. Jude is slow to answer, and Mercer is afraid he's just made a big mistake. "Or, uh, whoever it is?"

"It's a girl. Of course it's a girl."

"But have you told her?"

Jude shakes his head.

"You have to tell her," Mercer says. "It's your responsibility."

"I don't know if I'm going to see her again."

"Still. You have to try to find her. Let her know."

"She's nobody," he says.

"I bet she doesn't think that," Mercer says.

"I bet you're wrong," Jude says. "She's disgusting. I don't know what I was thinking."

Mercer decides to stay quiet. Give the kid space to talk.

"It was at a party," Jude says. "I was drunk and I was mad. I told you there's this girl I love, right? I saw her with another guy. And I mean *with* him, with him. Everything I'd been telling myself—like, that I even had a shot with her—was a complete lie. I'm nobody to her."

And instantly Mercer is back at the hot tub again: the pile of white clothes, the slumped white boots, Kinnicutt's hands running over Kelly's wet skin, the white hat on his fat, bald, sweaty head somehow a taunt, a further insult. "I'm sorry," Mercer says. "That's tough."

"I wasn't thinking straight," Jude says. "And this other girl was there, you know? And she was all, let's do it. And I was thinking, fine, you don't deserve any better, anyway."

"You or her?"

"Does it matter?"

"So you didn't have any protection."

"Wouldn't have used it anyway."

"Decisions," Mercer says. "Got to make better ones. That's what being an adult is all about."

"I was fucked up," Jude says. "And mad."

"Doesn't matter," Mercer says. He knows how hypocritical this is; he should never have driven home from Owen's party. He should have listened to Mollie and stayed there. But thinking straight hasn't been his thing lately, either. "You need to keep yourself in a state of mind where you can make good decisions."

"Thanks, Mom," Jude says.

"I don't think you've ever had a conversation like this with your mom," Mercer says. To his surprise, Jude's mouth turns upward in a vague approximation of a smile. Better than nothing.

"So," Mercer says. "This girl you love." Jude looks down at the crumbs on his plate, and Mercer can see the kid tensing, his shoulders squaring up, his jaw clenching. "The same thing just happened to me. Similar, anyway."

Jude eyes him closely. "Yeah? Your girlfriend? The one you told me about?"

"No," Mercer says. "That's over."

"Sorry."

"Don't be. It's for the best."

"So what happened?"

"There's this other girl that I fell for pretty hard. I took her to a party. She ended up in the hot tub with my friend."

"They hooked up?"

"They hooked up."

"Did you beat the shit out of the guy?"

"Just because I'm a cop doesn't mean I go around beating the shit out of people," Mercer says. "Although I could have."

"Should have."

"Maybe," Mercer says. "It would've felt good. But I'm glad I didn't."

The waitress clears their plates, then comes back and replaces their empty glasses with full ones. Something clicks in Mercer's mind. How could he be so slow, even with the fog of withdrawal in his head? "Jude?" he says.

"Yeah?"

"Be honest with me, okay?"

"I am."

"These people at the party? Are they the ones who left you in the cemetery?"

Jude inspects his shoe again.

"Because if they are," Mercer says, "you need to stop protecting them. Think about it. All the bad things are happening to *you*."

The silence is long, and Mercer watches him carefully. He sees a series of expressions wash across Jude's face: at first they look like understanding and relief, but then his face hardens, his gaze at nothing intensifies, and Mercer can see all the stifled emotion churning inside him: sadness, frustration, anger in a thousand directions. He hears Toronto's voice: *Kid's fucked up. He's all fucked up.* Jude pushes himself away from the table, his chair scraping against the floor, which turns people's eyes to them. "Bathroom," he says. "Where is it?"

Mercer tells him, and when the boy disappears into the back, he wonders if he should follow, just to be safe. Relax, he tells himself. Nothing's going to happen here, and you won't get anything else if you don't show trust. Five minutes pass. Mercer has nearly exhausted his capacity not to worry when he sees Jude returning. At the table, Jude hands him a folded piece of paper towel. He doesn't sit down.

Mercer unfolds it and sees a Daly City address written in shaky, childish handwriting. "Thanks, Jude," he says. "You're doing the right thing."

"Make sure nothing happens to Reyna," Jude says.

"I can't make promises like that," Mercer says.

"It's not her fault."

"I'll tell the detective."

Jude nods slowly, scratches his ear, pushes his hand back through his hair. "Thanks for today," he says, finally. "I didn't want to be alone."

"You're not," Mercer says, and he's surprised to find his own throat tightening. He swallows hard, tells himself this is not a time to appear weak. "Better things are ahead. Trust me. Take care of yourself, all right?"

Jude looks out at the darkening street, his eyes determinedly wide open. "Of course I will," he says. "I don't have any other choice, do I?"

They walk out to the street together and say good-bye. Mercer watches him walk the length of the block and then turn the corner onto Seventh. As soon as Jude is out of sight, Mercer calls Detective Funkhouser from his cell phone and reads him the address.

**T**welve hours later, warrants in hand, four Daly City Police units converge on the house. What they find: bottles and cans, a few needles, a used condom, boxes of Ramen, a moldy half-loaf of bread. No people. No one's been in there for at least a week, they determine.

"Ghost house," Funkhouser tells Mercer the next day.

**L**orna takes the long walk to the coffee shop from the pai gow table, her eyes cast down at the carpet, watching the black-diamond patterns go by under her feet. She's lost everything but the twenty-dollar bill she keeps in her shoe, and she needs to sit and think about what to do next. She's had a few bad nights in a row, but this has been the worst. It started terribly—junk cards every hand. Seven hundred dollars, gone in the first twenty minutes. She changed seats to try to goose her luck and got more junk. Once she whispered a prayer and immediately got a good hand—jack-high straight, pair of sixes— and the dealer turned over a flush and a pair of nines. She whispered another prayer and was blessed with more junk. *Every time I lose,* she thinks, *another child goes hungry. Another clean-water well goes undug. Another cleft palate goes unfixed.*

It's two in the morning, but the coffee shop is loud, full of people in their twenties, lots of Asians, and from the looks of them—the slouchy postures, the shrieking laughs, the sudden lurching movements—they've been in the bars all night. Such a waste of time. She's always thought so, and thank God, so did Wes. Wes was a lot of things, but a drunk wasn't one of them.

She sits in the only available booth. There are loud and beery kids on either side of her. She does her best not to listen to who effed whom or who wants to eff whom or who is whose *bitch*. She orders her coffee, then closes her eyes, blocking out all the noise and clatter and profanity and recklessness around her. Decadence. Complacence. Waste. It depresses her to see it.

What can she be doing wrong? Her card-playing is the Lord's work. She's been doing it for a while now, and she's never kept anything for herself—she's given it all away, and more. Sometimes in other people's names, like on her pledge cards. She doesn't need all the credit.

Maybe this is the problem: maybe she *enjoys* it too much. That moment when you first lay eyes on your hand. Deciding how to set it. Laying your cards down—the point of no return. Waiting to find out what the dealer is holding. The clack of chips when the house pays off. The feel of your arms brushing over the felt as you rake it all in. The feel of being a winner. Her bad streak could be a sign, a warning that she should approach her work here with detachment, even gravity. She doesn't quite believe it—Reverend Whipple enjoys himself as he's doing the Lord's work, doesn't he?—but this is the explanation that stays in her mind. Yes, she decides, that is the next thing to try: she'll tamp down that thrill when she feels it, she'll treat this as work, hard work on behalf of all those people who need her, who need the money she earns. It's all for them. Because *actual needy people* will get her money, not some hillbilly ghost-chasers who take advantage of old and sad and silly men. She doesn't want any credit. She just wants the Reverend to be proud of her.

She catches herself: no, she shouldn't be so selfish. It's not about what the Reverend thinks of her. It's about how much more he can do because of her efforts. There's no place for that kind of pride.

The coffee comes and it is bitter. The air is full of this smell of bitter coffee, and full of the sounds of drunk and fatuous and self-centered young people. She sips her coffee, emptying the cup even though she does not care for the taste—*it is bitter, but it will help me stay alert.* She slips off her shoe and takes out the damp twenty. She lifts herself up out of the booth, stands up straight and tall, and if any of those young people are snickering at her age or her weight or the pattern of her dress or the thickness of her ankles, well, let them. She has work to do. She must pay her tab, and then she must get more money from the ATM, and then she must sit down at the table again and play, because people need food and clothing and shelter and water and cures for their parasites, and she is going to do her part to help the Reverend make sure they get what they need. And the Lord will give her the strength she needs. Amen.

# TWENTY-ONE

# THE DEAD BUG

Mercer is lying on his back on the living room floor, groaning his way through an ab-strengthening exercise his physical therapist calls The Dead Bug, when he hears steps approaching the front door. "I'm coming in," Toronto says from outside. "Better pull your pants up." Mercer rolls out of the pose and onto his stomach, and he finds himself looking at the pile of sports gear in the corner, at the empty space where the softball bat used to lean against the wall. A reminder—yes, it's true, he gave the bat to a dead man who's out there bashing other dead people with it. And Mercer has a job to do; he has a posse to form and a gang of hardened criminals to thwart. It's totally Hollywood, not to mention insane, but it's exciting, and it ignites a spark of pride inside him.

The door swings open, and Toronto walks in with his meditation cushion under one arm and a rolled-up magazine in his hand. Before saying hello, he walks to the hall closet, where Mercer sees him put the cushion up on the shelf, bow to it, and close the door.

"I got some reading material for you," Toronto says, walking back through the living room. He drops the magazine onto the carpet next to Mercer. An issue of *Limn*. On the cover is a close-up photo of Marco DiMaio in a pose of intense thought, his fingertips laced together under a salt-and-pepper-goateed chin. His eyes are green and intense as a horror-movie hypnotist's. He's bathed in a stern lime-green light, and the background is a viscous dark green that fades to black at the edges. *Marco DiMaio: God Is in the Lens.*

"'God is in the lens'?" Mercer says. "What does that even mean?"

"Search me," Toronto says.

Mercer turns to the table of contents, where the title appears again, at the top of the page and in big red letters. Below, in black: A LIMN PROFILE. BY KELLY CHALESKI. Just seeing her name in print gets him excited, floods him with desire all over again. He remembers Toronto's advice and decides, yes, knows what he wants—and maybe this is insane, too, but he wants to give her one more shot. He's not even embarrassed about it. He hasn't felt an attraction this strong, this *consuming* in years, or maybe ever. He reads her name again, remembers her rosemary hair and peach-smelling skin, the way she moved her tongue, the overwhelming sense of *possibility* he'd felt with her in the DiMaios' gazebo. He sighs audibly, without meaning to, and then flips to the article. "Have you read it?" he asks.

"Skimmed," Toronto says in a bored voice.

"What did you think?"

"Read it for yourself." Toronto heads for the refrigerator. "You want a beer?"

Mercer shakes his head and starts reading. He intends to read carefully, to take in every word of hers as fully as he did her name, to visualize her on the movie set, or typing away in her Cow Hollow flat, but after the first few paragraphs, which describe a scene DiMaio was shooting in Belize, he gets lost. He doesn't know what to make of phrases like *visual semiotics* and *the hubris of deconstructionism.* He asks Toronto what they mean.

"Nothing," Toronto says. "Just a way to make boring movies sound more boring."

Instead of reading, Mercer scans the pages for his name, for Jude's name, for the words *Colma* or *police* or *cemetery* or *assault.* Nothing. He flips back to the beginning and skims the eight pages again, in case he missed something— but he didn't. There's no mention that Marco DiMaio even *has* a son. The closest the article comes is this:

> "To be an artist," DiMaio says, "you must have the gifts, you must work tirelessly, and you must be ruthlessly disciplined—which is to say adult—in your process. You must make decisions without doubt, self-consciousness, or regret. You must take responsibility for your vision, for your choices, and for all the consequences that flow from them, proximately or not. Every day I see evidence that young people today are unable

to do that. I worry for the future, that of cinema and that of the larger world."

In the following paragraph, Kelly asks him about his father, who also worked in the film industry, and she writes:

"Talent isn't genetic," he growls. "Neither is discipline. I've made myself who I am."

Mercer pushes himself up from the carpet. "Read this," he says. "Does it sound like he's dissing Jude?"

Toronto reads. He half-nods, half-shrugs. "Could be. Or you might be reaching."

"'*Every day*' he sees evidence," Mercer says. "What other 'young person' would he see every day?"

"What does it matter if he's talking about his kid? It's his opinion, that's all."

Mercer thwacks the magazine with the back of his hand, knocking it out of Toronto's grip and onto the floor. "So what the hell is this article *about*?"

Toronto eyes him closely. "It's mostly about your rider trying to prove she's smart by throwing around polysyllabic horseshit," he says. He shakes his head. "I read her wrong. Her rack must have clouded my judgment."

"I thought she'd say something about me."

"You weren't famous before, and you're not famous now. Nothing's changed."

"It's not about being famous."

"I know. It's about the girl telling you you're irrelevant—in the magazine, in the hot tub, and ever since. And that's a real nut-crusher, isn't it?"

"I thought she liked me," Mercer says. "I really did."

"You think you've got it bad?" Toronto says. "Shit, my fiancée disappeared."

Mercer nods. "Sorry." He raises his arms into the air and stretches until he can feel the staples pinch. He exhales deeply. *Exchange all your air*, the physical therapist likes to say. *Air of healing in. Air of injury out.*

"You been out for a walk yet?" Toronto asks.

"Not today."

"Why not?"

"Haven't felt like it." He has decided not to go out alone unless he has to. Not yet. He's going to follow Lillie Coit's instructions and wait until he's ready.

"You need to get out of here," Toronto says. He gulps the rest of his beer, tosses the empty, and then claps his hands. "All right, candypants. Exercise time. We're going for a walk. And don't give me the excuse that you can't tie your shoes yet. I'll tie the motherfuckers for you."

"'Candypants'? Is that Right Speech?"

"Apologies," Toronto says. "Candypants."

"Hang on. I have to do one thing before we go." He picks up the phone and dials Kelly's cell number from memory. Thinking about Lillie and Gage and Beachey has him suddenly feeling confident, capable. Ten feet tall and bullet-proof. Nothing to lose by trying. He and Kelly had *something* together, what-ever it was, and he's not going to let her end it by pretending he doesn't exist. If there's going to be an ending, there will be an *ending*.

The call gets bounced to voice mail—no surprise, but disappointing—and he delivers his message in a strong, even voice. A command voice. He wants her to call him, he says; he wants to have a discussion so they can understand each other fully; he likes her and respects her choices, so there's no need to shy away from talking with him.

"Bravo, Boy Thirteen," Toronto says after Mercer hangs up.

"You think it'll work?"

"Fuck, no," Toronto says. "Buttergirl has left the building."

They leave The Willows and walk eastbound along Serramonte, then turn onto a side street. "Double time, Private," Toronto says. "We've got to build you up and get you back on patrol soon. That kid Gomez is no fun. He does whatever Benzinger tells him to. It's an outrage."

"Did you take him to the panther?"

"Yeah. He wasn't scared, and he didn't think it was funny. The kid's a fuck-ing brick."

A roaring airplane rises into the sky above them, making it hard to talk. A real plane, not one of Beachey's, leaving SFO and turning a wide circle over the mountain and the Bay. Big black birds squawk and scatter away from one tree, converge in another nearby. *A murder of crows*, Mercer thinks. *A conspiracy of ravens.* He walks through a pocket of cool air, and his brain tells him: *dead person.* He looks up, but sees nothing out of the ordinary. During the day, he doesn't see quite so much. He's pretty sure they're not as active, either.

"What's our destination?" he asks.

"Molloy's," Toronto says. "If you make it all the way down there without bitching, your first beer is on me."

"Deal." This is an easy win. He can do this walk in his sleep. Literally.

He *should* be feeling good. It's March, and the spring weather is here to stay. It's early afternoon, so the fog is hours away from falling down on them. The sun is shining, and the breeze carries the smell of mown grass. Lobelia and nasturtium bloom in patches along the road. He got up the nerve to call Kelly. His body is healing. He'll be back to work soon. On both sides.

They pass a construction site where a sleek retail box, all glass and metal and out-of-place on this back road, is nearing completion. A sign in the window runs the length of the vacant storefront:

COMING SOON

~ETURNITY~

MODERN STORAGE AND DISPLAY SOLUTIONS

"Now that," Toronto says, "is just in bad taste."

Mercer's laugh is stifled when he hits another pocket of cold air. "You think there's such a thing as ghosts?" he asks. "That the dead don't leave? At least not right away?"

"'Not right away'? What does that mean?"

"Forget that. I mean, do you think there are ghosts?"

Toronto takes a few seconds to think. "In the Zen tradition, there are things called *hungry ghosts.* They've got empty, bloated stomachs and narrow throats. Always hungry and never satisfied."

"Really?" Mercer thinks of Gage, searching for his tamping iron for over a century. Of Barker and Ruczek and LoPresti and Eastwick, stealing and stealing in a place where there's no reason to, where nothing has value, apart from the sentimental. And spilling blood, too, for no good reason. It seems to fit. "So you think there are?"

"Well, it's a metaphor," Toronto says. "At least, I *think* I'm supposed to take it as a metaphor. For the human condition. Never satisfied with who we are, pursuing physical desires, et cetera. You know the drill."

"But they *could* be real?"

"I don't know," Toronto says. "It didn't say in the handbook."

"There's a handbook?"

Toronto shakes his head. "Boy Thirteen, you are the most credulous—"

Mercer holds up his hand, interrupts. "Wait. So how do you get rid of a hungry ghost?"

"You don't. That's the whole point. You invite them in and feed them. You show compassion."

"Compassion?" Mercer tries to imagine the results of trying compassion on Doc Barker. A great many stab wounds, probably. Maybe a throat full of Root. "That's crazy."

"It's about learning to deal with negative things. Understanding the darker aspects of yourself."

"I'm not interested in the metaphor," Mercer says. "I'm interested in actual goddamn ghosts. And feeding them is fucking nuts."

"That's my practice you're talking about," Toronto says.

He sounds genuinely offended, so Mercer murmurs an apology. They walk in silence for a few minutes. A truck rumbles past them on the narrow road. "I'd have popped that guy," Mercer says. "Truck's too heavy for the road."

Toronto stops suddenly. "Your rider was *hot,*" he says. "I can't believe you blew the deal. You should've popped her the night she rode with you. Speaking of ghosts? You're the fucking hungry ghost, buddy. You're going to spend the rest of your life wondering what it would've been like to be bone-deep in her."

"She might call," Mercer insists.

"Keep telling yourself that."

"What happened to Right Speech?" Mercer says. "Isn't it supposed to stop you from being an asshole?"

"Okay," Toronto says. "Truce. Let's keep going. Beer awaits. And we'll make sure we get you out of the house more often." He puts one hand between Mercer's shoulders and eases him forward.

Mercer pushes back, refuses to move. His pulse is throbbing in his head. "What did you ever do with the ring?"

"Ring?"

"Yeah. The ring your disappearing fiancée mailed back to you."

"That would be a low blow," Toronto says, "if I were still broken up about Mia and holding on to the ring in the hope she'd come back. Only I'm not. I sold it. Didn't take too much of a hit."

Mercer thinks about what he said, realizes he was being petty, probing for a weak spot. He breathes. *Air of healing in. Air of injury out.* "What are you going to do with the money?" he asks.

"Get a new apartment, once you're ready to be on your own. And go down to Cozumel with Hope."

"Hope for what?"

"Hope. The girl I told you about. From the Zen Center."

"Oh," Mercer says.

"Your memory is shot, Boy Thirteen. I don't know if that means you should kick the pills completely or go back to taking them by the fistful. Anyway, I'm going to be spending some nights at her place. As long as you're okay on your own."

"Of course I'm okay on my own," Mercer says. He kicks a rock in front of him. It scutters across the pavement before dropping off into the drainage ditch. "Is she hot?" he asks.

"Smoking. Of course."

"Spill it. How old?"

"What do you mean, how old?"

"Remember? 'You're only as old as . . .'?"

"It doesn't matter," Toronto says.

"Aha," Mercer says. "Meaning, she's older."

Toronto shakes his head. "She's twenty-one."

"You're going in the wrong direction. She's *younger* than your former students."

"You call that the wrong direction?" Toronto shakes out a cigarette and pops it into his mouth. "All bullshit aside," he says, pausing to light up, "I've got a feeling about her. I've got *that* feeling. You know what I'm talking about. You had it for Ms. Butterworth, and still do. Only difference is, when I get that feeling, I go for it hard. I'm relentless. I don't worry about being polite, and I don't worry about failing. Got to be willing to die like an aviator."

Mercer is pretty sure that Beachey didn't enjoy dying like an aviator, drowning while strapped to his seat in the frigid Bay water, but this is not the time to bring that up. "So you're telling me I'm not willing. That I fly safe. That I'm scared."

"You don't fly safe," Toronto says. "You don't even get off the fucking ground."

Mercer stops walking and stares hard at his friend. Behind Toronto, in the middle distance, are the stones of Cypress Lawn. Mercer's head goes swimmy, and a torrent of old, dammed-up fears come rushing over him. A new one, too: the fear that in his real life he has squandered too much time, too many opportunities, too many possible connections to people, none of which he can get back. He's nearly thirty, and he has nothing to show but a fresh scar in the small of his back, a modest savings account, and a nice letter from the DiMaios in his personnel file.

And speaking of files, his fuckups would fill a large cabinet. Too afraid to carve a middle-school identity apart from Owen's. Too afraid to even try to understand his father's disordered mind. Too afraid to fight for Shelby Laswell in college, when she fell for someone else. Too afraid to choose a path after graduation, instead wasting six years doing nothing. Too afraid to relax with Fiona, so he never found out if he loved her or not. Too afraid of conflict to stand up to so-called friends who crap on his loyalty. And then there are the infinite paths his life could have taken if he'd chosen more bravely, or chosen at all. He can feel himself flushing, sweating. There's a rushing wind and a chord of hearing-test tones in his ears. His fists are clenched.

"—because, come on, she was *throwing* herself at you," he hears Toronto say. "Her T-shirt might as well have said *Do Me.*"

"Fuck you," Mercer says. "She had her hand in my pants, and I left to go deal with your sorry drunk ass."

"That was your choice," Toronto says, not missing a beat. "No one told you to do that."

"You needed me," Mercer says.

"No, I didn't. You *decided* that I needed you. That's your own choice. Don't try to make me owe you for it."

Mercer is sweating freely now, and he crouches so he won't fall so far if he loses his balance. He feels his skin straining against the staples, imagines the incision splitting wide open.

"Trade-offs, Boy Thirteen. You make them, and you live with them. It's called *consequences*. It's called *adulthood*."

Mercer screws his eyes shut. The trouble is, Toronto's right. He's *right*. If there are any dead people around, they're probably laughing at him, laughing because he's only just realizing what they've known for years, decades, a century or more. "You should move out," he says, finally. "I need my space back. I have some projects I need to—"

Toronto touches Mercer's shoulder again, only this time his hand folds over his collarbone, this time soothing instead of pushing. Mercer shrugs it away. "I'm not trying to be a dick," Toronto says. "I'm trying to help." When Mercer doesn't respond, Toronto keeps talking. "I'll start looking for a place tonight. For now, let me buy you a beer. A deal's a deal. Although technically, you didn't make it to the bar without bitching."

"It's all right," Mercer says. "You go ahead. I'm not in the mood." He begins his long trudge up the hill.

"Come on, Boy Thirteen!" Toronto calls after him. "Don't be a pussy about it."

Mercer gets hotter and sweatier as he walks. With each step he gets madder at himself. He punches his thigh, once, twice, again and again, hoping to raise a bruise, hoping pain will sharpen him up. He *wishes* Doc Barker would show his blasted-out face right now, because Mercer wants to take all this anger out on somebody, and it's probably better if it's someone who's already dead.

A message is waiting for him when they get home. It's going to be Kelly, he knows—finally—and he decides to open a bottle of wine before he plays it. He watches the red light flash as he sips. By the time his finger pushes the PLAY button, the sky has fallen to night, and his nerves are dull and smooth, beveled by alcohol. So it doesn't hurt all that much when her digitally captured voice says *I have to apologize, I couldn't bring myself to call because you have such a black cloud around you, you're in the darkest place I've ever seen anyone, it's hard to be around, a little scary even, I didn't want to get sucked into it, I can't help you, I hope you find someone who can, I hope you can find a way to be happier.*

A click, a beep, and she is gone. The answering machine whines and clicks sharply as it rewinds. The sound makes Mercer think of a fly caught between two panes of glass, buzzing and popping until it drops, silenced. He won't get to talk with her. Everyone just disappears.

Three in the morning. Hours before the Zes-T-Mart clerk can go home.

He locks the front door and goes out the back to spark up behind the Dumpster. This is killer bud—from Mendocino, he was told. Red crystals. Sticky and sweet. He considers moving to Mendocino. He can't think of any reason not to.

He walks back into the store, thinks about turning off a few of the super-bright lights even though he's not supposed to. He walks toward the front doors, fumbling with his key ring, and when he looks up, he nearly jumps out of his skin. There's a dude in a bathrobe waiting outside and watching him, his eyes wide, a little crazed. He's tempted to leave the door locked, turn off the lights, pretend they're closed, but then he recognizes Bathrobe Dude as one of the local cops. He opens up, praying that he hasn't carried the smell of the smoke inside with him.

Bathrobe Dude walks past him without saying anything, without sniffing the air. He heads directly to the beverage fridge and carries four cans of KER-BLAM! up to the counter. He pays with a damp ten-spot. The clerk puts the energy drinks in a bag for him, and the dude turns and leaves without saying a damn thing. There's no sound of a car pulling away. Dude must have walked. Well, whatever tops your taco, hombre.

He decides to try something new: squinting and watching the cigarette case through his lashes. Ghosts will think he's not paying attention. Elbows on the counter, head in his palms, he watches. The light makes cool diamond patterns when you narrow your eyes. Mendocino, baby. Men-do-ci-no. The name sounds like a song. Or it could be part of a haiku. The first line would be *Mendocino bud.* The second would have some other words that sound good. The third, too.

He jerks upright when he feels something cold and wet on his wrist. He's drooling on himself. Idiot. He fell asleep. The clock tells him twenty minutes have gone by. The stack of Chesterfields looks smaller to him, although he can't say for sure because he forgot to do an exact count earlier. Goddamn, these ghosts are smooth.

Lorna awakens to pounding on her door. She rolls over groggily and sees the old clock's hands at 7:30. It's a nice old clock, one of the first electric alarm clocks that came out, very plain, with a round pink-orange glow behind the hands and a steady hum that's gotten louder in recent years, working harder to keep her company. Yes, it's an awfully nice clock. . . .

The pounding wakes her up again, and this time she swings her feet to the ground and stands, her knees crackling with the first motion of the day. She wraps her robe around herself and walks to the front door as the pounding continues. It irritates her, all this pounding, especially since she only got to sleep forty-five minutes ago. It was a long night of humbling cards and lost opportunities.

Officer Mercer is outside her door, wearing Wesley's old robe and holding more of her mail. His feet are bare, he smells like he's been drinking, and he looks so purple-eyed and squinty that he probably hasn't slept at all. She invites him in and seats him at the old kitchen table, where he hands her the mail. She quickly flips through them while his knee bounces nervously, shaking the table. The usual junk, plus a notice marked Past Due in red. Two letters from attorneys. A few suspiciously neutral-looking envelopes that she suspects are from collection agencies.

She wants to be left alone, but she can't be unneighborly, can she? She doesn't have much food in the house—she hasn't been baking at all, for one thing—but she fixes him a cup of instant coffee. She puts it in a travel mug, though, so she can send him on his way before he's finished.

His first sip scalds him. "I've had enough," he says.

"I know it's not gourmet coffee," she says, "but—"

"I mean I've had enough of pretending that I don't know you've got money trouble."

"Thank you, Michael, but there's no trouble. I just forget deadlines, some-times. When you're my age—"

"You're selling your *car.*"

"Yes, I'm selling the car. I thought I'd get something that can hold more, so—"

"You're not getting something else."

"I'm not?"

"No. You're selling your car so you can give that Whipple even more of your money. Then you'll walk everywhere and tell everyone how happy you are to do it."

"Office Mercer—" she says, her indignation rising.

"I'm not going to let you. No more money to him. Just because the Ser-geant gave a ton of money to some ghost-obsessed hillbilly oxy-freaks, you don't have to go out and waste what you have on that bolo-wearing fraud."

Lorna slams her palm down on the table, and he recoils at the sound, then sways woozily in his chair. "You are overstepping, Officer Mercer, and offend-ing me," she says. "This is none of your business, and you should know better. You *do* know better. So please *leave.*"

Officer Mercer pushes himself back in the chair and uses the table to push himself up. The fragile legs wiggle, and she wonders if it'll hold. He staggers a few steps toward the door. "Where's your tea table?" he says. "How much did you get for that?"

"Stop," she tells him firmly.

"I don't see your crystal wineglasses, Mrs. Featherstone. Where are your crystal wineglasses?"

"I don't *need* crystal wineglasses," she says, crossing toward him, trying to urge him toward the door.

He moves a few steps before planting his feet and pointing unsteadily at the empty spot on the wall. "Where's the clock?"

"What?"

"Didn't you *hear* me?" he says, altogether too loudly. "Where is the *cuckoo* clock, Mrs. Featherstone? The cuckoo clock that your *husband,* my sergeant, brought back from *Germany?*"

She takes hold of the knob and flings the door open. It's sunny and pleasant outside, and sparrows and finches are fluttering about. It's a morning she'd enjoy under different circumstances. "Go," she tells him. "Please. I don't know what you're mad about, but it has nothing to do with me."

"Nothing? How much did you *get* for it, Mrs. Featherstone? How much did you *give* that man? Probably not much, unless you found the *hands.*"

"Get out!" she shouts. "I'll call the police. You don't want that. It's not worth it."

"You lost the *hands,* Mrs. Featherstone!"

She tries to shout again, but her voice loses its power because she's crying now, for some reason. She really doesn't want to be, but she is.

"How could you lose the *hands?* You can't tell the goddamned time without *hands!* And he *bought* you those *hands!*"

She steps forward and pushes him out the door. His arms wheel as he backpedals crazily, but he doesn't fall. Thank God. It's hard to force words out between the sobs, between the scrapes and rales of her lungs, but she says, "Go home. You don't mean this. I'll forgive you sometime, but not now." She sees his eyes widen at the word *forgive*—she surprised him—and then she flings the door closed so it bangs in its frame, and she sits heavily on the couch—listed for sale on several bulletin boards, no calls so far—and cries into her terrycloth sleeve.

# TWENTY-TWO

# THE NEPTUNE SOCIETY (II)

**F**riday night, 2030 hours. Mercer steps into the shimmering green light of the bar. He has been avoiding the Neptune gang since the hot-tub fiasco at Owen's party, but he was desperate to escape The Willows tonight, to escape Colma, and his San Francisco friends felt like his last connection to sanity. He circles twice, checking all the tables, but he doesn't find anyone he knows. What's going on? Maybe they've chosen another bar and no one told him. Maybe they all took a getaway together, to Napa or Tahoe or Bolinas or Sea Ranch or any of the places where someone's family owns a vacation house. Whatever the reason, he's been left out. They've left him out. He heads for the exit with his jaw clenched tight and bright flecks of color sparking in his vision. He feels toxic.

Someone on a barstool grabs his arm, and he whips around. Mollie. A blond Mollie now, with thin blood-red streaks in her hair. "I didn't see you come in," she says.

"I missed you, too," he says. "Maybe it was the hair."

"What do you think?" she asks. She turns her head back and forth, a shampoo-commercial spin.

"I like it."

"Me too," an older man on the next stool says. "It makes her look feisty." He has a sweep of tidy gray hair and squinty eyes behind gold-rimmed glasses, and he's wearing a navy-blue suit. "Not that she needs any help in that department."

"Who are you?" Mercer asks.

"This is Bruce," Mollie says. "He's with the D.A.'s Office."

"I'm trying to get her onto the right side," Bruce says.

*Is Mollie having an affair?* Mercer wonders, even as he is locked in a vigorous handshake with the gray-haired man.

Bruce slides off his stool and offers it to Mercer, saying he has to get home to his family. Mercer watches their good-bye closely but doesn't notice anything out of the ordinary. He watches Bruce make his way through the crowd and disappear out the door before he eases himself up onto the stool.

"You know me," Mollie says. "Always networking. Even with the enemy. What are you having? Stout?"

"Bourbon," Mercer says. "Double. Where is everyone?"

"I'm not enough for you?"

"I'm just surprised. Where's Owen?"

"He's up north. 'Resolving some business,' he says. Many secrets lately. You haven't heard anything about it?"

"I've been underground," Mercer says.

"So he's keeping you in the dark, too."

"No one tells me much of anything anymore."

"Between you and me, he's on thin ice right now." She says it like she's joking, but he can tell she isn't. "I hope he's doing the right thing."

"Me too," Mercer says. "Where are the others?"

"Everyone has a big project, or just got back from Paris, or is scouting wedding sites, or seeing a play, or hosting in-laws, or whatever. I think Owen's party burned a lot of people out." She pauses. "Heath would've come, but he asked me if I thought you'd be here. I said you probably would."

"What's his problem?"

"He thinks you hate him."

"Well," Mercer says, "I do."

"He said he was afraid you'd use some kind of secret cop jujitsu on him. He's feeling bad about what he did."

"He should."

The bartender, the one who reminds him of the Irish dancers, asks them what it'll be. Mollie gives her their drink order when Mercer is slow to speak, then tucks her hair behind her ear and faces him. "You really liked her. I could tell," she says.

"The bartender?"

"Kelly."

Mercer shrugs. "Emphasis on *liked*, I guess."

"Well, good riddance, if that's the kind of thing she likes to do."

"I blame him," Mercer says.

Mollie raises her wineglass and drains the last few drops. "Yes," she says, setting the empty glass on the bar. "It was a terrible thing for Heath to do. But we've all known for years that he can be a self-centered jerk. Especially when he's drinking. Right? You know I'm right. And he's still our friend. Wouldn't it be easier to accept him for who he is? Maybe adjust your expectations?"

Mercer shakes his head. "Loyalty's not negotiable."

She sighs. "This is exactly why women should rule the world."

"I just thought—" Mercer says. "I mean, I felt—" Then his voice stops working.

"I know," she says. "I know." She reaches into her purse for her cell phone. "Tell you what. Let's liven things up here. I'm going to call a new friend of mine, see if she'll join us. Her name's Eileen. You'll like her."

Mercer tries to tell her no, he doesn't want any setups, but she punches in the number and holds one finger up to his lips. "Hush up," she says, so he busies himself tearing up a damp napkin on the bar while she talks. It's a brief conversation, and Mercer guesses that Eileen is saying she's stuck at work. Mollie doesn't lean on her too hard, and Mercer is glad. He needs to connect with someone one-on-one, someone reliable, someone he trusts. Mollie snaps her phone closed. "Oh well," she says. "Bad timing. Maybe next week."

The drinks arrive, and Mercer and Mollie clink glasses, a wordless toast to nothing in particular. After her first sip, she leans in close to him. There's a chemical smell in her hair, and he breathes it in. "How come you didn't say anything to the bartender?" she asks. "She winked at you."

"She winks at everyone," he says. "Tips." Also: he knows he looks terrible. He's bag-eyed and way too heavy, and he hasn't shaved in days. He's wearing his least-dirty shirt and least-dirty jeans, both of which came off a pile on his bedroom floor.

She asks how he's feeling, and he gives her the short version: back's better, still not sleeping much, anxious to go back to work next week. Off the pain-killers, more or less. He chooses not to mention that he has been fighting ghost-crime.

"What else, though?" she asks. "Tell me something I don't know about you."

"I'm worried about my neighbor," he says. He's been burning to talk to someone about what happened the other morning. Those aren't the first past-due notices he's seen, and a couple of days ago he'd read through a newsletter that came from Reverend Whipple's church. He'd found a photo of Lorna above an article that said she had set records for fund-raising in each of the last three months. "I don't think she's fund-raising," he tells Mollie. "I think she's giving him every cent she has." The car, the clock, the slowly emptying apartment: it all added up. He tried to talk to her, he says, but it went badly, and he upset her.

"I'm not surprised she got upset," Mollie says. "Money's personal. Plus, if you're right, she's probably ashamed."

"I have to do something. That sonofabitch is taking advantage of her."

She takes a sip of wine and rolls it around in her mouth before she speaks. "There's not a lot you can do if there's no fraud and she's not incompetent." He nods. He knows this, but he doesn't want to admit that he's powerless. "Let her know you're there for her," she says, "but her mistakes are her own mistakes."

"It makes me so mad," Mercer says. He doesn't care if Whipple was kind to him on the bus. Just part of the act. "Swindling old ladies for Jesus. What the fuck kind of person does that?"

She lays her hand over his. "Sssh," she says. "Try to relax. You might've helped her out just by noticing."

"He's a goddamned fraud."

"Maybe," she says, rubbing his knuckles with her thumb. "But you have to relax. You've been through a really rough stretch. And you've held up better than anyone else I know would have."

Immediately he feels pressure behind his eyes, and the green-glassed candle on the bar becomes an emerald in his blurred vision. "I should have found someone like you," he says, the words out of his mouth before he can consider them. It's true, though; if he had someone who understood him like Mollie does, who could see him at his most broken and still not judge him, he could really fall in love. It's totally theoretical, but it's true.

She closes her hand tightly around his again and gives it a shake. "Michael," she says, smiling, "sometimes I think you like to worry me."

He covers his leaking eyes with his other arm. "I have to go to the bathroom," he says. "Can you get me another drink?"


After his third drink, Mollie cuts him off and suggests they call it a night. Mercer, feeling spin-headed and free, protests vigorously. If he could keep drinking, he'd have to go home with her, for safety's sake. But she shakes her head, pays the bill with her platinum card, and hauls him outside, where she folds him into a hug. "Take care of yourself, Mike," she says, resting her head on his shoulder. "Call me if you need to talk. Whenever. Okay?"

Mercer grips her tightly, puts his nose into her hair, and inhales deeply. The smell is pungent, eye-watering, but it's what he wants. "Owen doesn't know what he has," he says.

She gently separates them. "Yes, he does," she says, putting her hands on his shoulders.

Her face is right there, close to him. Mollie. The one person who doesn't make him feel self-conscious. The one citizen that he can trust. The one person who might keep him from falling apart. Her eyes are focused on him, and her lips are right there in front of him. He leans forward, closes the gap between them just an inch. Mollie holds her ground and raises her eyebrows. *Don't make this mistake,* the look says. *Any other, but not this one.* She backs away from him and folds her arms over her chest. "Go home," she says. "Be careful on the road. Get some rest."

Mercer backs away, runs his hand through his hair, kicks at the sidewalk. "I'm going to have a talk with him," he says. "That bastard."

"What?" Her voice sharpens, and she steps away from him. "Owen?"

"I didn't mean Owen," he says, which is a lie, but other candidates come to mind, and he rattles them off out loud: Whipple, Kinnicutt, Bobby from Burlingame, Doc Barker, Ruczek, Eastwick, LoPresti. Aren't they all pretty much the same? And now Mollie is telling him he needs help, he should get some help, but Mercer talks over her, and he waits to turn away until the timing seems dramatic enough. As long as he he's fucked up his relationship with her—and with Owen, too—he might as well milk some satisfaction from it.

On his way to his car, he again passes under Leslie's billboard, and he flips middle fingers at the old people in the photo. The way they're smiling just makes him *sick*.

## MEMORANDUM TO FILE

Barker Investigation

4/22/05

At 0200 hours on the night of April 21, 2005, I was on foot patrol in plainclothes in Holy Cross Cemetery when I heard sounds of a disturbance from the southeast corner of the property. I followed the sounds in that direction to a building that was largely hidden by a stand of oak trees. The building appeared to be an airplane hangar.[4] A large, gray, dead horse stood outside and nipped at my arm as I walked past it to the door.[5]

I announced my presence by knocking on the door and identifying myself verbally. I received no response, and the sounds (raised voices, thrown objects) continued. I entered the building and found two individuals inside along with several old-fashioned airplanes in various stages of construction. I recognized one individual as Phineas Gage, as I had encountered him previously. I identified the other as Lincoln Beachey because I have seen many photos of him in a book.

Mr. Beachey appeared extremely agitated. He was crying and shouting and causing damage to his airplanes, workbenches, and unused materials with a sledgehammer. He said that "none of this matter[ed] without her" and that he had "had enough of this place." He blamed himself for being careless. He expressed feelings of worthlessness. I concluded from his words and actions that Mr. Beachey might be a danger to himself or others.

Mr. Gage was attempting to calm Mr. Beachey, but

---

[4]Any officers reading this memorandum in the event of my death should note that the hangar is difficult to locate and not visible from any roads or paved paths. A map is attached [Appendix A].

[5]See Appendix B: Photograph of Toothmarks (Equine) in Sleeve of My Jacket.

with little success. I made contact with Mr. Gage to discuss the situation. Several times we had to dodge engine parts flying in our direction, as Mr. Beachey was not paying attention to where he threw things. Mr. Gage said that Mr. Beachey was suffering intense grief at the recent loss of a close friend, one Elizabeth Fry ("Lizzie") Ralston, and blaming himself for her death at the hands of the Barker Gang.[6,7] According to Mr. Gage, Mr. Beachey faulted himself for encouraging her to go roller-skating unaccompanied, telling her it would be safe for her to do so, and for failing generally to keep her safe. As we spoke, Mr. Gage was hit by a piece of an engine that I think may have been a carburetor. He asked me if I thought it was a good idea to knock out Mr. Beachey with his aluminum bat (which in fact is mine) and I said there were probably better ways.

Having determined that Mr. Gage's efforts to soothe Mr. Beachey were having little effect, I intervened. When I got Mr. Beachey's attention, I reminded him that he had blamed himself for deaths before: those of the less-skilled aviators who had attempted to emulate his stunts, and those of two teenaged girls killed when his wing clipped an observation tent during a performance. In each case, he quit flying and fell into a depression. In each case, the depression only lifted after he got back into the pilot's seat and flew again. Therefore, I suggested, he would do well to shut up and die like an aviator. His initial response was hostile (understandable given that he already did so, once), but Mr. Gage intervened on my behalf and restrained Mr.

---

[6] See Appendix C, copy of Incident Report #05-0404-088.
[7] Arthur "Doc Barker" and his gang, which includes Wilhelm Ruczek, Giovanni LoPresti, and Eastwick (first name unknown), are suspects in hundreds of violent crimes and property offenses. See Appendix D, Chronological List-ing of Incidents Involving Barker Gang.

Beachey. Eventually Mr. Beachey calmed down and we were able to discuss the situation rationally.

I said I believed that there would be no way for citizens to live at peace while Barker and his gang were operating with impunity, and they agreed. I asked for their help in apprehending the suspects. They agreed to assist me.[8]

I asked if they had been aware of Sgt. Featherstone's attempts to apprehend the suspects. Mr. Beachey said he recalled Mrs. Ralston having mentioned Featherstone, but said he was too consumed with flying (and with Mrs. Ralston) to care much about some living person among them. Mr. Gage had no recollection, as he had been exclusively focused on the search for his tamping iron for the last century or so.

I informed them about Sgt. Featherstone's efforts to end the Barker Gang crime wave. I explained that Sgt. Featherstone believed that the key was to apprehend Barker himself. He attempted to lure Barker to a meeting site alone. He sent word through a neutral third party that a recently arrived physician had discovered a way to alter people's physical dead-selves, and thus would be able to remove Barker's fingerprints permanently.[9] The parties arranged a meeting at Cypress Lawn East; Barker was to come alone because the doctor did not want word of his abilities to get out. If it did, the third-party was instructed to say, the doctor would have too many people demanding his time and attention.

Sgt. Featherstone planned to conceal himself well in

---

[8]They were not, however, formally deputized, as I lack the authority to do so. For obvious reasons I was not eager to involve the San Mateo County Sheriff's office.

[9]See Appendix E, Handwritten notes of Sgt. Wesley Featherstone, March 2002. Sgt. Featherstone was unsure why S-Barker believed it so important to eliminate his fingerprints.

advance of the agreed-upon time and to take Barker by surprise. Sgt. Featherstone believed that Barker would come to such a meeting alone, for reasons that remain unclear to me. There is no record of why the operation was unsuccessful, as Sgt. Featherstone appears to have died in the process. I said I suspected that Barker had in fact brought his criminal associates with him, leaving Sgt. Featherstone hopelessly outnumbered. It is also possible that they arrived at the site even earlier and were able to surprise him.

I outlined my plan to Mr. Gage and Mr. Beachey: we would also lure Barker to a meeting place. If Barker had not previously been wary of an offer for him alone, he would be now. Therefore, the pretense had to involve the entire gang, and we would simply need enough manpower and resourcefulness to apprehend them all. Which seemed better in the long run, anyway.

We discussed the experiences that we and others had had with the Barker Gang. I had not determined what would be an effective lure until I saw Gage twirling the bat in his hand like a baton. If we spread word that Phineas Gage, one of the gang's favorite targets, had found the thing he had been searching for for a hundred years, the thing he wanted most in the world, they would want to deprive him of it immediately. For sport, humiliation, etc.

Both citizens expressed support for the idea. Beachey asked if we ought to recruit any others, so as to get numbers in our favor, or at least even. At that point, we were interrupted by Lillie Coit, who had been eavesdropping from behind a large scrap pile of canvas. She volunteered to assist us, saying she was tired of seeing harm come to good people. Beachey expressed reluctance to let a woman put herself directly in harm's way, but changed his mind when she demonstrated hand-to-hand combat skills, which she said she had been learning from a man in the Japanese Benevolent Society Cemetery.

Our next task was to figure out how to subdue the suspects once they arrived. Mr. Beachey suggested that we make use of any particular abilities or expertise we possess. It was clear he was referring to flying. Mr. Gage mentioned that he had started riding horses again and was very skilled. Ms. Coit had already shown her aptitude. It was not immediately clear if I would be able to contribute anything beyond my law-enforcement training and experience, but I told them I would keep thinking about it. I have not come up with anything yet, but I am still very excited about confronting the suspects. Justice has been a long, long time in coming to them.

# TWENTY-THREE

# THE SWEET FREE FALL
# OUT OF TIME

Arriving home from work, Fiona pulls into the driveway and glances at the curtain in the living room window, hoping to see it flutter and knowing it won't. Cricket hasn't been able to get herself up to the windowsill in a long time. As she fumbles with her keys on the doorstep, she listens for the cat's little chirp of a voice—again, knowing she won't hear it. Cricket rarely leaves the bedroom anymore; Fiona has moved the litter box and the food and water bowls into the room so she'll have all her necessities close by.

She sets the groceries on the kitchen counter, tosses her keys on the table, and calls the cat's name. She whistles. She makes the lip-smacking noises that used to bring Cricket running. Nothing. Again, not so much a surprise as a piercing disappointment.

She finds Cricket in the bedroom, curled up on a pile of dirty laundry in the corner, a little crescent of gray and white fur. She watches, as she has learned to, for the subtle rise and fall of breathing. She waits. She's just not seeing it, she tells herself; this is just her being nervous and afraid. If she keeps herself calm and watches carefully, she'll see. Cricket has to be breathing. She is old and dying, yes, but it's too soon. She can't have died yet.

Fiona watches and waits. She gets down on her knees and says the cat's name, strokes her fur, scratches her behind the ears, lays her own cheek against Cricket's side—that part where the gray fur of her back shades into the white fur of her fluffy underside—and feels the cool against her skin.

Be grateful, she tells herself. You should be grateful for the time you had with her. For the time your dad had with her. Yes. And never mind that you let her get sick, and never mind that you forced her to suffer in pain these last few weeks because of selfishness and fear. Don't think about that. Don't focus on that. Get that out of your mind before it takes hold. Get it out. Don't.

She gathers the cat into her arms. As she stands up, her knees crack. *God, she thinks. I am so goddamned old. All this time, and where am I? All this time, and for what?*

Jude closes *The Shenanigan Tapes* and rubs his eyes. The plot stopped making sense a hundred pages ago. And every single page is a wall of words. Would it kill this guy to use paragraph breaks? He'd give up and start reading something enjoyable, but he feels like he'll be disappointing Officer Mercer if he doesn't make it to the end and have smart things to say about it.

On the plus side, reading helps him keep his mind off Reyna. The cops must have raided the Daly City house by now. Did they arrest her? Did they arrest Bobby? Carlos? Yolanda and Ratgirl? Does anyone know that Jude's the one who ratted them out? What does Reyna think of him now? What did she ever think of him?

He did the right thing, giving Mercer the address. He knows this. He'd made the kind of responsible decision his parents had raised him to make, and he ought to feel confident, proud of himself, square with the world. Instead, he feels guilty and gutless, and his stomach knots up every time he tries to eat. He'd feel better if he knew what had happened. He wishes Mercer would call and let him know. Truth is, he feels a little abandoned. He considers texting Mercer, something innocuous, maybe just *Hi, I'm OK,* something to make the cop remember that he's alive. His thumbs are raised and ready to type when an incoming call rattles the phone in his hands.

Reyna's voice emerges from a blitz of background noise: voices, laughter, shouts, clinking glasses. "Jude," she says. "It's your dream girl calling. Hello? Jude? This is you, right?"

"It's me," he manages, finally.

"Did I wake you up?" she asks. There's a tease in her voice.

"I'm awake," he says. "It's only midnight."

"Come out with us."

He feels sweaty and jangly, like he's had way too much coffee. "Really?" he asks.

"Sure," she says. "It'll be fun. We're having a B and E night."

"What's that?"

"Oh, come on," she says. "You figure it out."

He has no idea. It's like his brain quits working whenever he talks to her. Bacon and eggs? Beer and Ecstasy?

"Here's a hint. Carlos found a house where we can party."

"Breaking and entering?" he asks.

"Smart boy," she says.

"Why not just go to Squid's?"

"This is more fun. That's the point."

"Right," he says. "Of course."

She says they're close to him, down on Haight Street, outside Murio's. Jude hurriedly puts on his shoes, grabs his jacket, checks his hair in the mirror. She wants to see him. He can't believe his luck.

His parents are easy to deal with. They're out on the patio with a producer and his wife, and they've gone through a few bottles of wine. Jude pulls the polite act with the guests, then tells his parents he'd like to go out for a few hours. "Wilson called," he says. "He wants to talk things out."

"That's wonderful," his mother says. Jude can see the hope on her wine-reddened face.

His father looks at his mother, and then at his watch. "Home by one," he says.

Before Jude backs the Prospector out of the garage, he takes several deep breaths and tries to steady his hands. He's going out to get fucked up and break into a house with a girl who might like him and some guys he can't trust. This is not a smart thing to do. He knows that. But he's done smart thing after smart thing for years, and he has a whole life of doing smart things ahead of him. He's *earned* the right to take a break from smart things. And this? This is pure excitement.

At a red light on Oak Street, Jude looks over at Reyna, who's riding shotgun. She's cut her hair short and dyed it a plain old dark-brown, like she decided she doesn't need to stand out anymore. She looks healthier than she did at Carlos's place, a few pounds heavier. Her brown jeans look tight on her, and he can't wait to get a glimpse of her ass in them. She's wearing a brown tweed cap pulled low over her eyes, which makes her look stylish and aloof and so hot it hurts.

Carlos is in the back seat, along with Yolanda and her silent new boyfriend. Most important: Bobby's not there. Jude couldn't believe his luck when he picked up the group of four, and part of him still expects that they'll be taking a detour to pick him up. Jude has been watching the minutes flash by on the dashboard clock, having decided to wait ten minutes before asking, so he could seem nonchalant.

Eight minutes. Eight minutes is good enough. Trying to strip all the eagerness out of his voice, Jude asks: "Where's Bobby?"

"He's out of town," Reyna says, putting her feet up on the dash.

*Shit, Bobby's in jail,* Jude thinks. Bobby's in jail, and this is a setup, to get back at Jude for talking to the cops. "Out of town," Jude says, squeezing the words from his constricted throat. "But he's okay, right?"

Jude watches Carlos in the rearview for any kind of reaction, but Carlos just looks the same amount of bored as always. He has grown a goatee, and with his long nose and sunken eyes, he looks like an evil magician from an old B-movie. But a bored one. "Bobby's another fucking rehab case," Carlos says. "He fucking ODed in his parents' bathroom."

"We broke up right before," Reyna says. "It was ugly." She scratches her nose and stares at the road in front of them.

Is this the best news Jude has ever gotten? Or is it bait?

"Bobby's got a lot of shit to deal with," Reyna says. "It was too much to be around."

"Big tough Bobby," Carlos says, "with a pussy-ass cry for help."

It's the cruelty in Carlos's voice that clues Jude in: Bobby really *is* gone, and Carlos wants to swoop in and vulch up Reyna. The old Jude would sit back, watch it happen, and mope about being alone. The new Jude is going to go after what he wants, for once. And he's not going to let Reyna make the same mistake again.

"I thought Bobby was your friend," Jude says.

"Didn't say he wasn't," Carlos says. "Just said he's a pussy."

"What about Trent? Was Trent a pussy-ass crying for help, too?"

"Nah. Trent was just a fucking amateur."

"Do you like *anybody*?"

"I like you, candypants."

Everyone in the back laughs, even Yolanda's dead-eyed and slouchy boyfriend, and Jude sees Reyna stifle a smile and look away. "Where the fuck are we going, Carlos?" Jude says.

"Colma," Carlos says. "Take 280. South. Ah, hell—you know the way."

Jude's stomach plummets again. He sees it all clearly: Bobby isn't in rehab, he's at the pit in the cemetery, lurking in the shadows with a roll of duct tape and a thirst for revenge. "No way," Jude says, steering the SUV back into the center of the lane. "You really expect me to go back there with you?" He looks over at Reyna, tries to read her shadowed face.

"Why not?" Carlos says. "It's just a party. Forget that shit in the cemetery. It was all Bobby's idea, anyway."

"But you thought it was funny."

"You would've too, if you'd been me."

"Exactly," Jude says.

Reyna swats him on the thigh with the back of her hand. "Don't worry," she says. "Tonight we're all just having fun. I promise." One tap on his leg and he's thinking about that night: the rain, the cold, the citrus tang, the swirl of sound, the kiss—*the kiss!*—the sweet free fall out of time.

"Okay," Jude says. "Cool. So what's the story with the house?"

"Guy died," Carlos says. "Family's out of state and not dealing."

"How do you find out stuff like this?"

"I listen."

"Carlos has magic ears," Reyna says.

"I got other magic parts, too, Reyna," Carlos says.

Jude pounds the gas pedal and takes the on-ramp curve as fast as he can, pinning Carlos against the door. "Sorry," Jude says. "I have a magic foot." From the corner of his eye, he sees Reyna studying him. What's she thinking? He wonders what if feels like to have people competing for your attention.

As they descend into Colma along Serramonte, the mountain looming ahead of them and shopping-center lights purpling the sky, Jude's uneasy feeling comes back again, stronger. (Jesus, does he ever get to feel good for more than one minute at a time?) This place feels like bad luck to him. It's juvenile to think that way—his dad always says we make our own luck—but that's what it feels like. *So maybe I'm still a little juvenile. Fucking sue me.*

Jude wonders if Mercer is out there patrolling. What would Mercer do if he pulled the SUV over right now and found Jude with Reyna, three back-seat riders, five open beers, and whatever drugs people have on them? Would Mercer look out for him and let him off easy? Would he be so let down that he'd come down hard on Jude? Would he apologize for not staying in touch?

It's Mercer's third night back on patrol, and while it's comforting to fall back into the rhythms of the job, he's disappointed at how ordinary it all seems. Ebbs and flows of activity. Radio codes and the Criminal Code. How to approach a stopped vehicle. How to give field sobriety tests that stand up in court. How to position the two-liter bottle for easy access and no spills. How to flip shit to Cambi. It's all *fine,* but it's no longer thrilling compared to what he sees around him as he drives: the dead, everywhere, dimmer than the living, their edges slightly blurred, some even flickering like cheap special effects. Root-miners pawing at the dirt; little boys skipping stones in reflecting pools; Comstock big shots James Fair and James Flood hurling silver dollars at each other's heads. On top of that, Mercer's mind is buzzing with scenarios for tomorrow night's confrontation with the Barker gang. He can hear Mazzarella's voice telling him that he should be spending his time pondering everything that could go wrong, but he keeps picturing them winning. He's not used to such optimism and confidence, and the feeling is intoxicating.

It's all he can do to keep his mind on tonight's action, and he reminds himself often to focus, to get it together, to *be here now* (as Toronto demanded earlier), because it's chaos out there tonight. Full moon, so the knuckleheads are out even more than usual—in Toronto's words, it's like there's been a goddamn harmonic convergence of knuckleheads here in the 94014. It's not even midnight, and all four patrol officers have already earned themselves hours of paperwork.

1145 hours: a domestic violence call, all available units. The residence is on

A Street, clear across town from Mercer, who's been making a pass through the landfill, watching moonily as the dead pick through the refuse of the living. Toronto and Benzinger radio that they'll be first on scene. *Do your job,* Mercer tells himself. *Focus.* He punches the gas, and the Vic takes off. He feels the engine's power in his feet, his fingers, his chest, and his adrenaline surges as the cruiser gobbles up pavement. He keeps his eyes on the road, ignores a dead boxer punching at nothing as he flashes by.

He screeches to a stop behind the two lit-up cruisers and radios that he's on his way in. All around, shadowy heads watch through windows; he can make out faces when the flashers spin light across them. The back of his neck prickles as he approaches the open front door and follows the voices to the kitchen. There, he finds Benzinger and Toronto herding the subjects—white male, 45; white female, 40—away from each other. Broken glass is strewn across the floor, and the table and chairs have been overturned. The sweat in the air is harsh and metallic. The subjects shout at each other incoherently over the officers' shoulders; they're both twitchy and crazed. The man is gaunt, 5'10" and 130 at most, with a picked-raw face, and the woman has the slackened skin of someone who has dropped weight too quickly. He studies her: she looks like the fat girl's mother, from the hospital, but fifty pounds lighter, in a meth-stripped body. He's not sure, but it *could* be her.

And if it is, then where's Layla? Just as the question hits him, he notices a flash of white in the window to the side yard—a round, white face? He turns and sees only night, but he has to check it out. The Book. "Got someone outside," he calls out.

"Is there someone outside?" he hears Benzinger ask the woman, but he doesn't wait to hear the answer. He races out and around the sagging house. He hears footsteps pounding away from him. He shouts a command to stop, but the subject keeps running. He gives chase. He imagines Layla running through the mottled dark ahead of him—short, heavy build, long copper hair whitened in the moon glow. There's a metallic *ching* as a gate slaps open, and he hears the footsteps pounding pavement, crossing Sandpiper Lane. Mercer breezes through the gate; across the road, he sees a gap in the fence that borders Olivet.

The cemetery is quiet. He scans the area: clear of the living, and only sparsely populated by the dead: several dozen stretched out contentedly in the grass as if they're being warmed by the moonlight, resting peacefully, just like they were instructed to; here and there people tending to the areas around their stones; a quartet of women jazzercising stiffly in business suits and Sunday dresses; a Root-miner plodding across the grass, trailing his spade, which *spinks* against gravestones as he walks. There is no sign of Layla.

In his earpiece, he hears Toronto spelling out names, addresses, DOBs. He creeps forward until he finds himself at the Sailor's Monument, a twenty-foot-high, stern-looking, black-granite helmsman. It looms above him, obscuring the splotchy moon. He walks a tight circle around the stone, watching, ready. *Spink. Spink.* His heart thuds. He pictures the girl: her pained face, the blue skin at her waist, the daisy barrette in her hair. He recalls the whine of the silver button bulleting toward his eye. He hears Fiona's voice, calming and strong. He finds himself hoping that Layla is here, hiding nearby; if that's her mom back there, then she needs help. The kid needs to be saved. Mercer has done it once, and he'll do it again, goddamnit, and for one moment, he thinks he hears the sound of a young girl sucking wind, but it's not from any particular direction, and just as quickly the sound is gone. "Layla?" he calls, and as he listens for a response, it dawns on him that he's exposed out here, vulnerable. Barker could ambush him. Grab him and do God-knows-what to him—maybe make his heart give out. He spins jerkily—*nobody there, nobody creeping up,* but he feels the familiar prickles rise on the back of his neck. He spins around again, and back again, and then a voice in his ear makes him jump: *Boy Thirteen, report,* the voice says. *Boy Thirteen, what's your location? Boy Thirteen?*

*Spink.*


The house is at the end of Windward Street, which rises gently uphill and dead-ends abruptly at the gated entrance to a service trail up the mountain. Brick, two stories, a fence dividing front yard from back. A few windows are lit in nearby houses, but the neighborhood looks like it's ready for sleep. Jude parks a block away, and they unload. Carlos points out that the wind is gusting hard from the west; any noise they make will get swept away from the neighbors and into the mountain. The five of them walk to the house, toting backpacks and grocery bags loaded with beer, trying not to clank too loudly, and when Carlos hops the fence, the rest of them wait in the shadows. Jude stands close to Reyna—closer than he's dared stand before, so close their shoulders almost touch—and he whispers, "Thanks for calling me."

"My pleasure," she says, not closing the distance, but not stepping away.

The front door swings open and Carlos appears. "Welcome," he says, sweeping his arm like he owns the place. They step inside, where the air is close and still and smells like dust and smoke and spilled beer.

Carlos snaps on a battery lantern, casting an indigo glow around them. Jude is surprised to see that the house is still furnished. Apart from the signs of an earlier party—stubbed-out cigarettes, empty bottles—it looks like the dead guy could be coming home any time. There's a worn leather recliner, a stained blue couch, a console TV, and a bookcase in the living room. A wedding photo of a young couple on an end table. He watches as Reyna sniffs the air and wrinkles her nose, beautiful and unself-conscious. Yolanda and her boyfriend race upstairs with a flashlight, and squeaks and rattles and whoops rain down on Jude as they jump around on a bed. The new boyfriend might not speak, but he sure can whoop. Carlos calls over to Squid's: *We're in, come on down, the place is great.*

In the dim hallway, Jude finds group photos of firefighters along with snapshots of the husband and wife, now aged and bulky, in vacation settings. They get younger and younger as the hallway runs deeper into the house. Near the end is a photo of the two of them, not much older than they are in the wedding photo, not yet gray or fat, standing in front of a long white car with fins. They have their hands on the shoulders of a little boy of four or five. It's the only photo that the boy is in. Jude wonders if he died.

And then Jude wonders: was this guy one of the firemen who got him out of the cemetery that night? He can feel the guilt gumming his blood, and he wishes he could leave. There's no way he's going to pass up his best chance to—

Someone grabs him from behind, shouts *Boo!* in his ear. He spins and finds Reyna grinning. "You jumped," she says. "Gotcha."

He tries to think of something to say, but his mind goes empty, and he feebly watches her as she hops away, laughing at him, and scampers upstairs to join the others trampolining on the bed. Too slow. Too much thinking. And now he's alone with Carlos in this still, blue room. He tries to avoid eye contact, but Carlos stares intently, and Jude can't ignore him for long.

"So," Jude says. "How've you been?"

Carlos doesn't answer. He plucks two cans of beer out of the twelve-pack and tosses one to Jude. "She looks good tonight, doesn't she?" he says, nodding toward the stairs.

"Who?"

Carlos laughs. "Come on, dude," he says. "You know who."

It's a challenge. Cards on the table. Each of them knows what the other one wants. Fine. "Yeah," Jude says. "She looks really good."

"She's a lot more fun without Bobby. He was dragging her down."

"I hear you," Jude says, and as they clank their cans together, Jude vows to make his move with Reyna tonight, before Carlos gets his bad-wizard hands on her. Assuming he hasn't already.

Fiona sits on her living room couch. The room flickers white and blue, lit by the movie that is playing on her TV screen. *Stockholm Underground.* She is staring at it but hardly paying attention. There is a woman. There is a man. There is snow. There are stairs going down from the white sidewalk. There is a subway car speeding off into a tunnel. There is an empty metro station with bare rock walls. There is a briefcase. There are echoing footsteps.

She has a pillow on her lap, where a cat should be. There is a balled-up blanket on the couch where a man should be—a man that she has gone forty-three years without meeting. There is an empty bottle of wine on the coffee table where a full one should be. She hits PAUSE, freezing a man in a dark overcoat as he reaches for the briefcase, and retrieves another bottle from the kitchen. The room flattens the sound of the popping cork. She gives herself a generous pour. Sometimes one out of three is the best you can do. And you have to get over that. Or at least get used to it. Because otherwise?.

. . .

There are five cruisers on-scene when Mercer returns, and Mazzarella is there, trying to shoo away a dozen onlookers who have gathered in pajamas, sweats, tank tops. The woman is in the back seat of Cambi's cruiser, staring straight ahead and fiercely working her jaw. She's not Layla's mother. She has darker skin and a sharp beak of a nose. How could he make a mistake like that?

Shaking his head, he joins Cambi at the end of the pitted driveway. "Bonanza," Cambi says. "Possession for sale. She's deciding whether she wants to talk."

Shouts fly from the house, and the man appears in the lit doorway, wrists cuffed behind his back. Benzinger pushes him forward; Toronto trails them. The man—Randall J. Denton, according to the radio—isn't going quietly; as he clomps along in his faded jeans and heavy work boots, he calls her a bitch dyke cunt; everyone else is a cocksucker motherfucker. "I told you to be quiet," Benzinger says.

"This is my life," the man says. "You fuck with my life, I'll fuck with yours."

"Relax, Mr. Denton," Toronto says. "Hostility doesn't help anyone. Especially not you."

"Eat me," Denton tells him.

"Or, in the alternative, you could try accepting responsibility for your actions," Toronto says.

Ten yards from the cruiser, Denton plants his feet and stops himself short, then spits in Toronto's face. Benzinger keeps her balance and tightens her hold, which makes Denton yelp—a high, girlish sound. "That fucking hurts!" he shouts.

"So calm down," Benzinger says. "And keep your bodily fluids to yourself."

"You really should listen to her," Toronto says, wiping his face with his sleeve. "She's tougher than you are."

"I'll sue all of you cunts," Denton announces as Benzinger pushes him forward again, his boots scraping loose gravel. "All of you. Fucking brutality. Pain and suffering."

Toronto steps up, grabs Denton's cheeks between his fingers, and presses his mouth into fish lips. "Listen up, ass-bag," he says. "Life *is* pain. Life *is* suffering. Accept it. And shut your goddamn piehole."

Cambi nudges Mercer. "Zen Cop," he says.

Denton drives his knee squarely up into Toronto's groin, dropping him to the pavement. A flurry of motion, then: Benzinger slamming Denton against the hood of the car, Mercer and Cambi rushing in, Toronto writhing on the driveway, Mazzarella furiously waving the crowd back to their homes and threatening to start making arrests.

Toronto picks himself up and chicken-walks toward Denton, who hacks out a rusty scrape of a laugh. "How'd you like that, ass-bag?" Denton says to him.

Mercer reaches Toronto and grabs him lightly by the shoulder. "Easy," he says, and Toronto nods, as if he's ready to let it drop.

His punch takes them all by surprise. Fist meets cheekbone meets metal, and the result is loud and lurid: a triplet of crunching bone and a brushy spray of Denton's blood over the white-painted hood. Mercer, all reflex, locks Toronto in a bear hug and yanks him backward, expecting resistance that isn't there, so he nearly hurls his friend down to the ground. As they stagger together in a clumsy dance, Mazzarella chugs toward them, his face siren-red. "Goddamnit, Toronto," he says, keeping his voice low. "You know I have to send you home. I have no goddamn choice."

Toronto flings Mercer's arms off him and spits into the patchy brown grass. "Yeah," he says. "I know."

"We've got citizens here, goddamnit."

"It's going to be all right, Nick," Mercer says.

"Shut it, Mercer," Mazzarella snaps. "There's going to be a shitstorm."

The new arrivals slip into the dead man's house in groups of two, three, four: peninsula kids with ripped-up jeans and good haircuts; retro-cool thrift-shop plunderers; girls with facial piercings and Eastern-themed body art; a white guy with dirt-brown dreadlocks. Ratgirl hasn't appeared, thank God. The last to come is a guy in his twenties who has subcutaneous devil-horn implants in his shaved head; while curious fingers trace over them and awe clouds the room like smoke, Jude thinks, *Dude, you're old. Shouldn't you know better by now?*

Right now, Jude is sitting on the couch next to Reyna, close enough that he can feel the warmth of her leg next to his. Carlos is on her other side, and Jude wishes he'd go shoot up or whatever and pass out and leave them alone. As the party has gotten louder, Jude has let himself drift into wordlessness, good and stoned. *They talk so much, and it means nothing. All chatter and bullshit.* Reyna turns to him—it's like she knows what he's thinking—and she smiles, then musses his hair, asks how he's holding up.

"Great," he says, as the world tilts on a new axis. He thinks: they should get away from these people. He thinks: they can help each other find direction, live the lives they want to live. He wishes: he could just hand her all the thoughts he's been having, and all the things he wants to say but doesn't know how to. He imagines: she opens her hands and takes those shining words and thoughts and she will know him.

Carlos takes a fat joint from the dreadlocked kid's fingers, inhales, and passes it along to Reyna. "Careful," the dreadlocked kid tells her. "It'll knock you sideways."

"Thanks for the warning," she says. "Fucking gallant of you." She takes a hit and holds it with her eyes closed and her arm held out to Jude. He picks up the joint from her fingers, but he's too busy watching her face to bring it to his mouth.

"Let's go, little man," Carlos says. "Don't kill the pace."

Jude puffs and passes and wishes Carlos would hurry up and disappear like Bobby did.

"So you really think we're cool here?" Dreadlocks asks Carlos. "The cops won't come?"

Jude jumps in before Carlos can answer. "We're cool even if they do come," he says, through a rolling wave of blue smoke. "I know them. They like me."

Carlos looks unbothered. "There you go," he says. "Little man's connected."

After the joint has been smoked to nothing, Reyna shifts in her seat, wriggles her way deeper into the couch, and arches her back, her white T-shirt tightening over her breasts. She catches Jude watching her and holds his eyes. She's expecting him to look away, he knows, expecting him to get shy and sheepish and apologetic, but not tonight. Tonight he holds her gaze, and he feels electricity run from his scalp and down his back. He rolls his thigh outward, letting it rest against hers, and she doesn't pull away. He holds still, maintaining the contact between them. His mouth feels dry and scorched, but his head is swimmy and Caribbean-blue, his body lapped by warm waves. Sweat rises on his forehead and his upper lip.

When he opens his eyes again, Carlos is watching them. Do it now, Jude thinks. Don't wait. "Follow me upstairs?" he says softly into Reyna's ear. Her hair tickles his nose.

"What?" she says.

"Follow me upstairs?" he says again, embarrassed. It's not the kind of line you should have to repeat.

She tilts her head back and looks up at the stilled blades of the ceiling fan. Her pale throat pulses, and he counts along with it. "You really want that?" she whispers back.

"Yeah," he says. "I want that."

"Little man's got secrets," Carlos says to the room, but Jude ignores him. He's in control tonight. He stands, and Reyna, smiling slack and sexy, holds out her hand to him. He pulls her up and into his arms, and for a sweet, clumsy moment, it's like they're dancing.

*Him?* he imagines the other guys saying as he leads Reyna down the hallway. Yeah, me. Believe it.

As they climb the stairs, Jude watches their joined shadows climbing along with them, twice as big as life, and he tells himself to remember the image. Someday he could use it in a film.

Distant purple streetlight diffuses through the windows of the master bedroom. He sees the hard outlines of furniture, picture frames, lamps, a TV stand with no TV, wrinkles rippling over the pale comforter. Reyna flops onto the bed, and he lies down next to her. She takes off her cap and tosses it across the room. Their faces are close. She smells like smoke and beer and jasmine. Like night. The voices below them are thick and muted, like they're coming through water.

"I'm surprised you asked me," she says.

"Tonight I'm taking chances."

"You like me."

"Always have."

"I know." She taps her tongue bar against her teeth. "You realize that gives me power over you."

"I guess," he says. This makes him feel uncomfortable, but he has to play along with her. "So what are you going to do with it?"

"I haven't decided yet," she says. "You'll just have to wait and find out."

"Should I be worried?"

"No. That's your problem. That you worry too much."

He wants to say, *What, so I should be more like Bobby? Like Carlos?* The silence between them is blue and heavy. It compresses the air in the room, and it forces words out of him: "I have Bobby's camera," he says. "I stole it."

Her smile spreads slowly. "No way," she says. "You don't steal things."

"I did. I stole it."

"It's funny," she says. "We never noticed it was gone."

Even though Bobby is miles away, Jude feels stung when she uses *We.*

"How come you're telling me?" she asks.

"Like I said, I'm taking chances."

"Good," she says. "I like the sound of that." She chews briefly on her lower lip. "Did you see the pictures on it?"

Tonight is not a night for hiding, for being afraid. "I've been looking at the pictures of you," he says.

"Did you like looking at me?"

He can tell that makes her happy. Which means he has some power, too. "Yeah," he says. "I liked them a lot."

"Did you jerk off?" she asks. "Did you come while you were looking at me?"

Their lips are close. He'd hardly have to move to kiss her. He nods yes.

"I like that," she says. "I'm imagining it. You jerking off to me."

He's glad he's wasted—he couldn't talk to a girl like this if he were sober—but now his heard whirls, his vision comes unlocked, and she slides in and out of his frame. He's a lot more fucked up than he thought. On the edge of losing control. A Seven Oaks mantra drifts into his thoughts: *When you're feeling overwhelmed, breathe deeply, and visualize your goals.* And he does. He breathes deeply and visualizes himself lifting her T-shirt. He visualizes the two of them on this bed, from a high camera angle. She is loose-limbed and cool, ignoring the lens as she raises her arms to help. Together they're dim and purple and grainy.

The bedroom door bangs open, and Jude spins himself into a sitting position. His legs dangle off the bed; his feet don't reach the floor. It's as if the room has gotten bigger and he's no longer to scale. Carlos's voice comes out of the murk. "Hey, kids," he says. "It's party time."

Springs creak as he plants himself on the corner of the bed. He's holding a little dark case, and Jude can guess what's inside it. *Get out,* he wants to tell Carlos, but he keeps quiet, waiting to see how she'll respond. She doesn't look upset that he barged in. Like she's used to this kind of thing. They have different boundaries, he realizes.

"We're busy," she says, and Jude's heart jumps.

"I know that," Carlos says. "I can see that. I'm just offering. Furnishing the means for a good time."

"We're having a good time," Jude says.

"A better one, then. You've never tried it, have you?"

Jude is quiet.

"You've never even had the chance to try it."

"Not really," Jude says.

Reyna turns to him. "Would you want to?" she says.

*What about Bobby?* he wants to ask. *What about Trent?*

It's as if Carlos can read his thoughts. "It's safe if you're with people who know what they're doing. Ask Reyna."

"You've done it?" Jude asks her.

"Now and then," she says. "When I'm in the mood."

"So, are you in the mood?" Carlos asks.

"Maybe," she says. She brushes her hand down Jude's arm, takes him lightly by the wrist. "We could do it together." The words are as soft as her touch, but there's something hard in her tone. It's a challenge, he thinks. He needs to prove to her that he's not afraid, that he doesn't have boundaries she lacks.

"So," she says, letting her hand drift down to his thigh. "Is this a night for taking chances, or what?"

. . .

The DVD player is off, and the blank blue TV screen shines on the green-glass bottles and bathes the room in a cold, even light. The pillow and blanket lie on the hardwood floor. The front door is slightly ajar. Outside, a swirling breeze pushes around the smell of low tide.

Fiona stabs her key into the ignition after missing on a few tries. She turns on the headlights. She makes sure the travel mug is secure in its holder. She checks her sideview mirrors. She puts on her seat belt. *Got to be safe,* she tells herself. Can't go around taking unnecessary risks, not at her age. She watches her face in the rearview as a tragic smile creases it, and then she turns the key.


The tourniquet pinches Jude's skin. The air around them smells scorched and sweet and gamy and brown. Carlos is on the bed with him and Reyna. He's sitting cross-legged, stroking his goatee and watching them.

"You don't have to do this," she had said, "just because Carlos and I are going to."

*Just because Carlos and I are going to.* That had clinched it.

It's strange, he thinks as he pumps his hand and watches the vein rise, how something that terrifies him can be routine for someone else. He has to remind himself to breathe. Everything feels heightened: the clamor downstairs more insistent, the light in the room more purple, Reyna looking hot in a way he doesn't have words for. Why does danger feel so sexual? Here he is, about to do the dumbest thing he's ever done, and if she so much as grazes his dick, he'll come all over himself. He realizes: you're never more alive than when you give up control.

"You're shaking," she says, taking his forearm in one hand. "Relax."

"It's all good," he says. Inside, he thinks, *I am not afraid. I am not afraid.*

She rests the cold steel against his skin, and he closes his eyes. "Good boy," her voice says.

He can feel blood surging in his groin. He wants to say *I love you,* but what comes out—in a high voice that hasn't been his for years—is "Ready."

A triplet of feeling: a prick, a burn, a cool damp dab on his arm.

*Oh.*

The wave surges over him and through him, silent and roaring, clear and golden, it spreads power and calm over him, a warm sweet melt of apathy, over him through him in him and Reyna is there, touching him, around him, feeling through him. One big warm wave. A sound surfaces from the back of his throat and swims through the blue to her, and when she hears it, she smiles, because she knows that even though it's not a word, it's a sound that he meant for her. She holds his hand as it unclenches and watches as his face slackens. Look at this boy. Look at this boy, and what he is willing to do for her.

# TWENTY-FOUR

# IT'S GREAT TO BE ALIVE IN COLMA!

No one wants to talk about Toronto. On the radio, everyone is iron-voiced and terse—the officers, the sergeant, the dispatcher. The banter is spare, the insults halfhearted. "This has been one sideways fucking night," Cambi says when the officers stop together for coffee, and Mercer and Benzinger nod quietly because that pretty much sums it up.

At 0100 hours, Sergeant Mazzarella tells them that he has asked the Gomez kid to come in so they can put another body out on the street. Like any rookie, Gomez is hungry for action, and by 0215, Mercer is backing him up on a traffic stop on a dark residential street close to The Willows. Driver and passenger, both black males, fiftyish, in a beat-to-shit Civic with a Jesus fish on the trunk. Driver on probation subject to search—narcotics offense. Shreds of scorched Brillo pad littering the floor of the car. Gomez has tossed the vehicle and come up empty; the Brillo screams out crack, but it's not enough to hold them. The two officers stand by Gomez's cruiser for no good reason other than Gomez wants to make the subjects sweat it out. Mercer can see the driver keeping an eye on them in his rearview.

"Driver says he's a youth minister," Gomez says. "Redwood City. Claims he's in recovery. He's supposed to be an example."

Mercer shrugs. "I'm not surprised," he says, thinking about Mrs. Featherstone. This morning, on the footpath outside The Willows garage, she pretended she didn't see him and scurried back into her apartment. Ridiculous.

She gets conned out of all her money by Whipple, and now she's mad at *Mercer* for noticing. For trying to help.

Gomez shakes his head. "Man of God, and he's using. I don't get that. My mind is clear because Jesus wants my mind clear. Because my mother wants my mind clear. Because people who love you want your mind clear. To me, that's a hint, you know?"

"Some people have an easier time clearing their minds," Mercer says. *And those people will never understand how lucky they are.*

Silence falls between them. Mercer's about to turn and leave the scene when Gomez speaks. "Fucking Toronto, huh?"

"Fucking Toronto," Mercer says dispiritedly.

"So much for Zen, huh?"

"He's dealing with some shit," Mercer says. "Maybe the Zen wasn't enough."

"He told me he had a hot new girlfriend. Is she not putting out or something?"

"More to life than that."

"Not much." Gomez shakes his head again, makes a sound that's part laugh, part *hmmph.*

"Is that what Jesus wants for you?" Mercer asks. "What your mom wants?" He watches as uncertainty descends upon the younger man: his smile recedes to a straight line, then curls up at one edge and quivers. It's a look that reads, *Is this guy screwing with me? He can't be serious, can he?*

"All I meant," Gomez says, "was that it's hard to believe Toronto busted up a suspect's face. You can't really fuck up much worse."

"Sure you can," Mercer says. "You probably will, someday." He's had enough of this kid, and he heads back to his cruiser. He imagines the look on Gomez's face as it dawns on him that he really did just offend an officer who could scuttle his chances for a full-time job.

Mercer has the door open and is about to drop himself into the driver's seat when he hears someone clearing his throat. He glances up and sees two dead people watching him from a weedy lawn across the street. The woman is Lillie Coit, wearing her fire helmet, as always. The man is roughly her age, mid-twenties. He's trim but bulked with muscle, filling out his plain black suit. He's wearing a fire helmet, too, only his is contemporary. Current issue. His face looks familiar.

"Jerry?" Mercer says, trying to keep his voice down.

"Boy Thirteen," the man says. His voice is Jerry's voice, minus forty years of age and smoke. "Good to see you."

Mercer turns his head, worried that Gomez might be watching, but the kid is talking to the driver of the Civic and waving him on his way.

Lillie is watching the cruiser's lights spinning on the undersides of the leaves above her. She is wide-eyed, entranced. "You're needed," she softly intones in that strange, high, backwards-sounding voice.

"My house," Jerry says. "Get there, quick."

"What are you talking about?"

"Shut up and go." Jerry folds his arms across his chest and stares hard at him. "Now."

Mercer looks at Lillie. "Am I still supposed to save my strength?"

Jerry answers for her. "Don't save a goddamned thing," he says. "Except the kid."

And then the two fire-ghosts are gone, swallowed by the dark. *Goddamn, Jerry*, Mercer thinks, dropping the Vic into DRIVE and punching the gas. *You are one cryptic dead sonofabitch.*

Through the air, pinged from relay to relay: a digital reconstruction of Reyna's voice, breathy and hurried, from the echoing emptiness of the ladies' room at the Crystal Springs Rest Area. The house is on Windward Street, she says. No, she doesn't know the street number. The 911 operator repeats it all back to her, her voice cold and uninflected.

Carlos is in the parking lot, waiting with the Prospector's engine idling. He hadn't wanted to stop until Modesto at least, but Reyna told him she was having an emergency, and if he didn't pull over, he'd have to clean her goddamn seat himself.

"Your name?" the operator asks.

"No," Reyna says.

"What's your name, ma'am?"

"It doesn't matter."

"Listen," the operator says, "you need to give me your name, now."

"I'm not going to fucking tell you," Reyna shouts into the phone. "Just get an ambulance there." She punches the disconnect button, then races into a stall and doubles over, feeling like she might be sick.

This is not what she wanted.

*Relax,* she tells herself. *Jude will be fine. Carlos gave him the Narcan. You're just being careful. Responsible. You should feel good about how you handled it. And Carlos says it was an accident, anyway. Accidents happen.*

Eventually, the nausea passes. At the sink she splashes cool water on her face. She'll ride with Carlos until she feels far enough away. Modesto, Fresno, wherever. She can vanish anywhere she wants; she's free.

She drops Jude's phone into the wastebasket on her way out and crosses the parking lot in the shadow of the sandstone priest, who still blindly points westward, floodlit and severe.


**M**ercer holds the steering wheel tightly and concentrates on the road as he speeds across town. He can't afford to get distracted right now, not if Jerry's tone is any indication. He feels feverish and jittery; the adrenaline running through him feels hot and spoiled.

He jumps when his cell phone rings, and he jerks the wheel. The phone is facedown in the passenger seat, and he snatches it up as it rings a second time. The display shows FIONA—CELL. He steers with one hand and lets the phone ring in his hand a third time, a fourth time. He should answer. He should. How gutless is he? A fifth ring. A sixth. *Stop thinking,* he tells himself, and he's about to push TALK when the radio in his ear squawks with an urgent call: medical emergency, narcotic overdose, north-side address. Jerry's address. Jesus. The hairs on the back of his neck stand up like darts. He pounds the gas pedal, hits his lights. He radios: he's on his way, all due haste. His phone, shining from the passenger seat, informs him of the obvious: MISSED CALL.

Cars make way and pull to the shoulder as he roars up Hillside. More info from Dispatch: the call came from an unidentified female, on a cell. Paramedics en route, but a few minutes behind. At Serramonte, Benzinger squeals in behind him, siren and lights.

"Jerry's house," he tells her on the radio.

Her voice crackles back. "Nothing's sacred."

"Roger that," he says, and the Vic's tires yelp as he accelerates into a turn.

At the sound of Mike's outgoing message, Fiona snaps her phone closed and tosses it aside. It bounces on the passenger seat and falls to the floor. Fuck. The fog line obscures the tops of the trees lining the road, but she feels them looming over her, blighted and dying and waiting for a wind to push them over as she passes underneath. She feels relieved when the road curls down onto the freeway, with its stream of lights and steady mechanical hums.

She doesn't want to talk to him, she tells herself. Not really. After all, what do they have to say to each other? He'll cough out some awkward condolences and fall back into silence. She just wants him to respond to her, to acknowledge that she exists. Or maybe to remind her that she does. But she does need to tell him about Cricket. He always liked her. Fiona remembers him in bed, smiling unguardedly as the cat pressed herself into his neck and purred, and she nearly starts crying all over again.

Her turn signal ticks and the car takes her down the Hickey exit ramp. Maybe she can find him. He'd want to know. She speeds into the turn at the bottom of the ramp, enjoying the screech of the tires. She'll have to find him on the street. If she goes to the station, they'll smell the wine on her.

She loops through the town, searching for his cruiser. Twice she comes across cops making a traffic stop, and she drives by slowly, trying to be discreet, but neither of them is Mike. She looks in parking lots, on side streets, behind warehouses. Junipero Serra, Colma Boulevard, El Camino, Mission, Lawndale, Hillside. Where is he? This goddamned town is *not* that big.

Around her, Colma holds its breath in the fog-filtered moonlight. The parking lot at the movie theater is empty, and broken glass crunches under her tires. The lights over the car dealerships shine garish and too-white; the cars are naked under them, polished and scratch-free, aggressively perfect. The cemeteries fling themselves out over expanses of grass. Her headlights flash over the sign for Pet's Rest, and it makes her think of Cricket again, and then her dad, and then the rest of her family, and then the man that Mike should have been, and then the kids she'll never have. So many holes in her life. So much emptiness. She lays on the gas, the engine whining, and rides the ass of a slow-moving sedan up Hillside. It's GREAT TO BE ALIVE IN COLMA! the bumper sticker says. FUCK YOU, she thinks. She swerves across the double yellow into the oncoming lane and zooms past, the driver a blurred head of white hair.

The front door of the house at the end of Windward Drive is slightly warped and for years has hung out of true. The night wind squeezes in through a narrow crack in the wood, which vibrates with a tone like a bowed middle C. Inside, it is still; the last echoes of a panicked exit have dropped away; scattered empties and ashes are the only proof of the beery laughter and reddened voices that earlier filled the house. A curtain rustles faintly when the draft catches it; a mouse scuttles through empty kitchen cabinets; a shard of a broken bottle clinging to the label plinks to the floor. Up the staircase, it is quiet. Down the hallway, it is quiet. In one bedroom, the wind gently rattles a window. In the other bedroom, a puddle of sick ticks wetly as it settles into carpet. A brief and faint glottal noise comes from the sixteen-year-old boy stretched out on the bed. A slow pulse taps quietly inside him. A shallow, labored breath dwindles away.

Then: a rush and tumble of noise: the door banging open; two voices, one male, one female, sharp with authority and urgency; boots pounding floors; locations called back and forth from rooms found empty; and, when a flashlight beam cuts across the limp form on the bed, a shout: *Found him!*

Then: *Jesus, Mercer. It's your kid. Again.*

Fiona flies down F Street, her foot steady on the gas as the oldies station plays Eddie Cochrane or Duane Eddy or one of those other Eddies who made music to drive fast to. She cuts a hard right on Hillside, surprised at how well the tires hold the road. Yellow light. Her foot hovers briefly over the brake but lands on the gas again, and she speeds through the fresh red. A siren whoops, and red-and-blues flash in her rearview. She sees herself in the light reflected off the mirror: a corner of her face, garishly flushed then cold pale. She feels her hackles rise, and she remembers what Mercer told her: listen to the back of your neck. Trust your instincts. She is absolutely certain now that he's the one in the cruiser that's chasing her down. She pushes the speed to sixty-five, seventy, testing his nerve. She shouldn't be doing this. Dangerous. Nothing to gain. Her father's voice: unbecoming of a woman her age. *Unbecoming.* A funny word. *Un-becoming.* The un-becoming of a woman her age.

Up ahead on the left: Cypress Lawn West. Where Mike found the kid. It flashes through her head, not in words but in feeling, that that night was when everything started to go wrong. The idea feels perfect: she'll lead him back there. When he pulls her over, he'll ask her *why?* and she'll say *you know damn well why.* It's not the kind of thing you can put into words, anyway.

Three. Two. One. *Turn.* She jerks the wheel left and shoots across the street in front of an oncoming car, and then she is skidding into the driveway, past a flash of green grass, past the black duck pond, toward the stone archway, still skidding. The smell of burnt rubber wakes her up to her reality: she has lost control. Which is maybe what she wanted all along. She relaxes and lets gravity work its force upon her.

The back end crashes against stone, throwing her sideways, and the car spins, she is spinning, her vision a twist of green black red-blue gray. Time bleeds into one long moment. *I'm okay with dying,* she tells whatever god might be listening, *but let me stay on solid ground. I don't want to drown in a duck pond.* Another crumpled-metal sound then, and the world turns over, red-blue green black gray red-blue, and then a sound like a gunshot and a blast of white all around her, everywhere.

**W**hite male, sixteen. Has a pulse but is in respiratory arrest. Unresponsive to pain stimuli. Moderate cyanosis. Found on floor: length of rubber, disposable lighter, 0.2-mg/mL vial of naloxone, hypodermic needle. Narcotic overdose, likely heroin. Unknown individual who presumably delivered the shot of naloxone no longer present. "Fucking idiots," Mercer says, between mouth-to-mask breaths. You don't just give an opioid antagonist and run away. You have to keep the victim breathing. Jude's been abandoned, again. *Breathe.*

"Save it, Mercer," Benzinger says. She punches a needle through the rubber skin of another Narcan vial, draws the liquid into the barrel.

*Focus,* he tells himself. Breathe. *Keep his airway open. Watch his chest rise and fall, and try not to think. Breathe. Try not to think about how Jude let himself get into this. Try not to think of how badly you've failed the kid, failed the parents. Try not to think of how young he is.* Breathe. *Don't look at his face. Don't think about all the anger and confusion and sadness that you've seen on it. Don't replay your conversations with him, and don't wonder what you missed. Just breathe. Watch chest rise. Watch chest fall.* Breathe.

Mercer hopes to feel movement when Benzinger sinks the needle into Jude's biceps, but the boy remains still. It's not like the movies. They don't just pop awake. You breathe for them and watch and wait and hope. *Breathe.* Watch chest rise. Watch chest fall. Don't look at his face. Focus. Rhythm. With each breath, he feels as if he's giving away something of himself—but it's something he doesn't deserve to keep, anyway.

At first he doesn't even feel the paramedic tapping him on the shoulder. It's only when Benzinger shouts his name that he gathers himself up and steps away. He keeps his eyes on Jude's chest while the paramedic looks the kid over. "Don't let him go," Mercer says, punching the air with a finger. "He's got to come through."

"We'll see," the paramedic says.

"Don't let him go," Mercer repeats.

Behind him, slouching against the wall, four firemen are talking. "In Old Jerry's house," one says. "That's a goddamn shame."

"Two-bedroom, two-bath, one dead kid."

"Wait. Isn't that—?"

"From the cemetery?"

"Looks like."

"Shitboy."

"Captain Bare-Ass."

"The Duct-Tape Wonder."

Mercer advances on them. These are guys he's friendly with—together they've hoisted beers, bullshitted about women and baseball and TV police procedurals, ragged on citizens and on officers like Landau and St. Cyr, but his vision is flashing red and sparkly; he can't see their faces, and he doesn't care. "If you don't have a purpose," he spits, "why don't you get the fuck out of here?" Benzinger grabs him by the back of the shirt, but he rips himself away from her. "I'm fine," he tells her. And he is. He could've gone into that pack of guys fists-first. He's fine, and they're goddamned lucky.

"Go," Benzinger says. "I'll meet you downstairs."

He pauses halfway down the stairs and leans against the wall with his eyes closed. *You have to breathe, too,* he tells himself. *Even if you don't want to.* His inhale is shallow and juddering; his exhale tight and just as shaky. He pushes himself through a few more cycles of breath before the raised voice sounds from above: the paramedic, telling people to clear away, clear away, the kid's gone tonic, give the kid space, he's gonna seize. Mercer feels the darkness fall heavily on his shoulders, and he lowers himself down the rest of the flight with one hand gripping the banister. He settles himself onto the bottom step and rests his head on his knees, listening—heavy thumps overhead, and more raised voices—and waiting, knowing that this is all he can do. He imagines Lorna telling him *no, pray, you can pray, you should pray,* but really. Come on.


The face Fiona sees is not Mike's. It's too wide. The angles are all wrong, and it sits neckless on a thick slab of shoulders. Where is Mike? Why isn't this him?

"Do you know what your name is?" the hulking cop asks.

She's not upside down, which is good. She was expecting upside down. "Yes," she says.

"What is it?"

She closes her eyes and lets herself drift. If she's patient, maybe she'll see Mercer the next time she opens them.

"You're supposed to pull over when you see the lights," the cop says. "You could've hurt yourself. Or other people on the road."

She opens her eyes and watches flashes of red and blue strobe across his face. "I know."

"Have a few drinks tonight?"

She smiles, because it sounds like he could be asking her out.

"Wait, I know you," he says. "You were Mercer's girlfriend, right? Jesus." The pissed-off and condescending look on his face softens.

"Is he here?" she asks.

"He's on another call right now. Emergency."

"I wanted him," she says.

"You got me instead," he says. "The paramedics are going to be a few minutes. For now, sit tight. Don't move. All right?"

Can she move? She wiggles her fingers. Then toes. Yes.

"How do you feel?" he asks.

"I want to go home."

She feels his hand against her shoulder. "You need to keep your head *still*," he says.

"I'm aware," she says.

The cop hesitates before answering. "That's Mercer's phrase. He says it all the time."

Damnit. She doesn't even have her own words anymore.

"I'm Officer Cambi," the cop says. "What's your name?"

Cambi. Which one is he? What has she heard about him? "What are your stories?" she asks.

"I don't know what you mean."

Behind him: glass kick-scattered off the pavement. Metal complaining. Another cop's hand reaching into the car. *Got it,* a voice says, and she hears the voice reading out names as if they have something to do with her: *First of Frank Ida Ocean Nora Adam; Middle of Charles; Last of William Edward Lincoln Lincoln Sam.*

Officer Cambi speaks to her again. "Relax," he says. "We got you. Me and Sergeant Mazzarella."

She tries to say *Mazzarella,* but her mouth is clumsy around the name. "He talks about dying," she says.

Cambi smiles at her. "All the time."

"Am I? Dying?"

"We got you, sweetheart. Don't worry."

"Thank you," she says. He called her *sweetheart.*

"Do you remember what happened?"

She knows what he's really asking: did you crash because you're drunk? Or on purpose? Were you trying to die? She has no idea what to say. It's not a one-word answer. She couldn't explain it in a thousand. "Lost control," she says.

# TWENTY-FIVE

# THE REDEMPTION EXPRESS (II)

0700 hours, Good Shepherd Hospital. A thick fog curdles the air over the valley, blocking out the sun's first rays; inside the windowless emergency room, though, the endless fluorescent daytime continues, and tired and worried-looking people blink in the hard-luck purple light. Mercer, still in uniform, is trying to stay awake in a rigid plastic chair. His head droops, and he immediately jerks back awake. On the chair next to him is a Styrofoam cup of coffee. When he drinks, he holds the cup with two hands so he can keep it steady. Fiona? Banged-up and in a lot of pain, he's been told, but everything will heal. Air bag saved her. Jude? Flatlined on the way in, but they brought him back. No word beyond that. No way to know what shape he's in. So Mercer watches the clock and waits for news. Looking up at the buzzing light tubes, he decides that he used to have a lot more incandescence in his life, and he was happier then.

He scans the other faces in the waiting room and doesn't see any people who look like they're here for Fiona. She should have people close by: family, friends. But maybe some of her fellow nurses are back there, huddling around her, talking to her, keeping her company. She deserves more support than he'll ever be able to give her by himself. He sighs deeply, enjoying the sensation of breath leaving his lungs. He drifts into sleep, awakens sharply, drifts off again.

The next time he opens his eyes, Susan DiMaio is sitting across the waiting room from him, fidgeting as she tries to get comfortable in her seat. She looks puffy-eyed and shaken, but her clothes are perfectly ironed. Nothing on this woman wrinkles. Next to her is the grotesque neighbor with the lime-green glasses who, while she may not have ruined Mercer's life per se, bears some guilt for the current miserable state of things, as far as he's concerned. He stands up woozily and approaches them. "Mrs. DiMaio," he says.

"Officer Mercer," she says. She's wearing a light, grassy perfume that doesn't quite cover the stale aura of last night's alcohol. He extends his hand, but she doesn't offer hers. Her eyes are fixed on a point above his shoulder.

"I'm sorry," he says. "I don't know what to say."

"This had something to do with the antidepressants," she says. "I just know it."

"Maybe so," Mercer says. "I wouldn't know about that."

"We never should have listened to those doctors."

"Where's your husband? Is he coming?"

Susan shakes her head.

"Is he out of town?"

"No," she says. "He's home."

Her tone reminds him of the weariness that used to weigh down his mother's voice when people asked her about his dad. Had she heard from Rudy? Was she worried? Did she think he'd be coming home? How on earth was she making ends meet? How was she holding up? How was Michael holding up?

"How can he not be here?" Mercer says.

"Believe me, it's for the best," Susan says. "He's too angry."

Mercer snorts. "Some God-in-the-Lens," he says. He feels his body trembling and hopes he's keeping the shake out of his voice. "Can't even see when his kid needs him."

Susan's face turns confused. "'God-in-the-Lens?' What are you—?"

"Jude is just a kid," he says. "Not everything is his fault."

"He made a *choice*," the neighbor says. "When my boys made bad choices—"

Mercer cuts her off, jabbing a finger in her direction. "You don't know what the situation was. Maybe you should find out before you go blaming him."

"Don't you take the law seriously?" The neighbor raises her immaculately thin eyebrows, two black darts across her forehead. "Maybe you don't. Maybe that's why you never found those cemetery people. Maybe that's why your department has been so *inept*."

"Gracie," Susan says. "Don't."

"I'm just saying what you're too nice to say," Gracie tells her.

Mercer looks down at Gracie, at her scotch-plaid pantsuit, at the gray roots pushing up into her hyperplatinum mop of hair, at the roses on her cheeks that shine like lies. "Go to hell," he says. He's not feeling very nice himself.

Gracie's jaw drops slightly open, and Susan looks at him with stunned-fish eyes.

"Jude's your *son*," he tells her. "He needs to learn to stand up for himself. And he needs to learn that he's worth standing up for."

Susan nods. She's not fighting him. She knows all this.

"Thank you for the parenting lesson," Gracie says, laying her arm protectively around her friend's shoulders. "But this isn't the time or the place. Or any of your business."

A wave of dizziness hits Mercer then, so hard that he can feel his eyes roll back under his closed lids. He hears Mazzarella's voice in his head: *You're losing control. Take yourself out of this situation before you make a mistake.* The world tilt-a-whirls when he opens his eyes, and he steps backward to steady himself. "Excuse me," he says, raising his empty cup, using what's left of his emotional reserves to put on the politeness that The Book would demand of him. "I'm getting a refill. Would either of you—"

Gracie stares coldly; Susan gives him the barest head shake *no*. He's not even worth their words anymore. He turns slowly and carries himself to the door with careful, even strides.

With a fresh cup of bitter black coffee, Mercer leaves the building and follows the footpath that loops the hospital. The sky is still socked in, and mist cools his face as he walks through swirls of vapor. Primroses line the walkway in tight clusters of orange and yellow and red, islets of dampened color in the gray. The grounds are busy—patients, docs, techs, maintenance—but Mercer feels separate from them. He's thankful for the clouds; if the sun were shining brightly, he'd feel exposed.

He settles onto a stone bench with a memorial plate fastened to the backrest and hits a speed-dial number on his phone. After seven rings, Toronto answers. "Mercer. You all right?"

Mercer pictures him sitting on a couch in his new apartment, smoking, watching himself in the long mirror. "Not really. You?"

"Think I broke a knuckle. Hurts like fuck."

"You hear what happened? Jude? Fiona?"

"Yeah," he says. "Benz called me. Said you were taking it hard. What's the news?"

"Fiona's going to be all right. Sprains and bruises, dislocated shoulder. Broken nose, from the airbag. She got lucky."

"You see her yet?"

"I don't know if she wants—"

"Get over yourself," Toronto says. "She wants. Go see her already."

Mercer hears him suck on a cigarette, then exhale long and slow. Neither of them says anything. Static crackles softly over the connection before the noise gate kicks in, forcing a moment of dead air between them.

"So what about the kid?" Toronto says.

"Goddamn, Nick," Mercer says, and he's shaking his head. "He flatlined."

"But he's alive?"

"Alive, yeah. But nonresponsive. No one knows—he could walk out of here, he could be a cripple, he could be a goddamned cauliflower. No way to know."

Across the lawn, two priests approach the hospital's front doors. Behind them, a young girl and her mother, who's carrying a bouquet of irises. Over the phone, he hears Toronto take a long drag.

"He's alive, Boy Thirteen. Could be worse."

"It's about so much more than that," Mercer says. He's not sure precisely what he means, but the words feel right, and that's a rare experience.

Toronto puts on his field-training voice. "Listen to me," he says. "You didn't make that kid shoot up, and you didn't make your old girlfriend get trashed and crash her car." He puffs again before continuing. "There's a lot of shit that *is* your fault. Letting yourself get kicked in the head, yes. Not pulling the trigger on Buttergirl, yes. Driving your grandfather's six-cylinder bedpan, yes. But not this. Not other people's shitty, self-destructive choices."

"Nick," Mercer starts, but he can't go any further. He wishes he had his sunglasses; even with the fog cover, the sky feels too bright. He closes his eyes, rubs them, watches drifting patterns of red against his lids.

"Mercer, if you start crying, I'm going straight down to the station to tell everyone what I found under your mattress."

"There's nothing under my mattress," he says. "Dick-weasel," he adds, but his heart's not in it.

"Then I'll have to make it up. You *really* don't want that."

Mercer sniffs. Swallows hard. "He's a good kid. I hope he gets to live."

"Don't hope."

"What?"

"Don't hope. Hope destroys. When you're hoping, you're not in the moment. Best thing anyone can do is quit hoping. Fuck that. Fuck hope."

*That's wrong,* Mercer thinks. *You are wrong, Toronto, Zen or no Zen, you are one-hundred-and-eighty degrees wrong.*

"Coincidentally enough," Toronto goes on, "fucking Hope is what I'll be doing tonight."

"No more punch lines," Mercer says. "Not today. All right?"

A long pause as Toronto blows smoke. Then: "Life continues, pilgrim. Get used to it."

Mercer makes a vague noise of acknowledgment and snaps his phone closed. He heads back to the Emergency Room, where he will sit alone in his hard plastic seat in the austere light, across from two women who want him gone. He knows this, though: he is not going home. He'll wait for the news about Jude. He'll go find Fiona, too, once he's not so worked up. For now, he'll sit here and wait, no matter how much the raised voices and bad smells bustle around him, no matter how much more alone he feels with each loop of the minute hand. He's going to wait, in this place where pain swirls like the fog outside and fills all the space between intercom calls and cell-phone rings and complaints about paperwork and intimate, sharp-whisper voices. He's going to wait, and he's going to hope.


He awakens with a stiff neck and back and with Susan's hand on his forearm gently shaking him. "They've moved him upstairs," she says. "We're going up."

He understands that this *we* does not include him. "Is he—?"

"No better. But no worse. I wanted to thank you for coming. It's good to know people care. And no matter what Gracie says, I believe that you tried your best."

*Tried.* Tried and failed. "I hope—" he says.

"I know," she tells him. "I'll call you when we know more." She taps his arm three times, a soft good-bye, then leaves the waiting room, her heels clacking away on the tile.

He stands up to stretch out his back. It helps, but he still feels hunched and pinched, so he lowers himself to his knees to do a round of cat-and-horse exercises, and if anyone's watching and thinking he's crazy, well, fuck them. Maybe he is. Actually, he *wants* someone to look at him funny, to question him, to say anything with the faintest trace of judgment or condescension. It would feel so good to explode. But no one pays attention, apart from a couple of little kids, who watch him dully, then turn back to their personal DVD players.

What he is, he realizes, is invisible.

He stands up, drops his ass back into the plastic seat's depression, and wipes the floor dirt off his knees. His mind drifts to Fiona, and for the first time he understands that seeing her might not be some obligatory mission of mercy: she might make him feel better, too. They might feel safe together. He's turning this idea over in his mind, questioning his instincts, trying to analyze it from every possible angle, when he hears a familiar, gravelly voice in the corridor outside. He knows that voice. He jumps up to confront the man it belongs to.

In the white-white hallway is the Reverend Clifton Chase Whipple, pushing a cart filled with teddy bears of different sizes and colors and styles: brown and black and pink and yellow, scruffy and smooth, smiling and expressionless. Stuck to the front of the cart is a hand-lettered sign that reads BEARS THAT CARE. Whipple is wearing a seersucker suit with a bolo tie and a straw hat. He looks like he's raided the wardrobe of a community-theater company.

"Hello, young man," Whipple says when Mercer stations himself in the cart's path. "It's good to see you. Lorna tells me your back is better. That you're working again."

"I have a name," Mercer says. "You don't know my name, do you?"

"I'm an old man. My memory isn't what it was. But tell me, how's your—?"

Mercer stops listening to him when he hears a high-pitched voice down the hall, old-womanish but energetic and jumpily melodic. Lorna. Talking to a phlebotomist about what an interesting name they have for their job. "Phlebotomy," she says. "I just love saying it. Phlebotomy. Phlebotomy. How can you stop?" And she laughs her familiar little Lorna-laugh, like absolutely nothing is wrong in her world.

"She's here?" Mercer says to Whipple. "You're still using her?"

A pink bear in a striped green Mylar vest falls from the top of the pile. "Pardon?" Whipple says as he crouches to pick it up. His knees crackle, and Mercer hears him make a back-of-the-throat noise of old-man exertion.

"Still exploiting her," Mercer says. "Taking her money. Getting her to sell her stuff and gamble for more. Bleeding her dry so you can feel like a saint with all this fucking *kindness.*"

Whipple wedges the loose bear into a gap in the pile and rests his crossed arms on the cart handle. "I have no idea what you're talking about," he says evenly. "If you're trying to tell me that Lorna's in some kind of trouble, tell me straight."

"Nice," Mercer says. "Wise man playing dumb. I'll bet that fools a lot of people." He's reminded, suddenly, of how sweet the sound of Randall J. Denton's cheekbone being crushed was, and he reaches out and plants his hand in the center of Whipple's chest, then shoves the minister backward. It feels good, making that weight move. "You," Mercer says. "You're the problem. Shameless. You collect money and the rest of us collect shame. You're the goddamned problem, *Reverend.*" He doesn't know where these words are coming from, but his blood's pumping in his temples and he's getting those multicolored pinpricks of light in his vision again. He feels *inspired.*

"Let's sit down and talk," Whipple says. "Matthew? Is it Matthew? Something with an *M,* right? Let me get these bears out to the kids, and then I'll buy you a cup of coffee, and we can talk everything through. If there's something about Lorna that I need to know, I want to know. And I want *you* to know that the last thing I want to do is exploit anybody. I know I'll have to earn your trust, but—"

That first shove felt so good, Mercer does it again. And again. Whipple is backpedaling now, stumbling away from his cart of bears, and Mercer likes having him on the run. He keeps advancing. "You. You're the problem," he says. He is vaguely aware of Lorna's voice behind him, calling his name and some other words, but he presses forward, driving the holy man back through the sliding glass doors and out onto the pavement of the drop-off area, where *The Redemption Express* is idling in a charcoal-colored cloud of exhaust. He feels hands clutching at him from behind, and he wrenches himself free, propelling himself forward, forward. This feels right, he has waited a long time to feel this right about anything, he takes another step forward, and another, he wants to see fear register in those deep-set shadowy eyes, he won't stop until he sees it—fear, or at least uncertainty, *something*—and he takes another step forward. Forward. Always forward.

**CPD MEMORANDUM**

To: Chief E. J. McCandless

From: Sgt. A. P. Mazzarella

Date: 05-08-05

Re: Officer Mercer's actions of 05-07-05 (1830-1915 hours)

[Page 2]

When Officer Mercer pushed Rev. Whipple up against the side of the bus, the driver, Dwayne "Dusty" Biggins came out of the vehicle and told Officer Mercer to stop what he was doing. Officer Mercer threatened him with legal consequences and/or bodily harm if he did not get back in the bus. Officer Mercer then applied a submission hold to Rev. Whipple and handcuffed him.

According to Mr. Biggins and other witnesses, Rev. Whipple attempted to engage the officer in conversation. He said he understood the officer was upset about the harm that had come to the DiMaio juvenile. Officer Mercer held Rev. Whipple against the bus and said nothing.

At no time did Officer Mercer unholster his weapon.

At 1905 hours, Officers Benzinger and Cambi arrived on scene. They called to Officer Mercer, at which point he released Rev. Whipple, sat on the pavement and cried. Officer Benzinger drove him back to the station and delivered him to the watch commander's office.

We are fortunate that Rev. Whipple, Mr. Biggins, and Mrs. Featherstone have all expressed empathy for Officer Mercer and are disinclined to pursue legal remedies.

[Statements of Mrs. Lorna Featherstone, Rev. Clifton C. Whipple, Dwayne "Dusty" Biggins, and Officers Mercer, Cambi, and Benzinger are attached.]

*A. P. M.*

**CPD MEMORANDUM**

To: Chief E. J. McCandless

From: Sgt. A. P. Mazzarella

Date: 05-09-05

Re: Officer Michael Mercer (CPD Badge 13)

Per our conversation this morning: I respectfully request that you order a Psychological Fitness for Duty evaluation for Officer Mercer to be carried out as soon as possible.

In light of yesterday's events, I do not think that Officer Mercer is fit to carry out his duties at present. [See attached statements of officers, witnesses, and complainant.] I am concerned that this Officer may be a threat to public safety, to the safety of other employees, and may interfere with the City's ability to deliver effective police services.

I have observed in the Officer's recent behavior the following criteria listed in department guidelines:

Impatience and impulsiveness

Irrational verbal conduct and behaviors

A pattern of conduct indicating a possible inability to defuse tense situations, a tendency to escalate such situations or create confrontations

Excessive tiredness, with sudden bursts of hyperactivity

Change in behavior pattern: inattention to personal hygiene and health

Memory loss

Officer Mercer has also exhibited what seems to me an unhealthy preoccupation with death and dying.

I am unaware of any inappropriate use of alcohol, medications, or other drugs by Officer Mercer. He was taking narcotic painkillers for an extended time earlier this year per physician's advice, due to a back injury suffered in a traffic accident in a Department vehicle. I have no evidence that he has been continuing to use or abuse them.

However, Officer Mercer has been under significant strain. In addition to that injury, he has endured several instances of head trauma. He ended a romantic relationship with a woman who subsequently assaulted him on the street. He was a friend of Jerry Fahey's and was saddened by his death. As you are aware, he became emotionally attached to the victim in the DiMaio case. Also, his close friend (and Field Training Officer), Nicholas Toronto, was suspended from duty and is facing disciplinary proceedings.

Officer Mercer is an intelligent young man and has shown both enthusiasm and aptitude for law enforcement as well as a commitment to the community. I personally find him agreeable. When I explained my concerns to him in a private meeting, he was both remorseful and cooperative, filling in details re the events in question, although he still appears very troubled.

I sympathize with Officer Mercer, but it is essential that this department serve the community safely, effectively, and with absolute professionalism. I do not believe that Officer Mercer is capable of doing so at this time.

*A. P. M.*

## CPD MEMORANDUM

To: Chief E. J. McCandless

From: Sgt. A. P. Mazzarella

Date: 05-10-05

Re: Officer Landau's encounter with Officer Mercer on 05-10-05 (0615 hours)

I have forwarded your request for an official report of the incident to Officer Landau. He expressed some hesitation about writing it because he did not want to be responsible for the incident going into Officer Mercer's personnel file. I informed him that he did not have discretion in this matter.

I will forward Officer Landau's report once I have reviewed it in its final form.

*A. P. M.*

| COLMA POLICE DEPARTMENT  CA0043479 | | | 1. CASE NO.<br>05-1667-68 | |
|---|---|---|---|---|

| 2. CODE SECTION<br>148, 187, 241, 243 | 3. CRIME<br>Resisting Arrest / Homicide / Assault and Battery upon a Peace Officer | 4. CLASSIFICATION<br>Felony | 5. REPORT AREA<br>Beat One |
|---|---|---|---|

| 6. DATE & TIME OCCURRED —DAY<br>05-10-05<br>0300 Sat | 7. DATE & TIME REPORTED<br>N/A | 8. LOCATION OF OCCURRENCE<br>Cypress Lawn Cemetary (East), 1370 El Camino Real | |
|---|---|---|---|

| 9. VICTIM'S NAME—LAST, FIRST, MIDDLE (FIRM IF BUSINESS)<br>Mercer, Michael G. | 10. RESIDENCE ADDRESS<br>2525 San Sebastian, Apt. 8N, Colma | 11. RESIDENCE PHONE<br>(650) 555-7631 |
|---|---|---|

| 12. OCCUPATION<br>Peace Officer | 13. RACE–SEX<br>W-M | 14. AGE<br>29 | 15. DOB<br>11-04-75 | 16. BUSINESS ADDRESS (SCHOOL IF JUVENILE)<br>1198 El Camino Real, Colma | 17. BUSINESS PHONE<br>(650) 555-8321 |
|---|---|---|---|---|---|

| 18. NAME—LAST, FIRST, MIDDLE<br>Fahey, Gerald D. | 19. CODE | 20. RESIDENCE ADDRESS<br>Holy Cross Cem., 1500 Mission Rd.,Colma | 21. RESIDENCE PHONE |
|---|---|---|---|

| 22. OCCUPATION<br>Fire-fighter (ret.) | 23. RACE–SEX<br>W-M | 24. AGE<br>25ish? | 25. DOB<br>12-30-27 | 26. BUSINESS ADDRESS (SCHOOL IF JUNENILE)<br>NA | 27. BUSINESS PHONE<br>NA |
|---|---|---|---|---|---|

**28. DESCRIBE CHARACTERISTICS OF PREMISES AND AREA WHERE OCCURRED**

Cypress Lawn Cemetary (East) Fern Grotto, Children's Section, and other locations

**29. DESCRIBE BRIEFLY HOW OFFENSE WAS COMMITTED**

Officer and de facto deputies were attempting to effectuate arrests of S-Baker, S-Ruczek, S-LoPresti, and S-Eastwick.

**30. DESCRIBE WEAPON, INSTRUMENT, TRICK, DEVICE, OR FORCE USED**

Root, plus various knives

| 31. MOTIVE—TYPE OF PROPERTY TAKEN OR OTHER REASON FOR OFFENSE<br>Resisting law enforcement action | 32. ESTIMATED LOSS VALUE AND/OR EXTENT OF INJURIES—MINOR, MAJOR<br>Abrasions on knees and elbows. Sharp pains in abdomen. Lingering sensation of extreme cold. Disorientation and loss of consciousness |
|---|---|

**33. WHAT DID SUSPECTS SAY—NOTE PECULIARITIES**

The usual cruelties and anachronisms

**34. VICTIM'S ACTIVITY JUST PRIOR TO AND/OR DURING OFFENSE**

Staking out area in anticipation of suspects' arrival. During offense: chasing S-Baker on foot through cemetery

**35. TRADEMARK—OTHER DISTINCTIVE ACTION OF SUSPECT/S**

See appendix (all previous Barker cases reported by Sgt. W. Featherstone and Officer M. Mercer)

**36. VEHICLE USED—LICENSE NO.—ID NO.—YEAR—MAKE—MODEL—COLOR (OTHER IDENTIFYING CHARACTERISTICS)**

N/A

| 37. SUSPECT NO. 1 (LAST, FIRST, MIDDLE) | 38. RACE–SEX | 39. AGE | 40. HT | 41. WT | 42. HAIR | 43. EYES | 44. SSN OR DOB | 45. ARRESTED |
|---|---|---|---|---|---|---|---|---|
| Barker, Arthur ("Doc") | | | | | | | . | |

**46. ADDRESS, CLOTHING, AND OTHER IDENTIFYING MARKS OR CHARACTERISTICS**

| 47. SUSPECT NO. 2 (LAST, FIRST, MIDDLE) | 48. RACE–SEX | 49. AGE | 50. HT | 51. WT | 52. HAIR | 53. EYES | 54. SSN OR DOB | 55. ARRESTED |
|---|---|---|---|---|---|---|---|---|
| Ruczek, Wilhelm | | | | | | | | |

**56. ADDRESS, CLOTHING, AND OTHER IDENTIFYING MARKS OR CHARACTERISTICS**

**57. CHECK IF MORE NAMES IN CONTINUATION**

X

| REPORTING OFFICERS | RECORDING OFFICER | TYPED BY | DATE AND TIME |
|---|---|---|---|
| | | | |

**OFFENSES INVESTIGATED AND RECOMMENDED CHARGES**

CPC 148—Resisting arrest

CPC 187—Homicide

CPC 241—Assault committed upon a peace officer

CPC 243—Battery committed upon a peace officer

See also Appendix for suspects' prior offenses.


1) SUMMARY:

On 05-10-05, at approximately 0300 hours, I was on foot in plainclothes at Cypress Lawn (East), supported by unofficial deputies Gage, Fahey, Coit, and Beachey. Deputy Gage positioned himself so as to lure Suspects to the location. Suspects arrived and attempted to rob Deputy Gage of his "tamping iron." I and the other deputies revealed ourselves and attempted to effectuate arrests of all four suspects. Multiple pursuits ensued.


2) VICTIMS AND WITNESSES:

V-Mercer, Michael G.

W-Gage, Phineas

W-Beachey, Lincoln

W-Coit, Lillie Hitchcock

W-Fahey, Gerald X.


3) SUSPECTS:

S-Barker, Arthur "Doc"

S-Ruczek, Wilhelm

S-LoPresti, Giovanni

S-Eastwick (first name unknown)


4) VEHICLE:

N/A

5) STATEMENT OF REPORTING OFFICER:

On 05-10-05, at approximately 0300 hours, I was on foot in plainclothes at Cypress Lawn (East). I was not officially on duty because of certain recent events. I was unarmed, having surrendered my weapon and badge on the afternoon of 05-09-05 pending administrative review.

I was accompanied by sworn-but-unoffical deputies Gage, Beachey, Fahey, and Coit. Deputy Fahey and I concealed ourselves behind overgrowth at Fern Grotto. Deputy Coit was concealed behind a mauseoleum to the northeast. Deputy Beachey was in his aeroplane several hundred yards away to the southeast, ready to provide aerial support. Deputy Gage, riding a horse ("Jamaica Farewell"), trotted around the nearby open spaces. He loudly and continuously expressed his joy at recovering his "tamping iron" (which he had not done, as the real tamping iron, according to a recently-arrived citizen claiming knowledge of such things, is in a medical museum in Cambridge, Mass., along with Deputy Gage's skull.)

Suspects, having heard of Deputy Gage's alleged good fortune, soon arrived to rob him of the (false) iron. As they advanced on him, Fahey and I revealed ourselves. I informed suspects that they were all under arrest. Suspects laughed.

At my signal, Deputy Coit lit a large fire made from old bedsheets and flammable materials borrowed from the landfill. Suspects were distracted by the fire and the Deputies and I took advantage of this opportunity and engaged them. Deputy Gage charged at S-LoPresti on the horse and swung his (false) iron (i.e., my softball bat), hitting S-LoPresti in the head and knocking him to the ground. While Suspect was incapacitated, Deputy Coit approached him with a quantity of Root and forced him to ingest it. There was a blast of heat and a greasy, gamy smell. S-LoPresti was thus eliminated.

S-Ruczek fled to the south, and Deputy Coit pursued him.

S-Eastwick (a very large man) wrestled with Deputy Fahey and subdued him, then stabbed him repeatedly in the abdomen with a knife he had been concealing. Then S-Eastwick fled in a northerly direction. Deputy Beachey reports that, now aloft, he maintained visual contact with S-Eastwick as the suspect ran. Deputy Beachey then targeted the suspect with a payload of heavy flour-sacks he had on board the aeroplane. Several sacks scored direct hits on S-Eastwick, knocking him unconscious. Deputy Gage, providing backup on Jamaica Farewell, dismounted and dispatched S-Eastwick with a quantity of Root.

I was unable to render aid to Deputy Fahey as I was engaged with S-Barker, who laughed and advanced on me in a threatening fashion. He said I looked like a useless chickenshit candy-ass like the late Sgt. Featherstone. I maintained my position. He held out his hands, which were dripping blood from the fingernails. I informed him that he would be unable to frighten me, since pretty much everything in my life had already fallen apart, so I didn't have much to be scared of. He came closer and closer and then dived at me. He knocked me to the ground. At each point where our bodies made contact, I felt an intense and painful sensation of cold. S-Barker also appeared to suffer pain, and I believe I smelled his skin scorching. We separated, both of us startled and in pain. I informed S-Barker that if that was the best he had, he was in trouble. S-Barker hesitated, then fled to the southeast. I went in pursuit up the hill through the cemetery in a southeasterly direction.

At the western edge of the Children's Section of Cypress Lawn, S-Barker leapt out from behind one of the larger stones and knocked me to the ground. S-Barker apparently was aware of my suspension from active duty and expressed amusement at my expense. S-Barker remarked that at least Sgt. Featherstone wasn't so dumb as to lose his job. I informed S-Barker that I had not lost it but that I was subject to administrative review and evalutaion. S-Barker said, quote, "Don't kid yourself. You've lost it, son." I informed S-Barker that he was to address me with respect and not to call me son. S-Barker raised his goddamn hands in a threatening fashion. I asked S-Barker why his hands were always bloody. S-Barker said, "Guilt's a bitch, ain't it, son?"

In one hand S-Barker held a quantity of Root and informed me that he was going to make me eat it, no matter how much the heat would hurt him to do it. I asked him what he thought that would do and he said we'd find out, wouldn't we? At this point I was hit by an unseen assailant and knocked to the ground. This assailant was S-Ruczek, who had evaded Deputy Coit and circled around behind me. S-Ruczek stabbed me in the abdomen with a seven-inch blade and then sat on me while S-Barker approached with the Root. Again, I felt extreme discomfort from the cold (and Ruczek seemed to be experiencing an uncomfortable amount of heat). I was unable to free myself. S-Barker approached close enough that I was able to smell both the Root and the blood on his hands.

There was a sudden, bright flash of orange, and a surge of heat, and S-Ruczek rolled off of me. He rolled in the grass screaming as his clothing (tuxedo separates made of flammable synthetics) burst into flames. S-Barker fled again, deeper into the children's section, and I pursued. Deputy Coit stayed with the burning S-Ruczek to finish him off once the flames died down a little. Deputy Coit's lighter was on the grass, and I picked it up before I commenced pursuit.

I was unable to keep pace with S-Barker due to extreme pain from the stab wound and from the cold, which felt like it had gone deep inside me. I stopped in the middle of a field of small stones where I had a clear 360-degree view but could not find him.

It was very quiet in the Children's Section, and I thought no one else was around at all until I saw a small boy (W-M, 7-8) leaning against a headstone very close to me. He was tossing and catching a baseball in one hand. A black dog lay in the grass next to him. Without saying anything, he pointed in the direction of a large, crumbling mausoleum under the cypress trees to the south, along the fence line.

I disregarded all recommended procedure and ran straight at, and into, the mausoleum, not wanting to give S-Barker an opportunity to escape. It was dark inside. I listened for breathing and then wondered why I was doing that, since S-Barker was dead. I flicked Deputy Coit's lighter. S-Barker was standing right next to me, and he had a fistful of Root that he forced into my mouth. He pushed some it into my throat, causing me to choke (and to suffer intense cold in my mouth and throat). I grabbed at the wounded area in his face, and we both fell to the ground.

I was choking on the piece of Root that was lodged in my throat, and I tried to cough it out but couldn't. S-Barker let go of me and pushed me into the corner. He said he wanted to watch what happened. I didn't know what to expect either.

What happened was this: I felt terribly sick to my stomach. That's all. And I'm pretty used to that due to a lifetime of worrying. But I pretended to be incapacitated. S-Barker was momentarily distracted when Deputy Beachey's plane came in low over the mausoleum, and I jumped out at him, wrapped him in a bear-hug, and wrestled him to the ground. I will never be able to describe the intensity of the cold that I felt, but I hung on to him, even as he was screaming and threatening me and his skin was blistering. I sensed that I was putting myself in grave physical peril, but I held on and held on because something told me for once I was doing something right. I held on and I froze and he smoked. At some point during the struggle I lost consciousness.

I awakened to find Deputies Beachey, Gage, and Coit at the doorway of the mausoleum. The air smelled strongly of burned remains, and there was a body-shaped scorch mark on the stone floor. Deputy Coit lent me her firefighter's coat so I could get myself warm.

We returned to Fern Grotto to find Deputy Fahey so we could share the good news. He was not there. Where he had fallen earlier, there was a greasy scorch-mark on the grass. I believe S-Ruczek was responsible. Deputy Coit blamed herself for losing the suspect in pursuit. I advised her that she had done her best and had nothing to feel bad about.

At some point, I must have lost consciousness again.

I awoke at or around 0615 when Officer Landau roused me. He wanted to know why I had slept on the golf course and conjectured that I was "one fucked-up motherfucker." I do not know if Officer Landau plans to report the incident officially.

I have no visible wounds but there remains a sharp pain in my abdomen. Also I am very, very cold, even with the heat all the way up. Still shaking.

6) EVIDENCE

N/A

7) PROPERTY

N/A


8) STATUS

Case closed successfully.


9) OPINIONS

All things considered, I feel pretty goddamned good.

[Additional sheet, stapled to Incident Report:]


UPDATE (05/10/03): Phone call from Officer Toronto re
Officer Landau, who asked him to inform me that he had
been ordered to write a memorandum about the incident,
and that in retrospect he should have kept it between
us, which he would have done if he hadn't thought it was
so funny. I asked Officer Toronto to convey to Officer
Landau that I appreciated the apology, although he
is and always will be a dick-weasel [or whatever the
current favorite term is].

◉

# TWENTY-SIX

# GERALD XAVIER FAHEY
# B. DECEMBER 1937
# D. MARCH 2005
# D. MAY 2005

Ishi, the last Yahi Indian, kneels alone under a willow tree, chanting an ancient song of mourning.

Lefty O'Doul lays his mitt on the grass, then removes his cap and holds it over his heart.

Emperor Norton stands on the top step of a nearby mausoleum, flanked by two sitting mutts, with his saber held high.

Lillie Coit leans against the chapel doorway, keeping her helmet tucked under one arm and wiping away tears on the sleeve of the other.

Lincoln Beachey flies past and dips his wings, and Phineas Gage salutes from the passenger seat. They land smoothly just over the next hill.

Michael Mercer is not in attendance, and he is missed.

# A TIME TO PLUCK UP

The coffeepot is full before Mercer realizes he has already packed his mugs. He cuts the tape on a moving box on the living room floor and digs into the wadded-up newspaper. He comes up empty, so he opens a second box, and then a third. Finally he locates two mugs, rinses them, and sets them on the table.

"You should label those boxes," Lorna says as he fills her cup.

"I'm aware," Mercer says. He's not sure why he didn't. Maybe he just isn't very concerned about his things right now.

"The coffee is wonderful."

"I'm supposed to be drinking decaf."

"So am I," Lorna says. "But everything in its time."

"Amen," Mercer says.

They sip their coffee quietly amid the chaos of Mercer's move. He told The Willows' office manager that he was breaking his lease and wrote a check for the balance on the spot. He could have negotiated, but it didn't seem worth the hassle. He only has two weeks to kill before his flight, and Owen and Mollie have insisted that he stay with them. And it's better to get out before the water stains on the bedroom ceiling coalesce into an image of Doc Barker. Or *any* dead person.

Jude, thankfully, is not one of those.

"Are you going to stay in touch with the DiMaio boy?" she asks.

He wonders how she knew what he was thinking. Maybe a look of concern had shown on his face. He nods. "Postcards, an e-mail or two, that sort of thing. Just a little support. It's probably better if I'm not too involved."

Lorna purses her lips. "Because you're a reminder of—?"

"Yes. I'm a reminder of."

How much more is there to say? Jude is alive, but he's been damaged. The ligaments in his legs are wrecked, so he's having to practice walking again, but that's nothing, really. The real issue is that something in him—spark, passion, acuity—is gone. It might just be dormant, hidden away somewhere safe while his brain and body heal themselves from the trauma, but the doctor Mercer spoke to told him that a complete recovery was unlikely. *Cerebral hypoxia*, the doctor said, *is a bitch*. Jude's no vegetable, but he's noticeably slower, duller. The worst part is that the kid is aware that he's different, that he's not the student or the musician or the reader or the thinker he used to be, that he's functioning at a level that is, at best, ordinary. There are far worse things than being ordinary, Mercer knows, but it's hard not to grieve what's been lost, and it's even harder to look into Jude's eyes and see him grieving it, too. Is Mercer responsible? He's talked this to death with the psychiatrist, who says he's responsible to the extent that he chooses to be responsible. And again: how much more is there to say?

He changes the subject, asks Lorna how her new job is going. Reverend Whipple has created a salaried position for her at the church as an outreach coordinator, feeling culpable for pushing Lorna into the trouble she'd gotten into. And he has crafted her schedule so that she can continue volunteering at the Historical Society.

"He's a good man," Lorna says, "and he does good work."

Mercer nods. He knows he owes Whipple, too.

"I hate to say it," Lorna says, "but this has all worked out well for me."

"Don't hate to say it on my account. I'm doing what I want to do. For now, anyway."

"I hope you'll have a good time. You'll be missed here. It'll be all up to Officer Benzinger to defend my muffins."

Mercer laughs. "They're getting better," he says. "Honestly. Even Toronto says so."

"I'm glad they let him back."

"The union really went to bat for him." One of the conditions for Toronto's return was that he take anger-management classes, which he's doing willingly, even eagerly. He says he's incorporated them into his Zen practice. "Yes," he said to Mercer over drinks one night at The 500 Club. "I'm a pissed-off Buddhist. So it goes." They had a good laugh over that. Toronto also swore Mercer to secrecy and said it was probably time for him to move on, too. "Hope's father is a bond trader," he said. "He offered to set me up in the business. How hard can it be? All the knuckleheaded dick-weasels I went to high school with are making millions. Imagine me as a bond trader. I'll eat those motherfuckers alive." Oh, and also? He got engaged again. "Goddamn, you're quick," Mercer said. Toronto did the shot of bourbon in front of him, shrugged, and said, "When you know, you know."

The doorbell rings, which is a surprise. He's not expecting anyone. He excuses himself and opens the door, where he finds Johnny G and Johnny K. They're all grins even though they don't look stoned, which is also a surprise. Johnny G's van is in the driveway, and Rae and April wave up at him through open windows. "What's up?" Mercer says.

"We're kidnapping you," Johnny G says. "Owen's orders."

"Put three days of clothes in a bag and come with us," Johnny K says. "No questions."

"Pack your toothbrush, too," Johnny G says. "I don't want to spend three days with your stinkbreath."

Mercer hears the kitchen faucet running and turns to see Lorna rinsing out her mug. "Go," she tells him. "What are you waiting for?"

Four hours later, they're north of Willits—the two Johnnys, the two girls, Mercer, and Johnny G's dog, a sweet old mismatched-parts mutt named Shadow who's been sitting with Mercer and drooling on his thigh. The rear of the van is loaded down with camping gear and cases of beer, wine, and liquor. They've left the highway and taken a series of turns that Mercer wouldn't remember even if he'd been trying to pay attention; around them is thick green woodland occasionally interrupted by modest houses far off the road.

"Hold on," Johnny G shouts, and the van bumps heavily onto a rutted dirt road. The road twists up a steep hill, then descends, then rises again. Dust the color of butterscotch flies up all around them, and the dry, earthy smell comes through the vents.

This is rural Mendocino County, and this is marijuana country. "I may not be a cop anymore," Mercer says. "But that doesn't mean I have to see everything Owen's up to."

"Relax your sphincter, Mike," Johnny G says, and Rae swats him from the passenger seat.

"Thank you, Rae," Mercer says.

Forty minutes down the dirt road, they come to a gate. Johnny K hops out of the van, opens the lock, and pulls the gate open for them. As the van judders down another slope, Mercer sees a sunny clearing ahead. Three white domes rise above the tree line around its perimeter. He looks out the window to his left and counts three more. "Yurts?" he says.

"Yurts!" Johnny G announces. "Yurts for all!"

Owen and Mollie are waiting for them at the far edge of the clearing, in front of a tired-looking outbuilding with a sagging roof. Mollie is in a tank top and shorts and has her hair tied back. Owen is wearing a seersucker suit with white shoes, apparently without irony.

"Miguel," Owen says. "Welcome to the compound."

"What is this?" Mercer says.

"It's Owen's big secret project," Mollie says.

Owen shrugs. "Just a matter of repurposing the land," he says. Mollie rolls her eyes at the false modesty.

"So that means the wedding's on." Mercer says.

"Yes," Mollie says. "It does."

"Yeah," Owen says, "I'm pretty lucky."

"And now I know he knows it," Mollie says.

"He'd better," Mercer says.

"I'm right here," Owen says. "Let's stop with this third-person business."

"Where's it going to be?" Mercer asks.

"Right where you're standing," Mollie says.

"I have another six yurts on order," Owen says.

"Six?" Mercer says. "Where are you going to put them?"

"I've got twenty acres," Owen says. "Hank needed a lot of room."

"Family and close friends stay in the yurts here," Mollie says. "Everyone else stays down in Willits. And the reception's going to be in the common hall."

"What common hall?"

Mollie gestures to the decrepit building behind them. "This lovely piece of architecture has, I'm told, served its purpose well, but it's coming down. The new foundation gets poured next month."

"So now we have a place to relax," Owen says. "All of us. If anyone needs to get away from the city, they can come up here. Any time. In perpetuity."

"When have you ever needed to relax?" Mercer asks. "What the hell do you have to relax *from*?"

"I have no idea. But it seems like a good idea to be prepared."

Johnny G unloads a cooler from the van and passes out beers around the circle. "To Owen," he says, raising his bottle, "and to his relative lack of sanity."

"Seriously," Mercer says. "Owen, I never thought you were serious about doing this."

"What's their money for if you can't buy your friends' love?" Mollie says.

"And proximity," Owen says. "Proximity's important."

They drink, and more toasts follow:

"To Mollie, for knocking some sense into him," Rae says.

"To Hank, wherever he may grow," Johnny K says, pouring a stream of beer onto the ground. "Poor, Smythed Hank."

"To our friend Michael," Mollie says, "who's back among the living."

Happy hour, which starts when the sun first nicks the tree line, consists of rum-and-guava-juice cocktails and a fevered bocce tournament on a long stretch of matted grass. Mercer asks Owen and Mollie where they're taking their honeymoon.

"It'll be a pre-wedding honeymoon," Owen says. "We don't feel like waiting."

"And it's good you asked," Mollie says, "since you'll be hosting us for part of it."

Johnny G tosses the pelota and calls over, "I can't believe you're moving back in with your mom, Mike."

"Johnny," Mollie says, "don't say it like that. It's not lame if your mom lives in Tahiti."

"You're right," Johnny G says. "Maybe I should move in with Mercer's mom."

"I'm not so much moving as I am going," Mercer says.

"Moving, going," Owen says. "Both are good."

"What are you going to do down there, Mike?" Johnny K asks.

"I don't know. Read. Go diving. Learn French, maybe."

"Meet Polynesian girls," Mollie says.

Mercer tells them about the phone message he got from his mother a few nights ago. She said she'd found the perfect girl for him working in the scooter shop across from their villa on Raiatea. Then there was a rustling sound, and his mother's voice, farther away, saying, *Allez, Sylvie,* and then a younger woman's voice, heavily accented. After a few rewinds, he figured out that she'd said, *Michael, I take you, ah, around ze island on ze scootaire. I am please to do zis.*

"Mike," Johnny K says, "you are definitely learning French. Tout-de-fucking-suite."

Rae mixes another round of drinks at the bar they've set up in the old outbuilding. When their glasses are full, Owen motions for Mercer to take a walk with him. Drinks in hand, they follow a narrow path into the trees.

"You really are looking better," Owen says. "We were getting worried."

"I'm sleeping again."

"And you're okay letting go of the job? Not being a cop anymore?"

"It's not what I thought I wanted," Mercer says. "But goddamn, it's been a tough year. It's time to rethink."

Owen nods and sips his drink. He points out landmarks along the way: the trail that branches off to the field that he used to call The Lower Forty; a deer path that leads to a pond; the cabin, hidden in a thick grove of oaks, where the ex-Coastie used to sleep. "He bought my gear and moved to Yreka," Owen says. "You don't know any Yreka cops, do you?"

"So," Mercer says, ignoring the question, "Kinnicutt was up here with you to help plan all this?"

Owen nods. "I know that pissed you off," he says. "But I knew there were some things you didn't want to see."

"So where's he now?"

"You really want to know?"

"Yeah."

"He's with Kelly."

"Kelly," Mercer says. Her name sounds strange to him now.

"They went to Cabo for the weekend. I told him we were going to surprise you up here, and he didn't think they should be part of the surprise."

Mercer thinks of Kelly again, of her mouth, her hands, the night air sweeping through the gazebo, and he feels his stomach tighten. *Let go,* he tells himself. *Time to let go.* "So they're together?"

"It won't be long-term. It's never long-term with him. Or with her, as far as I can tell."

"So they're a good match."

"Pretty good," Owen says, "although he's spending a lot on clothes. He's trying to fool her into thinking he has a fashion sense."

Mercer looks up at the sky, which is darkening to a rich purple. "Ah, hell," he says. "It would've been all right if they came."

"You mean that?"

"I mean it enough," Mercer says.

Owen shakes the remaining ice in his glass. "Should we head back?" Mercer nods, even though he still has half his drink left. He's pacing himself.

"Speaking of Kinnicutt," Owen says, "he saw your dad. In Santa Cruz."

"I know. He told me at your fucking party."

"No. I mean, he saw your dad again. At least he thinks it's your dad. Says he wasn't looking so good."

Mercer sighs. "I'm not surprised."

"Do you want to go down there, maybe look for him before you leave? I'll go with you, if you want. Just say the word."

Mercer stops walking. He stands still, holds his eyes closed. He hears crickets chirping and a large bird flapping through the trees above them. "Thanks," he says. "But I'm not ready for that. Maybe when I get back. Maybe."

"What would you think," Owen says, "if Mollie and I went down to look? Because I was thinking that if your dad needs a place to be, he could come up here for a while. Or if he needs more help than that, maybe we could steer him to it. Or it to him."

Mercer holds his eyes closed. Thoughts fragment and dissolve before they can come together. He listens to the crickets instead.

"We wouldn't tell him you knew anything. It would just be us. And we'd only put you in touch if you said you wanted it."

Still: no words. Crickets, and his own breathing, and his own pulse.

"It's just an idea," Owen says.

"It's not a bad one," Mercer says, and he hugs his oldest friend. "Thank you."

1130 hours. Seven friends around a campfire, bundled in sweaters and blankets, full of tri-tip and grilled red peppers and wine. Flames hula and jump, and smoke rises into the moonless sky. Wind rustles through the trees, and they hear deer running along one of the wooded slopes above them. Johnny G has just finished telling a story he learned at summer camp about a deranged small-town doctor who drank blood he drained from the villagers' livestock at night. He was killed by an angry mob, then came back from the dead and started sucking the blood from their children. At a tense moment—the hero stalking the ghost on a dark mountainside—Johnny K, who'd crept around behind them, let out a shriek of terror.

"That's the ending?" Mollie said, once she'd recovered. "That's not an ending."

"Sure, it's an ending," Johnny G says. "It's just not a happy one. Ghost wins. Hero's dead. The end."

"Not to mention," Johnny K says, "that you all nearly messed yourselves. Which means it's a damn good scary story."

"What about you, Mike?" Mollie says. "You must have heard some good ones."

"Yeah," he says. "I have." But what should he tell a story about? An aging cop stalked and killed in a ghost world? A younger cop face-to-blown-out-face with a ruthless dead gangster? A tormented ghost of a railroad worker, searching high and low for the piece of iron that once blasted through his head? He decides, finally, on a different one altogether. A brown-trouser moment that he himself lived through recently.

This one's true, he tells them, and it happened to him and to his ex-girlfriend, Fiona. She'd been in a bad car wreck at one of the cemeteries, and that got them talking to each other again. When she was ready to go back to work at the hospital, he found himself sitting around with too much time on his hands, and she suggested he come back and work security for a while, just to keep busy, keep his mind clear.

"Did you hook up again?" Johnny G asks. "Did you just skip a sex scene?"

"Shut up, Johnny," Mollie says. "Let him tell the story."

"Is anybody going to get laid in this story?" Johnny K asks.

Fiona's dating her physical therapist, Ed, Mercer tells them. Nice guy. Pretty much the nicest guy on the damn planet. Mercer's happy for her. He has no information on what their sex life is like.

"Make it up," Johnny K says.

Mercer flips him the bird and continues.

They're both working in the ER one afternoon when the Daly City cops bring in a 5150: an enormous Samoan guy—6'6", 350—who's out of his head on PCP. It takes four cops, two orderlies, and three security guards, including Mercer, to wrestle the guy onto a gurney, where he's strapped down and wheeled into one of the locked holding rooms, where Fiona shoots him with enough of a sedative to drop eight men. While the man doesn't go down immediately, he's slowed down enough that everyone thinks the crisis is over. Mercer is left to monitor the patient through the narrow window in the locked door. A few minutes later, the patient roars alive, and one by one, he breaks the leather restraints and frees himself, stomping around the room looking ready to kill. Fiona, waits by the door with Mercer, armed with another sedative, although she has no idea how she'll ever get it into him if he breaks out of the room. The man rages, ranting incoherently and punching the walls until his hands bleed. Then he flings himself against the locked door over and over, so hard that Mercer and Fiona can see it flexing in its frame. Spit dribbles down the window.

He might drop, Fiona says. Sometimes it takes a few minutes to really hit.

Emphasis on might? Mercer asks.

Emphasis on might.

Will the door hold? Mercer asks as the man lunges into it again.

It always has before, Fiona says. Translated: maybe not.

They find themselves holding hands. Translated: if the door doesn't hold, we're in trouble, both of us. And a lot of other people, too.

*Bam!* The door rattles again, and then there's a stretch of quiet. Mercer looks in the window and sees the huge man standing still near the door, wobbling slightly. Mercer and Fiona lean against the far wall, still holding hands, and they catch their breath. The silence is sweet. They're in the clear.

Just as they relax their grips on each other, they hear a tiny click coming from the door, and then another, another, and another. Click, click, click, click, over and over, always in groups of four. They realize what's happening at the same time. The murderous Samoan is standing at the door, still wobbling, but trying out combination after combination on the four-digit lock.

He might still pass out. But if he hits the combination, he's free, and he's coming after them. They hold hands again and pray that they'll live. And they're thankful, right now, to have each other.

"Where's the fucking ghost?" Johnny G says when Mercer finishes.

"That's not an ending," Johnny K says.

"It's an ending," Mercer says. "It's just a happy one."


The clerk from the Zes-T-Mart is on the roof of the store, stretched out on an air mattress with his new girlfriend. He's been seeing something strange in the sky, and he wants to show it to her.

It happens nearly every night: around two o'clock, an airplane dives out of the fog and goes down, straight down, nose-to-ground, and there's no question that that sonofabitch is going to make some serious fucking impact with the earth. But there's never a crash, and sometimes he thinks he can hear the plane's engine trailing off in the distance, flying low over the cemeteries. Last night, the plane fell out of the sky close enough to the store that he could see two men in it and read the banner it was trailing: BOSTON OR BUST!

He hopes they're not bound for Boston, because he likes having them here, and he can't wait to share his discovery—his *secret*—with Mindy. He checks his watch. It's nearly two. He stubs out the joint they've been sharing and points to the spot in the fog that she should keep her eye on. He folds his arm around her and pulls her in close. Together they watch, waiting for the show to begin.

## ACKNOWLEDGMENTS

I would like to express my deep gratitude to the many people and organizations that helped make this book possible. I am particularly indebted to: the Stanford Creative Writing Department and Continuing Studies Program, the Iowa Writers' Workshop and the James Michener/Copernicus Society, The MacDowell Colony, and St. Edward's University for their generous financial support; all of my teachers, especially Fred Haefele, John L'Heureux, Jim McPherson, the late Frank Conroy, and the late Gilbert Sorrentino; my friends and workshop-mates, expecially those who helped me grapple with this manuscript in its many stages of development: Ann Joslin Williams, Angela Pneuman, Matt Modica, Ed Schwarzschild, Ben Yalom, Jennifer Senior, Adam Johnson, Malinda McCollum, and Tony Varallo; my agent, Jay Mandel, and my editor, Sean McDonald, for their wise counsel and saintlike patience; the Colma Police Department, especially Officer Roger Arreola; the Hudak family; the T. Purser Bailey Foundation for the Arts; my friend Mark Young, without whose technical advice, enthusiasm, and generosity of spirit I could never have written this book; my brother, Jeff Dorst, and my parents, Charlie and Yvonne Dorst; and most of all, my wife, Debra, who has had my back every step of the way.

# ABOUT THE AUTHOR

Doug Dorst is a graduate of the Iowa Writers' Workshop and a former Wallace Stegner Fellow at Stanford. His work has appeared in *McSweeney's, Ploughshares, Epoch,* and other journals, as well as in the anthology *Politically Inspired.* A longtime resident of San Francisco, Dorst now lives in Austin, where he teaches creative writing at St. Edward's University.